THE
FIRE
ASCENDING

THE
FIRE
ASCENDING

CHRIS D'LACEY

SCHOLASTIC INC.

This book was originally published in hardcover in the United States by Orchard Books in 2012 and in Great Britain by Orchard Books, a division of Hachette Children's Books, a Hachette Livre UK company, in 2012.

ISBN 978-0-545-40293-4

12 11 10 9 8 7 6 5 4 3 2 1   12 13 14 15 16 17/0

Printed in the U.S.A.   40

First paperback printing, September 2012

This edition's book design by Whitney Lyle

"Time is like water; it finds its own levels."

the sibyl Gwilanna

And men will say to themselves, "What became of the last true dragon, Gawain? Did he die in flames upon the sword of a warrior? Did he spread his wings and fly into the sun, leaving nought but his perfect shadow behind? Did he cloak himself in the ash of a volcano, ready to emerge in glory one day?"

These stories, I can tell you, are all an invention. The truth is he died of loneliness. Solitude clawed at his aching heart and drew his fire to the cusp of his eye. His auma gathered in a single teardrop. And when he could no longer bear to look upon a world untouched by the beauty of dragons, he closed his eye and his fire tear fell.

Herein lies the way of it . . .

from The Book of Agawin,
a history of dragons

PART ONE
VOSS

I was a boy of twelve when I watched a dragon die. It was during the season of winterfold, when every morning the hillsides were brittle with frost and the peak of Kasgerden shone bright with snow. I was a cave dweller then, in the keep of Yolen the healer and seer. One morning, while I was tending a goat, the earth shuddered and the pointed shadow of the beast swept over the valley, bending every blade of grass to its will. The goats were disturbed and came together in a flock. They knew better than I that a dragon was near. I jumped up, spinning about. Between the clouds there was only pale pink sky. But I could hear the quiet scything of wings and smell the burned sulfur trail the beast was leaving, falling all around like unseen drizzle. Swiftly, I gathered my robe about my knees and hurried for the cave as fast as I could. Behind me the goat bells rattled. There was nothing I could do to protect the flock. If the dragon had wanted them, it could have had them all.

But killing was not on its mind that day. As I ran up the scree, calling out to Yolen, he was already standing at the mouth of the cave, staring hard across the yawning valley. His lips were drawn. There was a thoughtful look in his watery eyes. He raised a hand to tell me I should stop my panting. "Be calm, boy, there is no danger."

"But it's . . . a *dragon*," I blustered, my youthful voice overflowing with wonder. The beasts were so rarely seen those days. This mountain range had once been a breeding ground for them. They were legend here. Yolen himself had taught me this.

I saw him nod. His gaze narrowed slightly. "Then be quiet and *observe* it. This might be the only chance you'll get."

And I understood perfectly what he meant. Whenever men spoke about dragons those days, they spoke of them as if they were a finished breed.

So I sat upon the scree and I peered at the mountain. On the tip of Kasgerden I saw the beast in frightening silhouette. It was standing on a pair of stout hind legs with its wings stretched fully and its long neck funneled at the drifting clouds. I saw no flame, but out of its mouth came a cry I was sure would sever the air. I wanted to press my hands to my head, but Yolen had not moved to do the same and I did not wish to seem weak in his presence. So I bore the beast's rippling wail in my ears and tried, instead, to listen to its voice and make sense of its call.

Long ago, Yolen had taught me that all things natural to the Earth had auma. The great life-force, Gaia, moved within the most inanimate pebbles as well as through the river and the mountains — and me. Even the smallest grain of earth was aware of its presence in the universe, said Yolen. In essence, we were all one being, born from the fire of the true Creator (though he had yet to teach me who or what that was). This was a truth all men possessed but few knew what to do with, he would say. That day, I relaxed my thoughts and gave my auma up to the Earth so I might *commingle* with the dragon on the mountain. I built a picture in my mind from that distant silhouette and let the squealing enter my head. And long before my master had dropped his confident hand upon my shoulder, I knew what Yolen knew already.

"It's come to Kasgerden to shed its fire tear."

"Go to the cave. Gather food and clothing. There will be a pilgrimage," Yolen said.

I looked once more at the creature. It had not come hunting; it had come here to die.

And I was going to witness it.

That day, I became a follower of Galen. I had no idea when we set off down the valley that this was the dragon's true or real name. That I would learn from the mouths of other followers. The sun had barely moved through the narrowest of arcs when our path began to cross with a host of them, all making their way, like us, to Kasgerden. Yolen had led us straight to the river, which ran in a curve through the forest we called Horste. From between the Horste pines the pilgrims were descending, as if the trees themselves had lifted their roots and were moving as one toward the water and the mountain. They were simple folk, dressed in robes or common tunics. They wore sandals made of goat hide, and furs around their shoulders. I envied their children, who grew their braided hair far longer than mine and wore necklaces and bracelets made from cones and other seeds. Some of the men, I noticed, bore spears.

The name "Galen" bubbled up as we joined their throng. The last dragon from the Wearle of Hautuuslanden. A male. A bronze with white undersides. A feature that marked the beast down as old. Three hundred years at least. Maybe more. The men argued constantly about this fact. I heard one of them suggesting that the beast might not be old, but weakened. That its scales were losing their color due to some unusual condition or disease. (Yolen, I saw, took note of this.) But there was one thing they were in agreement on. There would be *fraas*, they kept saying. Fraas. Fraas. The sheer thrill of it glinted in their hungry eyes. They shook their spears and gave praise to Gaia. There was a dragon. And there would be fraas.

This word, like the dragon's name, was new to me then. I tugged Yolen's sleeve. "What is 'fraas'?" I asked him.

He drew me aside, close to the riverbank, a little away from the body of the followers. "It has been known," he said, "for a dragon to shed sparks when its tear is released or first strikes the earth. The older the creature, the more likely this becomes. A spark might travel far before it lands. At the place where it lands, its energy will linger. If a follower can reach that place before the spark descends into the crust of the Earth, he might briefly connect with the dragon's spirit. There are benefits and dangers associated with this. A dragon's fire, as you know, has been said to cure ills."

"And what are the dangers?" I asked. I looked nervously at the men with spears. Would they fight among themselves for the right to have fraas? Or were they simply wary of the dragon itself? Would its spirit rear up and haunt them forever if they dared to commingle with its untamed soul? The creatures, in life, were terrifying enough. How much more fearful would their specters be?

Before Yolen could reply, there was a sudden disturbance among the followers. Those at the rear began crying out a warning. I looked back and saw people stumbling and falling, children being picked up and rushed aside. The ground rumbled to the sound of galloping hooves. Horses were upon us. Arriving at high speed. The crowd parted like a flock of startled birds and I saw an old man knocked brutally sideways by the leading horse. It was as black as the unlit cave, with a mane that flashed around its neck like a blaze. Its eyes were full of blood and anguish. In the center of its forehead, at the level of the eyes, I thought I saw a stump of twisted rock, rough hewn at its point and oozing a kind of syrupy fluid. But my gaze was mostly on the rider, not his mount. Astride the horse sat a thumping brute of a man, with hair as long as the children of Horste. The menace in his eyes was as dark as the fists that gripped the black reins. And though I had no reason then to be afraid of him, a fateful chill still entered my heart. For even I, a boy of twelve, could tell he was mesmerized by the prospect of the dragon. He was hunting more than fraas, I was sure.

As he and at least six others swept by, the force of their gallop blew me quickly off my feet. I tumbled down the riverbank with panic in my lungs. Like the land, the river was harassed by the winter. The water broke my fall; its coldness, my voice. "Yolen-nn!" I cried, but he was already there, aided by another, stouter, man. Their sandals gouged lengthy channels in the earth as they clambered down the muddy riverbank after me. A hand took my robe and pulled me from the water. I slithered, legs blue and exposed, into the shallows. Yolen grabbed me and I grabbed him. I held tight to his body while his hand caressed my head. "Wh-who were they?" I chattered. I was struggling to keep my teeth clamped together.

"They were Premen," said the man who'd come to help.

"That's not possible," I heard Yolen say, but the fear in his voice contradicted his words.

"Trust me, seer, they were Premen," the man repeated. And he left us to recover ourselves back to the path.

I was too cold then to care about questions. Too shocked to ask my keeper what "Premen" meant. All I yearned for was the fur that the Horste man offered and that Yolen had wrapped around my quivering shoulders. But as we scaled the riverbank I quickly put away my own misfortune and turned instead to the people of the forest. The old man knocked down by the strange black horse was lying motionless on the ground. A woman was kneeling beside him, weeping. A tall man, rugged and handsome as the hills, looked at the body and touched the woman's arm. Then he rose up straight and called out loudly, "My father by marriage lies here, murdered. Who will support me in my rightful claim to vengeance?"

All of the Horste men shouted, "I!" Those with spears raised them high above their heads.

But as quickly as their roar had shaken the forest, their voices fell away to an anxious mumble. Out of the crowd stepped forth a woman, a dark green cape flowing off her shoulders. I felt Yolen's hand tighten slightly on my arm. It was a measure of protection, but I didn't know why until the woman dropped her hood and I saw her face. Her skin was as pale as the shimmering moon, the rims of her eyes so heavy with shade that the weirdly violet points within them looked as far removed from me as stars. Bones and bird feathers hung in her hair. There were more around her neck and ankles and wrists.

"What is she?" I whispered.

"A sibyl," said Yolen. "You must stay away from her."

The handsome man drew a sword from his belt. "Hilde, I beg you, put an enchantment on this humble blade so I might take that villain's head from his shoulders."

The sibyl walked slowly around the body. "Put away your sword," she said.

"But the honor of my family is —"

"You will have no *family*," the sibyl hissed, "if you lunge at this man with bloodlust and steel. He will shred you like a pinecone and hang you from a tree."

"Who is he?" someone shouted.

And I heard the word "Premen" on their lips again. The sibyl hushed them in dramatic fashion. With a sharp cry, not unlike the screech of a fox, she began to flap her cape. Yolen looked toward the forest. Four dark shapes had come out of the trees. Ravens. Birds I had always admired, though the followers, I noticed, huddled back in fear. The bereaved man drew his grieving wife aside.

The ravens landed by the old man's body and emptied their raucous *caark*s at the sibyl. She opened her hands and rasped at them in a language I did not know or understand. One immediately leaped onto the dead man's chest. It tottered to his face and hopped onto his chin. Without warning, it leaned forward and plucked out an eye.

All around us, the Horste made sounds of revulsion. Even the man who had lent the fur winced.

I pressed myself back against Yolen's body. *What kind of woman,* I asked myself, *instructs a bird to pluck out a dead man's eye?*

Hilde crouched down. She looked at the staring, muscle-torn orb, held tight within the raven's curving beak. "Find the rider," she said. "Drop it in his open

mouth while he sleeps. Make sure he swallows it —
whole."

And away went the birds on their grisly mission.

"He will be dead by morning!" Hilde cried. She
fanned her arms and spread her fingers like talons.
"Tormented by visions of his own sickly end."

The forest men muttered their approval for this.
Justice, albeit gruesome, was done. They gave praise to
Gaia and set off along the river again.

My stomach was churning and my knees felt colder
than they had in the water, but I could not take my
eyes off the sibyl and her stance. What's more, she had
now seen me. She crooked a finger and beckoned me
forward.

Yolen ground his teeth. He did not want this. But
he could hardly turn me away. Whatever powers my
seer could lay claim to, they did not match those of a
woman who commanded birds. "Go to her," he whispered, nudging my back.

I stepped up bravely, trying not to look at the dis-
figured face of the body on the ground.

"Cave dweller," she said, thumbing my robe. "Seer's
apprentice. Milker of *goats*."

How did she know this? "Yes," I said.

"What is your name, boy?"

"Agawin," I told her.

"Interesting." She cupped my chin. "A name that embraces the voice of dragons." She spoke it herself, forcing it against the roof of her mouth. *Aagg*-a-win. I smelled her choking breath and half-thought I might see fire on her tongue. She glanced at Yolen. "I like this boy. What do you want for him?"

Yolen stood forward. He shook his head. "I do not wish to give the boy up."

"What you wish has nothing to do with it, seer. Are you training him in your ways?"

"Slowly," said Yolen. "He is a simple boy. No use to —"

"Let us see how far he's progressed." The sibyl let go of my face and took something from a square-shaped pouch at her waist. It seemed to me nothing but a short piece of bone. But when I looked at it closely I saw it was etched with a number of symbols, the most prominent of which was a three-lined mark that twisted right around the shaft of the object.

Yolen sipped a little air through his teeth.

"Take it," Hilde the sibyl commanded. But as I reached forward she gripped my wrist with the strength of a hawk. "Choose your hand carefully, boy. This is a tornaq, a talisman of fortunes. Your death and your destiny are both within reach." Her piercing eyes stared into my soul. "Hold the charm tightly. Shake it three times with your eyes closed. Then you will tell me what you have seen."

So I took the charm. And I thought about death and destiny and hands. I milked with both, but favored the right for all other forms of manual work. Now and then, however, when a mood came upon me, I would dip a piece of wood into the embers of a fire and with the finely charred end draw images on the walls of the cave. This I always did with the opposite hand. For reasons I could not explain to myself, that was the hand I chose to hold the talisman of fortunes.

With the first shake, my head began to spin. By the second, I was flying down a tunnel in my mind. Images rolled before me — people (strangely dressed, and none of whom I recognized), land (a green hill surrounded by water), animals (a staggering *host* of animals, including a pack of bears not unlike the huge brown brutes

15

that roamed the woods of Druuvendier, but *white*, crossing vast sheets of ice). I saw birds formed in the likeness of dragons, but kinder-looking, with a softer eye and blessed with astonishing varieties of color. I saw an egg — large and glowing like the sun. Out of it I knew would hatch a true dragon. But the oddest sight of all was reserved until last. My journey came rushing to an end at the image of another, still stranger type of dragon. It was small, even compared to the birds, with pretty oval eyes as violet as the sibyl's and a wide, stubby snout. It sat upright on its tail and two flat back feet. In its paws it held a pad constructed of some kind of parchment and a writing implement that I thought for all the world was a larger dragon's claw. As I watched, I saw it make a mark on the pad. The same mark that ran around the shaft of the tornaq. When it was done, it held up the pad and in a voice that hurred like a sweet summer wind it spoke a brief translation: *Sometimes*. All of time seemed crushed into that moment. I sensed death, destruction, evil, darkness. I felt the auma of the universe turning.

I sensed a battle coming.

I dropped to my knees in front of Hilde. My hand was weak and my brain even weaker. But as I opened my fingers and the tornaq tumbled out, somehow it turned itself in the air and made its way back to her pouch. Once again, Yolen threw his arms around me. "Are you done?" he spat at the sibyl.

"Speak, boy, what did you see?" she demanded.

Nearly all of it had blurred, like mist upon the mountains. But I remembered the dragon and what it had said. As my breath came back I described the dragon's shape. All she did was sneer and say to Yolen, "You were right, the boy *is* simple."

Then she placed her foot upon the body by her feet and with one kick sent it rolling to the river. As it tumbled, the limbs began to crack and break away. By the time the water took it, the body had split into ash and small parts. They fizzled on the water before they sank.

Yolen and I looked in terror at Hilde.

"He was old," the sibyl said. And with the briefest of laughs, she pulled her cape around herself and melted into the background of trees.

Yolen quickly took my head into his hands and used his thumbs to pry my eyes wide. "Whatever you saw was a fantasy," he said.

"But —?"

"You must let go of it. These women are deceitful."

"But I saw a dragon *writing*," I said. And I bent down and drew the symbol in the earth. The wind stirred the tall green pines of Horste. Yolen spoke fiercely under his breath and put his sandal across the marks. He rubbed them out and pulled me away. "It was a fantasy," he said. "Do not speak of it again."

And I had to ask myself as we set off down the path, *If there was nothing unnatural about my vision, why does my master wish me to be silent?*

We walked through the morning and into the afternoon, this time with only the river for company. I wanted to talk, about Premen and the horse and the vision I had seen. But if I opened my mouth to muse upon these things, Yolen threatened to fill it with river mud and grass. So I did what my keeper wished of me. I walked straight and tall toward Kasgerden, now and then hearing Galen's soft roars as he sang his lament to his oncoming death.

By the late afternoon we arrived at the old stone bridge of Taan. The followers from Horste had made their way across it to the fertile farmlands on the other side. The Taans, like many of the ancient tribes, dwelled in places constructed of wood, usually cut from the forest of Horste. There was no thievery or conflict among the two peoples, but there was a sharp and persistent trade. What Horste gave in wood, Taan gave in sheep. One tribe slept among needles of pine; the other within timbers from the trees that dropped them. As we came upon the first of the kroffts, I noticed that the people, even the elderly, were leaving their dwellings and joining the Horste on the grassy undulations that were a feature of this land. Many of them were lying facedown upon the earth with their hands and feet spread out like stalks.

"What are they doing?" I asked.

Yolen shook his head and muttered to himself, "This is not right. Why are these people still here?"

There was a quiet roar in the distance. Dusk was drawing its dim skies upon us, but there was no mistaking the dark silhouette on the peak of Kasgerden. The followers, all of them, Horste and Taan, began to babble in appreciation. From a Taan woman's mouth, a song came forth. A strange, intoxicating hum that was taken up by most of the pilgrims present, especially the older ones.

Yolen dropped to his knees.

"What's happening?" I asked.

He nodded at the grassland and bade me place my hands upon it. And that was the first time I truly encountered the power of a dragon. Despite the season, the crispness in the air, the ground beneath my hands felt *warm*.

I took off my sandals and walked upon the grass. I danced. I laughed. There was *fire* in my feet. "How?" I said. "How is this possible?"

My keeper caught the hem of my robe and pulled me down. There was anger rumbling in his throat when he said, "You are a goat herder, not a god. In the presence of Gaia, you will kneel like the rest of us."

"This is Gaia?" I whispered, pressing the ground again.

"This is Galen," he said, through teeth bound with grit. "He is calling upon Gaia to draw up fire from the core of the Earth. It is a signal that he's ready to go back to the force that created him."

I let my fingers idle on the grass. Fire, coming up from the center of the Earth? Now my excitement was tamed a little. "How high will it rise?" Were we all to be consumed in the dragon's auma?

Before Yolen could speak, something whistled past my head at high speed. There was a thud against the side of the shelter nearest me. I looked up to see the bloodstained shaft of an arrow. A dead raven was pinned to the wall of the krofft, the head of the arrow right through its throat. The eyes of the bird had been removed. Three more arrows rained down and from each of them dangled a similar corpse. In the panic that followed I was drawn into a nearby krofft, for safety. As well as Yolen, three Taans were with us. A man, his wife, and their youthful daughter.

"Are they coming again?" asked the woman. She gathered the girl to her. They were very fine-looking, as Taans often were. The girl had eyes like the sheep she surely tended, large and soft and void of harm — but not of spirit.

"I don't think so," said the man. He had long yellow hair and a beard the same color. He was peering through a shuttered gap in the wall. "I can't hear their horses. But this is clearly another warning." He stepped away from the shutter but did not close it, allowing some light to fall across our faces. "You are welcome to shelter with us," he said. "Unless you confess to be allies of Voss." From his belt, he drew a large hunting knife.

"Rune!" gasped his wife. She could see the wild innocence splashed across my face and was shocked by her husband's show of aggression. He quickly relented and slid the knife back.

"Forgive me." He bowed his head. "Such a show of hostility shames the good name of the people of Taan. Twice today our homage to the dragon has been disturbed by riders bent on evil."

"We met them by the river," Yolen said. He briefly told the story. "You know this man as Voss?"

"That is how he announced himself to us. Voss, from the territory of the same name. You must have wondered why our people are still rooted here and not at the skirts of the mountain by now."

Yolen nodded. I remembered his puzzled question on the bridge.

Rune checked the shutter again. "He threatened us. Anyone leaving the district of Taan in search of fraas would be put to death."

"On whose authority?"

"On his. Did you see the black horse he rides?"

"I saw the horse." Yolen's back had been turned when the horses had charged us. But not mine.

I glanced at the girl. She was behind her mother, but her sheep's eyes were heavily intent on me. "It had blood in its eyes and a stump in its head."

The Taan man knotted his hands in anger. "That it did, boy. That it did."

Yolen shook his head, hardly able to believe this. "Are you saying it was a *healing* horse?"

Rune gave a grim-faced nod. "A unicorn, aye, from the slopes of Kasgerden, violated in the most appalling way. Its horn was sheared off at the base. Voss wielded the remnant at us. He commands some sort of dark power with it."

"Is he Premen?"

That word again. I was desperate for a meaning, but I held my voice in check.

Rune stalked sullenly across the room, stopping to light the wick of a candle with a splinter of wood he had taken from the fireplace. Above the fire hung a painted hunting bow. "I know nothing of Premen. But if the rumors of these . . . supermen are true, then Voss has turned all that is good in them to malice. No one dares leave the settlement. The leader of the Horste is aware of the threat. They have ended all thoughts of a pilgrimage for now and are looking to their sibyl for guidance. But I tell you, stranger, this sibyl will be no match for Voss."

And there were four dead ravens outside to prove

it. Hilde's enchantment with the dead man's eye had failed.

A heavy hand pounded the door. Without invitation, another man stepped in. He put a fist to his heart: the standard Taan greeting. "Rune, pardon this intrusion." His accent was more prominent than any Taan I had yet heard. A farmer, perhaps. A man of the fields. "The men are gathering now in the motested." He stared at Yolen and briefly at me. "Both tribes. No women — unless they be sibyls." He thumped his heart again and withdrew.

"What is a 'motested'?" I asked.

"Their meeting hall," said Yolen.

A meeting. A debate upon how to deal with Voss. My breathing quickened, but Yolen soon slowed it. He turned and put a firm hand on my shoulder. "Agawin, you will stay here." He glanced at the woman, who nodded her consent.

"No. I want to hear what is decided."

"You are two years from manhood. You will do as I command. Be aware that you are a guest of these people. You will ask nothing of them except their good grace." He ran a hand through a side of my hair. Then he headed for the meeting house with Rune of Taan.

"Agawin. That is a noble name." The woman spoke as the door closed in my face. I turned to look at her. It was impossible not to be impressed by her beauty. Her hair fell in two sweet braids to her shoulders and there were trinkets of bone in the lobes of her ears. Her dress was like nothing I had ever seen. Unlike the Horste women, whose legs below the knee were always exposed, the Taan wore gowns of decorated flax that bustled at their shoulders and swept around their ankles. At her waist was a graceful pouch, hung by a long strap across her breast. She put her hands into her sleeves and bent her knees slightly. It made me feel a little less anxious to leave. "I am Eleanor," she said, "and here is my daughter, Grella." I looked into her eyes. They drilled me with suspicion. She was older than me, but not by much, possibly just of marriage-able age. Her hair was fair and tied back in a tail. Her skin, like her mother's, was delicate and pink, as if she had been fashioned from fresh flower petals. She, too, wore a dress that reached her ankles and a pouch that was a little less subtle than her mother's. It was sewn with the same interlocking pattern that trimmed the neck and hem of her dress. "Please, sit," Eleanor said. She pointed to a flat seat carved from pine. It was covered with the brushed woolen hide of a sheep.

As if to claim an early advantage, Grella moved to the seat herself. But instead of sitting, she picked up something from it. A cloth, bound within a wooden frame. Strands of loose thread were hanging from the underside of the cloth. On its surface was stitched a picture of some kind.

"You like our tapestries?" Eleanor asked, as my eyes followed Grella to the better-lit side of the room. The girl tossed her hair and sat, cross-legged, on a low-slung bed freely covered with hides. She placed the tapestry frame across her lap. More examples of her work were pinned to the wall above her.

"Stop," she said as Eleanor drew me near. Grella held up a needle, made from a splinter of polished bone. "He's a cave boy. He smells of dung. I don't want it catching in the tapestries, Mother."

Her mother looked set to protest this rudeness but I countered it with a remark of my own. "Don't worry, my eyes are sharper than your nose. I can see your tapestries perfectly from here." And I stood where I was, some paces from the bed, and looked at the beautiful pictures they had made.

26

Scenery, mostly. Kasgerden and the white-tipped hills around it. The river. The settlement. The sheep being herded. The fields being worked. But the ones that opened my young eyes widest, and made me wish I hadn't planted my feet so far away, were those that pictured dragons.

When she saw where my gaze had wandered, Grella leaped up and stood before the tapestries. Her eyes were the color of amber stones.

"Have you met with all these creatures?" I asked. There were many types of dragon here, of many different shades, all in various stages of flight.

Eleanor answered for her. "The dragon that sits on Kasgerden is the first that Grella has truly glimpsed. But she has seen them in her mind ever since she was a child."

"How?" I asked the girl.

"I don't want him here," Grella hissed at her mother. "He asks too many questions." She lifted the needle, as if she'd like to prick my eye.

"He is a pilgrim," said Eleanor. "He has as much right to observe Galen as anyone. Be kind, Grella. Before this day is out, we might need all the friends we can get."

27

The girl wrinkled her nose. For one brief moment I thought I saw a glint of violet in her eyes, much as I had seen in the sibyl Hilde. She sat again and attended to the cloth, thrusting her needle into it with great ferocity, as if she wished she was stitching my eyelids together.

"Would you like to try it?" Eleanor said. She drew me away from Grella and opened a box in which there were a host of colored threads and needles. She picked a fresh cloth from a sleeve inside the lid. "Stitching is a Taan tradition." She invited me to sit with her on the pine seat. "Like most tribes, we remember our history in words, but we also preserve it on cloth. And everyone, even a boy from a cave, has to have a story to tell."

Across the room, Grella gave a sharp grunt.

Eleanor dipped into the box again. From a small compartment, she picked out a short black stick, whittled at one end to a dull point. It dirtied her skin as she rolled it through her fingers. "We call this a krayon. When moved across the flax it leaves a mark, which we then stitch over with a colored thread. Can you draw, Agawin? If I asked you to make a likeness of something — Kasgerden, for instance — could you do it? On the cloth?" She offered it to me.

I stared at it for several moments. At first, my mind was completely blank. I could picture my cave and the goats and the river — the great mountain, as Eleanor had said — but none of these held much appeal for me. Then an image did drift behind my eyes and I set the krayon to work on the cloth. Grella's curiosity hovered like the promise of brooding thunder, but she sat where she was until my drawing was done. It was only when her mother said, with some hesitation, "Is that . . . a *new* breed?" that the girl could no longer keep her distance. I had drawn, with some faith, the dragon I had seen on my journey with the tornaq. Grella snatched it from me. She studied it furiously and turned away to view it in a better light. "Where have you seen *this*?" She began to compare it to the tapestries already fixed to her wall.

Before I could speak or her mother could scold her, the door opened and Eleanor's man walked in. Yolen was a pace or two behind him.

Eleanor stood up. "Are you met so soon?"

"The meeting continues," Rune said brusquely. "The sibyl Hilde is asking for Grella."

The girl turned to look at him, her hand clenched tightly around my drawing.

Eleanor was at once both cautious and fearful. "What would a sibyl want with our daughter?"

Rune went to the girl and stroked her hair. "She wishes to engage with an innocent."

Eleanor of Taan at once shook her head. "But there are many young girls in the settlement. Rula. Katrina. Why choose Grella? She does not even know her."

"I offered her," said Rune. "The sibyl wants a girl that has been touched by a unicorn."

"Touched?" I muttered, but no one paid me heed.

"For what reason?" Eleanor asked her man.

"A way to reach Voss," he said.

For a moment our breaths fell as silently as snowfall. Then Eleanor spoke again, her voice charged with tension. "No. I forbid it. Let this . . . Voss have the fraas. Our daughter's life is more important than an old dragon's death."

"This is not just about the dragon," said Rune. He began to pace the room, pushing a hand through his thick yellow hair. He took my drawing from Grella and turned it through his hands, frowning as though it was the work of a goat. He put it on the seat where his wife had been sitting. "More pilgrims have joined us from Trooven. They come with a dire tale: Voss is attempting to seize control of all the settlements along the river."

"Control?" Eleanor was shocked. The word was in our language, but we rarely heard it used in the context that Rune was now implying.

Yolen said quietly, "All that has stopped him from attacking Horste and Taan is the appearance of Galen. But the dragon may be just a temporary distraction."

Rune poured himself a cup of water from a flagon. "Tell her the rest."

Yolen drew himself up to his full height. He looked frail and old beside the Taans. "The sibyl has cast the bones of a raven."

One of those that had been slain? I felt my knees weaken. She must have torn the bird apart to separate the bones.

"She reads in them Voss's greater intent." The walls seemed to lean in as Yolen took a breath. "He plans to slay the dragon. If he's successful, the prizes he will gain — scales, claws, any amount of fraas — will make him the most powerful man ever to walk the Earth."

"Stronger than Gaia herself," Rune growled, throwing back his drink.

"I will go to the motested," Grella said bravely. She stood forward. Her mother held her back.

"No, Grella."

"But the dragon must be saved."

"The dragon is in no danger." Eleanor frowned at the men as if they had dropped their wits in the river. "How can a man, even one with a tainted unicorn, get close enough to drive a spear through a dragon? At the first scent of evil it would turn him to ash."

A simple point, but a perfect argument. Even I had heard it said that dragons did not need to waste their energy commingling with men to read their intent. They could detect any hint of malice in a man simply from the odor given off from his skin. In Voss's case, that was as predictable as tomorrow's sunrise. My confidence was lifted. But not for long.

Yolen nodded politely and said, "Yes, I would agree — if the dragon was whole."

Once again, a wary silence gripped us. I had fully expected Yolen to announce that the burning of Voss would be just a merry spectacle, a blessed relief to faithful pilgrims and a lesson to foolish and arrogant men. But now I was reminded of his look of concern when the followers had discussed Galen's white undersides.

Could the dragon that was singing his flamesong on the mountain really be vulnerable to some devilish attack?

Yolen thought so. "The loss of color in the scales is a certain indication that its auma is fading. I believe the dragon has already shed its tear."

"But it would be dead," said Grella, echoing my words precisely. We looked at each other. For a moment we had unity, no danger of a needle in my eye.

Rune shook his head. "Brunne agrees with the seer."

"Brunne!" scoffed his wife. "That old fool? His teeth grind quicker than his brain these days."

"He is our keeper of legend," Rune said curtly, annoyed by his wife's poor show of respect. "He spoke briefly at the meeting — but well. He reminded us of an ancient detail: that if a dragon cries its tear through the eye it favors less, it may retain a small amount of its fire. Enough to enable it to fly a short distance and then sleep — like the winterfold animals do."

"Sleep?" said Grella.

"Until you and I are long dead," Yolen added.

"Why?" I asked him. "Why would it do that?" Had I not been taught that a dragon cries its tear so it may ascend to the spirit world, in joy? Why would it set itself down to *sleep*?

But all Yolen could say was "That I don't know."

"Brunne's visions have revealed that dragons the world over are doing this," said Rune.

Eleanor looked away, clucking like a hen.

"There can be very few left now," Yolen said. "This may be an act of self-preservation."

"Not if Voss has his way."

Rune knocked a fist against his mouth. Jewels of water glistened in his beard. He made no attempt to dry them. "There you speak all our futures, boy."

"Mother, I must go at once," said Grella.

This time her mother did not refuse. First, however, she looked hard at Rune — and even harder at Yolen. "What does this sibyl plan to do?"

"She wants to entice the unicorn from Voss. Without the horse, his power is greatly diminished. Hilde believes the right enchantment will draw it away."

"And what does Brunne say to this?"

"Brunne had retired to his krofft by then."

Eleanor extended a hand in despair.

"A song," said Grella. "I know a unicorn song!" She ripped a tapestry down from the wall. It pictured a child no higher than a barrel picking flowers at the edge of a woodland. A unicorn was shown approaching her. "My lullaby to Gaia attracted it," she said. She pushed the neck of her garment aside and showed us the first bare skin of her shoulder. To my surprise, there was the mark I had seen in my vision. The same drawing the dragon had made on its parchment, branded into Grella's soft flesh. "It touched me," she said. "I stroked its face and it laid the tip of its horn on my shoulder. Then it was gone. I never saw it again."

"How has this affected you?" Yolen inquired.

Rune gestured toward the tapestries. "Since that day, all the girl has stitched are dragons."

"I feel it," she said. "I feel its pain. The horse Voss rides is the same one, I'm sure of it. You should not have hidden me away when he came."

Her father said, "That was done for your safety."

"And how much less safe is this plan?" asked Eleanor. "Even if Grella can call the horse away, Voss will see it the moment it moves and instantly know of the deception."

"Not necessarily," Yolen said. He walked a pace or two, shaking the knotted ends of his belt. "The horse is greatly distressed. Its confusion is binding it to Voss's company — that and the fact he carries the horn. But if the lyrics of Grella's song are appropriate, the horse might be soothed and persuaded to run. They are fleet of foot. By the time Voss wakes, the horse will be with Grella."

"And then?" Eleanor looked at her husband, who had once again taken his knife from his belt.

"What are six against the men of three settlements?"

I saw a loss of color in Eleanor's cheeks. "You are not the warrior you once were, Rune."

"I will fight like a dragon for our freedom," he said. "I will not give up my homeland to any rogue Premen."

And with these brave words the decision was set.

Leaving Eleanor at home to muse upon our fate, we four — Rune, Yolen, Grella, and myself (this time, my master gave his consent) — made our way to the old Taan motested. We found the men in good heart and strident voice. They were passing around a flagon, drinking a brew prepared by Hilde.

"What is this?" Yolen asked the sibyl. He laid his palm across the neck of the flagon as it was presented up to Rune.

"A potion to give the men strength — and courage."

"Aye," said a man nearby. He was bending his

elbow, tensing his muscles. His upper arm, I saw, was greatly swollen, the veins wriggling about like snakes. "I feel it already. I am twice the man I was!"

"And three times as ugly!" another man called.

A roar of laughter rattled the pointed roof of the motested.

Without a moment's hesitation, Rune sank a long quaff, spilling rivulets down his beard again. He passed it to Yolen. My keeper shook his head. "I have my wits. That is all I require."

The men bellowed their displeasure. The sibyl took their cause.

"You more than anyone need it, seer. Sharp of mind you may be, but Voss's sword is sharper. He will run it through your chest as quickly as he passes a splint through a berry." She snatched up the flagon and held it to him. "Drink."

"Drink!" cried the men of Horste and Taan, pounding their feet till the motested thundered.

Yolen had no choice. He took a small draft, which I was sure he would have spat out had the sibyl turned her back. But I saw his neck ripple and the brew went down. Now the only male not to try it was me.

I reached for the flagon. The sibyl held it back.

The men bellowed, "Let him have it! Let him feel what it is to grow a hair on his chest!"

The sibyl thought long and carefully about it. Then she tipped the jug, and the dust on the floor had the last of her potion. "Someone has to stay and milk the goats, brave men."

They roared again and slapped their thighs. Even Yolen let a smile past his lips.

Now the sibyl drew Grella into view. She called for quiet while she spoke of her plan. In one hour, when the moon rose over Kasgerden, every man present would go with stealth to the forest of Skoga, which covered the western slopes of the mountain. Voss and his men were camped there, she said (more birds, sent as spies, had confirmed his position). The men would encircle Voss's camp but hide among the trees until the vital moment. Grella, the girl once touched by a unicorn, would enchant the dark horse and draw it away. This would leave the men free to attack. Voss and his followers were not to be spared.

But a hum of concern quickly rose among the Horste. The forest men knew of the Skoga pines and were deeply afraid to enter them. "What about the skog-katts?" they muttered. Those trees were the lair of legendary wildkatts. No one needed a tapestry to know that a skogkatt, with its haunting green eyes, could bedazzle a man, then rip out his throat with one slash of its claws.

A loud debate blew up. The sibyl ended it in one swift act. She threw the flagon to the wooden floor, smashing it. "Spineless idiots" she called the men of Horste. Did they really imagine that Voss hadn't thought of this? That he could sleep soundly surrounded by the threat of skogkatt claws? She raised one hand and opened it. Two bushy tails dropped out. She threw one at Rune. Another at a startled Trooven man. These souvenirs had come from her spies, she said. Voss had cleared the forest of skogkatts. But in doing so, had left himself vulnerable to spears . . .

So the men, their confidence restored, returned to their families to make what preparations they needed. The sibyl took Grella away for counseling. And my role in this battle was quickly defined: I was to stay in the krofft with Eleanor until the coming ugliness was done.

"But I will seem a coward in front of Grella!"

"You will be little use dead," Yolen chided. "Not even as goat feed."

"I can fight as well as any man!" I showed him my arm, growing rounder and firmer with every passing day.

"You're a boy," he said. "And you will do as I command."

And that was an end to it.

But he did at least allow me to wander the settlement. And in the hour before the moon, when darkness was upon us and the mood over Taan was strangely subdued, I found myself walking near the edge of the site. It was there that I came upon a tumbledown dwelling, buried among an isolated thicket of pines. A place so badly in need of repair that its occupants were surely wood chewers or rats. Yet there was a wisp of smoke from its chimney and a candle guttering weakly within. The door was bent and ajar. A crackling noise was passing out through the gap. I peered inside and saw a pair of hands resting on a pair of knees. Then a man's voice croaked, "Come in, Agawin. I've been waiting for you."

"Wh-who are you? H-how do you know me?" I stepped back from the door a little. I was sure I hadn't been seen. And other than Rune's family, who among the Taan tribe knew my name?

"I have seen the dragon that speaks through you," he said.

A terrible shudder ran down my arms. "Are you a seer?"

"I am Brunne. Some call me 'seer.' Some call me weak in the head. Perhaps I am, to be speaking to a *boy* of a creature that can shape the future — on parchment."

That was all the enticement I needed. I stepped in, leaving the door a little wider — if only to allow the escape of foul air. The place was repugnant with the smell of sweating fish. So rank that I had to pull my robe across my mouth. The seer Brunne rocked in his creaking chair. He was old and his eyes were like smooth white pebbles. Since I did not see him at the motested, someone must have guided him back. For when I passed my hand across his crumpled face the eyes refused to flicker or follow. But I learned that day that even a man who appears to be blind might see with the other senses he possesses. My heart almost stopped when his hand came up and he clamped my arm with the strength of a bear.

"Evil has settled on this world," he rasped.

His fingers were bound like rope to my flesh. Through them flowed an energy that crept along my arm and wove itself into my twitching neck. I could feel it running all through my head, like the roots of a plant might spread into the ground. A fine dust began to sting my eyes. The reek of oil from his mouth was horrendous.

"I am not a follower of Voss," I stuttered, thinking this was a test of my loyalty.

The old man grunted and let me go. I fell to the floor, startled by the sound of fish bones breaking against my hands. The runners of his chair came down to crush more. Now I understood the crackle — and the dust.

"Voss is nothing," he said.

Then why was every man sharpening a blade, about to risk his life in battle with him? "I am told he wields a dark power," I said, remembering Rune's description in the krofft.

"Or it wields him," Brunne said oddly. "Voss is in the grip of a shadow."

I rose to my feet. The man and his odor made my gut wrench. Even so I spoke up boldly. "A shadow is nought but a product of the light." Yolen had often soothed me thus when the shadows of the cave had tricked me as a child.

"Spoken like a wise apprentice," said Brunne. His lips creased into a smile. He leaned forward. The crackling instantly stopped. "Tell me, boy, does light have auma?"

I looked at the candle flame, bending to the window as if it, too, would be glad to escape. "Gaia blesses all things with auma," I said. "Why should light be any different?"

Brunne, I thought, gave a satisfied nod. "And which has more: light or fire?"

In the distance, I heard poor Galen roar. Was the dragon speaking to the rising moon? I knew I must be done here soon. I wanted to see Yolen before the men left. "I do not know. What has this to do with Voss?"

"When you can answer this question," he said, "you will illuminate the shadow in Voss and be a thousand-fold superior to him."

A hard wind whistled through the open doorway. Every panel in the derelict krofft began to groan. I did not wish to be crushed among fish bones, but my boyish curiosity would not take me out of there. "Teach me what I need to know, seer Brunne."

He sat back, pressing his fingertips together. "You are already learning, Agawin. The tornaq has shown you the way."

"How do you know about the tornaq?" I pressed. "Are you in league with Hilde?"

Brunne spluttered with laughter. He filled the air with another coarse belch. "Hilde would gladly empty my veins in search of the wisdom that I protect. The tornaq is not the sibyl's to command. It will leave her when its work is done."

Leave her? Was the tornaq alive? I thought back to my time by the river. How *had* the charm returned to Hilde? "Is it yours?" I asked. "Does it watch her for you?"

He tilted his head, but refused to answer. "You are a most unusual boy. What did the dragon reveal to you?"

Now was my chance to be a little wary, but I had nothing to gain by withholding the truth. "I saw it write," I said. "It made a mark on the parchment. The same three-lined mark that was on the tornaq. After that I saw a host of terrible things. Vile creatures made in the image of dragons. Darkness. A shadow on the land. Death."

"And it all begins here ... with Voss," Brunne muttered.

"If he slays Galen, will my vision come to pass?"

Brunne put back his head and spoke a strange reply. "Sometimes," he said.

And, oh, how my heart missed a giant beat. And I realized then that Brunne might well have let go of my arm, but he had not entirely let go of my mind. Some part of him, some part not really a man, was exploring me and seeking to take a hold.

"Are you Premen?" I asked the seer.

His lips parted and he took in a ghastly breath, as if a spear of ice had been passed through his heart. His dreadful eyeballs swiveled and locked. In one of them, a roving center appeared, more hideous than the egg that had been there before. "Not for very much longer," he croaked.

"What's the matter?" I asked. "Brunne, what do you mean?" His hands were shaking on the arms of his chair.

"Come closer, boy. A devil approaches."

A devil? What was he talking about?

"You need to understand the enchantments of time."

Time? What secrets did *time* hold? Every day, my fingernails grew a little more and the grass in the meadows rose a little higher and another of Yolen's hairs turned to gray. Time was a simple measure of change. The whole world moving forward as one.

I stepped toward him. But in that instant he seemed to change his mind. He swiftly raised a hand and some force pushed me back into the shadows of the krofft. He gave out a groaning sound like nothing I had heard from man or beast before — a rasp that rattled every bone in his chest, followed by a shudder that seemed to expel something more than air from his lungs. I gasped and covered my face. Whatever Brunne had concealed within his body was now in mine and sheltering there. The last thing I heard him say to me was this: "Keep Galen within your sight."

The door opened and a hooded figure stepped in. I could not tell if it was man or woman, but it seemed to know there were fish bones on the floor. I saw the figure pick up the full skeleton of a fish and draw it fast across Brunne's throat. The seer made a gentle gurgling noise. His head fell forward onto his chest. A dark stain ran down his shabby clothing.

The figure threw the fish bone aside and left.

For several moments, I was too petrified to move. Then I crept forward and shook Brunne's shoulder. His body slumped forward and tipped from the chair. I heard the zip of an arrow, and the next I knew the roof was alight. Through the open door, I saw the hooded figure running for the trees. The building burned while I gathered my senses. Then I started to shout. *"Fire! Fire!"* And I ran to Rune's krofft.

I burst in, calling for Yolen and Rune. Eleanor was on her knees, trying to stir them. Both men were on the floor, snoring like dogs.

"What happened?" I gasped.

"They collapsed in a stupor. I can't revive them." Foam was frothing on Rune's red lips. Yolen looked calm, but deeply asleep.

By now, I could hear a great clamor outside. I dived for the shutters and threw them wide. Women were running from krofft to krofft, calling to one another about their men. I saw a Horste man slumped against a water trough. A pan of water in the face could not bring him around. Nor could a hefty kick in the ribs. A woman spun past me, clutching her hair. "Sorcery!" she wailed. "A sibyl's work!"

All the men who had drunk from Hilde's potion

were asleep. Slowly, the settlement realized it was tricked.

"Eleanor, where is Grella?" I panted.

The worry in her pretty eyes gave me my answer: already taken, by Hilde.

"I need food," I said urgently. I opened the satchel I'd brought from the cave and looked around the krofft for anything I could eat. There was meat on a table and apples in a basket. I packed as much as I thought I could carry. I bent over Yolen and kissed his head. "Forgive me, but I must go." I slid Rune's hunting knife from his belt.

"No!" Eleanor blocked the doorway. "The sibyl will kill you, even if Voss doesn't."

I looked at this beautiful, sad-eyed woman and wished, in part, she could have been my mother. "Brunne is dead. I saw him slain. His dwelling is alight. All the world is in peril. You must let me go."

These words of heroism tumbled off my lips, but it felt like another boy was speaking them. Whatever life-force Brunne had just breathed into me seemed to have swelled me with courage — or madness. I had no idea how to avenge the old man or save a young girl I barely knew. But I glimpsed through the shutter and saw the moon rising and an idea suddenly sprang upon me. "I'm going to hail the dragon. Galen will defeat Voss and bring Grella home."

Eleanor rested her palms on my face. "Agawin, brave boy, listen to me. A hundred years ago, what you are saying might have been possible. But there are too many tales now of dragons being cruelly mistreated by men. Galen will not come to your aid. He will flame you as readily as he would burn Voss. All the creature wants is to die in peace."

"It can die when Grella is safe," I said. "What peace will it have with Voss on its trail?"

I moved for the door but she blocked me again.

"Very well. If I cannot stop you, let me tell you what little I know about dragons and give you two things that might help you in your quest." She walked to the wall and pulled down a tapestry. It showed a truly magnificent dragon, as monstrous and terrifying as it was stunning. "This is Grella's favorite. She says it is a queen."

A female. The fiercest of all dragonkind. On the bottom of the tapestry the girl had stitched a name. *Gawaine.* "How does she know this beast?"

Eleanor lifted her shoulders. "She claims they are real in her mind. They come to her on the wings of time. I've never known what she means by that, but perhaps this queen will be a charm to Galen. Take it. Keep it near to your heart. Pray that it brings you strength."

"And the second thing?"

She walked to the fireplace and reached for the bow. She fetched arrows as well in a sling for my shoulder. "The swiftest way to Kasgerden is through the Skoga forest. But you must swear to me you will not enter that place."

"Voss has cleared it of skogkatts," I said. But the moment those words were out of my mouth my new sense of being questioned their validity. After the deceit in the motested, why should I believe any of Hilde's claims?

"Use the edge of the forest as a guide," Eleanor said. "Keep it on your right hand and it will eventually lead you to a pathway up the mountain. The peak is well hidden till the final climb, but by the time you see its point against a clear sky, the dragon will know you are there.

"If you travel without sleep, you will reach the first trees by morning. After that, you have no more than two days to catch up with Voss. A dying dragon likes to wait until the moon is fully round before it commits itself to Gaia. The moon is almost at that stage. Voss will strike when the dragon is at its weakest, shortly before it closes its eye. My guess is they have taken Grella to calm it."

"With her lullaby?"

"Yes. She will be of no use to them when it's done."

"I'll find her," I said as a tear began to bloom in Eleanor's eye.

I turned and lifted the door latch.

"Wait," she said. "One more thing." She hurried back to the fireside again and opened a small, decorative box, the kind women used for personal things. She returned, rubbing her fingers in a pot of waxy lotion. She pushed back the sleeve of my robe and rubbed some into my wrist.

It had already disappeared into my skin before I asked her, "What is this?"

"A scent."

She saw my gaze narrow.

"Don't worry. It will not give you away to Voss. Only a Taan could detect it. It will last for three days. If you should get close enough to Grella, she will recognize it and know that help is at hand."

With that, she kissed my head and let me go.

I ran at a steady pace all night, guided by the moon and the shape of the mountain. Beyond the borders of the settlement the farmlands divided into fields of crops or open grassland grazed by sheep. I followed the paths the Taan had made, crossing the earth like a silent wave, flowing forward but never pulling back. For every steep hill there was a gentle valley. For every wayward bend another course that ran true. Even when the river curled its tail across me I was able to meet it at its shallowest point and skip across the boulders that sat up in its bed. And when the rain came to soften and puddle the ground I was nimble across it, too swift to be stopped. Yolen would have been proud of me.

But he would have been puzzled, too. Yes, I was young and able-bodied and naturally adapted to the land we inhabited, but I was a boy with limited endurance. How, he would have asked, could I have run until dawn?

The answer lay back in Brunne's krofft. As my feet beat their rhythm against the earth, I began to feel that I was not alone. Whatever had attached itself to my mind was cleverly adjusting the potential of my body to keep my heart pumping and my lungs filled with air. All I had to do was focus my intent. *The forest, by morning,* I kept saying to myself. And my "companion" strived to accomplish the task. Only if I tried to think too much did my muscles start to burn and my knees begin to ache.

But I had to know what Brunne had passed to me. So, as the morning light approached and the trees began to come within hailing distance, I dipped a little deeper into my mind. This is what I learned.

"What are you?" I asked.

My right thigh twinged, but only for a moment.

We are Fain, they said. I felt them in my head like a gentle breeze. Like a cloud of twinkling stars. Alive.

"Are you my enemy?"

No.

"Then why are you inside me? What do you want?"

We seek the fire of the dragon, they said.

"You are hunting fraas?"

No. We would be one with the beast.

"To kill it?"

To die with it and live again.

This sent my thoughts into a rapid spin and I felt the sharp taste of exhaustion in my mouth. The creatures said, *You must concentrate, Agawin. You must follow your intent.*

I looked up at the mountain and remembered my quest. Grella. Voss. Galen the dragon. With each of these thoughts, a fresh burst of energy surged through my body. "Show yourself," I said.

We cannot, said the Fain. *We have no form except that we inhabit. When we are bound to your form, men call themselves "Premen." We were Brunne. Now we are Agawin. We can roam freely if we wish.*

"I am Premen now?"

Yes.

My heart thumped against my chest. Premen. What would Yolen make of *that*?

"Where are you from? Are you even of this world?"

My rhythm picked up. I was smoother now. The Fain swarmed in and out of my memories. *We were like you once.*

"A boy?"

Human. We evolved and detached. We are thought without form.

The first tall spikes of the forest loomed up. I adjusted my course to keep them on my right.

We are consciousness, pure.

"Then why have you attached again — to Brunne and to me?"

Why not, in fact, attach to the dragon?

Although my thought was simply that — a thought, the Fain beings read it with ease. *We seek illumination, but the dragon's fire alone is not enough. The human form must also be present.*

And what would be the result, I wondered, when men and Fain and dragon came together?

Their reply was swift. *Perfection*, they said.

Sunlight flickered across the land. I was scurrying upward now, over a bed of bald earth and shale. To the east, nestled in the hollow of the hills, I could see the great lake of Varlusshandaan gleaming like a frozen eye. Farther north ran the wild reindeer herds that dragons of old had poached from sometimes. Was that another reason Galen was here? I listened for his roar but heard nothing other than my constant footfalls. The only sense truly alive in me was smell. In the clarity of morning the pine resin was so fresh it made my nostrils dance. At any other time I would have been lifted up like a feather. For there was nothing to touch the raw beauty of the stone and the swathes of green earth that served it — and the pines. This was Kasgerden in all its glory. But all I could think of as I finally stopped running and rested my hand against the first tall tree was the object of my journey, the warrior Voss. Brunne's words were coming back like whispers. *Voss is in the grip of a shadow. It wields him, not the other way about.* Bending double I said to the Fain, "Do you speak through Voss as well?"

They buzzed and circled around my mind. *Voss is tainted*, they said. *There is Fain within him. A dark form. The Ix.*

And there, all hopes of perfection burst. So there were beings, just as powerful as the Fain, that would use dragons and unicorns and innocent humans in the pursuit of evil?

We must triumph, said the Fain.

"That we must," as Rune might have said. That we must.

Tiredness had swamped my body by now. But I moved on, following the edge of the forest, this time keeping to a walking pace and taking water at regular intervals. I could see what Eleanor had meant about this trail. The general curve of the trees would bring me to the rockiest side of Kasgerden; already I could see its famous gray scarps. But the slope here, though it still required climbing, was the choice of the novice. I had once heard Yolen say that this approach was like "scaling a giant who had laid his hand, palm up, on the ground." For a nimble boy, aided by the Fain, it would be easy. But it would not be quick.

And the lure of the trees was profound. The pines had stood for many thousands of years, their secrets as dense as their thickening number. Sensing my desire to test the maze, the Fain counseled that to travel through the trees was quicker but the likelihood of going astray very great. Then there were the skogkatts, of course. Even supposing there was only one wildkatt for every two hundred trees, that would still be a multitude for Voss to have cleared. Something told me the katts were in there still. Maybe looking back at me. Waiting. Keen.

I put aside any thoughts of temptation. But as I adjusted my bow against my shoulder I saw something that changed my mind. A strand of blue thread was clinging to the bark of a nearby tree. I snatched it up.

Horses have entered the forest, said the Fain.

I looked at the bracken. I had never learned how to track a horse; I had never had any reason to. A hunting man, one of the Horste, perhaps, might have deduced from the breakage of twigs that the pattern could only have been made by hooves. But what I saw among the needles was not a row of prints but a small trail of horse dung, relatively fresh. Voss and his men had been here.

I stepped into the forest. The Fain inside me buzzed.

"Help me look for more thread," I whispered. If they had gone through on foot, maybe Grella had left a trail. The Fain, I could tell, were wary of the venture. Nevertheless, I felt a slight pinch in my eyes and the light in the forest seemed a little less dim. Straightaway, I spotted another piece of thread, ten trees farther in, positioned about waist height off the ground. I crept forward and took it. The same blue as before. Clever, clever Grella.

The forest breathed. A needle fell and made me look up. High above, in the few chinks of blue I could see, the points of the trees were ticking to the west. Suddenly, the bracken rustled. I quickly stepped back. My footfall made a crunch that could have been heard a small field away, but the bow was off my shoulder and loaded and ready. I had aimed at every possible gap in the trees before I realized the "rustlers" were only mice.

I closed on them, still tensing the bow. When they saw me, they scattered in all directions. Some seemed to leap from a shadowy hole at the base of a tree. As I drew near, I saw that the hole was an open carcass, festering and partly eaten away. An arrow was lodged between a set of dried ribs. The skull was stripped and the eyes removed. What was left of this unfortunate creature was covered in matted, blood-stained fur. It was a skogkatt. Several hours dead.

I lowered my bow and put the arrow back. So there was some truth in the motested story. Voss had been here, killing the katts on his shortcut to the dragon. And Grella, in her way, had recorded it.

Now I felt impelled to follow their path. So I hunted the markers with greater enthusiasm, but much less caution. And I learned two things about Voss in the process: that he was brutal — but above all, cunning.

I came upon three more threads and another dead katt before the trail spilled me into a small clearing, just a circular patch of ground no greater in width than Yolen's cave. I saw another thread on the far side of the circle and ran to pick it off. There was more, clinging to the neighboring tree. I picked it and saw another next to that. And another next to that. I turned and looked around the clearing.

There was blue on every tree.

My heart thumped.

The first skogkatt scuttled down a pine to my left, moving so fast he seemed almost weightless. His brown fur blended so well with the forest that all I could target was the sound of his claws. As I raised my bow, he spiraled around the dark side of the tree. My arrow whistled with murderous intent, nicking the bark and skewing away tamely without tasting blood. By then, the scratch of their claws was everywhere. At least one katt to every tree. And in the gaps at ground level, deadly green stars. A sea of eyes moving toward me. I was doomed.

Lay down your bow, said the Fain.

I was afraid to. I clung to it. Turning like a madman. Target to target. "Can we outrun them?"

Unlikely.

"Climb?"

They are tree dwellers, Agawin.

And the ground would be unforgiving if I fell.

Withdraw your weapon. They may show you mercy.

And kill me quickly? Without hindrance — or mess?

I rested my aim on the leading katt. It was three times the size of any other I had seen. Brown, as most of the skogkatts were, with streaks of black running through his thick fur. His ears were tufted, in the way of some owls. The intense green eyes were exquisitely savage. As he squatted down, ready to spring at me, I could have put an arrow right between those eyes. One last act of cruel defiance. But I went the way of the Fain instead. I fired my arrow into the ground.

Noble. But pointless.

The attack came, not from the front, but from a katt I could not see, to my rear. The Fain, which seemed to have awareness in all directions, warned me and I turned to meet the creature as he leaped. He wasn't heavy, but the shock of the impact made me stumble backward. I fell to the forest floor, using the arch of the bow as a shield. A paw flashed forward, eager to shred any part of my face. Several times I felt the draft as his claws passed my throat. If I had been in any doubt about the sharpness of those hooks I had only to look at my weakened bowstring, shredded at one end to a spider line. The katt hissed and showed me his fangs. They were as terrifying as anything I'd imagined on a dragon. I knew I could not hold this creature off for long. But as he lunged once again I saw a slim chance to gain an advantage. I moved the bow and let the katt's head poke between the arch and the string. The stink of raw meat from his gullet was foul, but in less than the time it took to blink I had the string around the katt's neck, looped in a twist. I paid for my courage with a claw that ripped a stream of hot blood from my arm. But as I pulled on both sides of the bowstring, snapping it, the creature squealed and I was able to roll with him. I had the skogkatt on his back and I could strangle him at will. The other katts knew it. They stopped their advance.

"I wish you no harm!" I cried out. "But I have no desire to die here today!"

The katt grizzled in fury and kicked a leg. I tightened my grip. The skogkatt gurgled and rested his body in surrender. The other skogkatts, I noticed, exchanged hurt glances.

They are intelligent, said the Fain.

"What does *that* mean?" I hissed. In the short time I'd had these beings in my head I had come to know how to be irritated by them. Were they my ally or just interested spectators? That question seemed to have been fearfully answered when, in the next instant, my mind went blank and I realized the Fain had gone.

But they had not deserted me. I saw one of the skogkatts throwing his head from side to side and leaping about as if all his fleas had bitten at once. The spectacle lasted just a few moments. Then with a sudden zing of awareness, I felt the Fain come back.

They recognize your victory. They do not wish to see a sacrifice. The katt you are holding down is a favorite. His mate was killed by Voss. This is why he alone attacked. Hold up your wrist. The one without the blood.

"Why?"

Let them scent Grella.

The Taan lotion. I did as commanded and waved my wrist. My arm tingled and I sensed that the Fain had loosened Eleanor's potion right across the clearing. Every skogkatt nose began to twitch. "I seek this girl!" I shouted. "Where is this girl?"

The katts sniffed on.

They do not understand your words, said the Fain, *but your intent is mixed with the auma of the scent. They know now that you are not like Voss.*

But there was a better way to prove it. I glanced down at the ailing skogkatt and released him.

The skogkatt jumped to his feet with more energy than I would have credited. He, too, had got the scent from Taan in its nostrils. As more of his companions swarmed to him to gratefully rub cheeks, the skogkatt looked me up and down and burbled at me.

"Can we speak to him?" I asked the Fain.

We will adapt your voice, they said.

I felt movement in the muscles of my throat.

Speak again, said the Fain. *Tell them who you are.*

"I am Agawin," I said to the katts, though it sounded to my ears like a meaningless rasp.

Every one of them pricked their tufted ears. Dozens of green eyes grew in size. A rare and rather beautiful sight.

The katt I had battled with padded forward. He tilted his head and observed me carefully. Then he switched his gaze to my arm and ran his tongue all along the wound. He cleared the blood, but left a trail of syrupy fluid behind.

Do not cleanse it, said the Fain. *There are healing qualities in his saliva. This is a mark of respect.*

"I am Tryst," said the katt. He raised a proud head. "You fought well — for a human child."

But I was more than a child. I was Premen now. Human and Fain, commingled together. I felt the Fain swarming around my wound. Examining. Learning. Spectating again. The entire scratch was burning like fury. Even so, I resisted the temptation to wipe it. "I was betrayed, as you were. We are not enemies."

I heard the skogkatts growling one name: "Voss."

"How long ago did he pass through here?" I asked.

"He did not," said Tryst. "The dark one you speak of came into the forest, slaying at leisure. His men attached thread to the trees. Then they left."

A trap. A simple trap. To draw pursuers in. To be slaughtered by the katts while Voss took a leisurely ride up the mountain.

He is cunning, said the Fain, coming back to my mind.

And Hilde, too. In league with him, surely. "Did you fight Voss?"

Tryst shook his head. His fur, I noticed, had thickened up again around his neck. "He has the wits of Premen and the magicks of a unicorn. Nothing but a dragon could defeat him."

But the dragon was weak. I put the thought aside. "Will you lead me through the forest?"

Tryst looked uncertainly at some of the others.

"I must reach the dragon ahead of Voss."

A few whiskers twitched. "Can you tame it?" asked Tryst.

"I must try," I said. "Or the girl will die and Voss will spread his evil over Skoga and Taan."

Tryst and three more went into a huddle. After a short round of intense chatter, during which one of the katts pulled away with a petulant hiss, Tryst turned back to me and said, "We will guide you to the Skogan Stones, which stand in plain view of Kasgerden's peak. The stones are not far, but the way to them is steep."

You must rest, said the Fain.

The soft patter of water drummed the forest floor. I looked up at the sky. A patch of marshy rain clouds were drifting south. The skogkatts were slinking back into the trees, already searching for warmth and cover. I was exhausted and wanted to be out of the rain as well. I said to Tryst, "I need time to sleep."

He licked a paw and said, "Katts sleep often, but not for long. Shelter where you can. Be ready when we come for you."

"Why were you arguing?" I looked at the katt that had walked off in anger.

But Tryst just repeated his last command. "Be ready when we come." And with a flourish of his bushy tail he was gone.

I found a place where the canopy of branches was thickest. I slept for what seemed like the second it took to lay my head on my satchel and yawn. I dreamed of Brunne. Over and again I witnessed the moment just before the fish bone was drawn across his throat and his voice was still able to croak about time. What wisdom had he not been able to speak? How did it connect to the dragon with the parchment? His final words swept through my mind. *Keep Galen in your sight*. And then Galen pushed his fearsome head into my dreams. His jaw unlatched and I raised my arms to welcome his fire. Everything I knew about myself was burned. But out of my ashes rose a new form. I was Agawin, the boy. And then I was . . .

. . . woken by bark chippings tickling my cheek. Spluttering like an idiot, I leaped to my feet, brandishing my knife at empty space. One of the katts was clinging upside down to the tree I'd been under. He spread a set of claws and idly licked them. *Nyeh*, he went, in a belittling tone. The katt looked a little pleased with himself.

Tryst was sitting on a root nearby, his thick tail wrapped across his stout front paws. The rain had stopped, but the ends of his fur were glistening still. His bright green eyes were wide and alert. "I bring news of Voss."

I rubbed the tiredness away and asked what he knew.

"The eagles have seen him, halfway up the mountain."

"You commingle with eagles?" It occurred to me then that I had heard no sound of birdsong in the forest. Winged creatures were too afraid to roost here, perhaps?

"During winterfold we leave them mice," said Tryst. "It pleases them — and keeps them out of the forest."

"They hunt you?"

"They try." He wrinkled his nose. "Voss is making no attempt to hide his presence."

"But Galen will see him."

"He already has. He sent two eagles to challenge Voss. Voss captured them and roasted them over a fire. Kasgerden weeps with their scent."

I shook my head in disbelief. "What kind of man would dare taunt a dragon?"

One that is confident of victory, said the Fain.

Tryst stood up and groomed his fur. "Galen has yet to retaliate. It's not clear why he waits; the eagles refuse to say. But no dragon would turn away from this threat." He looked me in the eye. "You, however, still can. Go back, Agawin. We will lead you to safety. You cannot hinder Voss. And you have no hope of defeating him."

"I defeated *you*," I said as more katts drifted into the clearing. Tryst raised his head proudly. I added at once, "Sometimes even the finest warriors meet with unfavorable luck. Voss has a weakness. Why else would he take an innocent girl and drug the men of three tribes so they could not follow him?"

An interesting argument, the Fain replied.

"Take me to the stones," I said to Tryst.

The katt stared at me as if I had a wish to be dead. But he did not question my bravery further. "Six of us will escort you. We cannot pass beyond the edge of the forest. Once the way through the trees becomes clear, you must face Voss and the dragon alone."

I nodded and picked up my satchel. A hole had been gnawed in the bottom. Out of it tumbled an apple core. "Mice," said Tryst. I heard the katts snicker. I sighed and picked up my bow. I feared for the cheese I had brought, but hopefully the tiny thieves had left me some meat.

Making the slightest of chattering sounds, Tryst flipped his tail and sprang into the forest. I followed him directly, though it wasn't easy. He was nimble and often bathed in shadow. I saw the other katts, too, but only in snatches, so well did their fur blend in with the trees. A small squeak now and then, followed by a fierce territorial growl, would alert me to the fact that one of them had caught a careless rodent. Always, they were ruled by the need to hunt.

Before long, I felt the Fain working my muscles to assist me up the gradients Tryst had warned about. For most of the climb my feet were able to gain good purchase and I kept to the katt's unerring pace. But as we approached the limits of the forest the plain brown bracken thinned like the hair on an old man's head and Kasgerden began to show itself, mainly in patches of loose gray shale that slid or broke away from my grasping hands. With little earth for their roots, the trees petered out. The light grew stronger. The ground, firmer. As we approached the final pine, several katts scampered up into its branches. Only Tryst came to the very edge.

He sat and dipped his head forward. The mountainside had become quite shallow, an escarpment of shale and rough earth and grass. Well beyond it were the harsh gray slabs of rock that soared up into the mountain proper. I saw a look of deep longing enter Tryst's eyes, as if he would like to go bounding up there. "Why can't you leave the trees?"

"Look at the stones," he said.

Among the shale were a number of large, weathered stones. They were not, as I'd imagined, tall fingers of granite, but a jumble of strange, misshapen boulders scattered over a widespread arc. "What happened here?"

Tryst was about to reply when we both heard the clip of hooves. I dived for cover, behind the same tree Tryst had quickly climbed. He laid himself flat on the branch above me. I reached for my bow and primed it.

Two men, said the Fain, sensing their auma.

Voss?

No.

Grella?

Just men.

"What's in it for us?" I heard one of them say. Dull. Disillusioned. Not too bright. I saw the first horse come into view. It was finding it hard to stay steady on its feet. The rider cursed and slid out of the saddle. He looked of Horste stock. Wild-haired and bearded. The color was a match for his dark brown jerkin. His pants were ripped. There were holes in his boots. He broke wind as he walked toward the stones.

"What's in it for us is a nasty end if we don't follow Voss's orders," said the other. He was thinner than the first man. Rangy. Mean. Hair that draped in lanky spikes around his bony, milk-skinned face. He had a lean, crooked nose. A mole on his chin. Sunken eyes, always on the lookout for danger. As they swept in my direction, I turned sideways behind the tree. The Fain slowed my heartbeat to keep me quiet.

The first man said, "I'm bored of looking for paths for the horses. I need something to *kill*."

The other man spoke in a soft mumble. "Well, there's a great big scaly brute up top just waiting to feed on a goof like yer."

"The old feller in the krofft, he was easy," bragged the man. "Ready for a dragon now, I am."

"You were seen, Egil."

"Nah," he said. "In and out like a shadow, I was."

"I'm telling you, I saw a kid run out."

My arrow hand began to shake.

"So what?" Egil said. He unbuttoned his pants. "The men was all drugged. We ain't gonna be followed."

"Get back on your horse," his companion said suddenly.

He's reading an auma wave, the Fain commingled. *I cannot tell if it's yours or Tryst's.*

I looked up. Tryst had bared his fangs.

"I need to pee," said the man on the ground. "When you gotta go, you gotta go."

"Hold it in," the other said, tightening his rein. "There's something hiding in the trees."

Egil turned his bearded face toward us. "Katts? So what? Let them look. They ain't gonna test the sibyl's curse, are they?"

Curse?

Agawin, you must remain steady, said the Fain.

"This is probably one, right here," said Egil. He jumped, two-footed, onto a stone and aimed a stream of urine at it.

The first drops had barely splattered the rocks when the branch above me twanged and Tryst broke cover.

Mercifully, Egil knew nothing of his fate — perhaps a deserved flash of pain as the skogkatt's jaws closed around his hand (the one aiming the pee) and the formidable teeth bit through whatever flesh they could find. By then, the other man had pulled a knife and whipped it with venom toward the katt. It struck Tryst cleanly in the middle of the ribs, but bounced off with a booming clang. It clattered down the hillside and came to rest not far from my hiding place. Egil's horse bolted. The knife thrower cursed. I looked on in horror. Egil, and the katt that had ended his life, had both turned to stone.

You must be decisive now, said the Fain.

I could have shot an arrow through the knife thrower's heart as he slipped off his horse to investigate. I could have avenged Tryst there and then. But I was not a killer. There was a better way, I thought. I stepped out of the trees while his back was turned. "Move, and you're next."

His body froze.

"There are five more katts in the trees and I can easily put an arrow through the back of your head."

"The boy," he said, as if he wanted to congratulate

his powers of intuition. His shoulders relaxed. I allowed him to turn.

"Where's Grella?"

He saw the glint of the arrowhead, the sweat in my fingers. His tongue swept nervously across his lips. "Whatever you plan to do you should do it soon, boy. Voss isn't far away. He'll crush you like a fly if he sees you're armed."

"Grella," I repeated.

"Bound," he said, grinning.

I aimed for the triangle of flesh below his chin.

"Unhurt," he added, raising his hands. "The girl's an irritation. Never stops talking."

"Take me to her."

"And what good would that do yer?" He looked up at Kasgerden's peak and laughed. "You and your katt band won't be jumping Voss. Even the dragon's scared of coming down for him."

He took a step forward.

I sucked in through my teeth, making sure he heard the bowstring stretch.

The hands came up again. He smiled, thinly. "Those things are dangerous, boy. It's not the wound they make, it's the infection they cause. Ever watched a man rot from an arrow wound? Trust me, it ain't pleasant. Put the bow down, eh?"

I aimed between his eyes.

He wisely stood back. "All right. I'll do a deal with yer. What's your name, kid?"

Do not tell him, said the Fain.

"I'm Eirik," said the man, putting his hands on his chest.

"Hands by your side," I growled.

"All right," he tutted. "No need to get twitchy." He put his hands out and showed me his palms. They were rough and dirty. A killer's hands. "Between you and me, I don't like Voss. The way he lords it over hard-working men like us. What's that about? What gives him the right? He was nothing before he broke the unicorn."

"How did that happen?"

"A pact with the sibyl."

So they *were* together.

"Some sort of sorcery. In exchange for a kid."

Kid? A child? Hilde wanted a *child*?

"The details" — he shrugged — "escape me. Look —"

He put a foot forward. I drew my fist back until the feathers of the arrow were scraping my cheek. "One more step and you're dead!"

"All right. Sheesh. Just hear me out." He was irritated now, but his gaze was never far from the point of the arrow. "I've got an idea. Something that might do for both of us, yeah?"

Do not trust him, said the Fain.

But I was young — and foolish. I jutted my chin.

"I know a way to set a trap for Voss. If it works, he burns. I get some fraas, maybe a scale or two as well. And you, cave boy, get to be a legend. I'll show yer."

I let him kneel — slowly. He found a patch of loose earth and scrubbed its surface with the palm of his hand. With one finger, he drew a rough image of the mountain. "Forest," he said, poking dots for the trees. "Voss." He made a *V* not far from the forest. "The dragon's here, in a cave on the far side of the mountain." He tapped the peak.

"How do you know?"

He pulled a strand of hair across his mouth and chewed it. "Voss captured two eagles. He squeezed it out of them before we roasted the meat off their bones."

From what Tryst had said there was truth in this. And the fact that I hadn't heard Galen for a while suggested he was hiding. A dragon, hiding. It made my stomach turn. I let the Fain calm me.

Eirik drew a circle above the mountain. "The dragon will expect an attack at full moon. Voss ain't gonna disappoint the beast, but only a goof like Egil would take on a full-sized breather, face to. So Voss is planning a little surprise." He looked into my face and smiled. "He's gonna go *through* the mountain, not up it. The dragon won't know until it's too late."

A few paces away, Eirik's horse snorted. We both momentarily glanced toward it. I saw Eirik tense, as if he sensed a chance to leap at me, but my aim was soon keeping him in check again. "How?" I said, grinding my teeth. "Kasgerden is solid. There are no tunnels through it."

Voss could imagineer a way, said the Fain.

"Imagineer" was a word I had never heard before, but Eirik was quick to support the idea. "He's got a unicorn horn," he said a little scornfully. "With the sibyl's help, he works all kinds of stuff."

And he'd got this far. I had to believe this evil might work. "Tell me your plan."

He moved his hand away from the drawing, but only to drum his fingers on the ground. "Even with magicks, it's gonna take time for Voss to tunnel through. And he's bound to leave a guard at the entrance hole. I'm the one he trusts to watch his back. When he's deep inside the hill, we call the dragon."

"How?"

"Make a fire. The eagles will see it and come to investigate. They'll see the tunnel and warn the dragon. The rest is easy. The breather comes over, flames the cave, and Voss goes up in smoke. Job done."

"But Grella will die."

He shook his head. "Voss told me himself that he won't risk taking her close to the dragon. I think he's taken a fancy to her. Wants her for a bride, I reckon."

"Bride?" My right arm weakened. Some slack crept into the bow.

"Oh, please," said Eirik, spreading his hands. "All this for a crush on a pretty Taan girl? Well, trust me, if you love the wench, I'm your best hope of getting her back."

I weighed it up again. I either had to kill Eirik now or assist him. The Fain favored me putting an arrow through his heart, but curiosity — and goodness — stayed my hand. "What would I have to do?"

"You're a cave boy. You know how to gather wood, don't yer? You set the fire. That's all there is to it. When the blaze is lit, you signal the eagles."

"They'll kill me after what you did to the others."

"Nah, you're an innocent. A kid in a robe."

"And what about you? Where will you be?"

He tapped one side of the picture. "There's some scrub just here. Should keep me covered, even from an eagle's beady eye."

"You're going to *hide*?"

"'Course I'm gonna hide," he snorted. "If the birds see me, they'll think it's a trick." He gestured to the drawing with his right hand. "It's a good plan, boy. Look it over again. Think about it. Take your time."

Foolishly, I did. I took my eye off him just for a moment, and in that moment he went to the ground with his opposite hand. By the time I'd seen him reach behind a stone he had the knife he had thrown at Tryst in his grasp. I panicked and released the arrow. It went straight through Eirik's wrist, the shaft lodging in his arm with the point sticking out. He howled and spilled the knife.

Fire again, said the Fain.

But even with their help there wasn't time. Eirik came at me in a wild frenzy. He bundled into me and carried me back down the slope. The bow snapped as we fell to the ground. By then he had a firm hand on my throat. His yellow eyes bulged with rage. Saliva dripped from his gritted teeth. My only hope was Rune's knife. My fingers flickered gamely for the hilt, but Eirik's body was too heavy to allow me to draw it. My will began to fade. My chest began to thicken. As my tongue swelled up and my head began to swim, I thought I felt the Fain desert me again. It was over. I was just seconds from death.

Then a surprising savior appeared.

I saw the dull shape of a horse behind Eirik, a blur of movement as its front hooves flashed. There was a thud. Eirik glugged. His eyes glazed over. His grip upon me loosened and he slumped to one side. I blinked, thinking I would see Eirik's horse.

Instead, I saw a deranged black unicorn.

"Get up," said the rider.

A blaze of sunlight at his back made him difficult to see. But I knew in my heart it was Voss.

Still spluttering for breath, I staggered to my feet. Another rider was sitting on a horse beside the unicorn.

He was overweight and stripped to the waist, despite the cold. He leaned sideways and spat at Eirik. A red stain was growing on the back of Eirik's head.

"Look well, boy, and learn," Voss said coldly. "Red is always the color of treachery." He glanced at the newly made stones, then the trees. "How did you pass through the forest unharmed?"

I gulped, which only served to burn my throat.

"Get the horse," Voss muttered to the other man, giving me a precious moment to think. If I told Voss the truth he would know I'd been aided by a force like the Fain. And where had they gone? I wondered. Perhaps he suspected I was Premen already, but there was no harm trying to mislead him a little. "I used an enchantment."

He grunted with laughter. But there was just enough doubt in his shrinking eyes to make me believe he was ready to be fooled. He rolled a hand, inviting me to please explain. My answer, he warned, had better be good. My life depended on it.

I slid my pack to the ground and opened it, keeping my hands in plain view. I drew out the tapestry Eleanor had given me. The one that Grella had labeled *Gawaine*. "The seer Brunne told me the skogkatts would fear this. When I showed it, they swore their allegiance to the dragon and guided me safely to the edge of the forest." I displayed Gawaine across my chest.

The unicorn immediately bucked, lifting Voss higher against the sun. He gripped the mane and violently pulled the thing under control. It sickened me to see a small amount of fluid oozing out of the stump of its horn. "How do you know this queen?" Voss growled. Like his mount, he was disturbed by the image.

I remembered Eleanor, talking of her daughter. "It came to me in a dream," I said.

Another horse pulled up with a clatter of hooves. Astride it was the sibyl Hilde.

"You know him?" said Voss, taking note of her squint.

"The seer's apprentice. He was at the river."

"The one you let journey with the tornaq?"

"Yes."

Voss nodded and steadied his mount again. He reached into a saddlebag and pulled something out. "You drew this, boy?"

I cupped my eyes. To my astonishment, it was the tapestry I'd started in Eleanor's krofft. The writing dragon was there, at its center. But there was also a kneeling child with it now. A young girl I hadn't drawn or even remembered. She was holding the dragon in the cup of her hands. Looking at her made me feel strangely dizzy. "Grella?" I muttered. Had she drawn herself into the picture as a child? Surely only she could have worked on the drawing?

Voss gathered up the tapestry and put it away. "Bring him," he said, and tugged on his reins.

The overweight man trotted his horse forward. Before I could open my mouth again, he had struck my face with the back of his fist. The world turned black and I fell to my knees. All I could think about before I passed out was the lingering image of that innocent child.

When I came to, my hands were tied tight behind my back and I was sitting up against a wall of rock. The air was so thin it hurt to breathe it. A few flakes of snow were clinging to my robe. My shoes had been removed and my feet and ankles were slightly blue, though not as cold as they might have been. Even here, at the very neck of Kasgerden, the rising heat of the Earth could be felt. Galen, it seemed, was still calling out, drawing Gaia's auma to him. Meanwhile, the sun was setting to the west of the mountain, pulling shadows across the far fields of Taan. Only the wetlands around Lake Varlusshandaan were easily picked out of the dusky orange landscape. It would not be long now before the rising moon was reflected in their calm, flat surfaces. With the moon would come the dying of the dragon — and the challenge to it from Voss.

He had camped on a ledge that was an overspill from a natural cave, a considerable height above the Skoga forest. From the position of the sun, I guessed it had taken half a day or more to reach it. If the ache in my back was to be believed, I had spent the entire journey slung across Eirik's horse. I could barely straighten my head to look around. When I did, there was Voss, sitting on a fallen rock just in front of me. In the background were the horses and three other men, playing dice. The unicorn was lying down, trying to sleep. Grella was beside it, stroking its mane. She was unharmed but clearly frightened. Every part of her face was screaming at me, *Idiot! What are you doing here?* The sibyl Hilde was nowhere to be seen.

"You must be hungry," Voss said. He was eating the meat I'd taken from the krofft, hewing off chunks like a bear might do. Despite this brutish display, he did not strike me as an uncouth man. The manner in which he held himself, the way he turned the joint of meat between his hands, even the ring of gold in his ear, suggested that he hailed from a noble tribe. Unlike Egil and Eirik, he took care of his appearance. His fingernails were clean and so were his clothes. His beard was well tended and close to his skin. Like the rest of his hair it was fully black, a shade that had also seeped into his eyes. He wore a plain padded jerkin, narrowed at the waist by a sturdy belt. In his belt was the unicorn horn. Rune's hunting knife was slid into the top of one boot.

"You'll forgive me," he said, "for stealing your food, but you've brought about the deaths of two of my men and inconvenienced my quest somewhat. A share of your provisions is the least you owe me." He spat a piece of gristle, which was picked up by a raven hopping around his feet. I watched the bird tear the gristle into strips. Every rip was echoed in the lining of my stomach. I had not eaten since leaving the krofft. "I should, of course, throw you off the cliff and be done." He paused and waved the meat around. The raven's keen eyes followed its arcs. "But you intrigue me, apprentice. I like a boy with spirit." He reached into his jerkin and pulled out my tapestry. He spread it out on the ground and weighted the corners with four loose stones. "You're going to tell me exactly what you saw with the tornaq. And I'd ask you not to dither. I still have a destiny to fulfil with the dragon."

I pitched a little and began to cough. A flare of pain all around my left cheekbone reminded me of the blow I'd taken. From the cave there came a high-pitched wail. A woman in pain. Voss ignored it, but took a little pity on me. "Give him water."

Grella looked toward the cave, then uncertainly at Voss.

He ran his knuckles down the side of her face, pushing back her tumbling yellow hair. "When I give an order, you obey me, remember?"

"Yes, Lord," she said. She hurried to my side. The unicorn let out a quiet whinny.

Grella took a water pouch from her belt and offered it up to my dry, cracked lips. "Don't speak to me," she whispered. "He'll be watching for that." I filled my mouth with the warlord's water. Its coolness was a welcome relief for my throat.

From the cave came another awful wail.

Voss swung his body toward his men. "Gunn," he barked. "Go and quieten the witch."

Gunn, the overweight thug who'd struck me, threw a wary look to the cave. "I ain't good with nippers," he said.

Voss drew the unicorn horn.

"All right," Gunn said, clambering to his feet. For a man with several layers of fat, he could run like a startled rabbit when threatened.

But even as Voss put the horn away, Gunn was back again, chased out of the cave by the sibyl's screams.

"It's coming," he said. "She wants you, Voss."

"I'm busy," Voss growled.

"Well, it ain't a pretty sight."

"Nor are you," Voss argued. "Now get back in there and stuff her mouth."

Gunn looked at his friends. They shrugged and went back to their dice.

Voss turned toward me again.

While their argument had been taking place, I had managed a swift exchange with Grella:

"What's happening in the cave?"

"Voss made a vile potion for Hilde — from the stem of the unicorn's horn."

The oozing fluid. "He poisoned her?"

"No. She's birthing a child."

So Eirik had not been lying about that. "Why did Hilde take you?"

"To calm the unicorn. When it passed through Taan it knew I was there and tried to leave Voss. Be quiet now. Drink."

"One last thing."

She frowned. Voss was about to turn.

"Why did you draw the child on the tapestry?"

Her face turned as pale as the falling snow. "I didn't," she whispered. "She appeared by herself." She thrust the water pouch back to my lips.

"Enough," Voss barked.

Grella, head bowed, pulled away.

"Well, boy? What have you to say about this?" He jutted his chin at the tapestry.

"I saw many things with the tornaq," I said. I swallowed and added, "Too many to remember."

Voss sighed. He stroked his beard twice. "It's a long drop, boy. You'll have time to remember every crack in every rock if you don't start talking." He pointed the joint of meat at the image. "The dragon is writing. What did you see?"

And suddenly, I knew a way to free my hands. "A symbol."

"A symbol?" He tilted his head.

"I can't describe it — but I could draw it for you."

He looked at me and chuckled, a clear indication that my plan was as plain as the night sky above. He pulled the hunting knife out of his boot and shaved off a sliver of meat from the joint. "If I have to ask you again, apprentice, I'll cut off your toes and make you hobble to your death. What did you see the dragon writing?"

I looked at Grella. *Just tell him*, she mouthed. But I didn't need to. I happened to glance down at the tapestry just then. And there, very small, but also very clear on the dragon's parchment, were the three curved lines that translated as *sometimes*. How they had appeared, I did not know. But Voss had followed my puzzled gaze and he could now see the lines for himself.

He stood up, throwing the meat aside. The raven cocked its head in hope. It danced what it knew could be a ritual of death, then *caark*ed once and stole the entire joint, dragging it away to a sheltered lip of rock. Voss put the knife away and drew the horn again. He pointed it squarely at me. Out of its tip came three dark lines of twisted light.

The unicorn neighed, setting off the horses.

The men stirred and began to call, "Voss, what's 'appening?"

I heard Grella scream, "No, leave him alone!"

But by then the dark light had struck my forehead. I jerked and kicked as the shadow force the Fain had warned me about swarmed through my mind. I saw Voss's mouth curl around the words, but the voice I heard came directly from the Ix.

You will tell us what you know about Isenfier.

They probed my memories and pulled out the image I had seen with the tornaq. I saw the dragon and I saw the child. She had wings on her back. A human girl with feathered wings. She was kneeling on grass. In a valley between hills. There were other humans with her. And dragons like Galen in the sky above.

You will locate this timepoint, said the Ix.

I screamed as darkness pressed upon my auma from a thousand different points of space.

But just as quickly, I was free of it again. When I shook myself back to full alertness, Voss was staring at the peak of the mountain and his men were trying to control the horses and the unicorn was even more demented and the moon had risen and there were eagles in the sky and there was so much heat coming out of the rocks — and so much snow coming down the rock face.

The first slide took Gunn's friends over the cliff. It gathered them up like pieces of fluff and carried them into the empty sky. They made no sound as they fell. All that could be heard was a distant *whump!* as their bones smashed against their unmarked graves. Voss leaped back and turned the horn upon the next fall of snow. A bolt of the dark light struck it. The air filled with crystals of sparkling black ice. I lost sight of Voss, but saw an eagle swoop down and sink its talons into Gunn's chubby face. He let out a shrill, gut-wrenching cry and turned a circle with the bird still fixed to his head. I didn't see what became of him and I did not care to imagine. By then, Grella was at my side. She hastily untied my hands.

"The cave!" she shouted. "It's our only chance!"

But as I got to my feet, a vast shadow appeared behind the crystal cloud. Every living thing present — me, Grella, Voss, the horses — must have thought we had breathed our last. Galen had come, with his wings spread wide, hovering in the way that Yolen had described to me in stories in the cave. He flipped his wings once and we were scattered like seeds to the back of the ledge. Through the swirling ice, I saw his jeweled eyes lock onto the unicorn. It was neighing at him with all its might.

I heard Grella crying, "No, no!"

But before I could wonder what she meant, Galen had brought his giant tail around and driven his triangular isoscele into the unicorn's anguished heart. I had never seen a more appalling sight or heard such a brutal squelch. But as the unicorn buckled, its body turned white and its eyes shone blue. It collapsed onto its side and crumbled into ash. In death, Galen had given it peace.

My thoughts immediately turned to Voss. I remembered Yolen saying, *With the unicorn gone, his powers will be diminished.* Yet Voss was showing no sign of fear. I was shielding Grella tight in my arms when I saw him approaching the lip of the cliff. Three eagles circled, wanting to attack. Galen snorted, keeping them back. This was going to be the dragon's kill.

Then Voss did a very strange thing. He raised his arms high above his head, holding the unicorn horn between them. I thought, *Why would a man, even one controlled by the Ix, come this far and not attempt to fight the dragon?* Right away I knew the answer. "He wants to die," I muttered.

"What?" said Grella, shaking in my arms.

"Voss *wants* the dragon to kill him."

So that he could live again. But in what form?

"Go to the cave," I told her.

"No, don't leave me!"

But I knew I had to.

I tore myself away from her and ran toward Voss. What was I to do though? What was I to do? Any impact would take us both off the cliff. I could try to draw the hunting knife from his boot, but would I have the courage to plunge it into him? Thankfully, neither of these options arose. With a thunder of hooves a horse ran in front of me, blocking my approach. I looked into its eye and saw a sparkle of life that did not belong there. The Fain. So that's where they had gone.

We had to shelter from the Ix, they said, coming back to me, commingling all their intentions at once. *Voss would have seen us in you with ease. You must leave and take Grella. Voss and Hilde have planned a great evil. We cannot defeat it. And the dragon has few reserves of fire.*

No. I slapped the horse and it moved away. "Voss!" My heart thumped with youthful defiance. My mouth filled with ice. My eye was on the dragon. I saw Galen in all his monstrous glory. Claws undressed. Nostrils flaring. Crescent fangs coated with sulfur and bile. The smell of him scoured the back of my throat. The heat of him stoked my fear — and my pride. What did it matter that his color was fading? That his scales were not shining green or bronze? Every muscle in his vast, incredible body was primed to wreak destruction on Voss. But he would not fight this villain alone. Or be tricked by any false sacrifice. I started to run for Voss again, but was thrown back by Galen's deafening roar. There was heat in my ears, possibly some blood. My skull felt like the egg of a bird that had had its yolk blown out through a hole. The dragon had called and the Earth had answered. A giant crack had appeared in the ledge. It ran toward the cave and split the lintel of rock above it. The mountain shifted a little. Out of the fissure came a burst of flame.

The Fire Eternal, the Fain commingled. I did not recognize or know the term then, but I felt the reverence they gave to it. If we died here now, in the fire ascending from the core of this world, we would be taken into the arms of Gaia.

But Gaia was not ready to take me that day.

I saw the flames roll toward Voss. He must have been using a powerful enchantment to keep himself in front of Galen, for he was still positioned exactly as before, with his arms raised high, holding on to the horn. He seemed unaware of the approaching danger. Or maybe he was simply waiting for it. Without warning, he switched the horn to one hand and pointed it at the dragon's breast. Finally, Galen responded with force. He closed one set of claws around Voss and popped him like a ripened berry. I turned my head as the pulp began to run. When I looked again, the claws were encased in fire. There was nothing to identify Voss the man, barring a glimpse of burning skull. But he had left a deadly thorn behind. With a squeal more akin to a rabbit than a dragon, Galen pulled back, drawing a trail of the Fire Eternal with him. In the flat of his foot was the unicorn horn.

He is poisoned, said the Fain, *and the Ix are within him.*

The dragon thrashed his tail and squealed again.

The cave, said the Fain. *Agawin, we must hide.*

No. I would not desert Galen now. I shook my head and ran to the cliff edge. "Galen! Galen! Look at me!" I roared. I had no idea what I was doing. I was just a boy who wanted to aid a dragon. A child befuddled by seers and tapestries and the beauty of a girl and the lure of a quest. Perhaps it had always been my destiny to stand on Kasgerden on the day that Galen died. Or perhaps I was just the lucky one. The voice that would carry his name into the future and one day illuminate the world about dragons. I called once more. Galen turned his head. A hideous and cruel metamorphosis had gripped him. His body was shrinking and turning black. Every crack of his bones put a twist in my gut. His striking face had contracted into ugliness. Where there had once been dignity was horror.

But in his eye, there was still a measure of goodness. I saw his wretchedness and he saw mine. A small teardrop appeared on his lower lid. The final remnants of his spirit, his fire tear. As blackness flooded the soft tissue of his eyeball, he roared a last time and tossed his head. The auma of the dragon flew toward the mountain. It sparkled once and struck me in the eye.

"Agh!" I fell back, covering my face.

The Fain swarmed around Galen's auma. For several moments the entities wrestled, leaving me shaking and jerking on the ground. The fire raged and the mountain moved. But in my head a strange calm began to settle. With it came a heightened power of awareness. A blossoming sense of universal truth. I sat up and looked at the enemy in the sky. I knew what it was. Antidragon. Darkling. A thing without conscience. Physical evil. Its transformation was now complete — apart from one thing.

It did not have fire.

I touched its auma wave and felt its frustration. Voss's frustration. He had died and been born again with wings and needle teeth. Yet Galen had thwarted him, right at the last. Voss had not been able to trap the dragon's tear and adapt it into what the new creature needed: dark fire.

It turned on me and clicked its claws. Unafraid, I picked up the hunting knife, the only thing Voss had left behind. From the cleft in the rock the fire still gushed. I held the knife by the blade and plunged it in. When I withdrew, my arm was unaffected but the knife was a cross of fire. I saw the darkling hesitate. But down it came, an untamed ball of spitting hatred. I launched the knife and my aim was true. The creature veered, but not quickly enough. The knifepoint entered under one wing and the flames of Gaia engulfed the beast. The darkling skriked and turned onto its back, then exploded in a mass of burning flakes. Voss was gone. And so was Galen. I touched my heart and wept inside.

I was twelve years old.

I had seen a dragon die.

But that was not the end of my adventures that day.

As the fire receded into the mountain I heard a voice say, "Agawin, is it safe?"

Through the smoke, I caught sight of Grella. She was just outside the cave mouth, holding a baby.

"Where is Hilde?" I shot an anxious glance at the cave.

Grella shook her head. "The flames . . . they took her."

Hilde gone, too. But not her child.

An innocent, said the Fain.

Despite Voss's potion.

"It's a girl," said Grella. And she was wrapped, of all things, in the tapestry of Gawaine. "I will care for her, Agawin, no matter what she is."

She will grow to be a sibyl, the Fain responded. *Be wary of this child. You may meet her again.*

"And there was this." Grella lobbed something small toward me.

"The tornaq," I muttered, catching it cleanly. I turned it in my hands. It wasn't even scorched. And that was not all that had survived the fire. As I took a pace forward, my foot became caught in something on the ground. It was the tapestry Voss had laid before me. It, too, was undamaged, but the drawing had grown again. *How is this happening?* I asked the Fain.

It is being imagineered, they said. *We believe these are your memories — or future visions.*

I looked at the image. It was just what I'd seen when Voss had questioned me. A wide valley patrolled by natural dragons, the strange writing dragon, the young child holding it, two people behind them, two more in the distance — one carrying a katt, of all things. I looked at the man who was closest to the child. There was something about him that resonated powerfully with my auma. The dragon inside me was strongly drawn to him. And yet it was the child I was most intrigued by. Whenever I looked at her, my head began to spin and the tornaq began to feel strangely warm.

"Sometimes . . . ," I whispered, looking at the symbol. And I thought I heard a child's voice in my head, as if the girl on the tapestry was speaking for both of us. *Sometimes we will be Agawin*, she said. *And sometimes we will be —*

"LOOK OUT!"

I heard Grella scream and turned to look for danger. But I had turned the wrong way. What felt like a roaring bull rammed into me. It was Gunn — I could tell from his bare, bloodied chest. He clamped his arms and his foul sweat around me. His face was nothing but ripped flesh and holes. My feet left the ground. I dropped the tapestry. Even with my newly found powers of awareness I had no time to stifle the assault. Grella screamed again. A wail of pure terror. A sudden rush of cold air hollowed my cheeks. Over Gunn's shoulder I saw Kasgerden's peak in the sky. A beautiful point of ice and rock, steadily growing smaller and smaller.

Gunn's weight had carried us off the cliff.

He howled like a madman and let me go. He went to meet ground he could barely see and I closed my eyes so I would not see. The sensation of falling was not unpleasant, like floating in a pool of salted water.

Had it not been for Galen's auma, that might have been the feeling I took to my grave.

The tornaq, his spirit said. *Use the tornaq.*

It was in my right hand and falling with me. Any moment now, we would hit the ground.

I shook the tornaq.

This time, I did not see visions. And I *did* hit the ground, though with barely enough force to flatten a daisy. When I opened my eyes I was in a green valley, in the shade of a tree. There was no sign of Kasgerden, and certainly no Gunn.

My heart was warmed to hear the tinkle of bells. I sat up, shaking a leaf from my hair.

"Hello. Where did *you* come from?"

I whipped around, startled by the voice of a pretty young woman. She was older than me, probably by as many years again. "Where am I?" I asked.

"Iunavik," she said, as if I ought to know. She looked up at the tree, wondering, perhaps, if I'd been hiding there. If I had, I felt sure she would have forgiven me for it; she had such a pleasant and trusting nature. "Do you know anything about goats?" A dozen or more were grazing on the hill.

"Yes," I burbled.

She smiled and said, "Then maybe you could help me. They need to be milked. I have to take milk to a woman in the caves." She pointed to an elbow of pale gray rock, jutting out of the hillside farther up. "What's your name?"

"Agawin," I told her.

"I like that," she said. She put out her hand and helped me up. She had stunning red hair and skogkatt eyes. "Welcome to Iunavik, Agawin. I'm Guinevere."

PART TWO
THE FLIGHT OF GIDEON

She sat down, cross-legged, beside a goat. She was dressed, like me, in a single garment — made, I thought, from hides, not flax. It was belted at the waist, though I couldn't see a clasp. On the belt hung a couple of rabbit-fur pouches. Like any hill dweller, she traveled light. Her legs were bare, a little tanned by the sun. On her feet she wore ankle boots, also made of hide. Her arms, likewise, were naked to the shoulder, though the flesh above her elbow was caressed by her hair. I had never seen a girl quite like her before. And yet, in a strange way, I felt I knew her.

She put a silver pail underneath her goat and started to collect its milk. "So, how did you get here? I thought I knew everyone in these hills."

We have moved through time and space, said the Fain, swarming into my consciousness again.

I picked up a spare pail and took it to a tame-looking goat nearby. "I'm . . . a Traveler," I said, opening my hand. There was the tornaq, resting on my palm. How could a simple piece of bone have brought me from Kasgerden to this hillside? I put it away in the pocket of my robe.

"Have you come far?"

"I'm not sure."

"Are you lost?"

I was looking around, not really listening to her. To the west of the hill we were on, a long spine of mountains ran into the distance, none with a shape I remembered or recognized. And there was something else, too. On the horizon, a vast gray shimmer. "Is that . . . *the sea*?" I asked. I had heard about this endless stretch of water and always hoped I would visit it one day.

Guinevere looked casually over her shoulder. "If that surprises you," she said, "you really are a long, long way from home. That's the Great Sea of the North. My favorite place in the world. When I die, I want to float out there and let my spirit gaze at the stars." She cleared her throat, making me look at her. "The milk?" she said, smiling.

"Um. Sorry." I sat down and put my hands to work. That was when I noticed a change in myself. My hands were larger and nowhere near as delicate.

You have aged, said the Fain.

"How much?" I said aloud.

"Sorry?" said Guinevere, raising her head.

"I . . . was . . . wondering how much milk you wanted."

She tilted her head and looked at me oddly. A warm breeze caught the sides of her hair and lifted it back, away from her face. "Till they're done, of course. But don't leave them sore. You do *know* how to milk a goat, don't you?"

I nodded like an oaf and looked down at the pail.

By now, Galen's auma was spreading through me, growing more active as it melded with my mind. I could sense my surroundings like I never had before. I was measuring distance in all directions, through lines in the Earth I never knew existed. I drew a mental image of Mount Kasgerden and was able to calculate how far we'd come. A whole landmass. Thirty days' ride on horseback. Though why the tornaq had delivered me here was yet to become apparent. Just then, a small bird flew into the tree. My nostrils swelled and my ears moved back. I could smell the creature in every detail, from its waxy neck feathers to its stalky little legs. I could detect its movements from the heat trails it left. More importantly, when I pitched those senses farther afield I was able to register a human form. Higher up the hill, in a set of small interlocking caves, was the woman Guinevere had talked about.

"She's called Gwilanna."

My ears flexed again, making me wince. "Gwilanna?"

"I thought I saw you looking. Up there. At the caves. You'll meet her soon enough. She probably knows you're here already."

"How?"

"She's a sibyl."

She saw my face change.

"You've met one before?"

"Briefly," I said. "Are you an apprentice to her?"

She moved the goat and whistled to another. The goat trotted forward. Guinevere began to milk her. "You speak as if you know about such things. Are you a seer's boy? You dress like one."

Boy. So I was still not a man, despite the shift of time and the look of my hands. "I was on a quest. I had to leave my seer behind." And what had become of Yolen? I wondered. Would he be looking for me now — or still?

"And it brought you to Iunavik, this 'quest'?" she said.

"It's a long story."

"I like stories, Agawin." She flipped her hair and went back to her goat. But this time, instead of conversing with me, out of her mouth came a beautiful song. There were no words to it, just a spiraling melody that seemed to bend the hill flowers and charm every cloud in the sky to a stop. The dragon within me began to stir. But rather than rise up or twist my ears, all I felt was calm flowing through me. Before I knew it I was falling sideways. I slumped over, kicking the pail down the hill.

I came to in Guinevere's arms. She was carrying me, *carrying me*, toward the caves. "H-how are you doing this?" I asked. Though I was young, I had to be heavy. And she was so slight.

"I don't know," she said. "When I ran to your aid I found you were no heavier to lift than a bird."

The dragon, said the Fain, sounding distant and wuzzy. *Galen is able to suspend his mass.*

How?

By commingling with the universal energy field. A procedure that enables him to step outside of time. We do not fully understand this yet.

And neither did I, though it made me think of Brunne and the secret he was trying to reveal. "Where are you taking me?"

"To Gwilanna. She heals all ills."

Be wary, said the Fain. *Be wary of this sibyl.*

"What happened? Back there, on the hill?"

"I was singing and you collapsed."

"Singing?"

"*Laaa* . . . and then you fell over."

"Where are the goats?" I tried to look back for them.

"In a pen. Don't worry. They can't stray or be taken."

"Pen?" I said. The hillside was broad and mostly grassy; I hadn't seen any sign of an enclosure. But when I looked back I saw four square sides of fencing poles with the goat herd gathered inside them. "How did that get there?"

"I made it," she said, with a gentle shrug.

I gave her a questioning look.

"Don't you imagineer, where you come from?"

112

Before I had a chance to query that, she said, "Can you walk now?"

I nodded and she set me down.

"Promise me you won't float away on the breeze?" She smiled and pointed to the caves. "This is it. We're here."

We were standing in front of a rocky outcrop about halfway up the hill, facing into the valley. Apart from a ragged slit in the stone, barely wide enough for a goat to slip through, there was nothing to suggest that anyone lived here. "It's bigger inside," she said.

As she made to go in, I held her arm. "Tell me about the pen. Are you saying you imagined it in your mind and it appeared exactly the way you saw it?"

She nodded. "It's not a difficult construct."

"The sibyl taught you this skill?"

"Everything I know I learned from Gwilanna."

"How long have you served her?"

She tossed her hair and looked toward the mountains. "She found me, abandoned, on the shores of the sea. I remember nothing before Gwilanna. She's the closest thing I have to a mother. Come on."

We dipped our heads and squeezed inside. The entrance was tight, but within a few paces the rock had opened up into a natural void and I could move around freely without the pressure of stone against my chest. There was a slight smell of dung, as though something wild had sheltered here once. But the overwhelming odor was of charred wood and smoke. The only light was the daylight that followed us in and a faint amber glow from a passage to our left. From the back of my throat came a stream of clicks, too fine for Guinevere to hear but strong enough to bounce off the walls of the cave. They described in their echo every dent and swollen curve of our surroundings. At the same time, the muscles behind my eyes began to stretch as the dragon reworked their limited capabilities. Well before we had entered the final chamber, where the sibyl sat tending a modest fire, I could see the entire shape of her dwelling. Larger than mine in the hills beyond Horste. Strewn with furs and bones and pots, all containing seeds or dried-up plant life. And on a ledge hollowed out of the rock in front of her was a skull, sitting on a folded piece of cloth.

"You're late," she said, without looking up. She was hunched over the fire with her back to us. I thought I saw a black-winged beetle crawling in the knots of her crusted hair. A stone cooking pot hung over the heat. Something like rabbit was stewing in it, casting its sickly-sweet scent around the walls.

"I found a boy," said Guinevere. "He needs your help."

The sibyl sat up, slow and straight.

She knows you are Premen, the Fain said warily.

Can she read the dragon?

Too early to tell.

She wagged a finger at a boulder by her right knee. "Let me see you, boy."

I looked at Guinevere, who gave a quick nod. I sat down. The sibyl slanted her gaze my way. She had a downturned mouth and shaded crescents underneath both eyes. Her cheeks resembled the skin of a plum that was just about ready to sag and wither. At first glance she appeared to be as old as the cave. Yet, in her eyes was the liveliness of youth. And though I had no memory of her faded face, strangely, like Guinevere, I felt I knew her.

"What ails you, boy?"

"He had a fainting sickness," Guinevere said, perching on a rock at the sibyl's other side.

"I wasn't talking to you. Where's my milk?"

"I left it so I could bring him here. It's safe. The bears won't find it."

"Bears?" I sat up, mildly alarmed. If a bear had strayed toward Yolen's cave, we would have been out with firesticks, scaring it.

"From the woods, farther north. They snuffle around the cave mouth, foraging for scraps. They're harmless as long as —"

"Be quiet," said Gwilanna. She turned to me again. "Give me your hand."

Show no aggression, the Fain advised. I could feel them keeping the dragon in check.

I extended my arm. The sibyl took my wrist. Her touch was light, but as cold as death. Her fingernails curled like the toes of a bird, drawing the blood to the surface of my skin. "What were you doing when this sickness struck you?"

"We were milking," Guinevere put in again, "and I was singing him an old lullaby. The dragon song. The one you taught me. Maybe he just fell asleep?" Her green eyes shone. She put her hair behind her ears.

Gwilanna tightened her grip on my arm. By now, the Fain had completely shut down, masking Galen's presence. But I was sure the sibyl was searching for something she wouldn't expect to find within a normal boy. "Where are you from?" she asked, barely parting her lips. She leaned forward, shaking dust from her clothes. She wasn't dressed like a hill woman should be. Her garment was long and filthy and ragged, severed at the knee for ease of movement. But it wasn't plain: There was stitching around the neck. It struck me that it could have been made in —

"*Answer me.*" The sibyl's hand burned against my skin.

"Don't hurt him," said Guinevere. "What harm's he done to us?"

"I think I've Traveled far," I told Gwilanna. "But . . . I'm not sure how I got here." And perhaps because there was some truth in this statement the sibyl decided to let me go.

"The boy is not ill; he's hungry," she said, throwing my hand back into my lap.

"Can he share your stew?"

"No, he cannot. I will prepare him an herbal broth. Go outside, girl. Pick some mushrooms. Do not dally or talk to bears."

I shot a glance at Guinevere. "You talk to bears?" She made objects out of nothing and she *talked* to bears?

"We share a love of the land," she said. "What resonates in Gaia, speaks through Gaia. Where *are* you from, if you don't know that?"

"Leave us," said Gwilanna, batting a hand.

The girl jumped up. "By the way, he doesn't imagineer."

"I said, leave us."

Guinevere sighed and hurried out.

The sibyl picked up a twisted branch and poked the fire as if she was stabbing an old wasp's nest. "I must intrigue you greatly, boy. Your face is full of a thousand questions."

I straightened my mouth. "Will you answer one for me? How does 'imagineering' work? How can you make an object appear just by . . . thinking about it?" I was picturing Guinevere's pen around the goats, but remembering that the Fain had also used the term to tell me how my tapestry had developed. From nowhere, the child's voice swam into my mind. *Sometimes we will be Agawin. And sometimes we will be . . .*

"Tell me," said the sibyl, "have you ever seen a dragon?"

My thoughts about the child dissolved. How should I answer the sibyl's question? I felt the Fain coming into my consciousness again, like a timid sheep poking its head above a wall. *Do not speak about Galen,* they said.

But if I lied, I felt sure the sibyl would know. "I . . . I saw one die once."

A piece of loose wood tumbled out of the fire. Gwilanna paused before snuffing out the fizzing embers. "Did you find fraas?"

I shook my head.

"Well, if you had, you might not be asking how imagineering works."

"You need dragon auma to imagineer?"

"No, boy, you need to be one with Gaia. And nothing achieves that quite like a dragon."

After a pause I said, "I honor dragons and respect the Earth spirit."

"Then you can imagineer," she said.

"Will you teach me this wisdom?"

"Perhaps. If you serve me well."

"And if I don't?" I glanced at the skull.

"Fear not, boy. I doubt you could do me nearly enough harm to warrant ending up like that."

"Who was she?"

"How do you know it was a she?"

I looked again. I was guessing, but . . . "The skull is small." And mostly undamaged, but blackened around the mouth and eyes, perhaps burned.

Gwilanna poked the fire. "Well, it's none of your business."

Be careful, said the Fain. *Do not provoke her wrath.*

But I couldn't help myself. I sensed a curious connection to these bones, as if I'd been part of this person's story. "Who was she?"

"I said it's *not* your business."

"What did she do to become like this?"

"She was —" The sibyl turned angrily. For one moment, I thought I saw grief in her eyes. And I was sure I'd heard a whisper from the mouth of the skull, like the swish inside a hand cupped close to the ear. "The skull . . . belonged to my mother," she said.

There was a terrible, terrible coldness in her voice that half-inclined me to speak of something else. But now I had begun, I had to pursue this. "Is it a charm? Was she a sibyl, like you?"

"No," she replied, short and to the point.

A souvenir, then? I had heard of people keeping the ashes of their loved ones after death. Was Gwilanna shading the truth a little? Could these sockets have once been filled by the actual face of her mother? The thought of it made me shudder. What kind of person, even a sibyl, kept the skull of a parent on show?

"Where was she from — your mother?"

Gwilanna thrust the stick into the fire and left it. "Why would a hill boy want to know?"

I was struggling to say. But some kind of powerful auma was drawing me closer and closer to the skull. "What was her name? Tell me her name."

. The sibyl met my gaze. "Who *are* you?" she growled.

Her answer came from a shout near the cave mouth: "Gwilanna! Agawin! Come quickly! Come quickly!"

"*Agawin?*" Despite the low light, I saw her eyes pinch.

I took note of her shocked expression, but I had no chance to question it then. I sat up sharply, triggered by Galen. All my senses were tuning to an auma source outside the caves. I had the oddest feeling that I could travel through the rocks to reach it if I tried, dissolving through the particles that held them together to reappear smoothly on the other side. But in the end, my exit was much more conventional. I simply leaped up and sprinted for the opening.

"Look!" Guinevere beckoned me to her the moment I emerged. She pointed to the sky, where an eagle was circling.

I cupped a hand above my eyes to block out the sun. "What's it carrying?" There was something between its talons. Something large.

"An egg," she said.

I squinted again. "How can it be? Eagles don't carry their eggs."

"Then there is not an eagle inside it," said Gwilanna, who had come out onto the hillside with us.

She is right, said the Fain. They were buzzing like a nest of summer bees. *The auma wave is almost too strong for us to bear.*

"It's a dragon egg," I breathed as Galen locked onto it.

One of great power, the Fain reported.

"It's coming down," said Guinevere. "It looks exhausted." She started tying up her mane of hair, in readiness to run to the eagle's aid.

"It's hatching," I muttered. "The egg is hatching."

She paused and looked across at me. "How can you tell?"

I could see it as Galen expanded my vision. Cracks were developing all over the shell. A rivulet of bright green fluid seeped out and flowed around the eagle's foot like a vine. There was a flash of light, and for several moments the bird was lit in a halo of rapidly-changing colors. Twice it tossed its head and squawked. Its wing-beats faltered. But it didn't drop the egg.

"Come on," urged Guinevere. "We've got to help it."

"No." The sibyl pulled her back.

"But it needs us, Gwilanna. It's —"

"Let the boy see to it."

The sibyl jutted her chin. And away I went, with the breeze at my back, feeling for all the world like I might fly. I skidded to a stop a good distance from the caves. The bird flapped down, arching its golden-brown wings for balance. With another soft squawk it released the egg, which rolled against a tuft of grass and stopped. A few pieces of the shell had become detached. Through the gaps, I could see the young dragon struggling.

The eagle sensed me then. It turned and opened its bright yellow beak, warning me off with a fierce spray of spittle. Despite its fatigue, it stood up tall with its talons forward, spreading its wings to their fullest extent. The white tips of its feathers were glowing, in peace. But in the beaded orange eyes there was only conflict. It would fight to the death to protect its cargo. I understood plainly. And so did Galen.

The muscles in my throat adjusted again. The words, when they came, burned the roof of my mouth and seemed to rip the inner lining from my lungs. But they were effective. This is what I said:

"I am the spirit of the dragon Galen. Lord of Kasgerden and the land beyond. Your work is done. You will deliver this wearling to me."

The eagle shuddered. It was almost spent. "I am Gideon," it panted. "I have traveled far. I was sent to find shelter by the queen, Gawaine. This is her only surviving son."

A pitiful growl bubbled up in my throat. Gawaine. I knew the name, of course, and it was clear that Galen did, too. His sorrow swept through me like a burst of rain. "Is the queen dead?"

"No," said Gideon. "She was attacked and had to enter stasis, helped by a healing horse. One of her eggs was stolen and destroyed. Her auma has been trans-ferred to this one. . . ."

With that, the eagle collapsed. Once again, a strange light flashed around him. He twitched a few times and curled his toes. I put out a hand and stroked his feath-ers. The auma of the dragon he'd carried for so long instantly began to commingle with me. There was a spark inside him, absorbed from the egg. He was going to live — and he was going to transform. But for now, all he would do was sleep.

A quiet skrike turned my attention to the dragon. I knelt and sat the egg in my hands. A head had just poked out, with a jagged piece of shell still attached to it. A foot broke through, then a whipping tail. Slowly, I pulled each piece away until all that was left was a baby dragon, covered in a film of slippery gloop. It skriked again and wobbled its wings.

This is the son of Gawaine, said Galen. In his rough-ened tongue it sounded like this: "Guh-wen."

And he unveiled to me the way her offspring should be named. Traditionally, in dragon culture, a firstborn son was named after its mother.

And so I called the wearling Gawain. "Guh-wane."

And Galen approved of this.

Guinevere could not hold back any longer. She came sprinting to my side, only to have her attention divided between the little dragon and its weary guardian. Eventually, she knelt at Gideon's side. In a craking voice she attempted to speak to him. His eyes remained closed, his wings still. "I think he's dying, Agawin. We should take him to the caves. Gwilanna might be able to — uh-oh. This isn't good."

I followed her gaze and saw we had company. Along the hill, poking its snout into the air, was a large brown bear. It had a look of cheery wonder in its deep-set eyes, and massive strength in its bulky paws. It sat up tall and squinted at us. My skin tightened all over my body — the equivalent, I guessed, of a dragon's scales lifting.

"That's a young male. They're trouble," said Guinevere.

"Tell it to stay back. You said you could talk to them."

"The old ones — the wise ones — yes. He's curious. He could be a serious threat."

I closed my hands around the dragon to keep him stable. "Do we run?"

"Only if you want his claws in your back."

The bear dropped down again and padded forward.

"What do we do? We're a long way from the caves. Why isn't Gwilanna helping us?"

"I don't know, but she's never liked bears."

"What's that got to do with it? She's not the one who's about to get mauled!"

This is a test, said the Fain. *The sibyl is waiting to see what you do.*

The bear snorted and tossed its head. I felt Galen measuring the sway of its shoulders, judging its strength, agility, and pace. Bones began to click all around my face as though he wanted to unlatch my jaw. Surely he couldn't make fire in me? One belch would fry my brain to my skull.

Guinevere stood up with Gideon in her arms. "We need to distract it, but my fain is still weak after making the pen."

"Your fain?"

"A term we use when we imagineer constructs. It means . . . a higher way of thinking. A deeper, more focused form of concentration."

Can we do this? I said to the Fain in me.

All living creatures are capable of it.

But? I sensed a definite "but."

Your intent must be strong. You must form the image clearly and you must not waver.

The bear had broken into a lolloping trot. The thought of being crushed in its brawny grip was beginning to sharpen my intent well enough. A believable distraction. I had an idea. "What do they eat?"

"Huh?"

"Bears, Guinevere. What do they *eat?*"

"Us, if we don't get out of here." She backed away up the hill.

"No, I mean what's their normal diet?"

"Berries. Any form of bright berries."

"All right. Keep moving. If this doesn't work, I'll let Gawain go."

Gawain? she mouthed.

I nodded at the dragon. Its scalene eyes had just blinked open. Amber gems in folds of green. I prayed they would never get close enough to see the bright pink lining of a brown bear's mouth. "I know they can fly soon after birth. He'll get away — and you can take care of him." I stopped walking and squeezed my eyes shut.

"Agawin, what are you doing?"

"Imagineering." I pictured a bush sprouting out of the hillside. A green bush, laden with shining red berries, glistening with early-morning dew. The Fain sharpened the image and Galen flowed his auma into it. But what made the thought materialize strongest of all was a burst of energy from the young dragon himself. I felt no physical sensation of his help, no tingling in the hands or pulsing in the head, but for one intense indescribable moment, when all of time seemed to come together and light itself seemed to bend to my will, I saw the vastness of the universe as a great sheet of energy. A limitless field of interconnected forces from which I could draw down any information I required and shape it into any form I liked: instantly.

I heard Guinevere gasp. When I opened my eyes, there was the bush, just as I'd imagined it. I had created a construct, straight out of my mind. The bear blinked twice, then with a grunt sat down to graze the berries.

And that surprised Guinevere even more. "He's swallowing them."

Wasn't that the point? To make him feed? "I hope they don't poison him." I had given little thought to the type of berry, still less to what they might taste like.

"But that means the bush is not an illusion. It's real. You *grew* something, out of the Earth. Not even Gwilanna can imagineer like that."

I looked back at the caves. The sibyl was still there, studying me carefully.

"What do you know about Gwilanna's mother?"

"Her mother?"

"Or the skull she keeps by the fire?"

Guinevere lifted her shoulders. "Gwilanna doesn't talk about her mother much, though I've heard her mumbling to the skull at night. All I really know is her name: Grella."

My heart thumped, making the dragon skrike. Could this be *true*? That the tornaq had moved me through time and space but kept me in touch with a strand of my past?

Gwilanna is Hilde's child, said the Fain.

The child Grella took from Mount Kasgerden.

A daughter fashioned by Voss — and the Ix.

Saying nothing of this, I followed Guinevere back to the cave mouth. The Fain, having put their all into the construct, were too exhausted to comment further. But as we approached the sibyl again, she clapped her hands in silence and said, "Very impressive — for a boy who's never imagineered before." She rolled back

Gideon's eyelid. In the center of his eye was a vital glint. "Take it to the spring," she said to Guinevere. "Give it water. The bird will recover. When it does, let it go. Then return here."

"Wouldn't it be safer inside the cave?"

"Birds do not like caves," said Gwilanna. "Dragons, of course, are a different matter. . . ."

Her eyes grew large as they took in Gawain.

Guinevere sighed and started up the hill. "Look after him," she whispered, touching my arm.

"And don't forget the milk this time!"

"I won't."

The sibyl turned her gaze on me. "What are you gawping at, boy?"

Her dress. It was soiled by years of accumulated dirt but I was certain now that it was not the clothing of a humble cave dweller. The garment had been made by a hand skilled in needlework. I thought back to her reaction on hearing my name and knew there was no point dancing around the truth. With a surge of boldness, I lifted my chin. "I know who you are. You were raised by Grella of Taan."

And just as audaciously the sibyl countered, "And you, if I'm not mistaken, are the boy who disappeared after a fall from Mount Kasgerden. My mother always spoke so fondly of you, *Agawin*."

So she knew. And she truly believed that Grella was her mother, a falsehood invented by Grella, perhaps, to make the upbringing easier. But did she know what part Voss had played in her birth, or of the evil that lurked inside her?

Leaning forward she sneered, "What are you, boy? A construct? A spirit? Or some other wonder?"

I did not have to answer that. Gawain threw out his wings and went *hrrr!* in her face.

A gobbet of spittle landed on her cheek and fizzed along one of her many wrinkles. "Little monster!" she squealed, pulling back. She rubbed her face dry and swept toward the cave. "Bring that inside. Put it by the fire. When the sun goes down it will need more warmth than *you* can give it."

I looked down at Gawain. He was indeed shivering. But it would not be long before his scales began to show, before he would get the insulation he needed. Dragons grew fast, if I remembered Yolen's teachings correctly. He might look surprisingly vulnerable now, covered in juvenile pimply skin, but in just a few days he would be battle-hardened. "Plated" was the term the old ones used.

So I did as Gwilanna instructed. I went inside and set him by the fire. Right away, he scented the stewing rabbit and leaped into the pot, devouring every chunk, using his tail to skewer pieces up. To Gwilanna's annoyance, he lapped up all the juices as well. Then he licked his feet and isoscele clean and settled in the pot with his tail curled around him, unconcerned by the heat from the flames.

Gwilanna cussed and went to a place in the wall from which she pulled some poorly baked bread. She tore it in two and grudgingly threw one half at me. "Eat. You don't look much like a ghost."

"I am not a ghost," I said to her, plainly. "Tell me how Grella died."

"Tell me how you *survived*," she snapped back. She ripped at the bread with her crooked teeth. "In my mother's stories, you were carried down a mountain. Nothing human could escape the fall she described. And yet here you are, gladly eating my bread."

I broke off a chunk and tried her "bread." It tasted of mold, but at least it was food. "People speak badly of women like you. Why should I tell you anything, sibyl?"

"Impertinent whelp," she said with a snarl, spitting flecks of bread off her ghastly tongue. "My mother always said you were an arrogant snipe. I'm surprised she searched for you as long as she did."

That stopped my bite. "Grella searched for me?"

"A pointless quest, spurred on by your seer."

"Yolen?" I gasped. "Yolen was with her?" So the men of Taan had survived Hilde's potion. And Yolen, sweet Yolen, had not given up on me.

She wrinkled her nose. A touch of indifference. "That is the name I remember, yes."

"What became of him? Where is he? I must go to him at once."

"Spare yourself — unless you can wriggle like a worm." She wiped her bread around a bowl of fat. "He's dead." She pushed the bread into her mouth.

I buried my face in my hands. And even though Galen strived to give me courage, I could feel my poor heart wanting to shatter. "What happened? How long ago was this?" How long, I wondered, was I lost in time?

"Look at my face," the sibyl croaked. "Is your history not measured in these ugly creases?"

134

I did look at her, but only for a moment.

She is not all that she seems, said the Fain. And although they could offer no real explanation, I understood what they meant. There was such deep bitterness embedded in her words, as if she blamed me for making her old. Once again in her eyes I saw a hint of youthfulness, as though she was wearing a cloak of wizened years and underneath was nought but a resentful girl. "Please, Gwilanna, what else can you tell me?"

She belched at me loudly. I had to turn away from the stench of her breath. "I note your eagerness for conversation when *I* have something to offer *you*, boy."

I put my hand in my pocket and touched the tornaq. "I am young. Forgive my lack of respect. I will tell my side when I know about Yolen."

The sibyl found an awkward morsel in her teeth and spat it sideways into the darkness. "My mother, myself, and the horse she rode back were the only survivors of the battle at Kasgerden. She met your seer at the foot of the mountain. The men of three tribes were with him. They had recovered from a sleeping spell, put upon them by a sibyl — whom you must have met."

Your true mother, I was thinking. The Fain made sure I kept my mouth from blurting it. But I did say this: "I barely met her; she did not use her magicks on the women or the children. Tell me now about Grella."

Gwilanna chewed on her thoughts for a moment. She belched again and said, "My mother told Yolen all she had seen, but he always refused to believe you were dead. They spent one turn of the moon together, hiding from the Taan —"

Hiding? I thought, but I did not interrupt.

"— searching the plains around Kasgerden. In time, the seer became ill with grief. His heart broke and his spirit left him. He is buried under stones at the foot of the mountain. I cannot say exactly where."

I closed my eyes and swooped through Galen's memories of the land. In doing so, I made this pledge to myself: One day I would find that cairn of stones and bless them with the auma of the dragon that Yolen had fought to protect. "Hiding?"

"What?" the sibyl grunted.

"You said they were hiding. Why would Grella need to hide from her own tribe?"

The sibyl flexed her foot. "Because of me."

The flames leaned toward the watching skull. I felt my heart muscles guttering with them. I thought back to the moments just before my fall. Grella saying she

136

would care for the baby — Hilde's baby — no matter what it was, no matter what the cost.

"When they saw me — the good men of Taan and Horste — they wanted to throw me over the cliff. I was the child of a villain, they said. A monster, fathered by darkest magicks. Most of them pitied my mother, but they also feared the woman she'd become. A dear girl robbed of her innocence, forced to give birth on a timescale not even a dog could master. Some said Grella should see the cliff, too. Is this turning your stomach, boy?"

It was. But not for the reasons Gwilanna imagined. How brave (or foolish) must Grella have been to accept the child (and the prospect of death) when all she had to do was admit it wasn't hers?

"Yolen was the only one to take her side. He argued for my life, saying that a child could not be judged on its heritage alone, only by the deeds it went on to commit. The men of Taan muttered among themselves. They talked about honor and superstition. In the end my mother was spared, but banished. Even her father agreed to this. And a price was put on her head."

"How so?" My fingernails strained in their sockets. Galen would have spread his claws if he could.

"She was told she must return once a year to Taan, on the anniversary of that day, and show me to the elders of the tribe at the border. If they found me unholy, I would be slain. If she failed in this duty they would hunt her down and kill us both."

I looked at the skull. My spirit raged. After all their hospitality, was I now at war with the elders of Taan? "Tell me how she died."

The sibyl raked her hair. "I do not wish to talk about that."

"But I want to know."

"You do not," she snarled. "With Yolen gone, my mother . . . wandered. She traveled with me until the Great Sea stopped her. We made a life here, among bears and goats. *That* is all you need to know."

There is falsehood in this, the Fain said to me. *Her auma betrays her words. We do not believe this version of events.*

But I had no chance to question it. In a strange, almost mocking twist, she said, "Now I will hear *your* story, Agawin. And do not try to fool me, boy. I can spot a lie as clearly as a pebble in your eye. I know you are Premen. That much was clear from the way you entertained that idiot bear. How did you survive the fall?"

The Fain said, *Do not give in to this.*

But once again I ignored their advice. If my adventures had taught me one thing, it was that boldness sometimes brings the greatest rewards. I reached into my robe and drew out the tornaq, curious to know how the sibyl would react. "This is what saved my life." I let it sit in the palm of my hand. And though the Fain implored me not to let her touch it, I allowed Gwilanna to pick up the charm.

She closed her mouth and breathed out through her nose. A crumb of bread fell from the end of her chin. "Where did you get this?" She sucked the words in with a greedy relish.

"Grella gave it to me," I told her truthfully.

Gwilanna stared at me in disbelief.

"She found it in a cave on Kasgerden, I swear."

"Was it my father's?"

I shrugged and looked away. Maybe it had once belonged to Voss. But I wasn't going to speculate. And I wasn't going to mention my encounter with Hilde.

The sibyl ran her thumb along the whorls, digging her nail almost enviously into them. For one anxious moment I thought she might shake it and disappear with a hideous cackle. Instead she asked, "Do you know what this symbol means?"

I shook my head, which was honest enough. I remembered what I'd heard when the writing dragon had drawn the symbol — *"sometimes"* — but it made little sense to me still.

"Then I will tell you," Gwilanna said, in a voice that seemed oddly detached from her own. "You may hear other, more fanciful explanations, but they will only be variations on this." She rolled the tornaq between her palms. "The three lines are the three dimensions of this world, held in place by the same forces that allow us to imagineer constructs. The spaces represent the flow of time, both forward and back, spiraling infinitely around one another, twining into the eternal now. But if the lines are moved, even by the smallest amounts, the dimensions of the universe flicker and change. The results, as you have found, are quite . . . spectacular."

Sometimes I will be at Kasgerden; sometimes I will be at Iunavik. One blink within the eternal "now."

I looked up and said, "How do you know what you know?"

She is drawing upon the unicorn's auma, said the Fain. *This knowledge has always been with her.*

The horn. Of course. The three-lined pattern. So strange to think that this woman, by virtue of her sinister birth, possessed the ancient knowledge of unicorns. And it was frightening to know that the shadow of the Ix must be in there somewhere, all mixed up with Hilde's magicks. But which of those influences drove her the strongest? And which was leading her now?

She ignored my question and asked one of me. "Were you holding the charm when you fell?"

I shifted on my rock. "Yes. But why should it deliver me here, to a place I never even knew existed?"

"That is a very good question," she muttered. She brought the tornaq close to her face, turning it in front of her searching eyes. "I have heard it said that if you cut a dragon open, you would find this symbol etched on its heart." I cast my eyes warily toward Gawain, but she did not appear to intend him harm. "All I can tell you is this: It was not a piece of bone that brought you to Iunavik, but what that piece of bone is hiding."

And then she did something quite unexpected. She hurled the tornaq at the wall above the skull.

"No!" I cried and was about to jump up when I witnessed an extraordinary transformation. The bone dissolved before it struck the wall and a small, birdlike creature fluttered free.

Grrraaarrkkk! went Gawain, raising his head.

"There," crowed the sibyl, pleased with herself. "There is the agent of your destiny, Agawin. You are looking at a being that can change its shape and carry you across time, maybe even worlds."

"How, though? How does this . . . creature . . . change time?"

"Dragons are masters of the energy field. What we do when we imagineer is a jot compared to the power they command — even one as small as this."

The creature fluttered down to my hand. It did not look entirely like a bird, but it wasn't quite a dragon either. It was white with a sheen like frosted snow. I could see the flames of the cave fire through it and its weight upon my hand was no more than a breath. It observed me with a keen, well-focused eye, as if it saw in that glance not a boy sitting on a rock in a cave, but everything that boy had been and would become. It peered at Gwilanna and its bright gaze narrowed. She drew back, adding more wrinkles to her face. The creature tilted its head and purred in warm admiration at Gawain. Then it turned into bone again, melting from one shape to the other as if it was nothing more than smoke.

"A lucky find," said the sibyl. "It seems quite attached to you."

And I didn't need dragons or Fain within me to know how much she desired to have it.

At that point Guinevere rushed back in, her airwave bending the flames again. Gawain sat up and made a fresh *graaarrkk*.

I put the tornaq in my robe and stood up to greet her. "What's the matter? You look worried."

"The eagle," she panted.

"What about him?"

"Burned."

"Burned? How?"

Gwilanna turned her head. "Speak plainly, girl. I do not like riddles."

Guinevere dropped to her knees. Her hands gripped her thighs to stop them quivering. "I took him to the spring water, as you said. All the way I could feel a great auma wave from him. Whatever he absorbed from Gawain was very strong."

Gwilanna squinted at the dragon but said nothing.

"Lights kept glowing around his body. Yet there was no flicker of life from his eye. I set him down and opened his beak, so I might drop some water on his tongue. I cupped a hand under the spring. The water was cold and I prayed to Gaia that the shock of it would cause no harm to the bird. And I don't know how it happened, my knee must have slipped against the muddy earth, but the next thing I knew I had spilled the water all over his feathers. His wings. His head. His tail."

"Yes, yes," said Gwilanna, squirming with impatience. "We know where a bird has feathers. What *happened*?"

"A blaze," said Guinevere, looking at me. "A fire ignited and he burned like nothing I have ever seen before. A white fire took him and turned him to ash."

"White fire?" I muttered.

"I saw his body through it — but that's not all." She looked at the ground, her face lost behind a fall of her bright red hair. "A new bird rose from the ashes."

"What?" said Gwilanna, grinding her teeth. The noise could be heard quite clearly around the cave.

"A spirit bird. But not an eagle. It was changed."

"A dragon?" I asked.

"No." Her eyes widened. "Something in-between. It had a longer beak. A softer eye. Pretty little tufts on the top of its head. Colors more beautiful than any sunset — like his golden-brown feathers but speckled with orange and yellow and green. As he rose, he opened his throat and breathed the same white fire that had taken him to ash."

He died and lived again, the Fain said excitedly. *He has commingled with the dragon and made a new form. A bird of fire. A firebird. We must find it. We must learn from this, Agawin.*

But the Fain were not the only ones intent on that. "Where is this creature?" Gwilanna said coldly.

Guinevere shook her head. "I don't know."

I crouched beside her. "Which way did it fly?"

"It didn't," she said. "It just . . . disappeared. It tipped its head down and folded away. It made the air ripple. I waited and watched but it didn't come back. Then I ran here, to the cave, to tell you."

It has moved through time, as you did, said the Fain. *Where would it go to?*

We could not say.

I made a swift decision and said to Guinevere, "Will you take me to the spring?"

"I would . . . but it might be wiser to stay in the cave."

"Why?" said Gwilanna. "What's happening outside?"

I didn't wait for Guinevere's answer. I ran to the cave mouth and poked my head out. To my surprise there were animals all over the hill. Goats, rabbits, squirrels, birds, waterfowl, foxes. All sitting there, calm and untroubled. The bear I had stopped with my imagineered bush was mooching about, berry stains marking the fur around his mouth.

This is a vigil, the Fain said quietly. *They have felt Gawain's auma. They are here for the dragon.*

"Is this usual," I whispered, "when a wearling is born?"

No. But he is more special than most. Our analysis suggests he is the last known dragon in this world.

And there and then my destiny was set. I did not need the spirit of Galen to tell me that it would fall to me, a seer's apprentice, to stay close to Gawain and protect him from harm.

But there was still one thing I did not understand. According to Gideon, the queen dragon, Gawaine, had passed her fire tear on to her son. He had inherited most of her auma. Gideon, in turn, had absorbed some of that. But in the many legends Yolen had taught me, not one of them spoke about a dragon with the power to create a new form from the ashes of another. How could Gawain — or his mother — possess the ability to resurrect an eagle?

I sensed that Galen had an explanation, but Guinevere came alongside me at that moment and her presence distracted me from hearing it.

"See what I mean?" She nodded at the animals.

It was remarkable to see them settled together, with no threat from any one species to another.

"Will the bear be a problem?"

"Not now he's fed. Come inside. Gwilanna wants to speak to you." She tugged my sleeve and we returned to the fireside.

Gawain was still in the cooking vessel, but the sibyl was on her feet by now, gathering seeds from her collection of pots. She put a handful into a smaller dish and started grinding them with a blunt-ended stone.

"Guinevere has told me what is happening outside. You must leave here and take the wearling with you. The presence of so many animals on the hill will not go unnoticed by the tribe that inhabits the far end of the valley. If men come, they will seize the creature." She twisted her stone, pushing and crushing the husks till they ended their resistance with a deathly crack. I half-fancied she wished it was the bones of my neck turning to powder in the base of her dish.

"Where will we go to?" Guinevere asked.

"We?" the sibyl said brusquely.

"I wish to travel with Agawin."

I held my breath for the sibyl's response. Although I had been in Guinevere's company for barely one tick of the afternoon sun, the thought that she might be allowed to join me unexpectedly filled my heart with joy.

"No," said the sibyl.

My heart sank.

But Guinevere paid no regard to her. "We should take him to the Tooth." She twisted on her heels and faced me directly. Even in the dim light, her eyes were a stunning blaze of green.

"Tooth?" I asked.

"A small island, farther up the coast. A lump of jagged rock that looks like a bear's front tooth. It's no use to anyone but the seabirds that nest there. Perfect for a young dragon. It can be reached by boat or a land bridge that appears when the tides are right. It's dangerous to cross, but once we get him over he'll be safe, I'm sure. It's an easy roost for a dragon to defend. The villagers on the shore side will probably help us. They're an old tribe called the Inook. They know me well. In the summer, I trade with them. They follow the path of Gaia and respect all animals and their spirits. They will welcome Gawain to the island, I know it."

"Hmph," went Gwilanna, who didn't sound so sure. "The world is changing, girl. They might just put a skewer through its heart and roast its 'spirit' in the salty air." She put her stone aside and splashed a little water into the dish, stirring it with two of her grimy fingers. She looked at me. A little slyly, I thought. I was doing nothing, just standing there with my hands in my robe, when suddenly she seemed to have a change of heart. "But you're right, the island would be appropriate." She leaned forward and settled the dish into the fire. "Very well. I give this journey my blessing. You may guide the boy to the Inook tribe. I will do what I can to mislead pursuers. But you must leave tonight, under cover of darkness."

"We should rest," I said.

Gwilanna slanted her gaze. "I agree. Follow the dragon's example. Sleep now; be ready when the moon comes up." She nodded at the dish. Its contents were already beginning to bubble. "This potion will relax you, but also give you strength."

"I will not drink any of your potions," I said. Not after what I'd seen in Taan.

"Agawin?" Guinevere looked at me, shocked.

I started to fish for an explanation, but thankfully she went on to say, "Whatever you've heard about sibyls in the past, forget. Gwilanna's been healing people in the valley ever since I've known her. She cured my ailment, didn't you?"

"Your ailment?" I said.

"The girl has an eye condition," said Gwilanna, "which could lead to blindness, if left untreated."

"They change color," said Guinevere. "Green to violet. Violet's bad. That's why I take these." She went into the pouch at her waist and pulled out a piece of shriveled gray material. "Dried mushrooms. Strange cure. But they seem to work." She popped the piece into her mouth and swallowed it.

"There is a chamber behind this one," Gwilanna said, tilting her head toward the rear of the cave. "You'll find furs. Nothing worse than you've slept on before. If you want to relieve yourself, go outside."

"And him?" I nodded at Gawain.

"Take the wearling for company if you wish, but a dragon will always come back to a flame."

"Nothing's going to harm him," Guinevere insisted, shooing me away. "I sleep in this chamber. I'll be here all the time. Rest, Agawin. And tonight, we begin our adventure!"

"Wait, boy. You're forgetting something." The sibyl picked up a cloth, thick and grubby with ash, and lifted the potions dish from the fire. She set it down at her feet, then poured some of the brew into a drinking vessel. She added a measure of cooling water and a sprinkle of some kind of herb. She held it up to me. "Drink."

I looked at Guinevere. "Drink," she urged.

This is unwise, the Fain cautioned me.

But I felt I owed Guinevere a measure of trust. So I took the vessel — and drank the potion.

The Fain went to work on it straightaway. Every part of my head began to buzz as they searched for ill effects on my mind. Galen wasn't slow to react in me either. A little burp of wind erupted from my mouth as he hardened the soft walls of my gut, preparing for a possible poison attack. Several embarrassing muscle twitches followed. Guinevere folded her arms and sighed. When the twitching was done and I was still alive, she pointed tersely behind me and said, "Your bed's that way." She settled down on a hide by the fire, pulling another one over her. "Sleep well, Agawin. Try not to snore." She pushed her hair off her face and promptly turned over. I considered myself dismissed.

The only fur I could find was riddled with fleas and there was water dripping where I lay my head and the whole chamber stank of mold, but I did manage to sleep. My mind was active and my dreams were strong. I had never had a dragon in my auma before and Galen was making his dominance felt. Through his eyes I saw a gathering of dragons. Twelve of them, assembled in an ice-cold cave lit violet purely by the brightness of their eyes. Burned into the barren walls around them were marks like the three-lined symbol I had seen. One by one, each dragon came forward and shed its fire tear into a hollow in the wide cave floor. The only dragon present that did not shed its tear was the queen, Gawaine. I recognized her from Grella's tapestry. She, with one snort, imbibed the whole pool and turned herself into a dragon beyond dragons. She grew by half her size again. One beat of her mighty wings shattered ice spears hanging from the roof of the cave. Her eyes burst into golden flames. Dragontongue glowed in the walls behind her. Her scales rippled and shone so brightly that even in the dream I was almost blinded. I was terrified. I kicked out, wanting to wake. Then a scent as sharp as an arrow hit my nostrils. And I settled again. And the dream changed course.

I saw Gideon, in his new form, sitting in the window of a strange dwelling place, made from materials vaguely like stone. It had many, many windows, this place. Too many to see at once. I began to draw back from it. Back. Back. Floating, lighter than a mote of dust. The farther I retreated, the more windows I saw. The more birds, like Gideon, sitting in the windows. Until I was so far back that the building stretched from the ground to the clouds, and still, it seemed, it was higher than the clouds. I floated to the ground, where I found myself in a field of daisies. I picked one and looked into its yellow center. There was Grella, holding Gwilanna. The baby's face was wrinkled and old. Then I heard laughter all around me. In the middle of every flower was the image of the skull. The jaw was moving, laughing at me. I stamped on the flowers, but the laughter kept coming. And I didn't know why but it sounded like the way Gwilanna might laugh. And once again I was restless and fearful. I smelled mold and knew I was close to waking. But the dream had one more twist for me yet. The last thing I remembered before I stirred was the image of a darkling flying low across the daisy fields. Closing, closing . . .

Bang! Its claws were in my chest! I cried out and my hand closed around a stone. But as I brought the stone up to pummel the creature my eyes flashed open and there was Guinevere, kneeling beside me. Gawain was on my chest, raking his hooks through my covering fur.

"Hey!" the girl barked. "What are you doing?"

She slapped my hand aside and I dropped the stone.

I was sweating. Panting. Still waking up. "I was . . . dreaming," I said. "I'm . . . sorry."

She scowled and picked Gawain off me. The dragon made a quiet, guttering sound as she stroked his spine to comfort him. He clamped his feet to the perch of her wrist and tested his juvenile wings. He had grown a little, which seemed impossible in such a short space of time. And yet there were two clear bumps on his head, the first defining features of a dragon: his horns, or primary stigs. "It's time," said Guinevere. "Are you sure you can travel? Gwilanna says you were talking in your sleep."

Was that the value of her potion? I wondered. A serum to make me speak? "Where is she?"

"Outside, on the hill."

I sat up quickly and pushed the fur aside. "I need to look at the skull."

"What? No! Gwilanna will roast you on a spit if she sees you."

"I have to do this. I *knew* Grella."

That brought a puzzled frown to her face. "How?"

"I'll tell you later. When we're on the move."

"Agawin?" she called. But I was already gone.

The fire in the main chamber had been built up again. As I swept past and knelt beside the skull, a few flakes of ash spiraled up toward the roof. "Grella," I whispered, half-hoping her face might appear to me, "is this you?" I ran my thumbs along what would have been her cheeks.

"Are you *mad*?" Guinevere appeared at my side. "Put it back," she hissed, "or there's going to be trouble."

She is wise, said the Fain, swarming into my consciousness as if they had only just woken, too. *Do not provoke the sibyl.*

And I was all but set to do as they wished when my gaze fell upon the cloth the skull had been resting on. To Guinevere's dismay, I put the skull on the ground and picked up the fabric. Slowly, I unfolded it.

There in my hands was the tapestry I'd started in Grella's krofft. Finished. Stitched. In astonishing colors. An image so alive I could almost fall into it.

"Oh," said Guinevere, slightly overcome.

"You've never seen this before?"

"No," she said. "Who are these people? What does it show?"

And a new voice said, "It's a battle, girl. Surely that much is obvious?"

I whipped around. Gwilanna was perched on her stone on the far side of the fire. She must have crept in with the stealth of a fox, for not even Galen had warned of her approach. "This is how you repay my hospitality, boy? You eat my food, take refuge in my home, then steal what few possessions I have?"

"I drew this," I said.

"What?" said Guinevere, calming Gawain. The raised voices were beginning to agitate him.

"I drew it and Grella stitched it," I said. "This does not belong to you, sibyl."

"You forget," she snarled, "that a child inherits what its parents want to give it. My mother begged me in my crib to protect the tapestry. If you value your life, you'll put it straight back."

"In your crib?" said Guinevere.

And perhaps, like her, I should have paid attention to Gwilanna's strange admission, but I was too far down my chosen path. I said, "Tell me how she died or it goes on the fire."

"Agawin! Have you lost *all* your senses?" Guinevere quickly shifted position to put herself between me and the fire. "Give the tapestry back to Gwilanna."

"But . . ."

"Do it — or you leave here without me tonight." She offered Gawain up to show she meant it.

"All right." I folded the tapestry and put it back, placing the skull on top of it again. But when I turned I said to the sibyl, "Grella was my friend. Tell me how she died."

Guinevere switched her gaze between us.

I watched Gwilanna skewer some bread onto a stick and begin to toast it against the flames. "You should beware of this boy, Guinevere. His knowledge is far greater than he likes to make out."

"Can I trust him?" she said. A harsh question, perhaps, but I understood why she needed to ask it.

The sibyl threw a short laugh into the air. "He intends you no harm and would even have you love him. But he will keep things from you. Can't you feel his delicate auma? It radiates such purity of spirit — a quality rarely found outside of dragonkind . . ."

"Tell me how Grella died," I growled.

She pulled the bread off the stick and turned it over to toast the other side. "I will tell you something, boy, and that might be enough. My mother, as you know, was meant to return to Mount Kasgerden on the anniversary of your 'death.' "

"And show you to the Taan."

The sibyl nodded. Guinevere was looking dreadfully confused. But she held her tongue while the story unfolded.

"She did go back," Gwilanna confided. "But she did not take me with her."

"And they killed her? For *that*?" My knee joints locked. There was pain in my shoulders. Had there been wings on my back, I would have been tenting them now. Galen, as always, was ready to fight.

Gwilanna sighed with impatience. "No. For many years, she took another child in place of me. She made an arrangement with a local tribeswoman. A new dress in temporary exchange for her baby. Grella, as you know, was skilled with a needle."

"But . . . why swap a child for you? Why would she need to go to such lengths?"

"Look at me," Gwilanna said. The fire sizzled as her spittle fell across it. "I was like this from the day I was born."

I had seen it in the daisies. The baby, horribly wrinkled. Old, I wanted to say. But despite my intense dislike of this woman, I could not stoop to such cruel remarks.

"If Grella had shown me, a prune, to her father, I would have fallen under his sword."

"Gwilanna, your bread," said Guinevere.

"What?" the sibyl grunted.

"It's burning."

With a rumble of annoyance, Gwilanna whipped her stick to one side. The bread hit the wall, flaring on impact. As it dropped toward the ground, Gawain skittered out of Guinevere's hands. Even though he was just a few hours old, he instinctively unlatched his jaw and just about caught the bread in his mouth. It was a comical sight. A young dragon stumbling around the cave with a piece of burning bread too big to swallow. He thrashed it to the floor and began to shred it. Only Gwilanna did not seem amused. "Dragons . . . ," she muttered.

"You seem to know a lot about them, sibyl."

"Do not try to belittle me, boy. I know what you are."

"What is he?" said Guinevere, looking at me hard.

But neither I nor the sibyl would answer that. "If Grella's father did not end her life, what did? Did she die a natural death, or was she slain?"

The sibyl gave another derisive laugh. "Would you seek to avenge her, Agawin?"

"I would try," I said bravely.

To which she said, "Pah!"

"Why do you react like that?" asked Guinevere. She tossed her hair, looking incensed. "Does it not demonstrate Agawin's courage that he would seek to put right any ills to your mother?"

"I told you, he is full of deceits," Gwilanna snapped. She found another piece of bread to toast. "He knows of the past but keeps it from us. He knows things about me he will not confess."

"If I am full of deceit," I said, "what do you see in the mirror of my eyes?"

"Have a care, boy." She pointed her stick in the region of my heart. "You fascinate me, true, but you are nothing I could not do without."

And this was clever, for it riled me just enough to blurt: "Grella was not your mother."

A mistake. A terrible mistake. One that would come to haunt me for as long as I was to know Gwilanna. The Fain, who until that point had been quietly absorbing the dialogue, suddenly switched to full alertness.

Why have you spoken of this?

Pure vanity. I hung my head.

Guinevere said, "Agawin, you must explain this."

I shuddered. The only bright spark of relief was seeing Gawain burp a cloud of smoke as he chomped on the last of the smoldering bread.

With my head still down I said to Gwilanna, "Your mother was a sibyl called Hilde. Your father, Voss, was oppressed by a force called the Ix. I do not know exactly how you were conceived but he used the auma of a dark unicorn. All of them died on Kasgerden that day. Grella rescued you and claimed you as her own. That is all I know."

For a moment, the only sound in the cave was the crackle of wood and Gawain scratching dough from his primitive teeth. Then the sibyl opened her mouth and out of it came a howl so loud that the flames retreated high up the wall. Guinevere screamed and grabbed Gawain, running with him toward the cave exit. I backed away, too, fearing that the sibyl would come for me now. Instead, she stepped straight through the flames and snatched up the skull. Her hands shook as she put her thumbs into its eyes. A jagged line ran down the back of the head. With a crack, the skull split in half. The sibyl dropped it into the fire.

Gwilanna's eyes rolled. They were dark, almost black. The wrinkles in her face were like old battle scars. Her matted hair was fizzing where the fire had singed it. A small lick of flame had caught her robe. "Get out," she hissed, in a voice that reminded me all too well of her evil father. "Take your wearling and run while you can. Dark times are about to come down on you, boy. Our story isn't done."

She howled again and I felt the rocks move.

I needed no more reason to flee from her than that.

We ran into the moonlight, Guinevere, Gawain, and I, where we were almost struck by another foe. The brown bear reared before us, roaring and flashing its great hooked claws. I had no time to imagineer. All I could think to do was punch its nose and hope to get away. But as I raised my fist Guinevere cried, "No!" She stayed my arm. "I think he's reacting to the wailing, not us."

Sure enough, the creature dropped to its haunches. It squinted in abstract wonder at Gawain, then tried to peer beyond us into the cave.

A little recklessly, perhaps, I slapped its shoulder.

It threw its head sideways and opened its jaws, letting out a growl that practically shook my teeth from my gums. The foul stench of its breath was enough to knock ten men off their feet, but my nostrils closed like a dragon's spiracles and I survived the blast with a passing grimace. "Guard," I told it, pointing at the cave. I raised my fists as if I'd like to box. "You. Bear. Stop sibyl coming."

"No. She'll kill him," Guinevere said. She gave Gawain to me and put her hand on the bear's thick flank. "Go back to your home." She made signs with her hands. "Do not attack the sibyl. We must leave." (She indicated me and herself and Gawain.) "We go to the sea, to the island of your ancestors."

"We go to an early grave if we don't get out of here." I could still hear Gwilanna ranting in the cave.

Guinevere made another "home" sign, then gestured me away with a tilt of her head. We left the puzzled animal behind.

Or so we thought.

We'd gone barely six paces when we heard him speak. "Thoran come."

"Huh?" I grunted.

Guinevere paused. A smile lit her face. "So he *does* speak." We glanced at each other and turned to look back.

The bear lumbered toward us, stopping to urinate against a rock. "Thoran lead way. Guard girl. Guard dragon."

"What about guarding Agawin?" I muttered. "I was the one who gave him berries."

He blundered past us, bobbing up the slope like a weighty moth.

Guinevere gave a delighted smile.

"Is this wise? He's going to slow us down."

"He knows the land," she said. "He's strong. We could do worse."

I heard Thoran snort. Already he was looking back, waiting for us.

"Why is he taking us up the hill? Surely it's better to go through the valley to reach the sea."

He is using the stars to guide him, said the Fain. I looked up. The sky was full of bright points, like fish dancing in a giant ocean. The moon, too, was unusually bright.

Guinevere said, "There are many routes to the Great Sea from here. I'm willing to put my faith in him."

Thoran curled his paw to beckon us to hurry.

As we set off after him I said to Guinevere, "Are you happy to carry Gawain?"

"Yes," she said, taking him back. "He's so warm. I can feel his auma right down to my toes."

I nodded and thought about my dream. Gawain must have inherited his mother's fire, and therefore the power of a whole Wearle. The transformational effect on Gideon was clearly a result of that. I glanced at Guinevere again and thought about what she'd said, about feeling Gawain's heat throughout her body. What would the auma of *twelve* fire tears do to a human form? I wondered.

"Before we go on, just two things." Her eyes made open contact with mine. "No more secrets, please? I want to know your story, especially how you got here —"

The tornaq! I scrabbled in my robe and thankfully laid my hand on the charm. For one horrible moment, I thought Gwilanna might have stolen it. "Sorry," I said, hugely relieved. "Go on."

She ignored my panicked search and said, "I also want you to know that when Gawain is safe on the island, I'm coming back here to be with Gwilanna."

"*What?* Why would you do that? You heard what I said in the cave. Her parents were evil. All that's keeping her from going their way is the auma of a unicorn — and that was tainted."

"I don't care. She's looked after me. That's all I know."

"She threatened us, Guinevere."

"No, she didn't. She said dark times were coming. She didn't say she would bring them. If she'd wanted you dead, do you think we'd be out here breathing fresh air? She's hurting now, because of what you revealed. But she'll come to our aid if we need her. I'm sure of it."

"I killed her father." Suddenly there it was, as stark as the night. My mind flashed back to the fires of Kasgerden. "He turned into a demon, a creature called a darkling. She may have that within her, too."

Guinevere swallowed. My heart reached out to her. The day had still not fully turned and I had rocked her world like an unseen storm. She laid a hand on Gawain and patted him softly. He *graark*ed and rubbed his neck against her palm. "Then you and Gwilanna have scores to settle. But for now, our only concern is this wearling."

She hitched up her robe and fell into step behind the bear.

I looked back briefly at Gwilanna's cave, half-expecting to see another darkling slither out of the split in the rocks. A cloud shuffled across the moon. The nighttime thickened. Not a leaf rustled or a goat bell rattled. But the sibyl's last words lingered loud in my ears. *Our story isn't done.* I respected Guinevere's support for her, but I had never felt more aware of the need to keep my enemy within my sight.

Thoran led us to the crest of the hill, just one of several wide-girthed ripples in a land of softly rolling earth. Distant spots of amber light pointed out signs of human life. A little cluster near the water. A dot or two in the valley we were leaving. As we walked the ridge, I saw Thoran's purpose. He was guiding us toward a band of trees, far smaller than the Skoga Forest, which seeded a natural scoop between the hills and would give us cover on the long descent to a bay just visible beyond the tree line. A strange sight we must have made. Three silhouettes against the full moon. Two upright humans — one with a dragon in the cup of her hands — following a bear that hulked along on all four paws.

"What are you thinking?"

We were a goodly distance from the caves now and I hadn't spoken to Guinevere since catching her up. I shook my head. Not because I didn't want to talk, but because I wasn't sure where to start. "I still don't know what happened to Grella." In the turmoil surrounding my outburst, her fate had gone unspoken.

"You were close?"

"It seemed so — for a short time."

"Tell me about her tapestry. Why did you draw what you did? The characters are strange, like no one I'd recognize. And wasn't there a dragon, writing?"

A dragon who'd reproduced the swirls around the

tornaq. A dragon who commanded time, perhaps? I let the thought pass. As we started down the slope on the far side of the ridge, I began to tell Guinevere all that I knew, from the moment when Hilde had given me the tornaq to the point when I'd dropped the tapestry on Kasgerden. I tried to explain that most of the tapestry was a mystery to me. But it wasn't the drawing she first picked up on.

"You caught his *fire tear*?" She looped her hair with one hand. "You actually *held* a dragon's fire?"

"No, I . . . got in the way of it, really. It was only a remnant. A spark, I suppose."

"Even so. No wonder Gwilanna was wary of you. Does it burn?"

I laughed and ran my hands through my hair, sticky now with grease and ash. A dead, curled-up spider fell out, which I imagined was a regular occurrence if you dwelled in that cave. "I feel Galen inside me all the time. He reacts to things, especially threats. You put him to sleep with your lullaby."

"But he's awake now?" She skipped forward a little to look at my face, hopeful, perhaps, that my eyes would adopt the familiar scalene lines of a dragon.

"*Hrrr,*" I went, which made her grin. She was so beautiful. Just like Grella. My face, I felt sure, was telling her so.

She looked away, flushed. "So, the tapestry. What is it? A battle, Gwilanna said. How can that be?"

I felt in my robe for the tornaq again, rolling it between my fingers and thumb. "Hilde told me I would see my destiny with the tornaq. Maybe that's what I'm heading for — a battle. Sometime in the future. I think it's called Isenfier."

"But you weren't in the picture."

I rolled my lips inward and gave a slight shrug. "Maybe I'm dead by then?"

We walked on a way, counting our footsteps.

"Maybe you just weren't in the picture," she repeated.

At that moment, we heard Thoran growl and I saw him rear up on his hind legs. We were close to the trees and he had spotted something. Telling Guinevere to wait, I hurried down the slope to be at his side. All of Galen's triggers were firing. I could feel the Fain probing the shadows ahead.

What is it? I asked them.

An auma source. Faint. We do not recognize it yet.

I began reaching for an arrow that was no longer there. Then, among the branches of the very first tree, a bird appeared. Even against the darkened background there was no mistaking the shape of a raven. Galen's scent nodes scanned it in a moment. For a bird of its size, it was giving off very little body heat or odor. My vocal cords adjusted, ready for speech, but there was surprisingly little movement in my throat. Birds and dragons, it seemed, had a near common language.

"Greetings," it *caark*ed in an oily voice.

Thoran showed it his impressive fangs. "Fly, raven."

"Into the wood! Would if I could!" It hopped sideways and tried to take off. One leg was held to the branch by a tie. It fluttered crazily, sending a dead leaf spiraling to the ground.

Thoran, slightly confused by this, dropped back to a less imposing height.

"Who has done this to you?" I said.

"Ix," it croaked out, picking at the knot. "Ix did this."

My blood cooled. "Why? For what reason?"

"No reason. No reason."

No conscience. That figured. "How did they come to you?"

"Wolf! Like a wolf!"

Is this a form they favor? I asked the Fain.

The Ix will take any form that gives an advantage, particularly if it kills with ease.

Galen had obviously registered that. I felt his auma raking the tree line. For a creature with only one natural predator I was surprised how cautious dragons were. I swept his focus over the bird. I could see little of it, just the moonlight glinting in its roving eye. "I don't believe you, raven. How could a wolf put a bind on your leg?"

I had seen wolves. A small pack used to drift around Yolen's cave, passing on like wisps of smoke if we faced them. Their agility was legendary. I'd seen water struggle to navigate rocks that a lone male wolf could flow over with ease. But lively as their paws undoubtedly were, they could never have tied a bird to a tree.

The raven had a simple explanation for it. "Magicks!"

Under my skin, the dragon reared. The heat in my shoulders was almost unbearable. Galen was desperate to show his power, as if the mere sight of his cavernous wings would see away any symptom of malice. For the first time, I felt his utter frustration. Here he was, a giant of goodness, trapped in a form that could barely express it. I had to act.

"If I set you free, will you fly with us and keep a watch for this wolf?"

"Will kill Crakus. Ix will kill."

"Crakus is your name?"

Caaarrrk! he went loudly.

"Agawin, what's happening?" Guinevere was struggling to calm Gawain. The wearling was treading about in her hands, flapping his wings in the manner of birds that sense changes in the weather — or danger in the air.

I said to Crakus, "If you prefer, I could leave you here for the buzzards to find — or set my wearling upon you right now. As you can see, he has your scent."

Thoran grunted and tipped his snout upward.

I saw the raven shrink in fear.

"I have no quarrel with you, bird — but if I let you go, you *will* be in my debt. Pledge your help and I will calm the wearling's longing. Think carefully on this. Even I can sense your blood flowing faster. I'm sure you know the effect that has on a *dragon's* pulse, especially one still learning to hunt."

The Fain said, *The bird will easily outfly him.*

But did Crakus want to gamble on that? I sensed his cowardice as sharply as the cool night air on my neck. Promising allegiance to us was the bravest thing he would ever do. And a pair of eyes in the sky could be useful.

Before he could make his decision, however, a new and more potent threat emerged. I turned my head so suddenly to the east that Thoran huffed and backed off a little. I raised my hand to still him, at the same time using Galen's sensors to pick up a thudding vibration in the soil: a sound I hadn't heard since my walk by the long Horste river with Yolen — hoofbeats.

"Guinevere. Into the trees!"

She turned her head to follow my gaze. "Why? What's the matter?"

"Horses. I can hear them. I think he can, too." I nodded at Gawain. He flipped his wings and rose to the height of Guinevere's chin. She grabbed him quickly and drew him back down. "Two riders. Maybe more. Get Gawain under cover. And whatever you do, try to keep him quiet." I ushered her past me, explaining in broken sentences to Thoran that horses were approaching. I pointed out the direction from which they would come. *Horses. Danger. Hide.* His discontented rumble suggested he would rather stand up and fight. But he obeyed my urgings and melted into the trees with Guinevere. As for Crakus, I had no knife with which to cut his tie and no time to spend unpicking a knot. But I gave him my word that I would come back and free him if he stayed in the shadows and made no sound.

I was right about the number of riders. I was barely concealed at the edge of the wood when two figures, on horseback, scrambled over a nearby ridge. Even with Galen enhancing my vision I couldn't see their faces, but I could see their mounts. A unicorn and a horse. The horse rider, a man who sat slim and tall in the saddle, spoke. "Slow down," he said to the unicorn rider — a woman with waves of hair like Hilde. He reined his mount around and stared at different points of the horizon, lastly at the trees. "Can you feel that?"

The woman trotted the unicorn up. Its horn was complete, its white mane flowing. Its elegant body was silvered by the moonlight. "Is it her?"

I felt my chest muscles tighten. Her? Were they looking for Guinevere?

175

"No, I'm picking up dragon auma."

"In the trees? Is that a habitat they like?"

The man leaned forward and gave the horse's ear a tug. "Depends how young they are. Let your auma commingle with the ground."

She looked down, as if she was concerned about the drop. "Why?"

"Just do it. You'll understand."

But before she could speak, I knew what she would find. The ground was warm, like it had been at Taan when Galen was alive. The fires of Gaia were ascending for Gawain. There was no way we could hide from it. I readied Galen for a possible attack.

"Remember the ark, just before we left Co:pern:ica?" The man was staring at Guinevere's position, as if he could source her heat trail, like I could.

"The fire on the water? Is this the same?"

The man nodded, more to himself than to her. "They're connected, over the entire nexus. Gadzooks must have used it as a kind of fire star so we'd be transported to the right place — and right time — on Earth."

"Smart dragon," she said.

And somehow I knew without knowing she was talking about the writing dragon on the tapestry.

Agawin. At long last, the Fain had spoken.

By now I had shifted position a little, trying to see the man's attire. He was not as thickly clad as Voss might have been, and clearly not a natural horseman; he seemed uneasy in the saddle and he was also not wearing riding boots. I could see no sword hanging off his hip. No bow. No quiver of arrows at his back. If he was a warrior, he was unlike any I'd seen before. The woman, likewise, appeared to be unarmed. All the same, I could not take chances. *Are they hunters? I* asked. Was there a bounty on the wearling's head already?

The Fain paused before replying. *They are visitors here.*

Visitors? Explain.

They do not have an auma trail consistent with this world.

What? I almost spoke the word aloud. I thought I saw Guinevere cover Gawain's mouth to stop him hurring. A few trees to my left, the bracken crackled.

This makes no sense to us. The woman is a kind of sibyl —

The plague of my young life. I tightened my fists.

— but the man, in part, is kin to —

"Greetings," said a voice.

My heart all but stopped. The idiot bird had spoken. The sibyl had heard him, but had she understood? "Raven," she whispered in a strange, almost self-congratulatory way, as if she had never seen a raven before. I heard Crakus shuffle along his branch.

Despite the bird's call, the man remained calm. "They're common on this world."

"She's got memories of them. A place called North Walk."

"Yes," he said. "A party of ravens attacked Zanna there once. You're phasing into her auma already. How are you feeling?"

"Strange." She threw her hair across her shoulders. "Like I've just jumped into my own reflection. One minit I'm putting books in order and the next I'm leaping through a wall of fire and sweeping across the universe on the back of a unicorn, learning to be a different woman. Everything I see or smell or taste here gives me another connection to Zanna. It's like looking at the daisy fields around the librarium and instantly knowing every one of them by name. It's very confusing. Am I Rosa or am I her?"

"You're Rosa," he replied. "With shades of Zanna. But the longer you stay on this part of the nexus, the more like Zanna you'll become. Try not to think about it."

"Easy for you to say. How do you adjust so fast?"

"It's different for a construct. We don't have the same . . . emotional fluctuations."

"Hmph," she went.

"That was very Zanna."

She scowled like thunder.

"And that definitely is."

"Greetings," Crakus said again, scratching his branch. The horseman flicked his gaze at the bird. I was certain he'd understood the squawk, but as yet he was making no move to reply.

Rosa reached forward and played with the unicorn's silky mane. "I'm frightened of what Zanna means to you. The . . . love she brings. The powers she has. I'm scared I won't be able to live up to her."

"You don't have to," he said. "You just be what you are."

The sibyl raised her head proudly. Just for a moment I was able to catch a glimpse of her profile. She was not as fair-skinned and appealing as Grella, but even the darkness could not conceal the striking, feral lines of her face.

"Is she prettier than me?"

The man turned his horse, unsure of how to answer. "Physically, you're almost identical."

"Almost?"

"Rosa, it doesn't matter." There was a pause. He said, "We need to get on."

But she was not done with him yet. "You've got a daughter, haven't you? Zanna's child."

This must have been true, for it made him swallow. "We're way too early in the timeline to meet her."

The sibyl laid her fingers across her bare arm. A slight blue glow came off her skin. "Then why do I feel her auma so strongly?"

He shrugged and said, "Alexa is . . . special. She's recorded as a primary being in the Is, so —"

"No," she interrupted him. "Forget all that 'Is' stuff. I mean she's very near."

"That's not possible."

"Well, I'm telling you, I *feel* her."

For a third time, Crakus called out.

Relieved to have a reason to end their conversation, the man slid off his horse. "I think you're picking up a forward memory. We'll talk about this later. Wait here a moment. I'm going to see what's bothering this raven." He patted the horse and approached us on foot. I half-expected Galen to burst from my body and throw his spirit self into the attack. But the dragon, like the Fain, seemed somewhat awed by this gangly man with the loping stride. The whole wood fell silent as he saw that Crakus was tied to his branch.

Quickly, he drew a knife.

I was clear in my mind that he simply intended to cut the bird free. But Thoran saw it as a provocation. He crashed through the trees and roared toward the man, flashing his paws and barking out of the pit of his throat. The unicorn reared, almost throwing the sibyl off. The raven squawked in high-pitched fear, as though *he* was the one about to be swatted. Meanwhile, my heart galloped forward with Thoran. I had never seen an overweight lump of fur move as fast as he did that night. But the visitor was faster still. He dropped, rolled sideways, and was on his feet again before Thoran knew where his foe had gone. Had the man

181

been swift he could have leaped forward and plunged the blade into the bear's thick neck. But he rolled the knife to improve his grip and just waited for Thoran to scent him and turn. Indignant at being out-maneuvered, the bear gave a yawning howl of a threat, delivered from a tilted, open jaw.

To my amazement, the man roared back. "Stay where you are. I've no wish to hurt you."

The Fain read the roar and immediately said, *A bear's voice comes naturally to him.*

To add to my bewilderment Rosa said, "Change. Quickly. Show him what you are."

"I can't," he said, dancing in an arc to keep Thoran turning. "We're too early in the timeline. He doesn't know about ice bears. He'll be confused, possibly traumatized. I can't risk that."

"Oh, and you'd rather be dead?" She threw out her hands. A huge net materialized in the air and fell with a clatter over Thoran's body. The bear punched and struggled and fell down and rolled, but every move only wrapped the net tighter around him, until he was imprisoned and out of fight. "Hah," went the sibyl, pleased with her effort. "You never told me Zanna had magicks."

At that point, I broke cover.

"Enough!" I called, running out of the trees. The sibyl whipped her unicorn around. I braced myself, expecting some form of attack. But a strange kind of motionless moment passed between us. My eyes were in hers, hers were in mine. Then the world clicked back and I was running again. But I was not alone. I felt a sudden breeze at the side of my head and saw Gawain go fluttering past.

With one of his now familiar *graaark*s the wearling crashed feetfirst into the man, flapping his wings like a pair of loose robes drying out in the wind. The man staggered and fell onto his back. He had the last known dragon in the world on his chest and the means to kill it still resting in his hand. I cried out, "Throw the knife aside or I'll command him to flame you!"

The unicorn reared.

"Rosa, do nothing!" the man called out. And when she was calm, he lowered his knife and dropped it on the ground.

I ran and snatched it up.

"Save your threats," the man said, without caring to look at me. "You couldn't kill me if you tried. And I doubt that a dragon as young as this will have found his fire, let alone a wish to kill." His hands came up to the spindly neck.

"No!" I yelled, fearing Gawain was about to be throttled.

But all the man did was run his fingers down the wearling's spine.

Gawain gave out a gravelly trill and dragged one foot across the visitor's heart.

"I know," the man said tenderly. "I never thought I'd get to see *you* either."

I hovered like an idiot, unsure of what to do. *Who are these people?* I said to the Fain.

Before they could answer, Guinevere stepped out of hiding.

The woman on the unicorn gasped, "Look at this."

Guinevere cast her a puzzled look but addressed her words to the man on the ground. "Please, traveler, let the dragon be. We are simple hill folk, we mean you no harm."

"Don't be afraid," he said. "We have no plans to hurt you — or the dragon. We're here to help you save his life."

"I heard you talking," I snapped. "Who are you? Where have you come from?"

The man put a finger into Gawain's mouth and let the dragon nibble it gently. "We are Travelers from what you might call the future, Agawin. It is Agawin, isn't it?"

"You know me?"

"We feel we do."

Guinevere gathered up her robe and knelt beside the man. "Your face . . . it's familiar to me," she whispered. She traced his cheek with her fingertips. I saw him blink, as if from that contact he had learned a truth about her that even she did not know herself.

The unicorn whinnied. "Tell them," said the sibyl.

The man reached out and held a few strands of Guinevere's hair. He looked into her face and his eyes shone violet, filled with all the love it was possible to imagine. "You're the image of someone dear to me. You don't know me in the future and you never will. But if our mission here is successful, you will bring about the birth of a woman called Elizabeth, who will carry your auma — and your legend — forward."

"Legend?" I said.

Guinevere wasn't listening. "What is your name, Traveler?"

"David," he replied. "And this is —"

"Rosa," she cut in quickly.

The moon emerged from behind a thin cloud and the hills grew measurably brighter. For the first time I saw the visitors properly. To my astonishment, I immediately recognized David. I had to look closely at Rosa to be sure, but there was no mistaking the sibyl either. These people, these so-called Travelers from our future, had already been in our present. They were the "strange characters" Guinevere had talked about on our way here.

They were both on the tapestry of Isenfier.

PART THREE
JOSEPH HENRY

He was as tall as Yolen, perhaps a thumb's length more, and walked with a similar willowy gait. His face, though handsome, was nothing extraordinary. It radiated kindness and a slight air of worry. Dark hair flowed almost straight to his shoulders. He had long and noticeably delicate hands. Once again I asked the Fain what they knew about him. *Kin*, they had said. But kin to whom? The violet in his eyes had now receded. Did he suffer, I wondered, from the same odd malady afflicting Guinevere? Could he even be related to the red-haired girl? The Fain could not give a definite answer, but were hopeful that David would reveal himself in time. *Is he a bear in human form?* I pressed.

He is illumined, they said. *He could be many things, Agawin. Like you, he is commingled to the spirit of a dragon. But not just any dragon . . .*

Tell me, I insisted. *Tell me what you know.* Hesitation in the Fain was very unusual.

I felt them reading David again. *The auma we detect in him matches Gawain's....*

"Jeans," David said.

"Huh?" I grunted. He was attending to his horse and not looking at me.

"You were staring, Agawin." He tapped his left leg.

In truth, I'd been staring at nothing in particular. I was just dazed by the Fain's revelation. How could a visitor who had journeyed from the future be commingled to a dragon barely hatched from its egg?

"Pretty standard clothing where I come from."

I nodded, though his words meant little to me. His garments did intrigue me, though, especially the way his "jeans" were woven to the shape of his legs. I picked at the metal studs around the pockets and the clever little loops his belt passed through. I noticed Rosa was wearing "jeans," too. And other adornments. A thin scarf of flax. Charms at her wrists. A half robe showing a glimpse of her waist. She wore strange red boots, laced to the ankle. A bag with a metal clasp hung at her hip. I had never seen a woman quite like her before, not even in Taan. "How far have you traveled?"

"That's difficult to say." He touched the neck of my robe, testing the fabric between his fingers. He seemed as fascinated with me as I was with him. Before he spoke again he glanced beyond my shoulder, as if there might be something crawling up my back. Puzzled, I let my eyes drift sideways, but there was nothing lurking in the corner of my vision. "It wasn't our intention to meet you and Guinevere. Your lives, your destinies, are complex enough. You are not the one we came in search of."

"Who, then?"

His eyes adjusted to the dark, moving in spirals the way a dragon's eyes changed, though from where we stood it was easy to see the others. Guinevere, with the wearling settled on her shoulder, was conversing with the sibyl about her boots. Thoran, calm and freed from his net, was sitting alone, grooming, nursing his pride. Crakus, the raven, was still on his branch.

Tightening a saddle strap David said, "Can you set a fire?"

I shrugged. "Of course."

"Of course," he repeated, smiling at his thoughtlessness. "Do it. We'll camp in the wood. I'll tell you everything you need to know in there." He called to the sibyl, "Zan — Rosa, we're going in."

She nodded and gave an instruction to the unicorn. Bending one of its delicate knees, it knelt, allowing Guinevere to climb onto its back. David gripped the horse's bridle and turned toward the trees.

"Why are you so uncertain of her name?"

"That's also hard to explain," he said. "On the world we came from I know her as Rosa. On Earth, her auma is slightly different. Here she would be Zanna — a reflection of herself with an altered life. I think I'll just stick to calling her Rosa."

"A reflection?"

"The universe is a strange place, Agawin. There's a great deal to learn. But you will learn. One day."

He walked on a little and was two steps ahead before I managed to ask, "And you? Are you a reflection — of another David?"

He paused and patted the horse's neck. "I just . . . Travel a lot," he said, without really saying anything at all.

Like an eager sparrow, I pressed him again. "How did you come here — from your other world?"

This time he turned to face me. A cold breeze wavered across our path. I shivered and pushed my hands into my robe. My fingers touched the ends of the tornaq. Did David carry such a charm? I wondered.

"If my memories are correct you're a seer's boy, Agawin. You must have been taught that certain species, three in total, know the enchantments of time?"

I shook my head, feeling slightly inadequate. Brunne had been about to instruct me before he was cruelly murdered, and Yolen, no doubt, would have taught me soon. All I could do for now was guess. Three species? One of them had to be dragons. I blurted their name. All the world knew they had extraordinary gifts. Was this, after all, not one of the reasons rogues like Voss sought to steal their fire?

David smiled as if all I had done was to tell him that dead leaves fall from trees. "Unicorns are similarly blessed," he said, "though their willingness to travel depends on their rider. We're fortunate that Rosa has Terrafonne's trust."

I glanced at the sibyl and her unicorn, Terrafonne. For such a fragile animal he was bearing two riders on his back with ease. When she asked him to move, he flowed like dust motes falling through sunlight. It wasn't difficult to imagine him slipping through time. "You said a third creature knows the enchantments?"

"Yes." He spoke sweetly to the horse, telling him we would be resting soon. "There is a type of bird, like a small dragon, that monitors ripples or changes in time."

The tornaq, said the Fain, becoming excited.

Instinctively, my fingers closed around it. An unwise move, perhaps. David's gaze had dropped straight to my fidgeting hands. "They're called firebirds. They rarely visit this world. But you'd know one if you saw one, trust me." He clicked his tongue and pulled the horse into a walk.

"Wait!"

"Agawin, my horse is tired. And the others are waiting." He pointed to the unicorn, treading his hooves by the tree line. Guinevere was petting his glistening mane, clearly wondering what was delaying us. "We'll talk when we're settled."

"There may be wolves lurking."

"Wolves?"

I told him what I'd heard from Crakus.

I felt his auma wave scanning the trees. "There are no wolves here. The raven lied to you."

Much as I'd expected. Maybe it *wanted* to be dragon food, this bird. "What shall I do with it?" It had not kept to its word and it could not be trusted. I told him of the terms I'd offered.

He thought a moment, then handed me the horse. He approached the tree slowly and pulled his knife. Crakus squawked and huddled back into the shadows. David reached up and severed the tie.

But as quickly as Crakus tried to fly off, David caught the loose end of twine and wound it swiftly around his fist, reeling the raven in again.

"Murder!" he croaked, flapping like fury. Somewhere in the trees, I thought I heard another bird returning its call.

David tightened his fist, trapping the wrinkled toes against his knuckles. "You know," he began with a sigh, "every time I meet a bird like you, there's always a sibyl nearby controlling it." He tugged the twine. "Who's working you, Crakus?"

"Ix was here" was all the raven would say. A look of spite glinted in his berry-shaped eyes.

David nodded slowly. I got the impression he could have squeezed more from the bird if he'd wanted to, but all he said was this: "You struck a deal with my friend. I expect you to keep to it. If you meet the Ix again, you let us know."

With that, he released his grip. The ungrateful raven pecked at his hand, missing it by the width of a leaf. "Traveler! Traveler!" he squawked as he flew. All the world from here to Kasgerden could have heard him. Rosa did not look pleased. But David merely grunted and gestured for me to lead the way. We said nothing more as we stepped into the thick strong shadows of the wood.

In a clearing, I set out a circle of stones and kindled a fire from dry moss and twigs. As it began to burn, I noticed the visitors were in hushed conversation. I glanced at Guinevere. She was busy keeping Gawain amused. Like any young creature, he liked to play. My gaze drifted back toward David and Rosa. It was wrong, I knew, to listen to their talk, but Galen was constantly reaching out to David and almost by accident I heard Rosa say, "Why, though? Why do I feel like this?"

"It might be a side effect — of the transition."

"A *side effect*?" She didn't sound satisfied with that. "David, every time I look at him I want to cry. Even I, naïve librarium orphan, know that isn't a normal response. What's he even doing in Guinevere's time? Zanna has perfect memories of the legend and he's not there, in any of it."

Not *there*? I wiggled my outstretched fingers.

"Agawin? Are you all right?"

I looked up. Guinevere had noticed me wiggling. "Just a little cold," I said. I bowed my head and tended the fire, pitching my hearing back toward David. "I've tried to read him," I heard him say. "It's clearly him, but his pathway is hidden."

"Hidden? How?"

"I don't know. It's very strange."

"But you read *The Book of Agawin* before we left the ark. He must have recorded something about this."

Write? *The Book of Agawin*? Now I was confused.

"I only browsed a few sections. Stuff about Co:pern:ica. And it's a living book, remember. It could keep things to itself if it didn't want me to read them."

Rosa sighed heavily. "This can't be right. What's he doing in a place where he has no history?"

"The history could be wrong. Much of what we know has been verbally passed down from generation to generation. Stories alter. That's why bears have a Teller of

Ways, so that their legends are faithfully recorded. Maybe the jolt in the timeline brought him here."

"Time," she tutted, as if she'd like to wrap it up and throw it away. "It still doesn't explain why he's making me weepy or why I keep sensing Alexa's presence."

"Yes, that is very odd," he admitted.

"Is she involved somehow? In this, our quest?"

He took a moment to think about that. "Alexa is always involved," he said.

Leaving the horse only loosely tethered, he strolled toward the fire. At the same moment, Gawain fluttered out of Guinevere's hands and dug himself a shallow pit close to the flames. He settled there, content to fall asleep again. Thoran, still a little grumpy from the fight, had already stalked off into the wood to look for the trail that would lead us to the bay. The unicorn folded his knees and set himself down at the side of the horse. And that, I thought, was all of us. Until something began to kick and punch inside the bag at Rosa's hip.

"Looks like the spell's worn off," she said. "Had to happen eventually, I suppose."

David said, "It's all right, let her out."

Rosa turned a clasp and lifted the flap.

Out of it popped another dragon.

It was small, no bigger than a handful of pine-cones — and every bit as spiky as them. Such a peculiar arrangement of scales. Such a strangely shaped snout and nostrils (wide, a little too big for the face). Such oval-shaped eyes. Such flat back feet (she sat upright on them, balanced by her tail). And *such* a furious scowl. I would have said I had never seen anything like her. But I *had* seen something like her. She was almost the image of the dragon on the tapestry. She had no writing tools or parchment, but carried a cluster of flowers in her paws and a quiver on her back containing more. She was the oddest "dragon" I had ever set eyes on, but definitely one of their kind. As Galen turned his attention to the thing, I detected a spark of their auma at her heart.

"This is Gretel," said David, breaking my thoughts. "A female dragon with the power to do magicks. She was made by the woman I described to you."

"Made?"

"From clay." He spoke to the creature, inviting her to show me what she could do. She huffed for a moment, then took a slight bow. Guinevere laughed out loud as she blew rings within rings of smoke. Then she performed her best trick of all: In the blink of an eye, she made herself solid.

With David's permission, I picked her up and turned her in my hands. The body was firm, even the soft places like the eyes — they made a quiet *clink* when I tapped them with a fingernail — and the scales reflected the light of the fire. Suddenly, the dragon became "real" again and flew from my hands to land on the row of stones nearest Guinevere. Like David, she reached up and touched the red hair. Guinevere was enthralled by the thing.

A remarkable species, the Fain said, buzzing. *A unique combination of dragon auma, clay, and physical imagineering.*

Which posed one obvious question: "How did this . . . Elizabeth . . . give it life?"

David looked at me thoughtfully. "I can't tell you, Agawin; it could compromise your future."

"Like Thoran — and the ice bear?"

He smiled at my attentiveness. "Something like that."

I was desperate to know what an "ice bear" was, but he was clearly not going to say. "Why did you bring this . . . flower dragon here?"

"You try keeping her away," Rosa muttered, a slight edge creeping into her voice.

David said, "Gretel was drawn to this place, like we were. We don't know exactly how she got here or why. But she may be able to help with our quest."

I watched the dragon rearranging her crop of flowers. She flipped them neatly into the quiver. A skillful trick, but what possible use could she have for flowers? "Will you tell me, now, the nature of your quest? You said when we met you were searching for someone."

"It's Gwilanna, isn't it?" Guinevere said.

Fssst, went Gretel at the sound of the name. She splayed a row of claws and started weaving the ends of Guinevere's hair into a series of short red twists.

Giving away nothing in the tone of his voice, David asked, "Do you know where she is?"

Guinevere picked up a broken twig and began drawing patterns in the soil around her feet. "I could take you to her dwelling place before the sun rises, but how just would it be to betray a woman who has cared for me since I was a baby girl? What harm has she ever done you?"

"She gave Zanna *this*, for a start." Rosa pushed back her sleeve and showed us her arm. At first, there was nothing to see. But as she brought her fingers closer to the skin, a scar began to form in the flesh near the elbow — the same three-lined mark that ran around the tornaq. "It's getting deeper," she said to David. "Taking longer to fade every time. I'm becoming her, aren't I?"

David chose not to comment. "You know this symbol, Agawin?"

An owl hooted, making me jump. The night wind played with the tips of the fire and the treetops all leaned in to listen. David had seen me peering closely at the mark and now I had to give a reason why. "It . . . follows the pattern of a unicorn horn."

"To the exact — and infinite — twist," he said. "You'll see it wherever dragons have roamed. It's the most potent and powerful sign in their language. It can work many wonders — when used with the right intent. In these regions you will even hear it given a name. The Inook call it the mark of Oomara."

"But this is an old scar," Guinevere said, carefully examining the wound. "Have you met Gwilanna before . . . in the *future*?"

"The witch is as old as these woods," said Rosa, growing more assured with every toss of her hair. "She keeps herself alive, or so she claims, with the auma she absorbs from a dragon scale — one of his, when he grows." She nodded at Gawain, who snorted and rested his snout on a stone. "She seems to be immune to death."

Guinevere let that smear go by. "I have served Gwilanna all my life and seen her perform many acts of healing. Her powers are strong and she is feared by some, but I have never seen her stray very far from her dwelling place — other than to snare food or gather water. How, then, can she travel through time?"

The unicorn auma inside her, buzzed the Fain. *She must eventually learn how to harness it.*

And I, in a moment of blunt stupidity, had made her aware of what she was. I had unleashed the sibyl on the universe and sent the dark Ix forward through time, along with the sleeping spirit of Voss. David saw me shudder. I pulled my robe into my shoulders and he let it pass.

"That's the question we're here to answer. We have no wish to harm Gwilanna. We simply need to . . . alter her plans."

"Show them the picture," Rosa said.

David dipped into a pocket of his jacket and drew out a piece of yellow parchment. "This is a drawing of something you might recognize." He unfolded it and turned it around.

"The tapestry picture," Guinevere gasped.

I sat back, stunned.

"It's called Isenfier," David said, still not asking questions of us. Once again he'd noticed my reaction, but for now he seemed happy just to talk. "It's the scene of a battle between dragons and a life-force known as the Ix. What you see is the battle at a critical stage, suspended over a nexus of time. A clever move by the dragon holding the pencil."

Guinevere wrinkled her pretty nose. "That little creature stopped *time*?"

"Mean crossword solver, too," Rosa said. To ease our confusion she added, "He's smart."

"Is the writing dragon kin to Gretel?" I asked. He looked of her breed, though his eyes were less striking.

"Yes," said David. "His name is Gadzooks. He, too, was made by the woman, Elizabeth."

"And she is *my* kin?" Guinevere asked, just to be clear about this again.

"If the timeline remains unaltered, yes."

And if it changes? I asked the Fain. But I knew the answer before they spoke.

The woman, Elizabeth, might not exist. Or any of the dragon breed she makes.

"May I?" Guinevere held out her hand.

David allowed her to take the parchment. Fireflies danced all around her hair as she held it closer to the light of the flames. After studying the drawing for a moment she said, "Gwilanna has a proper tapestry of this."

"Not the original, surely?" said Rosa, pitching her question quietly at David.

He turned to Guinevere. "How did she get it?"

"I don't know, but Agawin claims he drew it from a dream."

"Is this true?" asked David, turning to me. "You had this vision of Isenfier?"

I lifted my shoulders as if it was nothing. "I was traveling with my seer and we stopped in Taan. A woman there encouraged me to try their art. I was thinking of dragons and the next thing I knew . . . this was in my head."

"How is that possible?" Rosa asked.

David didn't reply. Instead, he asked, "Did you stitch it, Agawin?"

"No," I replied, looking down at my feet. "It was finished by a girl I met in Taan. Her name was Grella."

"Gwilanna inherited the tapestry, then?"

"I suppose so," I said, which was at least half true. Therein lay the story of Grella. I still had no idea of her fate, or the truth about that skull. And I didn't want to go into it again.

"It's not right anyway," Guinevere said.

We looked toward her.

"The drawing, I mean. The mountains and the dragons are exactly the same, and the girl, and the writing dragon. You were on the tapestry, too," she said to David. "But you're not on this. And what's Gwilanna doing there?"

"Gwilanna?" I rudely snatched the parchment from her. Sure enough, the sibyl was on the hillside. But in the place where David should have been standing was a wiggly line, as if he'd been squeezed right out of existence. And in the corner, more like a smudge than a drawing, was something else. I put my finger on it. "What's this?"

David said, "That's probably a firebird, arriving too late to protect the timeline."

"Firebird?" Guinevere looped her hair.

"They monitor the time continuum," he said, making no attempt to simplify his words. "I was telling Agawin about them earlier."

"Are they colorful?"

"Very. Though some of the early ones were almost translucent, like moving wisps of light."

"Gideon," she said. She slapped her knees and sat up smartly.

"Gideon . . . ," Rosa muttered.

"Search your memories. You'll find him," David said. "You've met him, Guinevere?"

"Yes," she said. "He flew here with the egg Gawain was hatched from. He came to us an eagle, but his body was changed by a fire the like of which I've never known before. He rose from his ashes and disappeared into the shimmering sky."

"Portal?" said Rosa.

David hummed in thought.

"Do you know where he went to?" Guinevere asked.

"He was taken to our world," David said, though

from the set of his features he wasn't sure why. "Every firebird there is descended from him."

"But he was an eagle, first — on Earth?" Rosa repeated it, just to be clear.

David nodded. "According to the legend, he was in the air for several days with the auma of Gawain between his claws. He was always going to be changed by it."

"He had tufts, like an owl," Guinevere chirped. "His colors were amazing."

"Once seen, never forgotten," David said. He looked pointedly at me.

"Only Guinevere witnessed this change," I insisted, desperately trying to save my blushes. I knew it would make little difference now. David would be wondering why I hadn't mentioned Gideon when we'd talked about creatures that traveled through time. I hastily turned him back to the tapestry. "What does this picture actually tell us? Why is a battle happening here?"

He took the drawing out of my hands and spread it by his feet, using stones to hold the corners in place. "This is a place called the Vale of Scuffenbury, though its name might be different in your present day." He waved his hand above the cluster of hills. "In the foreground is Glissington Tor, a smaller hill than the rest but still large enough to hide a queen dragon. Gawain's mother went into stasis here after giving up her fire to her unborn sons."

"That must be very recent," Guinevere said. "Two seasons at most."

I glanced at Gawain and grunted in agreement. A dragon's egg, once laid, took six and one half cycles of the moon to hatch.

"The Tor is a long way south of here," said David, "but word about dragons travels fast. It won't be long before you start to hear rumors of a betrayed queen dragon sending her surviving egg north, guarded by a trusted eagle. . . . Shall I go on?"

"Yes. I want to hear all of it." Guinevere reached down and rested a soothing hand on Gawain. He gave a quiet *graark* and wrapped his spiked tail across his back.

David said, "The Isenfier tapestry describes events much further down the timeline. Thousands of years after the queen goes into stasis, for reasons that would take too long to explain, her sleep is unlocked and she rises again to do battle with the Ix. After a bitter struggle, she forfeits her life in an effort to defeat the

Ix:Cluster for good. The sacrifice, though brave, is only partly successful. A unicorn sent mad by the dark forces at Scuffenbury plunges itself into the Fire Eternal and infects Gaia, the Earth spirit, producing the Shadow you see emerging from the hill."

"The dragons are losing?" I asked. Galen's auma stirred uneasily. I had to work to keep him under control.

"Yes," David said. "And Gadzooks is aware of it. He knows if they surrender the fight to the Shadow, the Earth and every species on it will fall under its spell and the Ix will become the masters of a force called dark energy. They would use this force to create or imagineer a dark fire from the unseen matter of the universe and set it in a physical form they call a darkling. These darklings, a kind of antidragon, will attempt to invert the very nature of being. Imagine a life that is a mirror of this one, where evil dominates every thought and goodness is crushed at every turn."

My mind raced back to the ledge on Kasgerden and the transformation I'd seen in Voss. I pictured a flock of the darkling creatures and began to feel very sick at the prospect.

David went on, "So Gadzooks does the only thing he can. Using every spark of his creative power, he inscribes the unicorn symbol on his pad. This has two effects: Time stops, and a beacon is transmitted across the universe, even into worlds you could barely imagine. In one of those worlds, a place called Co:pern:ica, I — or a version of me — hear his cry for help. That sets off a course of events which culminates in me and Rosa Traveling here. This is difficult to understand, I know. But it is the truth."

Guinevere puffed her cheeks. "And all this is because of *Gwilanna*?"

"More her equivalent on Co:pern:ica."

"Her what?" I said.

David steepled his fingers for a moment, seeking a way to explain. "Do you understand what I mean by 'imagineering'?"

"Yes," said Guinevere and I together.

This seemed to surprise Rosa. "Really? This early in Earth's history?"

To which David replied, "It was a limited, but natural, ability once." He turned to me and said, "Co:pern:ica is an imagineered world, very similar to

Earth, but not quite identical. Some . . . copies of the people here exist there. Gwilanna is one of them."

"A world?" said Guinevere, leaning forward. "Who could imagineer a whole *world*?"

A Collective, such as the Higher, said the Fain. My head tingled as they vibrated faster.

Explain "Higher."

A multiple gathering of Fain beings.

Why would they imagineer a whole world?

We do not know. We are an isolated cluster.

And all David would say to Guinevere was, "Just go with it, Guinevere. Under the right circumstances, it can be done."

"And Gwilanna exists in this place?"

"Sort of. As a result of what she did there, Gadzooks is now struggling to maintain control and Gwilanna, as you can see, has put herself into the Isenfier scene. If the battle restarts according to this picture, or Gwilanna attempts to manipulate the outcome, there will be serious repercussions all along the timeline."

"People will die?"

"Or simply fade out of existence."

"How you can stop this?"

David shifted his position to look me in the eye. "There are options involving the firebirds. Ways we might nudge things in our favor. But that would involve a confrontation with the Shadow and many birds could die as a result. It's far better that we undo Gwilanna's influence — here, at the earliest stages of the timeline. Gwilanna is what we'd call a spoke in the wheel. She acts impulsively, for her own ends. We know she's gained awareness of the way time works, but what she may not know is that any distortion of the forward timeline causes an echo back through history. All our knowledge points to the fact that the seed of change begins at the dawn of Gawain's birth. We think she's acquired an advantage on this timepoint that she didn't have in the original legend. If we can find out how she learns to meddle, we can restore the timeline, keep the legend secure, and save a lot of needless suffering."

Guinevere hummed in thought. She crossed her legs and pulled her robe over her knees. "But I don't understand why she'd want to do this. She seemed content with a life healing others. What ambition could serve her so well that she would risk the lives of so many people?"

"She wants illumination to a dragon," said Rosa. "She'll do anything she can to get it."

"But there *are* no dragons now," I said, "except —"

And we looked at Gawain, snoring gently. In him was Gwilanna's entire purpose.

"All right," Guinevere said with a sigh. "She lives in a cave not far from here. I'll guide you to it, but I will not bear any prejudice against her until I know for certain she's a threat to Gawain. A meeting will prove her charity, perhaps. If she wants what you say, to be part of him, why would she send us by night to the sea to put him on an island where he'll be safe? Why didn't she just . . . take him from the cave? Or slay him and be done?"

"Because she's plotting something," Rosa said. "Whatever you think of Gwilanna, think again."

"May I ask a question?" A curl of wood smoke rose from the fire and twisted slowly beyond my face. I let Galen enjoy its charred gray scent, then I reached over and picked up the drawing. "Who are the other people in this picture?"

"The tall man looking on is named Tam," said David. "A friend to Elizabeth's family. The young woman with him is Lucy, Elizabeth's daughter."

"And who is the child holding Gadzooks?"

Rosa took a breath. "That's . . . David's daughter."

"Your daughter?" Guinevere looked at him, stunned. "This girl is your *child*?"

The one I'd heard them talking about. The one whose voice I had heard in my head. This little girl was David's *kin*?

Rosa fixed her gaze on the child. "She's the one in real danger if we don't stop Gwilanna."

David shook his head. "We don't know that for sure."

"Look at her," Rosa snapped at him. Her dark eyes flared and she was suddenly more spirited, more like a sibyl. The bands of metal on her wrist clanged together. "Her face is vacant. There's nothing in her eyes. And Zanna remembers her with wings — doesn't *Daddy*?"

"Wings?" said Guinevere, echoing my thoughts.

The Fain said, *The child must be a new breed of human.*

Why do I sometimes hear her voice?

We do not know. This is unclear. Your link to this girl always ends in a paradox.

Explain "paradox."

An absurd twist in the layers of time.

"She'll be nothing like the girl we knew," Rosa said. "She might as well be dead to us, David."

"Us?" said Guinevere.

The wind gave a long, low moan.

Rosa turned her face away.

"She's ours — in a manner of speaking," said David. "Her name is Alexa. She's very . . . special. For some reason we're not quite sure of yet, Rosa feels her presence strongly."

I was about to ask how a child so young could ever be involved in the heart of a battle, when Rosa unexpectedly turned on me. "You." Her dark eyes swooped into mine.

"What?" I blustered, leaning back a little. "What have I done?"

"Who are you, exactly?"

"He's Agawin," said Guinevere, protective and perplexed. She sat up and shook her long red hair. Gretel, still braiding, huffed in annoyance and snatched back the strands she'd been working on.

"There's something weird about you," Rosa pressed, as if we were the only two people present. "Something you're not telling us. Something . . . deep."

"Rosa," David cautioned, but she wouldn't stop.

"You know about her, don't you? You know about Alexa."

"He can't," said David.

"What are you hiding?"

"Me?" I cried. "What am *I* hiding?" I stood up and threw the parchment down. It slipped toward the flames and one corner caught fire. Guinevere cried out, "Agawin! What are you doing?" She immediately bent forward to save the drawing, but David held her back and said, "No, let it burn. Its job is done. Let Agawin speak his mind."

His increasingly guilty mind. I knew what I should be telling them. Gwilanna was filled with unicorn auma; I had a tornaq hidden in my robe. The enchantments of time were all around me, but my vanity and anger prevented me from sharing it. Pushing my hand through my hair I said, "You Travel to our world as strangers in time and you dare accuse *me* of harboring falsehoods? Tell me how *you* are kin to Gawain." I whirled around and stared at David.

There. It was out. Now he knew I recognized the dragon in him.

The flower dragon, Gretel, blew a smoke ring or two. Gawain himself popped one eye open.

Guinevere pointed at the wearling and said, "Is this true? You share his auma?"

Gawain stood up and yawned. He beat his wings forward to stretch their muscles, sweeping debris and smoke at Gretel. I watched her spit a bright orange cinder off her tongue. She wrinkled her peculiar snout, unamused.

A spark of violet entered David's eyes. "Yes," he said. "But I can't tell you how."

"Why?" I insisted.

For the first time, I felt his anger rising. "If you knew what must become of me and Gawain you might try to alter the timeline yourselves."

From the corner of my eye I saw Rosa bow her head. Maybe, sometime in David's future, she would have been moved to change events herself.

"Sit down," David said.

"No. I will not be —"

"Sit *down*," he commanded, and I felt the full force of the fire within him. A power I could not hope to defy.

I hunkered moodily, but I did not sit.

"Now," he said. "Will Agawin, the seer's boy, speak what he knows or do I have to trouble the dragon inside him? Galen, if I'm not mistaken?"

You must speak truthfully now, said the Fain. *In one-twelfth part, he is your brother.*

I picked up a twig and flicked it at the fire. "I know how Gwilanna can move through time."

The temperature in the wood seemed to drop a little. The fire guttered. The treetops bristled.

I looked at Guinevere. She nodded her agreement.

So I told them what I knew about the sibyl's birth.

"*Unicorn* auma?" Rosa sipped through her teeth. "No wonder she's got delusions of grandeur."

"It's why she's being drawn to the Shadow," David said, picking up a scrap of badly scorched parchment. Ironically, it was the face of Gwilanna. Gretel stepped forward and turned it to ash.

"I foolishly revealed this to her," I said. "Whatever wickedness you predict might happen would not have come about were I not at fault. I have a spark of Galen within me, it is true. He would pledge his allegiance to the last true dragon and so do I. I would join you in your quest, David. I swear on the life of my seer that I will stop Gwilanna."

"Your request is favorably noted," he said. "First, I want to know about your vision of Isenfier. How did that come about?"

Must I show him? I asked the Fain.

We are surprised he does not already know, they said.

I dipped into my robe and pulled out the tornaq. "This was given to me when Hilde died."

Rosa stared at the charm in awe. "What the heck is *he* doing here?"

I looked sideways at her. "You've seen this before? You know about . . . the creature it becomes?"

"Zanna does," she said, staring at David. "He's practically part of the family, isn't he?"

"May I see that?" said David. He held out his hand. I put the tornaq into it.

"I don't understand. What creature?" asked Guinevere.

"The charm shape-shifts into a bird," I said.

David rolled the tornaq between his palms. "Not this one," he said. He raised his hands and let the charm fall. My natural instinct was to move to catch it. Then I remembered what had happened in the cave and I stayed my move, confident the little bird-dragon would appear.

The charm struck a rock and broke into two.

"No!" I dropped to my knees, scrabbling like a mad thing in the bracken. "Where is it? What have you done?"

"I've exposed it for what it is," said David. "It looks like a tornaq. It's not — it's a construct. It's a fake, Agawin. You've been deceived."

"So where's the real one?" Rosa said nervously.

"Stolen," I muttered, realizing what Gwilanna had done. "She must have exchanged it while I was sleeping. I *knew* I should not have drunk her potion!" I slapped the ground and stood up angrily. "I must go to the cave."

"There's no point," said David, grabbing my robe. "All you'll find is echoes and dust. Trust me, Gwilanna will be long gone by now. Sit down, Agawin. We need to talk this through — together."

"But we must go after her. We're wasting . . ." But I could not bring myself to say the word. Wasn't "time" what all of this was about? I looked at Guinevere. The lines of her face were drawn with worry. Any trust she'd ever placed in Gwilanna was slowly beginning to fall away.

David picked up the dialogue once more. "At least we know how she gained her knowledge of time. We need to find her now and get the tornaq back."

"Excuse me." Rosa raised her hand. "The tornaq is with a sibyl, you say?"

Her question was aimed at me. "Yes."

She tightened her lips and looked at David. "How did Groyne get into the clutches of a sibyl?"

"Groyne?" I asked, a little confused. "This is your name for the tornaq creature?"

"I could call him a few other names right now."

David steepled his fingers and tapped them slowly against his mouth. "It's possible he's part of the natural timeline. He was with an Inuit shaman before Bergstrom passed him on to me. We're close to an Inuit community here."

I looked at Guinevere, who simply shrugged. None of this was making sense to us. For now it was better to let the others talk.

"Come on, David," Rosa said curtly. "There's no way Groyne would have gone unnoticed if he'd been cast in Guinevere's time. He was with Gwilanna's *mother*. How could Gwilanna not have known about that?"

"She was a baby — an orphan, from what Agawin's just told us."

"I still don't buy it. If Groyne was around in Gwilanna's childhood she would have known and she would have got hold of him. No, he must have come here from the future, like us . . . but that doesn't make much sense either." She laid her fingers on her arm. The scars lit up. "My memories of this are slightly sketchy because of the time shifts and all that . . . spinning, but wasn't Groyne robbed of his powers by . . . ?"

"Gwillan." David narrowed his gaze sharply, as if a fly had landed on the end of his nose. "You're right. What's happened to Gwillan? He was with us at Scuffenbury, fighting the Shadow . . ."

" . . . but you don't see him on the tapestry, and you don't see him on your drawing either."

"Who is Gwillan?" I asked. I was *very* confused now.

"Another dragon, like the one in the drawing," David muttered. "There are many in Elizabeth's home."

"Tell him the rest," Rosa added. Not waiting for David, she turned to us and said, "Elizabeth conceived a son, but his auma left her body before he could be born. It entered her house dragon, Gwillan, who stole the powers of several other dragons, including the tornaq bird we call Groyne."

"What happened to this . . . boy-dragon?" Guinevere asked.

"That's a very good question," David muttered.

But Rosa had an answer. "He turned into a killing machine."

"A slight exaggeration," David sighed.

"He took out a darkling, as . . . Zanna recalls."

"A darkling?" I gasped, remembering Voss.

"That makes him pretty lethal in my book," she said. "And here's the best part of all: What if the bird that Agawin saw isn't the true Groyne? What if it's Joseph pretending to be Groyne? We know he can shape-shift. We know he's clever. We know —"

"Joseph?" said Guinevere. She pushed one half of her hair off her face. In the amber firelight, she looked so pretty.

"Joseph Henry: the name Elizabeth would have given her son." Rosa looked at David again. "It has to be him. What if he's turned?"

Gretel rattled her scales. A noise appropriate to everyone's mood.

David closed his eyes to think. When he opened them again, his gaze fell on me. "You say Hilde had the charm before you, Agawin?"

I nodded. "Yes."

"Did it bring you here?"

"I believe it did. I . . . fell off a mountain."

"It saved your life?"

I grunted at him. "Yes."

David looked at Rosa. "There's the answer to your question. If Joseph had been corrupted by the Shadow, Agawin would surely be dead."

"But why deliver him into Gwilanna's clutches? And how did he escape from Scuffenbury Hill?"

David's gaze settled on the heart of the fire. "More important, why is it only now that we've noticed it? He could be running this. He could be playing us all."

"Can you get a fix on him?"

"Not without help."

"From Gawain?" said Guinevere, seeing David looking. "Surely he's too young for any kind of quest."

"Gawain is no ordinary dragon," said David. "He has the auma of an entire Wearle inside him. He's going to grow rapidly. Very rapidly. By morning, he'll have found his wings and his fire. In a few days' time, he'll be the size of these trees."

I picked up a twig and flicked it away. "When he's grown, will you send him after Gwilanna?" In the eye of my mind the witch was a pillar of flame already.

David swept that hope aside. "No. I want you and Guinevere to stick to your plan. You're heading for the island, right?"

We nodded.

"Let Gawain see it. He'll settle there and be at peace for a while."

"For a while?" Guinevere looked up, worried.

"Till the end of his natural life," David told her. "Hopefully, if we can catch up with Gwilanna, the rest will fall into place."

"So how can he help you?" Guinevere asked. She put out a hand and stroked Gawain's neck. To my amazement, I heard a slight rattling sound and saw a fine row of scales come up. They were also appearing on his wings and back, spreading out and hardening like frozen water. In the time it had taken us to reach the wood he had completed the initial stages of growth. It would take most dragons a turn of the moon to get even near to that. He cocked a leg and passed some water, dousing half the fire.

David said, "I'll need one of his claws."

"You would injure him?" Guinevere picked the wearling up and squeezed on one of his four-toed feet. A set of talons promptly clicked out. Pre-claws, soft, like growing shoots, but they would soon be very capable of ripping out the heart of an evil darkling — or taking the head off a cheating sibyl.

David sat forward and ran his thumb across them, examining each of the hooks in turn. "If I took out the whole stem, yes, it would hurt him. But I don't need to do that. As the claws go through their early growth spurts they shed the armored casings around the main talon. By morning he'll be ready for his first real push. The casing is all I need. There will be enough of his auma in that."

"What magicks will you do with it?" I asked.

"I'll write with it, Agawin. Like you will, one day."

I scoffed at him and shook my head. I knew some properties of herbs and I could foretell when the rain would fall, but words had always been a mystery to me. "How can you say this when I cannot even write my name in the dust?"

Dragon ichor is a powerful tool, said the Fain. *With a claw and the right intent, you could.*

I was reminded then of David's conversation with Rosa, and how he had mentioned a book I had written. I asked the Fain, *What is* The Book of Agawin?

We do not know, they said unhelpfully.

And David was not about to explain. "One day, all of this will be clear to you."

"So, you'll make a spell?" Guinevere asked. She stroked Gawain's head. "With his claw?"

"One to catch a sibyl with, hopefully," said Rosa.

But none of this rested easy with me. The dragon inside me just wanted to fight.

And suddenly, I got my chance.

At that moment we were set on the alert by a screaming yowl from deep within the wood. Everyone leaped to their feet. The unicorn reared, neighing with fear. Rosa ran to attend him. Gawain, likewise, flapped away and landed on the branch of a tree, out of reach. "Gretel, keep him company," David said. The flower dragon zipped away and took up position on the branch above the wearling.

Another yowl ripped through the trees.

"That's Thoran," said Guinevere, biting her lip.

By now, Galen had probed the wood and found the direction the cry was coming from. "He's hurt," I said. I started to run.

"AGAWIN, WAIT!" David shouted.

But not for the first time in my life, I took off against the advice of another, propelled by anger — and perhaps a dash of vanity. For if I picked out the small grains of honesty in my heart, I would have to concede that the arrival of David had made me feel less important.

So I ran like a wild boy, crashing through the trees, beating aside any loose obstruction, listening only to the throb of my blood and the powerful urge of Galen's auma.

Before long, I came upon Thoran. He was a little way ahead of me, lying on his back between the roots of a tree. A large thorn was embedded deep in his foot. The warm scent of his blood swept into my nostrils.

The Fain said, *Poison has entered his heart.*

I stepped forward, hot and dizzy from the run. The air around me moved like thick, slow water. I thought I saw the shadow of wings go past. Then, out of nothing, *she* was there. Bent over, attending to the bear.

Gwilanna.

"Quickly, boy," she said, without looking up. She pointed to a gnarled old tree behind her. Growing around its base was a large gray fungus. "Pick off a cap and bring it here."

"You tricked me," I hissed.

She immediately snapped back, "Do as I say or the bear will die!" Thoran whimpered and threw his head to one side. He was genuinely hurt, but I hesitated still. Spitting curses, the sibyl fumbled in her robe. She opened her hand and showed me the tornaq. "Yes, I took it. What did you expect? I've been stuck in that cave since before you were born. Can you blame me for wanting to experience time?"

"Thief," I snarled.

"You can have it back, boy. The charm refuses to work for me. The dragon-bird doesn't like my auma. Now bring me the fungus. It's the only cure."

I looked at Thoran, sick and groaning. Through the trees, I could hear David calling. Any moment now I would have his support. I dashed to the fungus and popped the cap off the nearest stalk.

"Give it to me, quickly." Gwilanna fished for it with her outstretched hand.

I put the cap into it.

And my fate was sealed.

"Thank you," she said, gripping me tightly.

I saw the movement in her other hand and knew right away she'd tricked me again. I felt the pull of the universe on the first shake of the tornaq. On the third, David burst into view. Before my vision blurred and the charm did its work, I saw him go through a remarkable change, from man to dragon in the space of a breath. A tongue of flame burst from his roaring mouth. Perhaps he intended to kill us both, to sacrifice me in the knowledge of stopping her. But the sibyl had timed her plan to perfection. All that vaporized as Gwilanna and I disappeared through time was her laughter, ringing out around the woods. . . .

PART FOUR
THE CLAW OF GAWAIN

With a jolt, my eyes blinked open again. I was still holding hands with the treacherous sibyl, but the woodland and Thoran were no longer there. Instead, we were in an icy wilderness that stretched away from us in all directions, its surface as vast as the pale sky above. In the distance I could just see an island of rock, but nothing that looked familiar to me.

The sibyl detached herself from my grip, throwing me away from her as if I was dirt. I clamped my upper arms and shuddered. Needles of cold were pricking my skin. The sun was low and yellow in the sky. It looked on weakly, offering no comfort.

Gwilanna took a breath and stretched her arms. The robe she was wearing dissolved away, replaced by clothing made from furs. "Bulky," she muttered. "But

I suppose it will do." She looked at me scornfully. "You'd better imagineer the same for yourself or call on your dragon auma, boy. It won't take long for your body to freeze. Fingers and toes are the first to suffer. The cold gets in and eats them away like maggots in an apple. The eyes aren't pretty when they harden either. They set and shatter like the shell of an egg."

"Wh-where are we?" I said. My teeth were rattling like a bag of loose bones.

"Well, that depends where you are in the timeline." She broke up the fungus I'd picked in the wood and ate it just as if nothing had happened. "Some would call it 'Arctic' or 'Land of the Ice Bear.' Personally, I like 'Icelands of the North.' That has a ring to it, don't you think?"

"Ice bears?" I said, remembering that David had used the term when he'd first met Thoran.

The sibyl flapped a hand. "Oh, there is much for you to learn, boy. The stupid ice bears are just one part of it. I have Traveled far since you brought me the tornaq. And all in the blink of a dragon's eye. It's been very . . . illuminating."

"Why have you brought me here?"

"To show you your future — well, not *your* future. Yours is very much in doubt, I'm afraid. Look around you; what do you see?"

"Ice," I said plainly.

"Wrong," she said. "This is Guinevere's legacy to Gaia. And this is Gawain, right here." She crouched down and put a hand to the surface.

By now, with the Fain's help, I had also imagineered furs for myself. A brief dialogue with them had also warned me that aggression would be very ill-advised. The sibyl knew the territory. We did not. And in the tornaq, she currently had the only means out of there. Their advice was to let her speak at will. Do as she suggested: listen and learn. She might yet say something that would be her undoing. Then we might strike. I stubbed my boot against the ice but felt nothing. "What do you mean? Where is Gawain in this?"

"Well, I'm pleased you asked me that." She moved her hands again and imagineered a seat of pure ice. A beautiful construct, the like of which I had never seen before. It had a high backrest and finely sculpted legs. She set herself upon it in a manner which suggested that she and she alone was the ruler of this wilderness.

"Interesting material to work with," she said, meaning the ice. "Oh, do rest yourself, Agawin." She imagineered a three-legged stool for me. "It's a wonderful story. Well worth your attention. Really quite touching in places."

I cast a glance at the stool and slowly sat down. The ice crunched as it took my weight. Far to one side I heard the whole field creak.

We are floating, said the Fain. *The Great Sea is below us.*

I moved my foot through a gentle arc, scraping loose crystals into a ridge. *Can we use the ice as a weapon?*

Your power to imagineer is not as quick as hers. It would be dangerous.

The snap of her fingers called my attention.

"That's better," she said with a testy frown. "Anyone would think you didn't *want* to know about the legend."

"I want to know what happened to Grella," I said. I glared into her wrinkled face.

This made her grimace and fidget in her seat. "What is it with you and your awkward questions? This is not the way I planned it. Not the way at all. You're supposed to sit and be humble and be awed in my presence."

"Forgive me," I said. "Evil always makes me impatient for a fight."

"Save your energy," she spat, leaning forward. "I won't disappoint you in that ambition. Your greatest challenge is still to come." She thumped back, clawing at the arms of the chair. "You remind me so much of him."

"Him?"

"Yes, him. David Rain."

"Rain?" I said, genuinely confused.

"Oh, for goodness' sake! Further down the time-line, in the Earth's progression, humans usually choose two names to address themselves by. He, David, adds the name 'Rain.'"

"And why am I like him?"

"Because you constantly get in my way!"

The ferocity of this statement blew a thin cloud of mist in my direction. As I wiped my face dry, I had an idea. *Can we cloak ourselves? Blow the ice into a storm and escape within it, hidden?*

Our calculations indicate the ice field is immense. There is nowhere to run. She would track you with ease.

"Then David thwarts you — in the future?" I asked.

"Thwarts me? No one thwarts *me*, boy. He's just an irritating dog that won't give up its bite. David Rain will never defeat me."

"But you have clearly not defeated *him*."

Her eyes grew as dark as the hollows of her face. "You forget, I have the tornaq now. Thanks to you, I hold a distinct advantage. I can visit any place I choose in the timeline and soon, because of what I have learned, I will be able to change it at will. Time is like water; it finds its own levels. One little stir can cause endless fluctuations. This meeting, for instance, was never meant to happen. As a result of it, related events are becoming unstable. Some connections are starting to fade. Can't you feel the unhappy ripples in the universe? How big a ripple would it take, do you think, to eliminate David Rain *for good*?"

For the first time since my initial shudder, the cold of the Icelands seeped into my bones. There was so much venom in her eyes. So much desire for power. I moved the dialogue sideways a little. "He is kin to Gawain. That must make him a challenging foe."

"Kin," she snorted, kicking one foot. "Of all the undeserving twists of fate that should have been confined to the back end of history that was the one that should have brought up the rear."

"It was . . . an error?" I said, trying to understand. I frowned and felt the frost cracking on my eyebrows. Not an unpleasant sensation, just strange.

"It was a mockery," she said. "Useless Ix assassin."

Assassin? This was not a word I knew.

Killer, said the Fain. *There is a division of the Ix known as "Ix:risor." They kill without feeling. In the future, they must have been sent after David.*

"So David is . . . was . . . killed by the Ix?" I prompted.

"Should have been," she said, squirming her reedy frame against the seat. "Swatted. Wiped off the nexus for good." She struck the arm of the chair with her fist. A small piece, the size of a rock, broke off. It slithered toward me, stopping near my feet. "Instead he lived again and took what *I* should have had, what I *will* have — when the moment is right."

"And what was that?"

"The auma of Gawain, you fool."

And there was her ambition, as Rosa had warned me: She planned to be illumined to the last dragon on Earth. Glancing at the ice chunk, I said, "Tell me how David came to be so . . . fortunate. I want to know all of it. Right from the beginning. Did Guinevere reach the island with Gawain?"

"That was the easy part," she said, puffing air. "The dragon needed no persuasion to settle there. He commanded the island and the regions all around. He grew

241

and became a creature of legend. That was his attraction — and his downfall."

"He was killed — by hunters?"

"Hunters," she snorted. "What are men against the power of twelve dragons? He was pursued, it is true — mainly by farmers tired of losing their sheep to his gut. A large bounty was put on his head. Anyone who tried to grow rich from it is now just a pile of ash, blowing in the wind."

"Then he died naturally?"

"In a manner of speaking." She paused for a moment and let her gaze shorten.

While she mused, I quietly extended my foot and dragged the ice chunk closer to my hand.

Unwise, said the Fain, guessing my intent. *It will be hard to pick up or throw accurately from the glove.*

We must try. She has to be stopped. I mean to stun her and steal back the tornaq. I will need all the power Galen can offer.

She looked up suddenly. I had no time to pull my foot back, but flexed it as if I needed to stretch. Her gaze narrowed a little but she made no threat. "You were telling me — about Gawain?"

Her lips were blueing, showing the cold, but they still had the power to drone. "He gave up his fire tear because he was alone. This world, with its ghosts of dragons gone by, had nothing to offer a solitary beast. In the end, he was simply tired of the struggle."

"Struggle?" I said, to keep her talking. Again she looked away. Long enough to let me drag the ice within reach.

"He wanted to be loved, not feared, by men. In the final days, only Guinevere remained a friend to him."

"And me?" I asked, before the pause grew too great. "Was I not also a friend to the dragon?"

"You weren't *there*," she said harshly, close enough for me to smell the fungus on her breath. "You somehow disappear out of the timeline before Guinevere reaches the island."

I let my fingers loosen in my glove. I had a chance there and then to make my strike, but her words had made me itch with curiosity. "Why do I disappear? Is it because of you?"

She made a sound like a skogkatt and sat well back. "For once, I had nothing to do with it — though that will change when our lesson is over." She drummed her sticklike fingers on the chair. "There's something rather *odd* about you. You're a freak. A hiccup in the waves of time. Your name pops up all over the future, but no legend ever speaks of the heroic cave dweller, running to the aid of the last known dragon. You weren't even on the island the night Gawain died."

"Were you?"

"No. But Guinevere was. She would go to his aerie and sing to him when the moon came up. It was his only comfort in his final days."

"She helped him sleep," I muttered, remembering the time I'd collapsed near the goats, listening to Guinevere's lullaby.

"She calmed the beast, yes, when it shed its tear."

"Then . . . she must have been close to him at the end." The danger she must have faced was immense. "Was she consumed by the fire tear's flame?"

"Questions, questions, questions," whined the sybil. Nevertheless, she gave me an answer. "No, Guinevere did not die then. She spread her hands and caught the tear."

"Caught it?" My mouth fell open in shock.

"Some silly desire to preserve the auma of dragons on Earth."

I remembered us walking away from the caves, talking about my encounter with Galen. Her words of awe came swimming back. *You* caught *his fire tear? You* actually held *a dragon's fire?* Now, on this island, she had done the same. I was at once excited and terrified. Twelve dragons. There, in the cup of her hands. I forgot about attacking Gwilanna for the moment. This I had to know more about. "She was exposed to him then? To all Gawain's power?"

Gwilanna sighed. "This is tedious, boy."

Not to me. "She must have his auma. She must have absorbed some, just like Gideon. That makes her kin to the bird — and to David."

The sibyl immediately tightened her stance. "Do *not* mention that name. Why does everything come back to David? The fire tear had no effect on the girl. It simply . . . spilled from her hands and went back to the Earth."

"You're lying," I said. It was clear from the way she'd broken her words.

"Oh, very well. What is it going to matter that you know?" She pinched her lips together in a line. "The tear was carried here, across the Great Sea."

"By Guinevere?"

"Yes."

"She took out a boat?"

"No, not a *boat*. She was aided by that lump of blubber and fur that led her toward the island in the first place."

"Thoran?"

"Yes . . . Thoran. Whatever he's called. Somehow, she managed to extract my thorn and save his miserable, grunting life. He swam, with Guinevere on his back. Out to sea. Far out to sea."

"Why?"

"Never mind why!" she snapped.

But I had to know. "What happened to them, sibyl?"

"This did," she snarled, pointing at the ice. "She was carrying the tear in a drinking vessel. When the bear grew tired and could swim no more, she opened the vessel and poured Gawain's fire tear into the water. This is the result. Here. All around you."

The ice sheet formed from his fire, said the Fain.

And we, in effect, were sitting on his grave. "Did Thoran drown?"

"Unfortunately not." She ground her misshaped teeth in annoyance. "He climbed onto the ice and his fur turned white. His kind have been a plague to me ever since."

Ice bears. Now I understood. Thoran, like Gideon, had been altered by Gawain, creating a brand-new species of bear. "And —?"

"Stone," she interrupted, "before you ask. Gawain's tear did not return to the Fire Eternal, therefore his body turned to stone. For once, the old myths were actually correct."

I vaguely knew something of this. In my boyhood fantasies I had often imagined climbing up the tail of an old dead dragon and sitting on its back as though I might fly. But Yolen had quashed this in a few words. *When a dragon's tear falls upon the Earth*, he had said, *its body dissolves into the stuff of the Earth, there to replenish the spirit of Gaia.*

But if the tear had not gone back . . .

"Where?" I asked her. "Where did it happen?"

"On the peak of the island. Where do you *think?*"

I glanced at the distant point of rock. It had to be the Tooth that Guinevere had talked about, the place we'd been heading for. "He's there still?"

She snorted, scornful of my aspirations. "Don't waste your time thinking you can bring him back.

I tried once, well into the future. That idiot David got in my way. It was a particularly *chilling* experience, which I will take pleasure paying back to him one day."

"Gawain is gone, then? Lost for good?"

She licked her lips. Sadly, her tongue didn't freeze to them. "I did not say that. There is *one* way the dragon could rise again."

"How?"

A sharp *Caw! Caw!* split the air.

She smiled, but there was nothing pleasant about it. "I do believe you're about to find out."

I looked at the island again. Four black dots were on the distant skyline. Ravens. I readied Galen for combat. But there was one more thing I had to know first: What had become of Guinevere?

"How far along the timeline are we?"

"Far enough," she sniffed. "What is it to you?"

"Is Guinevere alive?"

She took this question like a slap in the face. A noticeable judder troubled her lip.

"What became of her when the ice was formed?"

"I am not in the mood to speak about —"

"Answer me, sibyl. I want to know."

"She perished," she snapped. "There is nothing else to say."

"Perished?" That seemed an odd word to use. All the same, it sounded final. My young heart tremored. And even she, Gwilanna, looked bitterly deflated.

"My perfect construct . . . gone," she said. "Lost, like a breath of wind, until . . ."

"Construct?" I almost fell off my stool. "You mean . . . Guinevere wasn't *human*?" The girl I'd befriended, the one I'd milked goats with, had simply come out of Gwilanna's *mind*? My thoughts flashed back to the moment by the woods when David had touched her long red hair. The sudden look of surprise on his face. He'd read her, and known. "She told me you found her, abandoned, by the sea."

"A tale, to ease her childhood," she muttered. "I *made* Guinevere. I imagineered her."

"No," I said. "I do not believe you. Even for a sibyl, how could such a thing be possible?"

"If you had suffered like I had suffered, you would not be asking that question, boy. Auma is energy. It can be shaped like clay. All it takes is extreme intent and some knowledge of the secret workings of the universe. I didn't understand the ability myself until I learned I was born from unicorn blood. . . ." She gave me a pompous grin of gratitude.

I was still struggling to take this in. "Are you saying Guinevere was born from your grief?"

Mockingly, she clapped her hands.

"From human auma? From the death of another?"

"Enough, boy. Cease your tiresome prattle. I do not wish to be reminded of this."

But I was on the tail of an old riddle now. This time, I wasn't about to let go.

"She's Grella, isn't she?"

"I said *guard your tongue!*"

Guard it? I was almost chewing it off. "Say it, sibyl. You killed poor Grella and from her auma you fashioned another. A perfect child who would always do your bidding. What was the skull for? More of your magicks? A charm to control her *eye color* by?"

With a whoosh that felt like a kick in the chest, I found myself landed on my back. I roared in anger — or Galen did — but for all that dragon's native strength I could not react fast enough to gain an advantage. With a speed so unnatural I did not see her coming, the sibyl reared over me like a demon, holding a spike of ice to my heart. "Guinevere is all that is precious to me. You will not speak ill of her. It's because of your *quest* that she dies out here. I visited the timepoint. I watched her body break into fragments and fly away into the northern wind. In the future I trace those pieces of her and watch over every child they spawn. Elizabeth Pennykettle. Lucy Pennykettle. All the other daughters of Guinevere and Gawain. And what do I get for my knowledge and vigilance? Interfering idiots like you and David Rain. *Don't* . . . try anything." She pressed down, denting my clothes with her spear. "This is how David Rain dies in this timeline. Killed by the work of his beloved dragon."

"Then I would be like him," I hissed. "In death, I would gladly commingle with Gawain. Kill me, sibyl, that I might be illumined. Kill me, that I might live a better life."

I closed my eyes.

Her craggy hand trembled.

I said my good-byes to all I had loved and prayed that Gawain would ascend into my heart.

But all that ascended was Gwilanna herself. With a cry of frustration, she stood up and threw the ice aside. "Get up," she barked.

I rolled onto my knees, but not in any hurry.

"You think I want another *bear* ruining my plans?"

I thought about this as I gathered my thoughts. The broken piece of chair was still within reach. Its appeal now was very great indeed. But my endless quest for knowledge was staying my hand. "You told me David was kin to dragons."

She sank into her chair, sucking air through her teeth. "Yes, but his dominant form is a bear. One of them was with him when he 'died.' I've seen it, in the future. It calls itself Ingavar. David commingled with its spirit."

Out of nowhere, a cold wind stirred.

"Ingavar?" I let the word drift into it.

Ice spicules ran across the space between us. I thought I felt the ice field tilt a little.

Just then, three ravens settled on the chair. They folded down their wings and eyed me with distrust. The fourth bird landed on Gwilanna's shoulder. Although one raven looked much like another, I was quite sure this was Crakus. He hopped to the chair arm and opened his mouth. A dragon's claw dropped into the sibyl's lap.

She picked it up, laid it on her palm, and stroked it. "About time," she said, eyeing it greedily.

Craaark! went Crakus, demanding payment.

"Oh, very well." To my disgust, she imagineered worms on her chair. The ravens plucked them off anywhere they wriggled, gulping them down their black throats, whole.

"So, boy, I suppose you'd like to know where this came from." She lifted the claw to the level of her chin, testing the springiness of its point.

"It's Gawain's." His auma was unmistakable.

"Correct," she said smugly.

"How did they get it?" The claw was too developed for a wearling's body. It had to have come from him when he was grown, though it seemed unlikely that a cowardly raven could get close enough to rip it from a dragon's foot. And wasn't he supposed to have turned to stone?

"They stole it," Gwilanna said, matter-of-factly, "from the Inook community near to the island."

I looked at each of the thieves in turn. One of them scraped its beak against the ice, leaving a smear of blood against the white. Another was shaking and holding up a foot, probably injured during the raid. Crakus was grooming his sleek black feathers. But the raven on the highest part of the chair had turned its round eye into the breeze, as though it was aware of something approaching. It paddled its feet a couple of times, uncertain of whether it should raise an alarm. I swept the ice with Galen's sensors. The wind was quickening, the ice field rumbling. Something *was* coming. Something . . . heavy.

"How did you know the Inook had it?"

"I Traveled along the timeline, of course." She sighed, as if she expected more of me. "I moved among the Inook as softly as a shadow and watched their history unfolding like a flower. They revered the dragon throughout his short life. When his eye finally closed they organized a pilgrimage. They went foraging for keepsakes and found his isoscele and one of his claws. He'd detached them before he'd turned to stone. A last gesture to remind this world that dragons were once a dominant force. The Inook, with their usual superstitious zest, treated the claw as a holy relic and put it away. A pathetic waste of its powers, of course. It was a simple matter to send my birds on a mission to retrieve it."

The bird that was shaking suddenly collapsed and fell off the chair arm, dead. Gwilanna paid it no heed, but both Crakus and the bird that had been cleaning its beak swooped down and began to peck at the corpse.

"What are you planning to do with the claw?"

"Well, that's where you come in."

At that moment, the raven on lookout gave a frightened call.

The whole ice field shifted again.

The sibyl sat forward. "What was that?" Her grin quickly dropped from her face.

To my right, the far horizon had vanished. A slow-moving cloud was rolling toward us.

"Fly!" cried the sibyl. "Find out what it is."

The raven on lookout backed away. And all of them proved to be as fickle to their sibyl as they were to their brethren. For they simply took to the air, circled once, and promptly turned back toward the island.

Crouching, I put my hand to the ice. "They're coming," I whispered. I could feel their auma.

"Who is?" said Gwilanna, twisting to see.

The Fain said, *A multitude. Answering to his name.*

The followers of Ingavar.

"Bears," I said.

"No!" The sibyl squawked in rage. "Not bears. Anything but *bears!*" She jumped up quickly. Her imagineered clothing dropped away and she reached into her old Taan robe — for the tornaq.

Now was my chance. In one movement I swept up the ice chunk and hurled it at her. It had no points or spikes to it, nothing that could skewer her or take out an eye, it simply struck her temple and broke into shards. The impact sent her stumbling sideways. The precious tornaq dropped from her hands. I saw my chance to preserve history and stop the sibyl meddling with time. All I had to do was recover the charm. If I had still been a humble cave dweller, a nimble-footed boy with no auma enhancements, I would have done no more than snatch up the tornaq, shake it thrice, and leave Gwilanna fuming for all eternity. But that was not the way of it. My act of aggression — the throwing of the ice — had caused the dragon within me to flare. A conflict set in. I wanted the tornaq; he wanted the sibyl. He planned to destroy her. And his will was strong.

My eyes swiveled as his triggers locked in. The sibyl's body scent flooded my nostrils. Blood rips appeared at the corners of my mouth. One of my damaged teeth fell out. A tremendous pressure passed through my knees as he squeezed the long muscles in my legs and propelled me into a forward leap. My knuckles cracked as my fingers swelled. My uncut fingernails stretched in their beds. The pain this caused was sharp and horrendous, though nothing like the agonies Gwilanna would have suffered if armored claws had grown out of my hands. I saw a real glint of terror in her eyes. Even she, with all her sibyl powers, knew she might be cut down in a stroke.

But her blood did not tint the ice that day.

Two things saved her life.

First, the tornaq changed. The strange translucent bird emerged — and flew away from my grasp. But the real damage happened when Galen attempted to make me fly.

I fell facedown, howling so loudly that any creatures swimming below the ice would have turned their fins in terror and fled. My imagineered clothing dissolved and I lay in the cold in the robe I'd grown up in. Along my back, following the line of my shoulder blades, the flesh had opened up in two long rips. The fabric had split, but no wings had emerged. Only muscle, blood, and a great deal of pain.

"Fool," Gwilanna hissed. Her hand came down and picked up the tornaq. It had changed back into its bone form again. Why? I wondered. Why did it favor her over me? Beyond her, the bears were fast closing in. I could see their faces poking through the mist, over-lapping one another as their spirits took form. And I thought I saw something else as well. Just behind the sibyl, a ghostly image of a young boy. He looked for all the world like a smaller David. I mouthed the name, believing it to be him. But the boy shook his head as if to say *No, I am not David.* Then the sibyl kicked me in the ribs for good measure and I felt her hand take a tug of my hair. The boy disappeared. The bears and the ice merged into a blur. The sibyl shook the tornaq and *whoosh!* We were Traveling through time again.

We landed on a bed of warm, hard rock, breathing air that was thick with dragon smoke. I was gripped by a strange kind of dizziness that had nothing to do with the cuts in my back or the soreness in my damaged ribs.

Where are we? I said to the Fain. The words seemed to hover outside my mind. And when at last the thought beings answered, they spoke as if my ears were expanding bubbles.

Kasgerden, they replied.

Terror gripped my soul.

A breeze blew across the face of the mountain. The smoke cleared. A familiar scene unfolded. There was

Voss, hovering in his darkling form. There was I, about to dip my knife into Galen's fire. But from that point onward, everything changed. Gwilanna raised the claw of Gawain and drew the symbol meaning "sometimes" from three wisps of smoke. "Good-bye, Agawin," she said. In an instant my two "selves" merged and my awareness was all with the physical body of the boy I had been, only this time I was not about to triumph over evil. As I tried to throw the knife, Gunn ran at me early. His brute force shouldered me over the cliff. A rock shower followed me down. Gunn teetered on the edge of the shaky precipice and he leered at me, fat and ugly in his triumph. Then the edge gave way and he fell with a scream that rang around the mountain long after he was silent. Once again, Gunn had plunged to his death.

But Voss had survived.

And I was surely going to die.

I fell and I fell, with no tornaq to protect me. But my life did not end at the foot of the mountain. It simply took a different course again. Gwilanna's dishonest use of the claw had sent signals rippling through the fabric of the universe, signals that Traveled infinitely faster than a seer's apprentice could chance to fall. As the darkling rushed away from my sight, three other creatures filled the space around me. Firebirds. One green, one red, one a beautiful cream color with apricot flashes around her ear tufts. It was she who spoke to my consciousness saying, *Agawin, we are monitors of time and the agents of Gideon. Do not be afraid. Joseph Henry is with you.*

Joseph Henry? I asked. My voice had the texture of thickened mud.

But all the firebird said was this: *You have been chosen for illumination. You will die and live again, through the auma of Gawain. All you have to do is give yourself up to it.*

I do not want to die. Panic gripped my heart.

It is a change, she said. *Simply a change.*

I was floating now, less aware of my body. All around me, the tiniest stars were glittering. I felt that if I let my consciousness touch one, I would instantly pop into another life. *What of Galen?*

He will always be with you. In your new form, he will not hinder your progress.

What is the new form?

A hybrid of human, dragon, and Fain.

But that is what I am now.

This time, the energies will be fully commingled. You will go back, to observe Gwilanna. Joseph Henry himself has decreed this. You will be hidden from the sibyl — but always within her sight.

How? How is that possible?

Choose a star, the firebird said. *There are many probabilities. Let your instinct guide you.*

So I reached out in search of a different life. And in a timescale I could not measure or estimate, I found the star that was right for me, at a point on the timeline of huge significance, located at a place called Wayward Crescent. I chose, for my dominant form, to be human. And I chose to be born to a very special mother, one who had cause to be close to Gwilanna. The last thing I remembered before I touched my mother's star was the memory of the child I had seen on the tapestry. And at last I understood her purpose and her words. *Sometimes we will be Agawin,* she had said.

But from now on, we would be called Alexa.

PART FIVE
IN THE LIBRARIUM

The first time I truly saw Joseph Henry, he was sitting cross-legged on a deep windowsill of the 97th floor of the Bushley Librarium — the firebird aerie in the heart of Co:pern:ica. Up until then, I had only seen the building in visions or dreams.

Even in silhouette with his back turned to me, Joseph looked like a very young David Rain — a fact he acknowledged in his opening sentence.

"There was a time when the ice was ruled by nine bears."

After a moment a reply came to me, perhaps inspired by the dusty shelves of antique books that seemed to be holding up every wall. "And one of those was a bear called Ragnar." I wasn't sure how I remembered this, but we were quoting from David's book, *White Fire*, one of only two my father had written before his ill-fated journey to the Arctic. It felt like a kind of security test, as if Joseph needed to be sure of who I was. His next two words were far more welcoming.

"Hello, Agawin."

"Hello, Joseph."

"How do you like being Alexa?"

He turned, like dust rearranging itself. He was dressed in a robe of shining white, which shimmered with the promise of dragon scales. He had shoulder-length hair and delicate hands and skin as smooth as pale pink silk.

I was five years old, almost six. A sweet little girl in a plain white dress. I had Zanna's dark hair and David's blue eyes. Neither of my parents were ever aware that I had once been Agawin or that my life had been saved by firebirds. The boy that had been the seer's apprentice had disappeared out of the Isenfier timeline, just as Gwilanna had correctly suggested. Now I was Alexa Martindale. And though just a child in mannerisms and speech, I had developed wings and the power of flight. I could speak (and think) in fluent dragontongue. I knew the enchantments of time.

And yet, as I thought about Joseph's question, I couldn't work out at first what had happened. I blinked and had a memory of a battlefield, where I was kneeling and holding Gadzooks. Then the first significant timepoint came to me. "I was at Scuffenbury Hill," I muttered.

"And before that, Wayward Crescent," he said. He moved his hand as if parting a mist.

Straightaway, my mind began to fill with scenes from my five years growing up in the Crescent, sharing a house with the Pennykettle family and their clutch of amazing dragons. The kitchen table where I'd sat and drawn pictures of a mammoth. Bonnington, the cat, eating food from his bowl. The listening dragon who'd sat on the fridge. The "fairy" door in the garden rockery. I remembered how the house had been swollen with grief, because David had disappeared in the Arctic, allegedly killed by the Ix assassin Gwilanna had openly crowed about. And as I sped through the years I remembered his return, until I finally arrived at the sequence of events that had led us to the battle at Scuffenbury Hill. I remembered a trace of dark fire, trapped in a misshaped block of obsidian. And how the obsidian had broken open and the fire had escaped and gone into Elizabeth Pennykettle's body. And how we feared for her life and that of the unborn child she was carrying. This child. Joseph Henry.

"Shall I tell you something about that?"

I sent him an inquisitive look. He could read my mind; he was simply being polite.

"I am responsible for what happened to my mother."

"I don't understand. What did you do?"

"I drew the dark fire into her. I felt its presence in the room as soon as the obsidian was broken. I drew it to my mother because I knew the only chance of transforming its evil was through the auma of Gawain. I had to leave her body to enable that to happen. I left her, Agawin. I went into the shell of the house dragon, Gwillan, and stole powers from the other Pennykettle dragons. I left my beautiful mother unguarded and went to fight darklings at Scuffenbury Hill, believing I was doing the Earth a service. But David could have handled the conflict with ease. I was vain, boisterous. I wanted a fight. But I should have been in the Crescent protecting her. And now . . ."

"What?" I asked. "What happened to Liz?" And Arthur, her partner, for that matter.

He lifted his face. Tears were filming his sparkling eyes. "Just tell me your side of the story," he said. "I can visit anywhere in anywhen, but if I try to go too close to my mother's timepoints I am tied to her auma and the events become fuzzy. I need to know what happened just before you flew to the hill with Gadzooks."

So I concentrated for him and it quickly came back to me. "I was outside, in the garden with Bonnington. We were watching a squirrel playing on the rockery. All of a sudden it faded from view."

"Like an untended construct."

Yes. Like a construct. I realized then that the squirrel was false. "At the same time, one of the dragons came out. I don't remember which. It said Agatha Bacon had come to the house and that Zanna had left to join David at Scuffenbury."

Agatha Bacon was the sister of our neighbor. A trusted friend. A good sibyl.

"I ran into the house and went upstairs to Elizabeth's room. There was blood. Your mother was on the bed, injured. Agatha wasn't there, but Gwilanna was. She lay dead on the floor. There were two small dragons on the dressing table. They were anxious to tell me what they knew. . . ." I shuddered as their terrified voices came back to me.

"Continue," said Joseph. "Gwilanna arrived in the guise of Agatha Bacon and tricked Zanna into leaving the house. What happened then?"

"Gwilanna believed you were still in your mother's body. She tried to deliver you. The dark fire escaped. The dragons say Gwilanna died of fear."

"And the fire?"

"It found a portal through the dressing-table mirror. I summoned Gadzooks and followed it to Scuffenbury. When I arrived, the darkness had infected a unicorn, which had plunged itself into the Fire Eternal and tainted it to produce an Ix Shadow. The Shadow turned on us as soon as we landed. But Gadzooks was quick. He wrote the ancient mark on his notepad. The enchantment favored by unicorns."

" 'Sometimes,' " said Joseph.

"Yes. When the Shadow struck his pencil it could not cope with the infinite ambiguities suggested by the word. So time was suspended and a call for help was sent across the universe . . ."

"And picked up here, in Co:pern:ica," he said.

Yes. By David and Rosa. My earliest memories were all coming back.

My mind began to puddle with dozens of questions. I had never understood the mirror world, Co:pern:ica. Why it was created. How it linked to Earth. The "alternative" templates — like Rosa, for instance.

Joseph, hearing my turmoil, said, "It was a project, Agawin. A failed attempt by the Fain to imagineer a paradise for humans to migrate to, while leaving the Ix in isolation. One day, you will understand it fully."

"How did David and Rosa cross the nexus?" I knew Rosa had her unicorn, but the enchantments of time would limit her movements to those lines common to Co:pern:ica. "How did they come to Earth?"

"I created a fire star for them," he said. "It was impressive. A beautiful ocean of fire. They couldn't really miss it. They had to step through."

"You wanted them on Earth?"

He pressed his fingertips together lightly, making a rainbow of color arc over them. "Let me tell you something about Gadzooks."

I sighed, thinking he had drifted off the subject.

He hadn't.

"There was more to his mark than you might have realized. One of the powers I stole from the dragons was Groyne's ability to move through time. As you know, he transforms into a tornaq, marked by the unicorn symbol you saw. Gadzooks's cry for help was also a coded instruction to the universe to free Groyne from the Scuffenbury timepoint. In other words, freeing *me*. I've been working with the timeline ever since, finding a way to resolve all this."

"Then it was *you* who allowed Hilde to have the tornaq?"

"And me who brought David and Rosa to Earth. And teamed them up with Gretel. I had to put her somewhere in the timeline to make her think she was being useful. She would have caused a dreadful nuisance otherwise. What's the matter, Agawin? Why are you scowling?"

"You moved the tornaq out of my grasp when I was fighting Gwilanna," I said. I remembered the shadowy boy on the ice, and also seer Brunne's words in Taan: *The tornaq is not the sibyl's to command. It will leave her when its work is done.*

"I know you're a little . . . upset," he said. "But if you had taken the tornaq then, it would have ruined or delayed the course of events. Trust me, Agawin. It's complicated. I can see resolutions that you can't."

Trust him? A little *upset?* I was deeply incensed. "You allowed Gwilanna to throw me off a cliff! And you changed me into this." I looked down at my body.

"Don't you like being Alexa? You never did answer."

And I couldn't find the words to answer it now.

"The trouble is," he said, before I could snap, "everyone has the annoying habit of using their . . . free will to get involved. David would have tried to cross the nexus without my assistance before very long. He had good cause, once Gwilanna had possession of the dragon's claw."

"I don't understand that," I said. "Gwilanna was dead when I saw her in the Crescent."

"On Earth, but not here. Not on Co:pern:ica."

"Did her mirror-form hear Gadzooks's beacon?"

He shook his head. "When Gadzooks suspended the timepoint, pressure was exerted on the membrane of space between Earth and Co:pern:ica. A small Ix:Cluster managed to break through it. They invaded a firebird, turning it black. The bird found and stole a claw of Gawain that had been hidden on this world long ago by the Fain. When the firebird and Aunt Gwyneth commingled —"

"Aunt Gwyneth?"

273

"That was the name of Gwilanna's alternate. When they joined minds, the Ix learned what the Aunt knew about Co:pern:ica, and Gwyneth learned about her counterpart on Earth. She took the claw and drew upon its powers of transformation to write herself back into existence on Earth."

In the sky behind him, I saw an image of a woman's hand writing words of smoke:

I, Gwyneth, sometimes known as Gwilanna, live.

"The universe has been in turmoil," said Joseph, "ever since these words were committed to the Is."

I recalled my discussion with David and Rosa in the woodlands of Iunavik. "This is why my tapestry differed so much from David's drawing. There would have been changes all along the timeline."

"Yes," he said. "There are few things more powerful than a claw of a dragon, especially one illumined by twelve fire tears."

I closed my eyes and tried to take in the enormity of Gwilanna's deceit. It was impossible, even for a mind like mine. "Why am I here and not on the battlefield?"

He laced his fingers and thought about this. "I wanted to protect you from what is to come. Please don't fight it, Agawin. I created a paradox and took you from Scuffenbury. It's not stable. We don't have long."

"What is to come, Joseph?"

"I can't tell you that."

"What about the others? What happens to them?" Zanna, Lucy, Tam Farrell. All of those caught in the darkness of the Shadow.

"Nothing, until I give Gadzooks the signal to let go."

"Are you going to?"

"You want to stop Gwilanna, don't you?"

There was a flutter of wings and Gideon landed on a lectern near the window.

"I promised David on the life of my seer that I would stop Gwilanna doing more harm."

"I know. I've visited the timepoint. I heard you." And just for a moment he seemed to take on the appearance of Yolen.

He saw my frail eyes puffing with sadness and softened his features back to David's. "Would you like to see your seer again? We still have long enough to visit his timepoints. It's all recorded here." He swept a hand backward. Behind him, through the open window, the sky filled up with millions of fire stars.

I shook my head. What was done with Yolen was done. I believed Gwilanna's version of events, but I did have doubts that the sibyl had been brought to the sea with Grella or that Grella had died a natural death. And I was still perplexed by Gwilanna's claims to have "made" Guinevere.

"I can show you what happened," Joseph said quickly, reading my mind again.

"You seem eager for me to know."

He shrugged, but I was sure he wanted me to see it.

"It will help you understand Gwilanna better. She was a baby, remember, in Grella's time. It's a powerful story, Agawin. But I warn you, it's not pretty."

"Grella suffered?"

He nodded.

Now I *did* want to know. "How can I see it?"

He opened his hands. The centers of his palms were as violet as his eyes. "We are at the heart of the Is. We can Travel anywhere in anywhen. Touching the appropriate fire stars will take you into Grella's timepoints. But first, you need to know more."

"About what?"

"About everything. Earth will be your world — once we've dealt with Gwilanna."

"*My* world?"

"Alexa will be the Earth's . . . guardian angel. You should begin with the ice bears."

"The ice bears?"

"*Mmm.*"

On a table in front of Gideon, a large, old book had just appeared. Waves of yellow parchment swept out from its middle. Its bindings smelled of the hide of a goat.

"There was no template created for the bears on Co:pern:ica. Their auma was sent to Ki:mera when the dark fire was first detected on Earth. Their ancestry with the fire of Gawain encouraged the Higher to protect them closely. But they're restless. They want to go back to their ice. You should make a note."

"A note?"

"In the book."

I heard a scratching of claws. Gideon twisted his nut-brown ear tufts. What looked like a delicate shower of ash materialized and fell across a page of the book, forming beautiful words of dragontongue. I had to flick my wings and hover just off my tiptoes to read them. They said, *In the final hours, the auma of Gawain is returned to its resting place and the children of Thoran walk freely on the ice.*

"You're writing a book?"

"No," he said. "Those are *your* thoughts — on every page."

I squinted at the book. A single page turned. Then dozens all at once, bringing with them flickering memories of ice bears, generations of them through centuries of time. "Ingavar," I whispered. The pages stopped and flickered back the other way. Out of the dragontongue rose an image. A striking male polar bear, sitting on an ice block, addressing eight others. I looked at Joseph again. "David talked about this book, but I don't remember writing it."

"You don't have to," he replied. "When you came to the librarium, your mind imagineered it. This place is clever like that. You know it all because of your links to the nexus. It's always been in your consciousness, just like the tapestry of Isenfier."

The Book of Agawin. A history of dragons.

"And bears. And the Earth. The whole timeline," he said. "Think of it as a kind of manual or guide — a *Theory of Everything*. It will help the new Premen, when we're done."

I was about to ask what he meant by "done" when a skogkatt appeared on a shelf beside me where a moment earlier books had been standing. It licked its paws then settled down to sleep, wrapping its distinctive tail around it.

"Floor Ninety-seven," he said. "Skogkatts and villhund."

I jumped aside as a large black dog came swaggering past.

"It won't hurt you. It looks mean, but it's just . . . territorial. You'll see plenty of those in Grella's story."

I watched the dog slink past the skogkatt's perch before curling up in a shady corner. As it closed its eyes it turned into a jumbled heap of books.

"A cloak," said Joseph. "This world will need more animals when the time is right. It's all in the book."

"Skogkatts and villhund?"

He tilted his head. Light was glittering in the strands of his hair. "I saved two of each species before the Dead Lands, here, became the waste they are now. I got the idea from this." In his hand appeared another large book, with gold-tipped pages and a ribbon to divide them. There was no dragon auma attached to it, but I could feel it fizzing with boundless energy.

"Did I imagineer that book as well?"

He shook his head. "Several Premen wrote this." He moved his hand in a gentle arc and the pages opened like fluttering silk. "I like the early stories best. In this section an old man rescues animals from a flood. They ride a boat with him until they find land. Then he frees the animals and the world begins again." He let the book go. It flew out of the window on silent wings. "Floor One Hundred and Eight," he said to Gideon.

The firebird shook some dust from his feathers and flew away after it.

"The animals are all here, hidden among the shelves. The whole building is a boat as well as a library. The cloak dissolves on a trigger set into one of the books."

As soon as he had said it, my consciousness jumped to it. "David's squirrel one." *Snigger and the Nutbeast.* He had written it for Lucy's eleventh birthday.

"Good," said Joseph. "You're tuning in."

I looked through the window at the open sky. Its color was changing from blue to black. "Is there going to be a flood?"

"Kind of," he said, without really saying anything at all.

Just beyond his head, some of the stars were coming

to the fore. "The timeline," he said. "You're thinking about Grella."

A desperate ache took hold of my heart.

"Don't be afraid of it. Come and see what *Is*. We'll watch it together. Then we'll talk some more."

So I fluttered up and sat on the sill beside him. In an instant, he'd turned us to look at the sky. "You've Traveled before — with Aurielle, of course."

"Aurielle?"

"The cream-colored firebird. The clever one."

"Yes." I remembered her from Mount Kasgerden. Here I was, as she'd promised, in my hybrid form, looking at billions of fire stars again. The instant I thought of Grella those fire stars connected to her sparkled brighter and arranged themselves in a matrix in front of me. I was hesitant to touch them. Whatever had become of the brave Taan girl had ended with a skull in Gwilanna's cave. If I thought about her final breath, most of the lights on the stars would dim, until I was left with the vital one that would have taken me straight to the moment. But I needed to see her entire story. I reached out toward a peripheral star.

"There are rules," said Joseph. "Here is the first."

My arm and the fire stars froze in space.

"You can witness any episode of Grella's life, but you cannot interfere. Do you understand?"

"Yes," I whispered.

"You will be there with her, right in the *when*. Use your fain to hide your presence. Ready?"

"Yes," I said.

And he set my arm free.

PART SIX
GRELLA

I began at the tragic chapter with Yolen. I asked the Is to show me Grella building his cairn. Several fire stars sparkled in front of me. I touched the nearest star and materialized behind her like a breath of wind, barely rippling the strands of her hair. Taking Joseph's advice, I quickly entered the body of a mouse that was tugging at the shawl around the baby, Gwilanna. The mouse squeaked but wasn't harmed in any way. The sound, however, made Grella turn.

"Hey, cheeky. Leave that alone."

She batted a hand. The mouse scuttled away. I hid myself amid a cluster of stones. When I looked again, Grella had picked up the child and was cradling it in the crook of her arm. It was twilight, almost dark. There was rain in the air, but the ground was dry and tightening with frost. The cold had left its mark on

Grella's face, but she was still as slim and beautiful as ever. The same could not be said of Gwilanna. Her ugly wrinkles were hard on the eye, but Grella seemed neither to care nor to notice. She sang a sweet lullaby over the child. The one that Guinevere had sung to me. Gwilanna made soft-happy gurgling noises. Grella touched the baby's nose, put the bundle down, and picked up another stone for the cairn.

I was in the process of blessing the stones, to pay my respects to my beloved seer, when I heard a stealthy movement nearby. A twig breaking. A rustle of leaves. The auma of another animal was approaching. Something far bigger and more threatening than a mouse. I could smell the hostility in its sweat, right down to the dirt between the pads of its feet. I looked at Grella. She had her back to the baby and was still singing. The mouse popped through a skittish circle. It squeaked again, much louder than before. It wanted to follow its instincts to run. But my overwhelming need to see what would happen kept it quaking by the rocks.

Remember, you must not interfere.

The primary law of Travel. Joseph's voice was in my head, reminding me of it. I was desperate to materialize and shout a warning, but all I could do was watch the timeline develop — and wait for the creature to pounce.

A wild dog, a villhund, slipped through the undergrowth. Its hot breath blew across my quivering whiskers. On any other night my host might well have been staked with a claw and instantly ripped to pieces. But apart from slanting a bloodshot eye, the hound walked by me and stalked toward the baby. In a silent, almost tender act of thievery, it hooked its teeth into the folds of the shawl, picked Gwilanna up and trotted away. Grella sang on and knew nothing of it.

It was the bark of another hound that alerted her.

Like the skogkatts, the villhund roamed in packs. As the scent of Gwilanna traveled, another dog rushed forward from a copse of trees. There was a bark. A savage scuffle. Fearsome growls. The dog carrying Gwilanna doubled back on itself, chased by two of its ruthless companions. They jinked and swerved and I heard a sharp yelp as a third dog gripped the hind leg of the leader. By now, Grella was also giving chase. She ran at the villhund with two large stones that should have been laid in memoriam over Yolen. Her first throw thumped against the flank of a dog, sending it away, yowling. Her second throw fell short. But by

287

then she had caught up with her quarry. Her threats and screams and flailing arms were enough to make the dogs let go of Gwilanna and shuffle back baring their rotted fangs. She kicked one chancer under the chin, drawing a spurt of blood from its jaw. For a moment or two, she was in control. But soon the entire pack had gathered, growling, wild-eyed, wanting revenge. They formed themselves into a ring around her. She had no bow, no arrows to fire. She had no savior.

Or so I thought.

I heard a whistle, thin and sharp as a blade. Every dog flattened its shabby ears. A man stepped into view. Short and dirty, dressed in rags. His hair hung loose in spikes across his face. His legs were red with insect bites. There were coverings on his feet like bandages of sackcloth. Spaces either side of his middle teeth. "Gurl," he grunted. He spat on the ground. "Lookee tha' way. Lookee at mounten."

"Who are you?" said Grella. Dogs all around her. A wild man in front. A quivering mouse so desperate to help her. She clutched Gwilanna tight to her breast.

The man clenched his teeth and whistled through the gaps. Every dog folded its knees and lay down.

Grella stared at the pack like a startled bird. "H-how did you do that? Are the villhund yours?"

The man narrowed his dingy eyes: two grubby little beads in a landscape of pitted, unwashed flesh. He licked his lips and gestured at the mountain.

This time, Grella turned her head.

"What?" she said. "What am I looking for?"

"Nuffin'." He put a short pipe to his lips. A feathered dart zipped through the air and landed in Grella's exposed neck. She fell instantly, collapsing in a bundle. She still held Gwilanna in her arms.

The fire star closed and brought me back to the Is. Right away, I reached out for the next.

"There is another rule of Travel," Joseph Henry said. "Beware, Agawin. If you venture too long at any one timepoint, there is a danger you'll become attached to it — or it will become attached to you."

"Attached?"

"Your consciousness will feel you belong there. Then there will be no possible escape. The Is will reshape itself, and you will live and die wherever you are set. You could go back to her. You could be with Grella and rescue her from her ugly captor. But you will not stop Gwilanna if you do."

289

My wings shuddered. I nodded, grim-faced. "I will keep to my purpose. But I must know what happens. Who was that man?"

"He is Stygg, from the wild lands of Nomaad."

I had heard of Nomaads. "Eremitts" they also called themselves, because they lived alone and kept no company. "Show me this man," I commanded the Is. Dozens of stars came out of the matrix. I let my instincts guide me to one.

I touched it and returned to the same clump of rocks. The mouse, perhaps wisely, had scuttled away, but a small gray squirrel was grubbing about among some nearby tree roots. I let my auma commingle with it. It sat up with a surprised chirrup. Hearing it, Stygg aimed another dart, which missed the squirrel's ear by the width of a blade of grass. The creature dashed around the back of the tree. I let it catch its breath and groom its tail before I guided it into a viewing position. There I watched the Nomaad dealing with Grella.

He was remarkably strong for his size. He lifted Grella up and threw her over his shoulder as if she was nothing but a coil of rope. For a moment, I thought he might leave Gwilanna. He grimaced when he saw her and muttered the word "rynkler." He nudged her with a callused foot and seemed disappointed to hear her cry. He wiped his arm beneath his nose, both ways. One of the villhund started to howl. "Neh!" he warned it, glaring at them. The pack picked themselves up and mooched away. The man poked Gwilanna again. "What Stygg do with you?" he grunted. But he'd made up his mind as quickly as he'd said it. Grasping the shawl in one hand and twisting it once to wrap the contents, he yanked Gwilanna off the ground and stumped away, swinging her along like a bag of rocks.

I sent the squirrel in pursuit.

The sun had gone down and night was upon us by the time Stygg had reached his destination. He had led me to a derelict shack set deep among a coppice of hawthorn trees. He whistled a greeting call. Given that the Nomaad usually lived alone, I was surprised to hear a woman's voice reply. "Where ya bin? Where ya bin?" She craked like a bird with a bone in its throat.

"I bin huntin'," he said. "I made me a catch."

"I cun smell it. T'ain't no fish nor hund."

"Be a gurl, and she be mine."

"Gurl?"

"Aye, mine."

"You live 'ere, you shares."

"I ain't givin' you nowt — not nowt o' this catch, Muther."

"You do as Griss sez. Lay it down. Let us see it."

Stygg let Grella slide off his shoulder. She groaned as the back of her head struck earth.

The woman poked her head through the window of the shack, illuminated by the lantern she held. She was the oldest, ugliest crone I'd ever seen. One round eye was poking out of her head like a sticky, overripe plum. There was a stitched-up socket on the other side. Wiry threads of silver-gray hair clung to the rear of her scalp like worms. I almost gagged in the squirrel's throat as she tipped her head to squint at Grella and the eye made a popping noise in the socket. "Taan," she said with a lick of her lips. "You bring that inside. We cun use that, we can. What ya got in yer paw?"

"Babby, I reckun."

"You *reckun*?"

"Ain't sure."

"Well, izzit or ain't it?"

"Babby, all right — but old, not babbylike."

"Can't 'appen, you loaf."

"Can, sez I."

"Show me." She wobbled a scrawny hand. "Griss wud see this babby, she wud."

Stygg opened the shawl.

The old woman leaned farther out of the window. Her nose was as hooked as a raven's beak. The nostrils twitched. The eye shrank back. "That be a babby wi' a curse yon its 'ead."

"Cursed? How be?"

"Witched by a sibyl. Be a wrong 'un, for sure. Lookee at them rynkles. T'ain't natrul, izzit?"

"She 'ad it, tho'." Stygg pointed at Grella. " 'Er. The Taan gurl. Weren't no sibyl anyways near. 'Eld it, she did. Tight, like her own. Sang to it. Pretty. *She* weren't frit."

"Din say I wuz frit. Din *say* I wuz *frighted*, jus' that it's wrong. That rynkler ain't no use to no eremitt. Throw it to the dogs, the accursed thing."

Stygg's sighs became a grunt. He bent down to do the deed.

At that point, Grella raised her head. "Stop." She sounded wuzzy, still suffering from whatever had been on the dart.

"Put a chain on that," said Griss. "Lay it in the barn. It cun side with the pig."

293

"Ain't chaining it. Wants it for a wife, I does."

"WIFE! What Taan's gonna whisper in *your* thick lugs? Chain it. Look at them long white legs. You don't put no chain on them they be off thru the trees like a scoldy rabbit. Don't wannit runnin' away now, do we? It cun work, it can. It cun cook. It cun clean. It cun prob'ly skin a rat, cun *this* pretty catch."

"My baby," said Grella. "Don't hurt my baby. . . ."

Griss replied with a soggy sniff. "You won't be needin' that babby no more. The dogs," she said to Stygg. "Or the mud pools. Go."

"No!" Grella scrabbled to her knees. The dart dropped from her neck. She gripped Stygg's legs.

"Strike it down!" his foul mother squawked.

Stygg was in two minds about that. But he gave in to his ma and swiped his fist across Grella's face. She fell sideways, dribbling blood from her mouth. I thought I heard one of her cheekbones crack.

Despite the hum of pain, she raised herself again. "If you take her you might as well kill me now. I'll do nothing for you. I'd rather starve myself than stir a pot for you."

"Idle, wicked talk," squeaked Griss. "I'll be 'aving the meat off yer bones fer that. An' yer pretty Taan hair." She ran a hand over her repulsive head. A spider that had made its web behind an earlobe scuttled away and hid itself inside the ear. Griss pointed to the baby. "Be rid of it, Stygg."

But Stygg was undecided again. "What's a babby eat?"

Griss shook the lantern, sending a flare of light into the trees. "What? What blether you sayin' to me now?"

"Scraps, ain't it? Leftovers is all."

"Milk," said Grella, holding her face. "The child needs milk. You've got a goat. I can smell it. I'll milk it myself. I'll work. I promise. I'll do what you ask if you spare the baby. I'll sew for you as well."

"Sew?" said Stygg. "What need 'ave we of —"

"Hold your fat tongue," Griss said to her son. "'Splain yerself, gurl. And makee quick."

"I'm Taan," said Grella. "I can sew things for you. Dresses. Tapestries. Things you can trade."

I looked at Griss. The crone was licking her blistered lips.

"I got 'oles," said Stygg, pulling at his rags.

"Give me a needle, I'll make you a robe."

A wide smile spread across his goofy face. "What sez you, Ma?"

"I sez you're a love-struck eremitt loaf. All right, be giving her the babby — then chain her."

They put her, as Griss had suggested, with their pig — or what was left of the wretched beast; it had festering welts where its ears should have been and hobbled around on three good legs. Stygg hammered a link around Grella's ankle and chained her to a post beside the animal's trough. He soon saw the error in this. When I returned, a day had gone by and he was drenching Grella with buckets of water to clean off the pig dirt she'd trailed into the shack. He moved her instead to a barn infested with scabby mice and insects which liked to suck blood from her flesh. (I spent my next few visits in the guise of a spider, eating as many of those parasites as I could.) Over several days, I saw her make a crib in a log pile for the baby. She herself slept on rough sacks on the floor.

I watched Stygg construct another chain. Not as stout as the first, but long enough to let Grella move around the shack or reach the well from where they drew water. They put her to work from the moment they had her. Scrubbing in the mornings, cooking in the afternoons. Stews. Always stews. Usually mice from the barn. Topped and tailed and boiled in their skins.

They made her catch woodlice and sprinkle them into the stewing pot, whole. If Stygg caught a pigeon or a squirrel in the woods she would be told to stuff it with spiders, for flavor. (Several times I had to hide my host away to avoid ending up in the pot myself.) Now and then Stygg slayed an elderly villhund. If Grella was lucky they would throw her a bone. Otherwise, she ate the same slop she made for them. And in case she ever thought of poisoning them, with fungus or some deadly leaf or thorn, they would always make sure she ate a bowlful first — then give some of the juice to Gwilanna. At every tasting, the sibyl cried. No matter how hard Grella blew on the juice, it always scalded the baby's lips. It was a wonder the wrinkled child survived.

In the evenings, they made Grella sew. For this, she needed basic materials. Griss sent her son on a mission. I did not follow him through the Is, but three days later he returned to the shack with a bundle of spoils. Across the floor he spilled tapestry cloths, needles, wool. I saw Grella blanch. She knew, as I did, what had happened. Stygg had crossed the border and raided a krofft. Taan blood was still drying on his hunting knife.

With a heavy heart, Grella set to work. Her only comfort, besides Gwilanna, was the tapestries she now began to make. She drew pictures of that last day on Mount Kasgerden. The glory of Galen. The darkling in flame. Her captors were awed, their greed ignited. From what I overheard of their eager conversations, they knew that a dragon had died on the mountain. And here was the story recorded on cloth. Ignoring their disinclination to trade, Griss bustled Stygg out with Grella's first tapestry, telling him she wanted a brush for it at least. Stygg did better than that. He brought back a brush and a mirror, too. Griss rejoiced. She ordered Stygg to hold Grella in a chair. Then she took a rusted, sickle-shaped knife and cut off Grella's long fair hair. From it she made a wig of sorts, which she plastered to her head with a thin layer of goat dung. She hung the mirror from a tree and went out six or seven times a day to admire her grisly reflection. I watched her from the body of a sparrow and encouraged the bird to sit above the mirror and loose its waste products over the glass. None of this bothered Griss. The repulsive old crone just wallowed in her newfound vanity and "wealth," and ordered Grella to produce more tapestries.

Grella stayed calm and worked steadily, sometimes taking a cycle of the moon to complete one piece. Sheer tiredness prevented her from working for long (many times I would come to the barn and find her asleep with a cloth in her hands, the mice nibbling at the edges of it). She was also aware that every time her supplies ran out, someone else in Taan could be murdered by Stygg. I watched her scratch marks on the wall of the barn to keep a tally of all Stygg's raids. If any chance of revenge presented itself, his punishment was sure to be multiply unpleasant. Daily, Griss screamed at her to speed things up. The incoming trickle of knickknacks and treats was becoming a way of life for the crone. Grella stuck to her rigid pace and was rash enough at times to argue with Griss that quality, not quantity, would reap the best rewards; it usually brought her a slap across the face. Or a kick in the ribs. Or a lash from a cane. It was all I could do not to call down a dragon and burn this foul place out of existence. I hated seeing Grella suffer like this. But I obeyed Joseph Henry and did not get involved — though I was once, unwittingly, almost the cause of both our deaths.

One night, when the fire stars brought me to the barn, I immediately sensed that something wasn't right. I commingled with my favorite host, the squirrel (it tended to wait for me now), but its limbs felt stiff and its auma strange. I looked up at Grella from the floor of the barn. "Ah, there you are," she said. "I've something to show you." She lifted Gwilanna and pulled out a tapestry she was keeping hidden. She turned it around and pointed to the picture. "Look, that's you. My only friend." It was a portrait of the squirrel eating a nut. The tail and the body were already sewn in. She was starting to work on the arch of the eye.

A fever raged in my head. I began to shake. The squirrel's teeth chattered. The space between me and the tapestry image began to melt into a murky gel. "What's the matter?" said Grella, puzzled and disturbed in equal measure. At that moment, the firebird, Aurielle, rushed into my mind. *Grella must not complete this image*, she said. *Or you will stay in the timeline in the form of the squirrel.* This was the price I had paid for repeatedly using the same host animal: Grella had grown familiar with it. She had pulled me too far into her consciousness. I was in danger of changing her timepoints.

At that moment, Stygg wandered into the barn. "Squir'l," he muttered, and picked up a lump of rotting wood. With a thwack that made the barn walls rattle, he brought the wood down and tried to squash me flat. Splinters flew in all directions, even into Gwilanna's crib. I was lucky to escape unharmed. Stygg was groggy and his aim was poor. I avoided the hit and found enough energy to skitter away and hide in the damp straw among the mice. But I knew I could never take a risk like that again. When he hauled Grella off to do Griss's bidding, I went to the tapestry and pulled every thread of gray I could find, gradually working the whole squirrel free.

When Grella returned and saw the piece ruined she fell to her knees, broke down, and cried. Griss beat her in the morning for being late and for damaging a precious cloth (in my haste I had made a hole in it). She told Grella this was her final warning. One more slip and the babby died. Maybe the ungrateful mother, too. Once again, Grella swallowed her pride. She offered an apology. This would not happen again. She lifted her head and saw me from the corner of her cherry-black eye. That was a terrible moment. After four months in captivity she was barely recognizable as the girl I'd met in Taan. They had beaten the beauty out of her and she looked no better than Griss at her worst. *Why?* her face asked me. *Why did you do that?*

There was still a thread of gray wool caught between my claws. At the risk of threatening the timeline again I sent her a signal I hoped would be of comfort. I lifted a paw and held it as near to my heart as I could. Grella's gaze narrowed. She made a fist of one hand and touched it to her breast. I let the squirrel chirrup quietly. She blinked in confusion and cried a little more. Perhaps she thought her wits had deserted her. For how, even in a time of dragons, could a squirrel have known the age-old salute of Taan . . . ?

"You were lucky," said Joseph, when I reappeared on the librarium window. So much time had passed in Nomaad; in Co:pern:ica, we'd barely paused to breathe.

I looked at the stars. There was more of Grella's story to see.

"Did I do too much, showing her the greeting?"

A daisy appeared in his hands. He caressed each petal with the back of his finger, making them lift and slightly change color. "She will believe for a while that magicks were at work. Then she will begin to question her sanity. Then she will tell herself a squirrel is a squirrel and that squirrels have a habit of holding one paw in a certain fashion. You did no harm. But there will come a moment when your limits will be tested. And then, Agawin, what will be, will be."

I resolved to be stronger. I would not tease Grella with hope again. "Tell me this: Why doesn't Gwilanna age?"

To my surprise he said, "She does. She is. There are just no physical signs of it. She's aging rapidly — and growing, too. Far quicker than a normal child."

"Because of the unicorn auma she was born with?"

"Yes. She is fully aware of her development, but she cannot break the curse Hilde put on her."

"Hilde did this? To her own child? Why?" If memory served me correctly, Gwilanna blamed Voss for her wrinkled skin.

Joseph looped his hair behind his ear on one side, reminding me a little of his sister, Lucy. "If you were to visit the timepoints of Hilde you would see that Hilde tried to prevent Gwilanna being born. Too late she realized that Voss had poisoned her with darkened auma and that she, the mother, would perish giving birth. If Grella had heard the sibyl's curse she might not have rescued Gwilanna from the cave. Hilde condemned the child to grow old in a sack of wrinkled baby skin, until someone showed her she was beautiful."

But who would do that? The child was as ugly as a common wart. "How did she become an adult?"

"The fire stars will show you. And there is something you've missed."

I turned to look at him.

He threw the daisy into the timeline and an image of Grella appeared before us. She was bending over Gwilanna's crib, making baby talk and waggling a raggedy doll. She had made the doll from sackcloth stuffed with straw and dressed it in a Taan-style robe. Gwilanna gurgled happily and reached for the toy. Grella had given it a beautiful face and attached red strands of wool for the hair. "This is your kachina, your spirit doll," said Grella. "It will guard your auma and be your guide. Are you going to say hello? *Hello, Gwilanna.*" She waved the doll's arm. "When you're old enough we'll give her a real Taan name."

"Guh . . . ," said the baby, taking the toy and shaking it as if she might bring it to life.

"Yes," said Grella. "Guh, like a dragon . . ."

The sound of Stygg clomping out of the shack stopped her happy chatter dead. She snatched the doll back and pushed it under a pillow she had made from a hollowed log. She looked anxiously over her shoulder. Her eyelids were puffy and purple-colored. Sores had formed in patches on her scalp where her hair had been continually severed. A red split that refused to heal marked where Stygg had broken her cheek.

The image faded away.

"You must prepare yourself for greater horrors," said Joseph, noticing a tear rolling out of my eye.

"Why did you show me this?"

"For the doll."

"What of it?"

"It's important," he said. "There is more you should know. You remember Rune?"

Grella's noble father.

"Four times she took a baby to the border to show to him."

To prove the child was normal or face his wrath. I remembered Gwilanna telling me about it. "She made an arrangement with a woman from Horste and showed Rune that child in place of the sibyl."

"Yes," he said. "She was afraid that Rune would kill Gwilanna because the baby was wrinkled and refused to grow. It was not long after their fourth meeting when Stygg ran across her near Yolen's grave. Remember this as you progress through the Is." He moved his hands and Grella's stars sparkled in front of me again.

Once more, I went back as the squirrel.

Grella did as she'd promised. She grew less rebellious and settled into her servile role. She did not argue with Griss anymore or complain about the baby's lips being scalded. She cooked. She skivvied. She mended cloth. More than once she had to fend off Stygg's attentions — which was easy, given that his mother was near. On the surface, she seemed to accept her confinement, and I feared she had conceded all hope of escape. Then, one night, she began to sing Gwilanna a brand-new lullaby. It told of a hero come to slay an ogre: a toothless beast with very little hair. I soon realized the ogre was Griss and the hero could only be Rune, Grella's father. It occurred to me then, as it must have done to her, that her promise to show her baby to the Taan would be broken — which meant Rune would be forced to come looking for her. I noticed her scratching fresh marks on the barn, marks recording the quarters of the moon. She was counting down the time to the next winterfold and the anniversary of their regular meetings. But Rune's chances of finding her in Nomaad were slim. It was untamed country with no set paths. Grella, however, had an answer to this. It lay, of course, in her needle and thread. With the tools of the Taan tribe at her disposal she had seen an opening that avarice had blinded her captors to. A picture could be more than a thing to look at. It might conceal a message. Or a signature.

Or a map.

I watched her carefully. The eremitts did not. Grella noted where the sun rose in the mornings and where it came to rest at night. She counted the trees and studied every possible curve of the land. She mentally copied down the layout of the stars. She picked out where the villhund barked and in which direction the spring birds flew. She studied the shack from every angle. The days grew shorter. The nights blew cold. Winterfold approached the land again.

And Grella's tapestries began to change.

They moved away from dragons to more "homely" scenes. Woodland animals. General landscapes. She even drew an image of Stygg chopping wood. Griss complained at length about this. Who would want to trade a tapestry of Stygg?! she demanded. Or a river running through an empty field? Or the shack poking through a thicket of trees? *Thwack! Thwack! Thwack!* Each picture cost the girl another wallop. Grella accepted it all. She simply replied that in her experience people liked views of things they could relate to, not necessarily things they'd never seen. Who among the Nomaads didn't chop wood?

To the eremitt's surprise, the pictures *did* trade. Stygg exchanged the river for a pair of old boots and brought home a saddlecloth in place of the shack. The chopping scene, however, he saved for himself. He told his mother he'd traded it for apples, but the truth was he'd actually stolen the fruit. Later, he went to the barn and shyly revealed the tapestry to Grella. To his dismay, she was angry with him.

"Go back," she hissed at him, scratching her ankle. The link around her leg had rubbed down the flesh. Blue ulcers were beginning to form underneath.

"Back?" he said, puzzled. "But Stygg like thissun. Ain't never seen no show o' me, afore. You makee look strong." He flexed his muscles till the blood vessels strained.

"Sell it, Stygg. Or your mother will be angry."

"Bah, Muther." He flapped a hand. He tucked the tapestry into his robe. (He had a fine robe now, made by Grella. She'd even inscribed it with her own mark.) "She don't be missin' one nibbly bit o' cloth."

"Sell it, Stygg, or I'll tell her you've got it."

That cast a dim shadow over his mood. He was about to respond when he saw me perched on the water trough, watching. "Darned squir'l," he muttered. "Al'ays round 'ere." He whipped out a knife, but I was under the trough before he could advance and from there up into the rafters of the barn. He thumped a post in frustration and blew aside his hair. He rolled the blade in his callused hand, then walked to the log pile and tipped it at Gwilanna.

"Stygg? What are you doing?" Grella's chain rattled in tune to her panic. She hobbled toward him as fast as she could. He stopped her at arm's length and held her by the throat.

"This babby be right unnat'rul," he said. He tapped the blade against the lice-infested shawl. Gwilanna made gurgling noises. Her hands reached up for the shiny metal. Stygg allowed her pudgy fingers to grip it, not caring that the baby might cut herself. "Why don't it grow? You bin 'ere ten moons 'n more an' it ain't spread a toe."

"She lacks food," said Grella. "Let her be. I beg you." She pushed against his hand. He held her back, squeezing a glugging sound from her mouth. Wisely, she relaxed and didn't try to fight him. "All right, you win. Keep the tapestry. I don't care."

"If I slit 'er," he muttered, "what wud I see?"

"You'd see her die," said Grella. "Please, let her be."

Gwilanna gave a gentle yelp. Stygg pulled the knife back and held it vertical. A trickle of blood ran down the steel. "Black," he said. "There be night in 'er veins."

"What have you done?" Grella squealed.

"Nowt," he grumbled. "It jus' be a fingernick. Weren't my doin'. Babby med its own mark on the blade."

At last Grella wrestled clear of his grip. Pushing him aside, she lifted Gwilanna out of the logs. The child had a minor cut on one finger. It was oozing a bubble of dark, dark blood.

"Why izzit *black* . . . ?" Stygg muttered again. He twisted the blade in front of his face. He put it under his nose and sniffed.

Gwilanna started to cry.

"Be quietin' that!" a voice shouted from the shack.

"Leave us," said Grella, cradling the child. She looked grimly at Stygg, urging him to go.

He sneered and wiped his nose on his sleeve. Suddenly, he pointed at a piece of cloth sticking out from under one corner of the shawl. "Whassat?"

"Nothing. A wrap to keep her warm." Grella tried casually to tuck the cloth back.

But Stygg, for all his idiot ways, wasn't going to be put off easily. He stepped up and tugged at the swaddling materials. "Thas a tap'stry, I reckun. Show it to Stygg."

"No," said Grella, struggling with him now. "No. It belongs to Gwilanna. Get away."

But he was strong and he'd pulled the thing free in seconds. I scrabbled along the beam for a closer look. Stygg's eyes popped as he unraveled the material. For he'd found not one, but two fine tapestries. And a new Taan dress.

The first tapestry was the image of Gawaine in flight, the one Eleanor had given to me in the krofft and I had carried through the Skoga forest. The other was the Isenfier tapestry, complete.

"Aar . . . ," breathed Stygg, as if he'd found a pure gold nugget in his teeth. "This be a pretty thing a'right."

He was looking at the roaring image of Gawaine. The Isenfier tapestry didn't impress him.

But he did like the dress. He let it dangle from his arm. A golden robe, fit for his beloved.

His tongue squeezed out like a slug between his teeth.

"Stygg, this is all I have of home," Grella begged. She stumbled forward and fell at his feet. "Give the tapestries back. I can make others like them."

"Nah," he grunted, with a shake of his head. "Stygg be doin' good trade fer these."

"Please, Stygg. You can't take them. You can't."

"You 'iding any more?" He jabbed his knife.

"No," she said, turning Gwilanna from the blade. The baby cried louder still. The kachina doll dropped to the floor of the barn.

"What's squawkin' that babby?!" Griss called out.

Stygg grunted. A fair impression of his pig. "Tell 'ee what. Stygg cud trade wiv Grella?"

"Trade?" She looked horrified. "What would I want of yours?"

His eyes ran the length of the dress once more. "This be right pretty to be wedded in."

"Wedded?"

"Aar." His dumb eyes glinted with hope. He brushed his lanky hair aside, as if he might appear more handsome to her.

Grella struggled to keep her revulsion at bay. "I wed you and you'll let me have the tapestries back?"

He nodded. "Aar."

She closed her eyes and gulped. "You'll take me out of these chains as well?"

He chewed a fat mole that was growing on his lip.

"Build us a shack to hang the tapestries in?"

He scratched a black spider off his neck.

"Take me away from here? Away from Griss?"

His left eye twitched. His shoulders shook.

"You'd care for my baby? You'd treat her as — ?"

"I don't be knowin'!" he cried. She'd rattled him now. He threw the dress down. Within seconds, the mice and the lice were at it.

"You don't be knowin' what, you loaf?" his mother called.

"Nowt!" Stygg shouted. "I not be knowin' nowt!" He tucked both tapestries into his robe. "You be sayin' no words to Ma 'bout this or I be soakin' my blade wi' yer rynkler's blood." He bent down and picked up the kachina doll. For one moment, I thought he would take

313

that as well. But he threw it in the crib and backed
away. "I'll be thinkin' on our weddin' night, I will."
And he curled his tongue and licked the black streak
of blood off his knife.

"No!" I gasped.

The fire stars brought me back to the window.

Joseph immediately said, "You have witnessed a terrible thing. It's recorded in the Is that Stygg has a trace
of Voss inside him. This is the beginning of the end for
the Nomaad."

"Does he kill her?" I couldn't believe what I'd seen.
Stygg could now be capable of all kinds of wickedness.

Joseph studied his fingernails. "You can stop any
time you want to, Agawin."

Having come this far? And not seen the truth? "Have
I learned what I need to know about Gwilanna?"

"No. Not until the very end."

"Then I have to go back. I must know what happened." I looked at the timeline and thought about
Stygg. A fresh group of stars began to sparkle. Once
again, I reached into the Is.

Within days, the eremitt was losing his mind. He
began to argue with anyone near him, crashing dement-
edly around the shack as if a weevil had burrowed

under his scalp. He shouted at corners, challenged shadows to fights. I watched him splash his face in the water trough, then push the trough over and scream at the moon. The turning point came when he bit a villhund. He'd been stomping around the barn with a rope in his mouth — chewing it as though it were a roll of bread — when he happened to see a rogue dog stalking the pig. He picked up a chain and whipped the dog's back. The villhund was swift to get even. With one bite it ripped off the Nomaad's toe (the big one that pointed through a hole in Stygg's boot). A howl as long as the great Horste River came pouring out of the eremitt's throat.

Then it got serious.

Any sensible dog would have run with the toe, spat out the nail, and enjoyed (if that were possible) the corn-ridden flesh. Instead, the hound dropped it and dived in again, hoping to get a whole foot this time. In a blood-curdling act of retaliation, Stygg fell upon its neck, sinking his teeth far into the juiciest part of its throat. The dog jerked, gave a rasp, and immediately went limp. Its yellow eyes rolled. It faded into death. Stygg drew back, shuddering a little. A dark light burned in his vacant eyes. Blood and fur were stuck around his mouth. He bit again. He ripped. He chewed. I thanked the universe I'd seen far worse on my Travels or I might have caused my poor host squirrel to vomit.

When she saw the wretched dog, even Griss was appalled. Grella, out of goodness or pity or both, tried to warn the crone that Stygg was changed. Griss would not listen. She accused Stygg of drinking mushroom juice, a common cause of coarse behavior among the lonely men of Nomaad. "Gettee gone and do sum tradin'!" she barked, pushing him and his blood-spurting foot toward the trees. She kicked his backside soundly for his trouble. For the first time in his life Stygg turned on his mother, snarling as brutally as the dog he had slain. "Gettee gone," she rapped again, completely unaware of the danger she was in. He lunged at her, but just a second too late. The door had slammed shut against his slavering mouth.

Stygg tumbled down the steps that led to the porch. He rolled over, beat the ground, and picked himself up. But instead of getting to his feet as normal, he righted himself on all four limbs. Swaying a little, he shuddered again. Then a strange transformation began to take hold of him. His black hair extended down his back and fur began to thicken on his arms and legs. The boot with the hole in it split around the seam. Claws burst out where his toes should have been. His other foot and fingers went the same way. There was little change to his upper body, and his robe, despite ripping, covered him still. But Stygg was not a man anymore. With one more horrible bone-cracking twist his face took on the shape of a villhund.

He roared at the moon and ran for the trees.

I quickly came back to the librarium again.

By now I had discovered I could ask the Is to filter the stars on different levels. If I instructed the matrix to compare the arrays of two individuals, the stars would change color where their lives overlapped. The colors gave no clue to the nature of the incidents, but significant events always showed up strongly. The last few stars of Grella's array overlapped with Stygg's, which warned me that her fate was tied up with his. But what about Rune? Was he involved? The Is moved in its strange, mysterious way and produced a new, and even more complex, array. Nearly all of the stars stretched into Grella's past and her long family life with

Rune and Eleanor. But a few of Rune's hovered over her future. And nearly all intersected with the last days of Stygg.

I touched one of those.

I materialized at night in a thunderstorm, on muddy ground served by a scrubby patch of trees. Rain was drumming down, puddling the dirt. Up ahead, I heard the splash of a hoof, followed by the whinny of a horse being turned.

"What is it?" said a voice.

"Thought I heard something." Rune of Taan glanced over his shoulder. His hair was plastered to his face in strands. His brow had gained a new furrow or two, but this was definitely the man I'd met in the krofft.

The second man turned his horse. He was Taan also. I'd seen him at the motested, but I didn't know his name. "Is that a katt?" he said, leaning forward in the saddle.

A scraggy excuse for one, yes. My new host had been huddled up under a bush, trying to find what little shelter it could. I'd made it step out into the rain and its wail of dissent had reached Rune's ears.

Spitting water off his lips, he looked around. "Where there's a katt, there's usually a hovel."

"There," said the second man, pointing.

Rune narrowed his eyes to a squint and saw it. A single-story shack, held together by crossed, nailed planking. Faint yellow candlelight flickered inside.

Rune tugged on his reins. "Let's go and introduce ourselves."

The horses walked forward. As they approached the primitive doorway, the second man let Rune go on alone.

Rune stopped his horse and bellowed through the rain. "You, inside. Whoever you are. I am Rune Haakunen, from the district of Taan. I seek shelter for myself and one companion."

I saw the companion lower his hand. It came to rest on the hilt of a sword.

There was a pause that seemed like the end of time. The door opened a crack. A face peered out. "No sheltur 'ere. Ain't no room to dizzy a katt. Be goin'. I want no truck with Taans."

"We're soaked and we've traveled far," said Rune.

"No room," said the Nomaad. The door began to close.

"We have money."

A spike of lightning divided the night.

As thunder clapped, the door creaked open.

Rune reached into a purse at his belt. A silver coin tumbled through the moonlit air. It landed in the mud with a tidy splat. The eremitt was out like a ferret. His hand splashed around and fished it out. He looked at it and rubbed it and bit it to be sure.

"Silvur," he said.

"For one night," said Rune, nodding at the door.

The man pulled his shabby rags around him. "There be two o' yer."

Rune threw back his hair. The wet ends slapped against his riding jacket. "Very well. Two kroat." He produced another coin and rested it on the nail of his thumb. The eremitt hopped and got ready to catch. But as Rune made to flip it he paused and said, "And food. Two kroat buys us shelter *and* food."

The eremitt wiped his blue-veined nose. "Ain't got no food. Water. Thassall. Jus' water, an' a place to lie."

"I've got a skyful of water," Rune said plainly. The rain was finding channels all over his face. "Bread. You give us bread, we pay two kroat."

The man sniffed and made a grizzling noise. "One pull. Thassall." (He meant one hunk ripped off a long loaf.) "An' I does the pullin'."

Rune's horse snorted. He tugged his reins and considered the offer. "Very well. One pull and a place to lie." He flipped the second coin.

It tumbled into the Nomaad's grasp. He bit into that one also. Satisfied it was genuine silver, he pushed the coin into a pocket of his rags and cautiously widened his doorway. While Rune and his companion tied their horses, I crept forward and managed to slip inside the shack, narrowly avoiding the eremitt's kick. There were empty rabbit traps everywhere and foul-smelling skins hanging out to dry. No fire and only one grungy fur, which the eremitt draped around his shoulders. He swept some loose traps into one corner, giving me a place to hide and watch. As Rune stepped in, the eremitt pointed to the space he'd made. It was barely wide enough for one man's bed, let alone two stocky travelers from Taan. None of this seemed to concern Rune much. He peered around, ignoring the eremitt's grunts. Right away, he found what he was looking for. On a wall of the shack, pinned above a table knocked together from branches and barrels, was one of Grella's tapestries.

Rune was there in three slow strides. His fingers trembled as he touched the cloth. It was another of

Stygg outside the shack — a pack of villhund crowding around him, begging for what looked like the leg of a pig. Grella had drawn the setting sun throwing its amber rays onto the roof. "A fine piece of work," Rune Haakunen muttered, doing well to control his rage. "How did you come by this?"

The eremitt wiped his scratchy mouth. His nerves were as high as the grim scent of rabbit. "You be wantin' that bread now." He tried to step past Rune to get it.

Rune turned his shoulder, trapping this ferret of a man into a corner. "I asked you a question. Where did you get this tapestry?"

The eremitt darted his eyes to the doorway, blocked, of course, by Rune's companion. Thunder clapped again, driving a wash of rain into the shack. The eremitt began to panic.

"I ain't dun no wrongin', I ain't. Murgo traded six skins fair. Nevur tricked on no one, I dint."

"Murgo. This is your name, yes?"

"Aye," said Murgo. "Whassit to you?"

Rune Haakunen did not reply. He ripped the tapestry off the wall, sending bone pins scattering over the floor. "How long ago did this trade take place?"

Murgo shrugged. "I don't be rememb'rin' easy."

"Well, let's see if my friend can help you."

There was a glint of light by the doorway. Rune's companion lifted a sword. It was as long as the space between him and the eremitt. He touched its point to Murgo's throat, lifting the terrified man by the chin till he was on tiptoe to avoid being cut. The fur fell away from the captive's shoulder. Unremarkably, his memory came back.

"Two moons. Two moons it were."

"With a Nomaad trader?"

"Nomaad, urr."

"Where did he get it?"

"Wunt say whereun 'e goddit. Dint ask on it, I dint. You can 'ave it. Be takin' it — bread an' all. Murgo don't want bother with Taans."

Rune examined the piece. In the bottom right corner was a knot of yellow wool. To the untrained eye it looked like a bunch of poorly stitched flowers. To a father desperate to find his daughter, it was a signature. "This place," he said. "The shack in the drawing. Where can I find it?"

"I not be knowin'."

The sword made a dent in Murgo's throat.

"I be truthin'," he squeaked through a bubble of drool. Stupidly, he shook his head. A small nick appeared in his jaundiced skin. A trickle of blood burst out of a vein. One of his hands began to shake. "Nomaad be ev'rywhere, wide as thuh sky. Keeps usselves to usselves, we do."

For some reason, this angered Rune's companion. He twisted the sword. The blood ran thicker.

Rune laid a hand on his friend's strong arm. "Easy, Truve. He's no use to us dead." He turned to the eremitt again. "My friend is a farmer, more used to plowing a field than torturing weevils who call themselves men. He's traveled far and his grip is tired, his hand could slip at any moment. He wields the sword because his wife and son were murdered by a villain who raided his krofft and took sewing materials. The rogue answered the description of a typical Nomaad. For all my friend knows, it could have been you."

"Not me! Not Murgo!"

"Then you have no need to fear us," said Rune. He picked a hair off one of the rabbit skins. "Tell us what we want and we'll leave you in peace." He looked Murgo hard in the eye. "The man we are hunting has left a trail of tapestries in other dwellings. Two of your countrymen were kind enough to . . . donate his wares to us, but not his likely whereabouts. I'm sure you won't be as unhelpful as they were." He held up another tapestry cloth, but I could only see the reverse of it. "Do you recognize the hills in the background of this picture?"

The prisoner's eyebrows pinched together. "Gray-backs."

Rune nodded and held up another cloth. "The same shack, from a different angle. The Graybacks are shown both here and here. You could save our horses a lot of effort by telling us the best way to reach this ridge, the one with the moon above it." He gestured Truve to pull the sword back.

The eremitt doubled up, coughing spittle. He put a hand to his neck and looked at the red smears greasing his fingers. "Murgo dunnee no wrong."

"The ridge," said Truve. "Or I'll chop off your ears."

"I showee on the morn," Murgo said defiantly. He threw up a hand. "Too murked now, even fer stars."

Rune and Truve exchanged a glance. "Sunrise it is, then," Rune said firmly. "Now, all that remains are the sleeping arrangements." He grabbed Murgo and threw him to Truve. "Tie him to a tree. If he's struck by lightning, that's too bad."

Murgo's protest was startlingly loud. "No, Taan! No." He did his best to scrabble free.

A slap to the back of his head stopped him wriggling. "Shut up," said Truve. "Or I'll bind you feet upward and watch your tiny brains dribble out of your ears."

Rune unclasped his knife belt and threw it down. "We've paid for your hospitality, eremitt. We'll be taking the shack. There's no room for three. A drop of rain might freshen your memory."

Thunder rattled the shack once more, making all the rabbit skins swing.

"T'ain't the rain," said Murgo. "Rain be nowt."

That was clear from the drips falling through the ceiling. Carpentry was not a skill the Nomaad were known for.

"What then?" Rune asked, mildly intrigued.

"Rummers. There be rummers knockin' in the woods."

I saw Truve scowl.

Rune walked to the window. "Rumors of what?" He looked out, as if checking for the first flowers of spring.

"A villhund, roamin'."

Stygg. My heart leaped. The shock of it made the katt give a hiss. He flicked his tail, rattling the traps. Rune flicked a glance at my hiding place but probably assumed it was just a mouse; their black pellet droppings were everywhere.

"Villhund?" Truve gave a scornful snort. The dogs, though vicious, rarely attacked men. He pressed the eremitt against the door frame, forcing his hands behind his back.

"Thissun ain't nat'rul," Murgo spluttered. "Large, they say. Big as a man. Cursed. Not proper. Not doglike, no. Beast wi' the fire o' dragons in its eyes."

Truve and Rune exchanged another glance. Though neither of them seemed quite ready to believe it, neither could they disbelieve the story fully. But the shack was small. And the eremitt stank. And the two Taan men were tired and soaked. "You say you've heard talk of this beast?" asked Rune.

Murgo gave a fretful nod.

"So you were lying when you said you keep your own company?"

Lines of guilt swept across the eremitt's face.

"Take him out," said Rune. "The night air should straighten his tongue by morning."

"No!" cried Murgo. "It be on the wind. I've 'eard its 'owl. I be truthin'! I be truthin'!"

But it was done and the eremitt was dragged outside. I watched Rune for a moment, knocking his fist on the window frame. Then, taking a chance that he didn't mind katts, I slipped out of hiding and leaped onto a box so I could see outside. He heard me and whipped around, reaching for his knife. I made the katt meow. Rune relaxed and caressed my fur. How strange it felt, being stroked by the father of the girl whose fate I was here to follow.

He was rubbing my ears when Truve came back. "It seems we are threefold after all."

"Let's hope it keeps the pests from our rations," Truve grunted, aiming his boot at a skinny mouse scuttling through the shadows. He was clearly not fond of katts (or mice), but not so averse that he wanted to toss me into the storm. "I tied him to a dead tree. He's sheltered well enough. I gagged him to stop his pathetic whining. You won't be hearing screams if his villhund comes. At least we should get some sleep tonight, even in this miserable, stinking dump."

Rune frowned and said, "I will never truly rest until I know about Grella." He stretched out Murgo's tapestry again.

"Leave it till the morning light," said Truve. "I'll persuade this Nomaad to talk."

If he was still alive by morning. Beyond the horses, through the rain, I could see Murgo pulling against his ties. His eyes were as big as two gray pebbles.

Another thunderclap drew my gaze into the room. "This is our man. I'm sure of it," said Rune. He tapped a finger on the image of Stygg. "This is the villain who murdered your family. What do you make of this line of silver stitches running from the shack toward the barn at the back?"

"A chain, perhaps?"

Rune nodded grimly. "They're holding her here. They're holding my daughter, chained, like a dog." He rolled the cloths and put them away.

"Get some rest," Truve said kindly. He was younger than Rune by a good five years. A swatch of dark hair above his top lip could not disguise his youthfulness. "When we find this rogue I'll cut out his heart. But what of your heart, brave elder? You rode with me intent on punishing Grella for not upholding your bargain of trust. Surely these messages have turned your head? Every new tapestry shows her plight. All of them a plea for her father's help. Who in Taan would reprimand you now for saving your daughter from a Nomaad captor?"

Rune took off his boots and tossed them aside. "Let us not forget that she pledged her allegiance to a child born with darkness in its soul. I still fear Voss's hand in this."

Truve sighed. He also removed his boots. One of his socks was soaked through, and stank. It left its print on the grubby floor as he shuffled around, looking for a place to settle. "We are doomed, Rune, if we stare into our souls and find no hint of forgiveness there. Promise you will talk with me before you strike."

Rune lay down, closing his eyes. "My sword won't be making any rash decisions. On this, you have my word."

And so they slept. When I returned to the katt the next morning, daylight was just about to drive away their snores. Rune was first to open his eyes. He knocked a mouse off his chest and sat up wearily, loosening a pocket of wind from his gut. He nudged Truve.

The younger man woke with a start. "Still raining," Truve groaned, hearing it drumming. He sank his head against the pillow of his coat, stretching and flexing his barely dried toes.

Rune grunted in the affirmative. "The storm has settled. The clouds are emptying their last. Riding conditions will be poor today. I'll check the horses."

He pulled on his boots and went to the door. My katt was on the box where it had been the night before, now with a mouse tail by its paws.

Smiling at me, Rune opened the door. The smell of drenched earth crawled into the shack, mixed with the clammy permanence of rain. I dropped to the floor and followed him out, settling myself just under the porch. I could see the whole clearing easily from here. The horses blinked and nuzzled Rune's hand. He patted their necks and looked across the puddled earth toward the dead tree. Murgo had his head slumped into his chest.

Rune walked over and slapped him awake.

"Uh?" The Nomaad jerked himself upright. He'd spent a trail of urine down his legs. Even from where I was sitting he now stank worse than he had before.

"Breakfast," Rune said, ignoring the stench. He tore the gag free and pushed the bread into the eremitt's mouth. "Eat. Far fresher than yours, I think."

Murgo chewed on it a couple of times and swallowed the rest in a slobbering lump. "Lemme go, Taan."

Rune shook his head. "Tell me what you know about this trader first."

"I knows nuthin'."

"I want a name, Murgo."

"Not knowin' a name."

"I think you do. Tell me his name and the way to the ridge, then you can go back to snaring rabbits."

"Why shud I trustee?"

Rune pursed his lips. He looked over at the shack. "We are honorable men."

"Pah!" said the eremitt and spat in his face.

Rune Haakunen sighed. He took a rag from his pocket and cleaned his cheek, taking more time than he needed to. Without making any overt threat, he pulled out a knife and polished the blade using Murgo's spit. He folded the rag and put it away. Then, in a sudden flash of fury, he drove the knife toward the Nomaad's belly, pressing his body up behind the thrust.

Murgo squealed and exploded breadcrumbs, but the knife was in the flesh of the tree, not him.

"His name," Rune Haakunen growled. He pulled the knife out and held it close to Murgo's nose. "I might not be so careful next time."

"N-no," said Murgo, shaking his head. He appeared distracted by something in the clearing.

"Look at me," said Rune. He gripped Murgo's chin and held it fast. "I *will* kill you if you don't speak true."

"No. Cut uz free," the eremitt gabbled. His gaze was anywhere but on the knife. "Lemme go. Lemme go!" He tugged at his ties. In a desperate eruption he suddenly cried, "He be named Stygg and he shacks wi' a crone. Don't let it 'ave me! Don't let it near!"

Rune stepped back. "What are you talking about?"

"Rune, look out!"

From the doorway of the shack, Truve called a warning. I had seen the danger, too, but couldn't have meowed if I'd wanted to.

The half-dog, Stygg, leaped through the air. A shadow must have flickered in Murgo's eyes, for Rune, despite his roundness of age, was quick enough to spot it and roll his body aside. Stygg missed the man of Taan and sank his claws into the Nomaad prisoner.

Murgo's screams nearly stopped the rain. Eight jets of hot red blood spouted from the points that had punctured his chest. His body spasmed. His eyes froze open. He looked into the slavering face of hell and his life-force washed away into the mud.

Truve by now was eating up the ground, both hands clamped to the hilt of his sword. He was a big man, a farmer, as Rune had said. He did not care for subtlety in swordplay. As the man-dog ripped itself free of Murgo, Truve roared like thunder and lunged at the beast, intent on putting an end to its life with one unstoppable swing of steel. The blade sang heavy in the rain, its angle savage, its purpose true. Stygg's gruesome head looked sure to be parted from its mutant body. But fortune favored the ugly villhund. Truve, in his haste, had run into the rain in his stockinged feet. One piece of grit, one treacherous nub of Nomaad stone, bit into his sole and made him tilt. The blade fell awkwardly, its target missed. Stygg's ear popped off in a crown of blood. A portion of the flesh underneath went, too. So neat was the cut that the villhund did no more than yelp. The rain lashed down. The horses panicked. A dead eremitt hung from a long-dead tree. Then the water and the mud and the weight of the swing all conspired to take Truve down. As he lost his footing and fell to the ground, Stygg was on him, tearing and thrashing and making all the damage he needed to make to hasten the closure of a brave man's life.

The sodden fields of Nomaad were wetted bright red before Rune could land a blow with his knife. His blade sank firmly into Stygg's flesh. Stygg howled at the sky and danced away sideways. But this time he did not fight back. Still yelping with pain, he loped into the trees, leaving a trail of blood in his wake.

Rune fell to his knees and gathered up his friend, pressing Truve's collar against the wounds. It was hopeless. There was a hole in the farmer's throat that was already sucking in air and rain. "I'm so sorry," Rune said, perhaps for a multitude of reasons, but right then, as he knelt in the bloodstained dirt, it was surely because he knew he could do nothing to save the life of a dear companion.

"Did you see it . . . ?" Truve croaked. "The robe . . . did you . . . ?"

"Don't talk," said Rune, rocking him gently. A tear ran out of his craggy eye.

Truve gripped Rune's arm with all the strength a dying man could muster. "Taan," he said. "Grella's

335

mark on it . . ." He gurgled and started to cough. A surge of loose tissue bubbled over his lip. "Follow it, Rune. Dog . . . take you . . . to . . . her. Follow, avenge my . . ."

And that was it. That was all there was. Truve's head fell sideways and he breathed no more. Rune gathered him tighter and held him close, speaking a quiet, angry prayer. After a suitable time he laid Truve down, setting the farmer's fist across his heart. "Rest, I will come back for you." He made the Taan salute, then picked up the sword and strode to the horses. He took the saddle and a hunting bow off Truve's horse and sent the horse running into the woods. Taking what he needed of Truve's possessions, he hid the saddle inside the shack. He saw me trembling on the porch. All the katt's fur was standing on end. Strangely he said, "Look after him for me." Then he went out and mounted his horse. He looked at the eremitt and shuddered over Truve. Then he kicked the horse once and galloped after Stygg.

In his altered state, and despite his injury, Stygg must have traveled as fast as the horse, for he appeared at his own shack several minutes before Rune did. By now, the fire stars had lessened in number and we were coming to the end of Grella's story. I was in the body of the squirrel again, watching from a tree where I could see it all. Stygg dragged himself to the edge of the porch, yowling like a katt that had brought home a mouse. Some tone in his voice must have spoken to his mother, for Griss opened the door and stepped out.

She was holding an ax behind her back.

"Gettee gone!" she snapped. "You ain't no son o' mine."

Stygg could not speak. A bloodstain covered his entire shoulder. His feet were bathed in a puddle of red. He flopped onto the steps and bayed at his ma.

"Gettee gone!" She showed him the ax.

Somewhere in the background Gwilanna cried.

Rain swept hard across the clearing.

The shack roof creaked. The treetops bowed.

Stygg raised a paw and crawled up a step.

"I'll cut 'ee. I'll trim yer," his mother threatened.

Stygg bayed for help.

Griss chewed her tongue.

"Ma . . . ," he croaked.

And she swung the ax.

One chop sent the end of his dog's paw spinning.

The need in his wild eyes turned to horror.

The storm rapped the shack front, blowing the door inward.

Then he was on her, like he'd gone for Truve.

Suddenly, an arrow scythed through the air and sank its point between Stygg's shoulders. He jerked upright and spat out a gobbet of blood. He swayed for a second not making a sound. Then a second arrow hit him, closer to the neck. Only then did he fall back, heavy and stiff, breaking the bottom step in two. His mother fell the other way, into the shack. Half her face had been shredded into strips by his claws.

Rune came running out of the trees. He threw the bow aside and drew his sword. "Grella!" he shouted. "Your father is here!"

From within the shack he heard her voice. Feeble as a sparrow, but alive. *Alive.*

Whispering a prayer, Rune ran to Stygg. With the flat of his foot he kicked him once to be sure he was dead. The man-dog rolled off the broken step. As his useless life washed into the rain, he shrank back into his Nomaad form. He had one hand missing and his back was split by a diagonal wound. His face was violently contorted, two askew eyeballs in a crumpled bag of flesh. Rune made the sign of the dragon over him, then bolted up the steps and into the shack.

I was down the tree in a flash, and there.

On the floor of the shack lay a slender woman, dressed in a fine Taan robe. Her face was in shadow but there was no mistaking her strong yellow hair, spreading out across the sagging boards. On her knees, bending over the woman on the floor, was another woman clothed in filthy rags. She had very little hair and she smelled of pig muck. A knife was clamped in her wounded hands. Its quivering point was aiming downward.

"No!" Rune Haakunen shouted.

In error, he thrust his sword.

The figure in rags gasped. Slowly, she turned her head. She had swollen eyes and broken skin. Sores on her scalp. Teeth chipped and missing. A yellow lesion had eaten one side of her nose. But the shape of the mouth, the fall of the ears, the glint of recognition in her tormented eyes were all Rune needed to know his daughter.

Grella dropped the knife and let it clatter to the floor. She put her hands instead around the point of the sword, which had passed through her back and out through her belly.

Rune let go of it. He staggered back, knocking over the chair where Griss liked to sit and pour scorn on the world. "What have I done?" he wailed. "What have I done?" Seeing Grella about to fall, he rushed to her and caught her and held her up. As tenderly as he could, he withdrew the sword and flung it aside. "In the name of Godith, forgive me," he said. And he wept openly, and vividly, and strong.

Somewhere in her mazy consciousness, Grella heard his sobs and found the energy to raise a hand. She touched her father's fatty cheek. Her lips parted and she tried to speak. Rune tipped his head and begged her not to. But she managed two words. "Thank you," she whispered.

Thank you.

For releasing her from her torture.

I felt so sick with grief.

Lifting her into his powerful arms, Rune carried her outside onto the porch. He went back for his sword and in one huge swing he cut through the chain that bound her to the Nomaads. Then he carried her into the rain. He was Taan; he was not about to give up hope, but he knew enough about life and death to be certain that all she had left was seconds. Laying her down in the rain-softened earth, he fiddled in the pocket of his jerkin for something. It was a small piece of rock. A tiny remnant of Mount Kasgerden, singing gently with the auma of Galen. Folding her hands together on her breast, he fumbled the rock inside her grasp and knelt to say a final prayer. He had barely begun when a sharp wail cut through the hissing rain.

A baby, crying.

Torment savaged his rugged face. Here lay his once most beautiful daughter, dying from a thrust of his reckless sword, and there in the background was the entire reason for the whole tragedy. The wind made another tour of the trees. Rune looked at Grella through wetted eyes. Even now he saw a twitch of motherly concern as her fingers stretched toward the sound. Groaning in confusion he thumped the earth. *Damn it! I heard him cry. Damn this ludicrous child!* He hurried to the barn, with me in pursuit.

There she was, in her woodpile crib. Gwilanna: no bigger than the day she'd arrived. No sweeter on the eye than an upturned louse. Rune looked baffled. He stopped short of the crib. He turned a quick circle, perhaps wary that he'd walked into a Nomaad trap. No. Just him and the child . . . and a squirrel. He looked at the squirming baby again. "No," he said, holding his head in disbelief. And I knew he must be thinking of his meetings at the border. The baby girl that had become a toddler, with no abnormal creases in its soft pink skin. Yet here was this ugly . . . troll again.

He reached in and lifted Gwilanna clear. Instantly, the logs gave way and the crib fell apart, exposing the few things Grella had hidden: a small pouch, presumably a gift for Gwilanna; a very rough pair of baby shoes; the dress Grella might have been "wedded" in. All of this added to his misery and grief. "What are you?" he hissed at the child. "What devil made you so foul?"

Gwilanna gurgled and clutched her kachina doll.

Growling like a bear, Rune turned her around. Supporting her under the arms, he walked out of the barn and showed her Grella's body. "Look at her, child. See what this . . . *deceit* has made me do. See what has become of my only daughter. What made her care for a wretch like you?"

Gwilanna kicked her feet and stretched her hands. "Guh . . . ," she gurgled. "Guh. Guh."

Something glinted across the clearing. It was the mirror Griss had used when she'd brushed "her" hair, still hanging by a thread from its place in the tree.

"Come," Rune said, marching into the rain. "Look, child. There. Behold your *beauty*." And he thrust Gwilanna toward the mirror.

A flash of lightning impaled the darkness.

The tree branch withered.

The mirror cracked.

And a different face flashed in the glass.

"Agh!" Rune was so shocked he let the baby slip. As her feet hit the ground she pitched forward and fell facedown into a puddle. And though he must have hated her more than anything, he still reached out to prevent her from drowning. But the child, like Stygg, was about to go through an incredible transition. Right before his eyes, Rune watched her grow. Large, beyond childhood. A youthful woman. Too startled to react, he allowed her to turn. Mud was dripping from the end of her nose. Her eyes were a harbor of loathing and menace. She was wrinkled still, but not as badly as before. This was the woman I had seen in the cave whose eyes betrayed her lack of years.

Unmistakably the sibyl Gwilanna.

Grella's father sank to his knees. He shook his head, struggling to understand. "Who are you? What vile magick is this?"

Gwilanna looked down at the woman she called "mother." Grella was a whisper away from death. The sibyl began to shake with rage. It was the only time I saw her wounded by grief. "Murderer. You will pay for this. . . ."

"No," Rune said. He tried to stand. "It was an accident, I swear. I . . ."

Before he could finish, Gwilanna opened her throat and squealed like a wild crow in his face. Rune was bent back as if he'd walked into a blizzard. By the time he'd managed to cover his ears, blood was trickling out of them. "What would you have me do?" he shouted.

From the shack came a long, low groan. Despite her mauling, Griss was alive.

Gwilanna picked up the kachina doll. Her hand trembled as she tidied the red woollen hairs. "Bring her," she ordered. "Bring me *Griss*." Her voice could have rasped the edge off the wind.

Rune Haakunen shook his head. "Why? What good would it do?"

"I need her auma," Gwilanna said darkly. She stroked the kachina's mouth.

Rune squinted in confusion. "No, there is evil in this. I will play no part in your foul iniquities."

"You already have — *Grandfather*."

Hearing this, Rune made a white-knuckled fist, as if he might strike the sibyl down. All that stopped him was a pure sweet sound, rising like a wisp from Grella's lips. A lullaby no louder on the air than a feather. "Daughter?" he whispered.

He moved forward, wanting to cradle her again, but Gwilanna snapped, "Do as I say if you want her to live."

Rune's eyes shrank back to points. "You can save her?"

Gwilanna glanced at the doll. Rune could not see the change in it, but I was in a lofty position by now and the squirrel could see what Gwilanna could see. The little stitched mouth had begun to twitch — making the shapes of Grella's song. "She was touched by a unicorn once," Gwilanna said. "She can call upon a trace of the healing horse. But she needs more auma. Quickly, man. Her time is running short."

Rune stood up, still in something of a daze. As he turned toward the shack Gwilanna spoke again. "Just the head," she said. "The rats can have the rest."

Rune, the hardened traveler, gulped. With a vacant look in his weary eyes, he staggered to the shack like a newborn calf, there to finish what Stygg had begun. And I could have changed the squirrel's position and borne witness to the slaying of the Nomaad mother, but that was one thing I could not watch.

All I heard was the clump of the sword.

At the same time, Gwilanna took a sharp breath of air.

I saw the kachina doll's eyes turn green.

Then out came Rune with his gruesome trophy. He was holding the head at shoulder height, the way I'd often seen Griss with her lantern. In the other hand he wielded his sword again, its blade now soiled with Nomaad blood. Having the weapon back in his grasp seemed to have renewed his purpose and courage. He lobbed the head between Gwilanna's feet. The stuck-on hair parted away from the scalp.

Rune made a bold announcement. "This deed I have done to avenge my daughter and the people of Taan who were robbed and murdered by these Nomaad wretches. I will have no alliance with you. Be gone, witch. Take yourself far. Leave me in peace to mourn my child. My mind is changed. I will not subject her to any of your magicks. She feels my pain, I know she does. In the next life, she will forgive my hand. I defend her right to a natural death."

"Then you die here with her," Gwilanna said, "which, incidentally, was always the plan."

Hearing this, Rune's course was easy. He roared at her and swung his sword.

Gwilanna spoke a sibyl curse.

The sky awoke like a great black cat. Out of it came a vein of lightning. It struck Rune's sword and passed along the steel blade into his arm, shaking him as if he were a piece of straw. For a moment or two, a halo of energy held him taut. Then the bolt retracted like a shriveled root, sucking all the color out of the man. A black tree in the shape of his final lunge now marked the spot where his daughter lay.

The kachina doll stretched its arms.

Gwilanna stroked its cheek, then knelt down and placed it on Grella's chest.

It began to kick its limbs.

"Feed," said the sibyl.

A small word, quietly spoken, but out of all proportion to the evil it suggested. What looked like trails of glittering smoke passed from the remains of Rune and Griss and entered the kachina doll through its mouth. The tree that was Rune remained unaltered, but the flesh shrank away from Griss's head until all that was left behind was her skull. I realized then why Gwilanna had been so evasive about it. It was Griss, not Grella, that had sat in her cave.

Gwilanna raised her mud-splattered arms to the sky. "I command a new life, for all I have lost!"

Above her, the heavens rumbled uneasily. The rain stopped and started. The moon turned gray.

Grella's lullaby began to falter.

"Forgive me, Mother," the sibyl said darkly. "My kachina needs your auma as well." A death rattle crept into Grella's breathing. The smoke trails began to leave her body. Gwilanna spread her arms and closed her eyes. "I have a name for my 'doll.' I always did. Guinevere. I hope you approve."

And I watched the kachina doll grow in size. Until it was a red-haired human girl. Beautiful, just like Grella had been. With one exception.

Its eyes were black.

At that moment, I could bear it no longer. The need to bring Grella some kind of comfort overcame Joseph's rules of Travel. I left the body of the watching squirrel and let Alexa materialize into the scene. Hovering in the air behind Gwilanna, I found the last thread of Grella's auma. I willed her to open her eyes. She was weaker than a blade of grass, but her lids flickered up and she glimpsed me there. A flying girl. An angel of mercy. A ray of joy to enter her failing heart.

She clasped her hands around the stone from Mount Kasgerden.

And as the smoke trails shimmered violet, she died.

Suddenly, the air fanned out in ripples as Gwilanna, aware of the presence of *something*, tried to whip around to see what it was. It seemed to require a millennium of moves, but by then I was back in the librarium, with Joseph.

"So now you know what became of Grella," he said, "and how the power of reflection broke Hilde's curse. It was Rune's misfortune to tell the child she was beautiful. That and the mirror set Gwilanna free."

"But did she see me?" I asked, knocking my fists together.

Calmly, he stared at the Is. The fire stars were speeding by so fast they were forming into streaks of infinite light. They were twisting into the spiraling mark which dragons and unicorns understood to mean "sometimes." "The timestreams are realigning," he said. "You interfered, Agawin — but the Is records that you always did."

"What?" I said, fluttering my wings to keep myself stable. "You *knew* this would happen?"

"Yes," he said, his voice unruffled. "The Is records that the sight of an angel appearing to Grella raises a powerful surge of light, enough to overcome Gwilanna's intent and make the baby's auma turn violet. Without you, Guinevere might have been evil and my mother, Elizabeth, a maker of darklings."

"So . . . I was a part of Guinevere's birth?"

"A vital part. And of the timeline she shared with Gawain."

The complexities of this, the paradoxes it raised, were too much even for an illumined mind. "Why violet?" I had never understood the significance of the color.

"A sign of the dragon," he said. "Their fire is called 'white,' but violet is a closer description. Gwilanna will always suggest that the color is merely an irritating defect in the eyes of anyone close to dragons, but that is because she could never admit that she came to love the child she'd created."

"Love?" I scoffed.

Joseph nodded. "Ultimately, what the sibyl considers a weakness will be the thing that saves her. For all her faults, Gwilanna is capable of feeling loss. You saw it briefly outside Stygg's shack. You know this instinctively, which is why you — as Alexa — have always reserved some sympathy for your 'aunt.'"

"But she was trying to imagineer a monster. A female likeness in Voss's image."

"She was young," he said, "and fueled by anger. She was obeying the only impulse she knew. Later, the goodness she experienced through living with Guinevere suppressed Voss and brought the unicorn forward, allowing it to self-heal to a degree. But the balance of Gwilanna's mind is delicate and readily affected by negative influences such as the Ix. The conflict is slowly turning her mad."

Misguided, not evil, as David often said.

In the Is, a giant image of Gadzooks had appeared.

"Isenfier is upon us," said Joseph. "You must return to the Crescent, where you will be safe." He stood up

351

and made a firebird call. Gideon and the three that had saved me at Kasgerden came flying down from the upper floors.

"Joseph, wait. You never did tell me what happened to Elizabeth."

"Just stay in the Crescent. For my sake now."

"But I vowed to stop Gwilanna."

"You can't," he said. "Only Gwilanna herself can do that."

I spread my wings with a determined *phut!* "I have a duty to Galen and the last twelve dragons. Let me be Agawin. Let me *fight*."

"What makes you think there will be a fight?"

No fight? "Then what is your plan?"

"Gwilanna has set the conditions for Isenfier. Everything now depends on her. We will give her what she craves and let the timeline adjust. It begins the second after she takes you from the woods."

Back in the dawn of history. With Gawain.

"Your book will record it all," he said. He nodded at the lectern, where the book was waiting.

But my mind was still hovering firmly on Gwilanna. "Give her what she craves?"

He signaled to Gadzooks. The dragon lifted his pencil.

And as I felt the strange tug of the universe turning, I watched Joseph Henry fade away and commingle with the body of the firebird Gideon. "We need to give her what she's always wanted, Agawin." He spread his wings and snorted fire from his nostrils. "Illumination to a dragon."

PART SEVEN
ISENFIER

1. WOODLAND, IUNAVIK REGION, UNRECORDED TIME

Rosa came crashing through the trees, rearing her unicorn up beside David. "I smell burning. What happened? Where's Agawin gone?"

"It was a trap," David said, kneeling down beside Thoran. "Gwilanna was here, with the tornaq. She took him."

The unicorn bucked again. "Well, do we go after her or what?"

David shook his head. "Thoran's hurt. He needs help. This thorn in his paw is going to kill him. We need to remove it. Is Gretel with you?"

The potions dragon zipped through the trees and came to land on an exposed tree root. Thoran was fading out of consciousness, but still awake enough to know the meaning of pain. "Knock him out," David said in dragontongue to Gretel. "Quickly."

"No, wait."

The potions dragon flicked her tail and blew an impatient smoke ring at Rosa. The bear, as David said, was fading fast.

Rosa slid off the unicorn's back. "Surely Guinevere has to be the one who saves him? If we interfere we'll be changing the —"

"*Hhh!* Let me see him!" Before Rosa could finish, Guinevere came crashing through the bracken and knelt down, pushing her hair behind her ears. Gently, she lifted Thoran's paw and turned it to examine the wound. "Where's Agawin?" she asked, suddenly aware that he wasn't with them.

"Taken by Gwilanna," David said bluntly.

"Taken? Why? Why would she do that?" Guinevere looked at them both in turn. "Is this supposed to happen? You know my legend, don't you? Does he always disappear like this?"

David touched his thumb to his lips. "When Elizabeth Pennykettle taught me your legend, Agawin's name was never mentioned, but Thoran's definitely was."

"So will I see him again — Agawin, I mean?"

David looked into her eyes. "I don't know."

Guinevere nodded but made no comment. She checked Thoran's wound again. The thorn had snapped off between two of his pads. Golden-colored pustules were starting to appear all around the entry point. "The thorn has been tipped with nightshade," she said. "I can see a trace that hasn't entered his paw." The bear groaned as she laid his foot down. "I'll need to gather leaves to make a healing poultice. Did I hear you say Gretel could make him sleep?"

David nodded at Gretel, who quickly took some flowers from a quiver at her back and wafted them under Thoran's nostrils. Within seconds, the bear had slumped sideways.

"Look after him. I won't be long." Guinevere jumped up and ran into the woods.

When she was clear of them Rosa whispered, "Now what happens to this crazy timeline? You can't tell me Gretel was around a zillion years ago to nurse . . . why do I want to say 'Winnie-the-Pooh'?"

"It's a book. One of Alexa's favorites. You're picking up Zanna's memories again. Winnie's a bear. And *this* bear is Ingavar's ancestor, remember. Part of him is in me. Try to have a bit more respect."

"Just answer the question."

"It doesn't matter how the bear is saved as long as Guinevere's influence is dominant. What's crucial is that she strengthens the bond between them, so he'll come to her aid when she needs him at the island." He stroked one of Thoran's small brown ears. "Gretel, remove the thorn."

Shrugging her shoulders, the potions dragon fluttered down and studied the wound. With a quick burst of fire she burned down the pustules and cauterized the flesh. Then, with an accurate pinch, she pulled the thorn out whole.

"But if Gwilanna's somewhere else in time," Rosa pressed, "he won't have a reason to *be* at the island. It's because of her that he swims out to sea with Guinevere. If Gwilanna's not around, will Guinevere even catch Gawain's fire tear, let alone drop it into the ocean?"

"She has to," David muttered. "Or Scuffenbury is lost. We'll have no ice cap and we'll have no bears. No Liz, no Lucy . . ." He glanced at Gretel. "No Pennykettle dragons. Maybe no me."

Gretel pretended not to hear that. *Hrrr*, she said, to alert them to the fact that Guinevere was coming back.

Rosa looked up and saw Guinevere running through the trees, clutching a handful of spongy green leaves. But as the girl broke fully into the clearing, the world seemed to tilt and motion slowed and all color became a blur of gray. The effect only lasted a moment. But when Rosa shook her head and her vision cleared, she saw not Guinevere coming toward her but a small pack of long-legged, thin-faced dogs.

"David!" she screamed. By then the first dog was flying through the air. Rosa fell back with her hands instinctively clamped to its throat, its gritty fur chafing the centers of her palms. It was lean and bony with little forward thrust, but the sight of blood on its needle-like fangs was a powerful aid to Rosa's grip. How long she could hold it, she couldn't be sure. The beast had a frenzied desire to kill, and the putrid stench from its open throat was rapidly making her insides fold. Grimacing, she turned her face aside and screamed for David again. Saliva dripped onto her exposed neck. Claws paddled and tore at her clothing. In a moment of panic it suddenly occurred to her she could not reach the mark on her arm and thereby save herself with magicks. Of greater concern was the feeling that the mark might not be there, for she couldn't sense Zanna in her consciousness now, only Rosa, the orphan girl from Co:pern:ica, who had stepped through fire to enter this world and who could, at any moment, die in it.

Then David came to the rescue. With a mighty thump, the dog was sent flying into the treetops, batted away by the paw of the bear he called Ingavar. One more was bitten and another mauled. Any more with any sense faded into the woods.

David switched back to human form and knelt down quickly beside Rosa. "Did it scratch you? Are you hurt?" He scanned her body. Some clothing was torn but she appeared unscathed.

She sat up and threw her arms around him. She was breathing too fast, but still managing to speak. "Tell me this is all just a horrible dream and we can go home to Co:pern:ica and put some books in order."

He placed his hand on the back of her head and let his mouth rest on the fabric of her top. Resisting the urge to kiss her, he said, "You're safe now. That's all that matters."

But it wasn't. And she had to tell him. "I can't feel Zanna anymore." She glanced along her arm. The mark was gone. With it, she sensed some hope had, too.

She felt him sway. Her grip tightened a little. "Are you okay?"

"I don't know. I feel . . . strange."

Momentarily, she closed her eyes. Then she pulled away, stroking one hand down his arm as if she needed to convince herself he was still real. "What happened just now? One moment Guinevere was running toward me, then those horrible . . . *things* appeared."

"Wolves," he said. "At least, they used to be."

She stared at the corpse that Ingavar had mauled. During the attack she had seen very little of the creature's face, only its jaws and high pointed ears. Now she understood what David meant. Part of the memories she'd gathered from Zanna contained images of things Zanna called "grotesques," ugly stone figures built onto churches. This wolf bore a mild resemblance to them. There were helical swellings at the side of its head and even small wings sprouting out of its back.

David crouched beside the wolf and lifted a wing. "Vestigial," he said.

She shrugged. The word meant nothing to her.

"A leftover trace from a line of evolution. Except I don't think this happened over millions of years. This wolf is an experiment. It's been crossbred with a darkling."

"A darkling?" Rosa felt a shiver of fear run through her. "But they don't exist on this timepoint, do they?"

"Look around. What do you notice?"

"The trees," she said eventually. "The trees look different. Have we *moved*?"

"No, but other things have. The timeline has altered."

The blur, she thought. *That peculiar tug.*

David stood up and turned a full circle. "We're fixed to this point because we're visitors here, but everything indigenous to the Earth has changed."

"So in this timeframe, Guinevere doesn't exist?"

"She can exist, but she might not be found in this place. The same is true of Gretel and Thoran." Who, like Guinevere, had both disappeared.

"And Gawain," Rosa muttered, looking back the way they'd come — the way she *thought* they'd come. There was no sign of the last true dragon. Or David's horse. Or, more worryingly, her unicorn, Terrafonne. "Do you think Gwilanna has him?"

"Well, he certainly isn't dead. I can feel his auma. It's radiating out from somewhere close — probably the island. Even though the legend is bound to have changed, it will gravitate to its original setting."

"So what are we waiting for? Let's go. Let's track him down. If we find Gawain, you can bet we find Gwilanna."

"Yes, but do we want to?" he muttered. He crouched and stared at the woodland floor. "Gwilanna might not be the whole cause of this."

"She must be. She has the tornaq."

"This is not Groyne's work. Groyne is just an agent of time. She will have used him to hunt for one of Gawain's claws, maybe even the isoscele. Nothing else would have the power to stir the Earth. But why would she go this far . . . ?" He put a hand flat to the ground.

"David, what are you doing? What are you feeling for?"

"Gaia," he said. "The fire is ascending. The whole *core* of the Earth is realigning. . . ."

Rosa pushed her hands back through her hair. "David, you're not making any sense. What are you *babbling* about?"

"I can answer that for you," said a voice.

Rosa whipped around. David jumped up, ready to

protect her. But he did not assume his ice bear form and Rosa knew he was just too stunned to attack. Sitting on the unicorn that had carried them across the nexus was none other than Lucy Pennykettle. On the horse that David had ridden was Tam Farrell. On foot, and quickly surrounding David and Rosa, was a party of unknown beings. They had the physique of ordinary men, but . . .

David stared at the girl he had known as Lucy. "In the name of Godith, what have they done to you?"

She had gone the same way as the wolf. A human girl with a darkling imprint. Tam was the same, but slightly less recognizable. "Don't try to resist," he said. "We've coded the auma from the bear known as Thoran. His threat is nullified. You cannot escape the Shadow."

Two of the darkling men stepped forward. They grasped David's arms and sniffed him as if he was just fresh meat. "Coded," he said. "Interesting choice of word. I would have used 'corrupted.'" He looked at Lucy again.

She gave the unicorn's mane a short, sharp tug, making the animal whinny and rear. "The Pri:magon is expecting you." She barked an order at the men as she rode. "Bring them."

2. WAYWARD CRESCENT, SCRUBBLEY

I materialized in the kitchen, the room my mother usually referred to as the "center of operations" in the Pennykettle household. On the fridge top was the listening dragon, Elizabeth's "radar" for anything and everything that happened in the house. For the listener, like everyone else, the suspension of time had been no more than a blink. It wasn't surprised to see me in the kitchen and must have assumed that I'd run in from the garden. I spoke a word of greeting and dashed upstairs, almost tripping over Bonnington on the landing. I poked my head around the door of the Den and saw G'reth, the wishing dragon, shaking his head as if trying to remove some fluff from his ear. Then I heard a voice from Elizabeth's bedroom. Arthur whispering, "Please, no . . ."

I ran in. Elizabeth was lying on the bed. Arthur was

kneeling on the floor, reaching over her, pressing a nightdress to her tummy. I wasn't sure if Gwilanna had cut her or not. There were clothes and coat hangers on the floor, as if someone had fought their way out of the wardrobe. The dressing-table mirror was shattered so badly that only one piece of glass was hanging in the frame. Pieces of clay were scattered about the floor. I noticed the clock on the bedside table. 3:15:22. And at the foot of the bed, curled up dead, her face contorted by fear, was Gwilanna.

"Arthur," I said.

He turned. His eyes were as sad as a kitten's. "She's gone," he said. "She's gone. She's . . ."

And then the timeline changed, just as it had for David and Rosa in their where and their when in the woodlands of Iunavik. Everything blurred and the room readjusted. The furniture disappeared, the curtains with it. The pastel wallpapers faded away, replaced by violet painted walls. A rack of lights shone down from the ceiling, illuminating a large, unfinished sculpture on a turntable in the center of the room. The room was cold, on the point of freezing. The sculpture seemed to be made from ice.

A woman walked in. She was clearly Elizabeth, though her hair was considerably shorter. One eye was violet, the other green. "Hey," she said kindly, "you shouldn't be in here without a sweater on, at least."

I held the hem of my T-shirt out in front of me and stared at the fabric for several seconds.

"Agawin, are you okay?" she said.

Agawin. I looked up, feeling my face. "Am I . . . a boy again?"

She laughed and said, "Sweetheart, you've always been a boy."

"My wings?" I whirled around, trying to see them.

"You are funny," she said, laughing. And from nowhere she had a sweater in her hands, compressed and ready to slip over my head.

"Where's Arthur?" I was almost panting.

"In the kitchen, at his food bowl, where he usually is."

"His food bowl?"

She shrugged. "A cat has to eat."

She stepped forward and drowned me in wool for a second.

"Arthur's a *cat*?!"

She pushed my hair from my eyes as I stretched my arms straight. "Four legs, a lot of whiskers, and a curly tail. Still blind in one eye. You've been having those timeline dreams again, haven't you?"

I didn't know what to say. My memories of Alexa and Yolen, and the seer's apprentice I had been so long ago, were fading away like lights in fog. This . . . altered reality . . . seemed to be all that mattered now. But one name was still very prominent in my head.

"Muh —" I began, then changed my mind. This was Elizabeth, not Zanna (and where was *she* now?). "Grand . . . ma . . . ?"

"*Hmm?*"

At least I'd got that right. "Tell me about Gwilanna."

"Great-*aunt* Gwilanna," she tutted. "She'll think you impolite if you refer to her so bluntly. What about her?"

"Is she alive?"

"I beg your pardon?"

There was a fluttering sound and a firebird flew in. It landed on the table beside the sculpture. It was not as big as Gideon or any I'd seen before, more the size and color of a Pennykettle dragon. A stunning shade of green with turquoise ear tufts. *Rrrh?* it went, through its elongated beak.

Elizabeth said, "It's all right, Gryffen. Agawin seems to have stepped out of the wrong side of his sleep chamber this morning. You can go back to your tree."

Rrrh, went Gryffen. And he zipped out again.

Elizabeth took my hand and swung it. "Would you like to see a counselor? You seem to be on another planet this morning."

"Co:pern:ica?" I said, a little uncertainly.

She blinked at me, uncertain whether she should smile or not. "Is Co:pern:ica the world in your comix?"

This wasn't going well. So I laughed out loud (as convincingly as I could). "Only joking. Got you, Grandma."

"Phew," she sighed falsely, flapping a hand. "You nearly had me worried there for a moment. You and that big imagination of yours."

"Sorry." I tightened my hand around hers. "So . . . you were saying — about Aunty Gwilanna?"

"Well, she's on her way. That's all I can tell you. I had a :com yesterday to say she's . . . close. I hope I get this finished in time."

"In time for what?"

"Her birth day, silly."

"Sorry," I said again. "Brain's gone to sleep. I'm a bit . . . cold now." Colder than she knew. Almost freezing in terror. Something to do with the way she'd said "birth day."

She slipped her arms around me. "Come here," she whispered, giving me a hug. She turned me to face the sculpture. "What do you think? Coming along, isn't it?"

"*Mmm*," I said. About a quarter of the ice block now had form, but I didn't have any idea what it was. At the risk of being sent to a "counselor," I said, "So . . . ?"

"It's a gathering of angels," she said. "I've got a name for it, too. A really good name. Do you want to hear it?"

More than she knew.

She squeezed herself together, in the way people do when they're pleased with themselves. She was so very pretty when she spread her mouth and smiled. "In the old tongue it would translate as 'the fire that melts no ice.'"

"And in the new tongue?" I tentatively asked.

She walked forward and unveiled a temporary plaque. On it was written Isenfier.

3. Capture

It wasn't just men and wolves. On the long trek down to the shores of the sea, David saw birds, rodents, and even a wild deer displaying signs of the darkling template. Some of them had wings (the deer did not), but those that did — like a mouse he spotted turning worried circles — appeared to have no use for them or no idea what the wings were for. Many animals lay dead or rotting in the foliage, all of which was losing its shades of green. Like the animals, the plants were physically changing. He saw leaves without symmetry. Roots knotted aboveground. Flowers that stank of something unholy. As the party reached the edge of the wood, a long gray vine with helical nodules snaked down from the trees and fixed itself around Rosa's neck. She screamed and was heard by Tam, who galloped forward and chopped the vine through with a knife.

"Take the rest of it off her," Lucy said. "The Pri:magon won't be happy if she thinks the girl's lost any auma to the Shadow." The nodules were oozing a gooey black fluid.

"So the Shadow got clear," David said. "And infected everyone at Scuffenbury Hill. But why has it drawn you here? Why has it pulled you back through time . . . ?"

Lucy angled the unicorn toward him. "Scuffenbury," she said. It wasn't a question.

He let his mouth form into a smile. "Of course, you won't remember the battle. Or the 'Pri:magon' won't allow you to. That's what playing with dragon claws does for you. Think back, Lucy. Somewhere in that strangely inverted mind you'll find a better place." He let his gaze drop, inviting her to follow. With the toe of one boot he had scratched the number 42 in the soil around his feet. He saw a flicker of movement in her eyes. The first hint of confusion. The first sign that he might have a chance of saving her. "Wayward Crescent," he whispered.

She looked up fiercely. "My name is not Lucy. I have no name. I only exist to serve the Pri:magon."

"No, you don't," he said, which earned him a thwack across the head from Tam.

"No talking," Tam said. "Move."

By now the sea had come into view: a widespread, unsettled slate of gray, fixed between a characterless sky and land. It was raining as they made the descent. Rosa, whose footwear was barely adequate for the slippery terrain, lost her footing because of the enforced pace and had to suffer the ignominy of being slung across a shoulder and carried the rest of the way down. On the flat, they entered what had once been a village, though, rather like the mammals with wings, the darkling people seemed to have no awareness of what to do with their dilapidated shacks. They were moving in clusters, scavenging for food. A whole crew of them were using their bare, clawed hands to tear at what had once been a whale. David and Rosa were ushered through quickly, into fishing boats oared by the men under Lucy's command. Rosa was planted back-to-back against David. As the rain lashed down and the boat struck open water, she whispered over her shoulder to him, "Where are we going?"

"The island," David said. "I'm guessing it's around that headland." He nodded across the water, even though she couldn't see from where she was sitting.

"Can't you do anything?"

"There are too many of them. And Tam and Lucy are still there under that . . . façade. The only way to free them is to get to Gwilanna and reverse all this."

"Hmph. Easy as that. Remind me to brush my hair before the showdown."

That brought an irritated sigh from his chest. "You know, you really are more like Suzanna than you realize."

Rosa shivered and shook the wet hair off her face. "Suzanna? Why did you call her that?"

"It's her name, Rosa."

"But you *never* call her that. Why here? Why now?"

"I don't know," he said. "I was . . . thinking about Alexa. And Suzanna sounds more . . ."

"Feminine?"

"Motherly."

"Oh." Rosa looked away, over the ocean. The boat hit a wave and bumped them apart for a second. "Do you think Alexa will be at the island?"

"I hope not. I hope she got away."

"What about us?"

"Us?" he said as a rower struck an elbow against his knee and growled in fury at losing his rhythm.

"You! Seven! Keep rowing," barked Tam.

The darkling growled and heaved at the oar.

Rosa waited for the fuss to settle, then whispered again, "We, or rather 'they,' were at Scuffenbury Hill. David and Zanna. I know you have this ability to flit between timepoints, but what about her? Am I going to see *her*? Won't that create a massive paradox?"

"Only if you touch."

"What happens if we do?"

"You two!" This time it was Lucy shouting. She turned, stern-faced, to Tam. "I said they weren't to talk. Separate them."

"What happens if I touch her?" Rosa hissed again as Tam came forward from the back of the boat. He yanked her upright and told her to be silent. Spray from a loose wave slapped her face but her eyes met David's and she mouthed again, *What happens if I touch her?*

"You'll fade from time."

She had a moment of time to think about that.

Then she was dragged away out of his sight.

4. ERTH

She made angels in this timeline. Angels, not dragons. Flying humans, inspired by the firebirds, she said. She liked to experiment with different kinds of media. Paper. Cardboard. Strangely, not clay. Clay was not appropriate here, she said. She painted them, too. In various states of flight. Hands lifted to the sky. Soft violet in their eyes. Just like the beautiful tapestries of Taan, they hung in every room throughout our "pod." Wherever I looked, a new one would appear. Yet I saw no signs of brushes or paints, even though she was wearing a paint-stained smock. More puzzling still, no hammer or chisel for the Isenfier sculpture. No "stuff" existed at all in the pod. Just us, the firebirds, and Elizabeth's creations. I had yet to see Arthur the cat.

On the second day, after a very long sleep, she sensed

I was finding the pod confusing and asked if I'd like to use the tele:computer.

The *tele:computer*?

"Where is it?" I asked.

"Right here," she said.

There, taking up the whole of one wall, was a huge screen. How, I wondered, could I have missed it?

"Watch for as long as you want to," she said. She tousled my hair and straightened a piece just above my ear. "You know where to find me."

As she drifted away, a gradient of colors swept across the screen, leaving behind a small row of icons. I stepped forward and touched an image of a pod. Its title was simply HOME.

It told me I lived at Wayward Crescent, in the "burrow" of Scrubbley, "position" 42. A clock with a dateline faded up. The year was the same as the one I'd left behind, right down to the nearest second (for some reason, I seemed to instinctively know it).

42.

Wayward Crescent.

Scrubbley.

3:15 and 22 seconds.

Home.

Next to "Home" was a flashing icon of a planet. Blue one moment, gray the next, but not keeping to any regular pattern. The wording underneath was flickering, too, between "Earth" and the slight alternative, "Erth." I prodded it with a finger.

The icon stayed gray. The screen came back with a strange message:

Information pending

I pressed again, trying to turn the planet blue.

The icon stayed gray.

Then flickered again.

Gray.

Flicker.

Gray.

Flicker.

Information pending

"Grandma, this isn't working," I shouted.

I looked over my shoulder. She wasn't there.

But on the opposite wall, sitting on the floor like a misplaced vase, was a brown tabby cat.

"Arthur?" I said.

Brrr-up? the cat replied, sounding peeved.

Not Arthur, then.

He flicked an ear. A triangular piece was missing from it.

"I know you," I whispered.

N-yeh, he burbled.

But no matter how I tried, the name wouldn't come to me.

Suddenly, two firebirds went flying past, drawing my gaze away from the cat. When I looked again the cat wasn't there.

Nor the screen.

Annoyed, I went in search of the firebirds and quickly found myself in Elizabeth's room, though how I'd got there I couldn't say. I seemed to be floating around the pod. I had no memory of the room I'd come from or of the layout of the rooms nearby. Time was all the while passing, I thought, but all I ever had was the feeling of "now."

Elizabeth was sitting on a cushion on the floor, facing the sculpture, six feet away. She had her legs crossed over, the way I'd seen Arthur Merriman meditate. Her thumbs were making a circle with her fingers. Her eyes were closed, but she knew I was there.

"Shh," she said gently. "Don't speak, Agawin. Not while the birds are busy."

I saw then how the magick happened. She was picturing the carving in her head. And through some means of interspecies telepathy, three birds were using short bursts of fire to melt away the ice that wasn't needed. They were working on the base of it, creating what looked like a sleeping dog. Though it was large for a dog. A bear, perhaps.

Elizabeth shook her shoulders and let out a single puff of air.

The birds stopped working and came to hover in a line in front of her.

"Thank you," she said.

Rrrh, they went, and zipped out of the room.

She extended a flappy hand sideways to me.

"You okay, Grandma?" She looked a little tired.

"Yes," she said. "I'm very happy here. But I can only concentrate for so long. Then the tiredness comes and they make me stop."

"Who?" I asked. "Who makes you stop?"

She smiled and tugged at the ends of my fingers. "Are you having a good day?"

I wasn't really sure. What made a good day, here? "Grandma, can I ask you something?"

"Anything you like."

And it should have been about the cat or the screen, but I heard myself saying, "Where are . . . the others?"

"Others?" she said.

"I can't remember their names, but I know there were others." I was sure I'd shared this pod with *someone*.

She looked at me kindly. The green in her left eye grew a little brighter. "The others will come for you when they're ready. I think they've sent you here because they know you'll be safe."

Or they'd made a terrible mistake. If Gwilanna was coming, I must be on my guard. I had to *warn* someone . . . Henry? Joseph? *Joseph Henry*. Yes, that was it. That was the name. But how?

I was almost punching the air with my thoughts when an idea struck me. "Grandma, is the listener still in the kitchen?"

"Probably," she said. "Why do you want to know?"

"Just . . . y'know, curious."

She looked past me to the door. A gray-haired cat had just strolled in, different from the one with the damaged ear. This one had a black patch of fur across one eye and walked with a slight, left-sided limp. He padded straight past me and curled into her lap, meowing as she smoothed her hand along its back. "It's all right, Arthur, I'm with you," she whispered. And she hummed a gentle lullaby to it. And the walls of the pod responded to the sound and began to glow with life-sized scenes.

I saw a beautiful red-haired girl, singing along while she tended her goats. Then the same girl on a mountaintop, a sudden explosion of light in her hands. And again on the back of a huge brown bear, emptying that same light into an ocean. Then there was ice as far as I could see and as many white bears as the ice could hold. All of them squinted proudly at Elizabeth. They planted their claws and held their heads high, but in their hearts I knew they were bowing to her.

A single drop of water ran down the ice sculpture and dripped with a fiery plink onto the table.

And I wanted to cry and cry and cry.

"Grandma, what does this *mean*?" I begged.

She stroked Arthur's head and finished her song. "Isn't it time you were in bed, Agawin?"

And placing a soft kiss on my head, she carried Arthur out of the room.

5. DARKLING ISLAND

They landed, not on the island itself, but on the curved strip of rocks that joined it to the mainland, only visible when the tide was low. Some leveling had been done on the upper surface to make a passable breakwater. "The Bridge of Souls, how appropriate," David muttered. "You remember the legend, don't you, Tam?" He was being held by Tam while the boat was moored. He nodded back toward the land. "Gwilanna stands on the shore and creates a wave that carries Thoran and Guinevere out to sea. The rest is . . . frozen in the Earth's *proper* history, not in this sordid side-step in time."

The darkling commander looked at him oddly, the growths on his temples straining like warts. He attempted the closest thing to a frown. "You talk too much," he said eventually, and bundled David off the boat, onto steps hewn crudely out of the rocks. Every one was riddled with dark gray weed and the slime from another marine "experiment." Behind him, through the rain, David heard Rosa shouting, "Get your hands off me, you ugly excuse for a human being!"

"She's going to give you trouble, that one," he said.

Tam hauled him up the steps and onto the bridge. "The Pri:magon will deal with her. Walk."

A powerful thump in the center of his back persuaded David to do just that. As he stumbled forward he let his gaze pan across the island. He had seen it before, in its appropriate timeline, locked in ice, mostly blanketed in snow. A place for bears to winter their young. They called it "The Tooth of Ragnar," because its famous tip hooked over like a canine. It was as sacred to the bears as it was to the people who inhabited the north. The legendary resting place of the last known dragon, Gawain.

A plume of fire suddenly erupted from the peak. It boxed with the low cloud hanging overhead, then scrolled into an orange ball and fizzled away. The gray sea arched its back. David looked to the northern shore. The swirling patterns of water there confirmed his worst suspicions.

They had Gawain and they were using him, some-how, to draw out Gaia.

They were working on the Earth's magnetic core.

"How are your hands, Tam?"

"Shut up," he growled. "Or you'll die drinking salt."

"I doubt that," David said, with confidence. "The Pri:magon wouldn't like to lose me, would she?" The darkling man nearest them began to cough. The heat falling back toward the water was bringing down a filmy cloak of ash. The man cursed and spat a lump of phlegm onto the stone. Dotted throughout his murky saliva were small dull spots of yellow sulfur.

"So . . . hands. How are they?" David repeated. "Not the reptilian skin, of course; the chemistry of the inversion doesn't really interest me." Or does it? he wondered, glancing at those spots of sulfur again. Maybe there was a weakness there. He could hear more coughing farther back along the bridge. "It's what's under the skin that matters."

"What are you talking about now?" Tam snarled, betraying a hint of his once-Scottish accent.

David stopped abruptly. They bumped together, eye to alien eye. "Under the skin," he said again quietly, looking as deep into Tam as he could. "We were allies once, Tam and Ingavar. I gave you a gift to help you kill darklings. All you have to do is look for it."

With a rasp of steel, Tam brought out a knife. It was pressing at the border of David's neck when Lucy bellowed, "Stand down! Now!"

Tam growled, showing his changing teeth. The enamel, David noticed, was already breaking up, splitting into the familiar darkling "needles."

"Now!" Lucy barked.

Tam stood aside, kicking a dead fish back into the sea. The tide had dropped them all along the bridge. One or two men were scooping them up, eating the heads and throwing the rest back. Ravens, likewise, were dropping like stones, helping to clear the path ahead.

"That must hurt — being told what to do," David said. He ran a hand inside his collar, relieved, perhaps, that Tam had not cut him. "Then again, she was always feisty. It's the dragon in her. She'll never be entirely rid of it — agh!"

Lucy's fist came up and struck across his cheek, almost rearranging his top row of teeth. "One more word from you and I'll kill you myself."

David straightened up and looked her in the eye. A trail of blood was running down his cheek. A gift from the calluses spread across her knuckles. "Gwendolen sends her love," he ventured.

And thankfully she didn't kill him. She made a muted gesture at Tam, and David was made to start walking again.

At the junction between the bridge and the island, a wooden ramp had been laid to even out the final part of the join. The drumbeat of approaching men brought others running from the bluffs and crags like ants spilling from a hole in the ground. Still the rain came sweeping down. The darklings seemed oblivious to it and lined the rocks to watch and sneer, clinging to the wetted surfaces like lizards. An unsettled rumble from the belly of the island signaled another belch of fire. Nearly all the darklings coughed. Several of them turned and spat at the mountain. David, wondering how Rosa was coping, tried to look over his shoulder for her. Another whack to the back of his head kept him focused on the path in front. They were heading for an opening where the slope was less steep. Until then it had been hidden from view by fallen rocks and the angle of approach. Tam went in first, dipping his head, even though the space was high enough for him. Two of the party grabbed David's arms. They flung him through the hole but didn't follow. Shortly afterward Rosa was hustled in as well, followed by Lucy, pushing all the way.

Lucy strolled on ahead. "Pri:magon, we have them. They were in the woodland, where you predicted."

Tam grabbed Rosa and hauled her into line beside David. He shoved them forward as one.

To David's surprise they had entered a hollow. It obeyed the shape of the island so well that he wondered if the layers of granite and earth had been plastered onto a conical bubble. For once, there was an element of color present. The ragged walls of the chamber were glowing amber, reflecting a pool of clinkery lava swirling in a crater at the center of the void. David glanced upward, wondering at first how the heat and fumes were being channeled away from the island floor. Then he realized this was no ordinary fire. There was an element of natural magma present, but it was heavily mixed with dragon auma. A violent *blup!* made Rosa squeal. She gripped his arm and said, "We've got to get out of here. If that explodes, we'll all be dead!"

"Clearly, you know nothing about dragons," said a voice. As if to demonstrate that, the pool was sucked loudly into the crater. A second later, a column of air and gas was ejected toward the dome of the island. It ignited before it hit the open air and swirled around the walls of a man-made caldera before escaping into the sky. The interior rock face shook like a tissue. Already, cracks were beginning to show.

A figure moved through the shadows. A woman, dressed in a floor-length gown, pinched at the waist by a knotted cord. She had long wild hair and her feet were bare.

Tam and Lucy knelt to her, bowing their heads.

David said, "Rosa's right, Gwilanna. The island is unstable. It *will* be destroyed if you —"

The woman began to laugh. "Oh, David. Has it been that long?"

She stepped forward into the light.

And David saw her altered face, but the bangles gave her away to him first.

Rosa gasped and covered her mouth.

A darkling clone was standing before them.

Not Gwilanna at all.

Zanna.

6. GANZFELD

I didn't go to bed. I didn't feel tired. I went chasing out of Elizabeth's room, thinking I would run downstairs to the kitchen. I wanted to speak to the listening dragon.

But as soon as I emerged, I realized I hadn't seen a stair since I'd been here. I looked left and right. There wasn't even a door. Then I heard a gentle muffled sound and saw the brown tabby cat in the floor space ahead of me, the one with the damaged ear. He was sitting down, scratching his collar with a paw. "You must know the way to the kitchen," I said.

He looked up and frowned, the way cats do.

"Bowl," I suggested. "Food."

That did it.

N-yeh, said the cat. With a twitch of his whiskers, he turned and trotted away.

I followed him — or rather the tink of his bell, for the cat himself was always too far ahead. All I saw now and then was a flash of its tail. Doors opened up where they hadn't done before. Walls changed color. Lights came on. A potted plant with red and green leaves appeared (KOLEUS written on a label in the soil). Tele:screen images flashed up on the walls. The first I saw was a stuttering lecture about the history of the planet Erth. I glanced sideways at it as I ran. A man in a plain white suit was explaining that a change of timeline did not have to disrupt the advance of learning. In our particular history, for instance, a stroke of serendipity had brought the discovery of electricity and the invention of silicon-based circuitry much closer together. Since "our" seventeenth century, technology had grown at a furious pace. Thanks to this, the Pearlygates Interactive Tele:computer was now a feature of every . . .

I ran on. I had almost lost the sound of the bell.

The second time I saw a tele:screen, I did.

It felt as if I'd been following the cat for hours. Yet the only time I could think of was "now."

3:15:22

No bell. I paused for breath. In front of me, another tele:screen lit. A documentary feature about firebirds.

Likewise, said a slow voice-over, *every species on Erth has experienced a changed evolutionary path. Some for better. Some for worse. One of those that have come to major prominence, of course, is the firebird. Here we see three, in their natural aerie. What draws them to structures such as this isn't clear.* An image of a giant building appeared. It had thousands of square-shaped windows, all identically spaced apart. I knew that I knew this place — but from where? The camera zoomed in and came to rest on a cream-colored firebird with apricot ear tufts. *Females*, said the voice, *like this fine example, are often attended by two or more males.* A grumpy-looking red one was in the window to her right; a mild-mannered green one in the window on her left. *Rrrh!* went the red one, making the female jump. She leaned forward and squinted — at the lens, or at me?

"Who are you?" I asked.

But the screen had cleared, and the next thing on it was a series of schematic diagrams, aiming to describe how the birds had evolved their strange ability to generate fire. *By filtering small quantities of hy:drogen from water and collecting it in tonsillar sacs in the throat, these highly intelligent birds are able to throw a jet of flame by rapidly expelling the stored gas. What benefit this has is not entirely clear, for the birds appear to have no natural predators. And their extraordinary progress does not end there. Evidence has recently come to light of another remarkable physical development....* Up came another set of images, which appeared to predict that the next stage of firebird evolution might be a hardening of their feathers into scales. *Were we to extrapolate from here*, said the voice, almost beside itself with scholarly excitement, *who knows what magical creature might result....* The beak morphed into an extended jaw. The tail feathers coalesced into a kind of whip. The wings grew out into powerful canopies. Small arms emerged from the breast. A glint pinged out of a jeweled eye. A burst of white fire clouded the screen.

"Dragon," I breathed.

Hrrr, went a voice.

I jumped around.

In front of me was a tall white refrigerator. Two doors, top and bottom, hinged to the right. On top of the fridge sat the thing I'd come to find: the listening dragon.

It was, as my mind had expected it to be, tall and green and spiky and cute. It had trumpet-shaped nostrils, large oval eyes, a wide curling tail, and flattish back feet.

And the most enormous petal-like ears.

It smiled, almost ruefully, and looked down at the fridge.

"Should I open it?" I asked.

The dragon sniffed. It looked around and drummed its claws.

I reached for the top door and pulled it open.

On the middle shelf of three was a small box.

Meow, said a voice from the floor.

I pushed the door half closed and looked down.

The cat I'd been following was sitting beside an empty food bowl. It flicked its ears when it saw I'd noticed it.

I opened the door again and took out the box. It didn't look big enough to store any food. All I found inside was a folded piece of paper.

It said WRONG DOOR.

The listening dragon shrugged.

I put the box away and opened the bottom refrigerator door.

A blast of icy air swept out. As it cleared, I saw an amazing scene inside. A young polar bear was sitting on a sheet of ice, with water lapping gently in front of him — an image more real than anything I'd watched on a tele:screen. I felt that if I climbed inside the fridge I would hear the crunch of ice underfoot. I shivered and rubbed my arms. "Who are you? What is this world?"

The ice bear tipped his head to one side. His small brown eyes were packed with wonder. "This is Ki:mera," he said. His voice was gruff, but as sharp as the pale blue sky around him. "My name is Avrel. I am the Teller of Ways."

"Ways?" I asked.

"Legends," he said.

I thought about this. "Are you here to tell a story?"

He tilted his head to the opposite side. "You *are* the story, Agawin. And we have been waiting for you." A slight wind swept across him, tugging at his fur. A host of bears was behind him now, sitting, paws together, like the cat by his food bowl, as if they had an appointment with destiny.

"What do you want me to do?" I whispered. I feared this perfect image might crack if my voice was raised any louder than that.

Between his feet, a book appeared. The pages flickered until the wind dropped. On one leaf was a beautiful sketch of the listening dragon. I recognized the ears, even though the drawing was upside down to me. On the opposite page was what looked like a scorch mark. Avrel blew on the book. It turned right around.

"You must lead us to Ingavar," he said.

I looked at the mark. On the page, it was just a simple squiggle: a wavy line with a shorter line through it, thicker at one end, finished in a slight triangular spike. It looked like it might have been a signature. The longer I looked the more structured it appeared, until I could see real depth in it and something began to trigger in me. A memory of a language.

Dragontongue.

"Agawin, where are you?" Elizabeth's voice. She sounded close. Very slightly concerned.

I closed the fridge door, shutting out the bears. The cat's food bowl vanished. The cat himself was twizzling his ears, trying to locate where the voice was coming from. He scuttled away, low down, looking guilty. Likewise, the listening dragon gulped, as if he should not have been a party to this. He dibbled a paw and disappeared in a blink. The fridge he'd been sitting on disappeared with him.

"Ah, there you are." Elizabeth slipped her hand around my shoulder. We were back in a plain square room again. Warm pink walls. Friendly. Soothing. The kind of place where an active mind might put away any worrying thoughts and drift on an ocean of eternal calm. I smiled at Elizabeth and she at me. The firebird Gryffen landed on her shoulder. He poked his inquisitive gaze here and there, but I was fairly sure he had seen nothing. Already, my memories of the bears were fading, but I was clinging to that mark as though my life depended on it — or someone else's did. For in that very thin slice of time, that tiny shudder in the unity of "now," I had managed to find a translation. With it came a whole new raft of meaning. I had unwrapped a very great secret. I had seen the name of the listening dragon. I held Elizabeth's hand and repeated the name over and over in my mind.

Ganzfeld.

Ganzfeld.

Ganzfeld.

7. THE ILLUMINATION OF GWILANNA

Y ou look surprised," Zanna said, squaring up to David. "Or do my gothic roots still make you cringe? Suits me, don't you think? The dark. The Shadow."

He stared at the crusted scales on her cheeks. The coils at her temples. The row of thorns on the back of each hand. In some ways, she did look strangely alluring. But the Ix in her would always be repellent to the Fain in him. "You're not her," he said quietly. "You're not Zanna."

She flicked a spiteful glance at Rosa, who could do little more than gulp and shy away. "Am I beautiful, Commander?"

"Yes," said Tam.

"Would you die for me and give me your *shade*?"

"I would." He touched a hand to his darkling heart.

Zanna stepped forward, dabbing a finger at the trickle of blood on David's cheek. "Would you desert me in the heat of a battle?"

"Never, Pri:magon."

David tried to look away, but she caught his chin and applied enough sideways pressure to make him face her again. "Hear that, David? He wouldn't run away." She angled her dark lips close to his. "He wouldn't disappear across a huge time nexus, leaving me and my friends to fend for ourselves."

"I warned you things would be different," he said, trying not to flinch as her nails dug in.

Burying a snort in the back of her throat, she brought her mouth up close to his ear. "Don't try to be brave. The war is won. The Shadow controls this part of the nexus. Very soon we'll have the rest — and more." He heard the slither of her darkling tongue. "Now, be a good Fain and tell me what you've done with Alexa. . . ."

He thought about this, then whispered back, "Shouldn't you be asking Gwilanna that? Where is the evil old witch by the way?"

"Pri:magon, the dragon is rising," said Lucy.

Zanna pulled away and turned toward the crater. "Behold, David, the last dragon on Earth!"

"*Hhh!*" gasped Rosa as Gawain's studded head emerged from the lava pool, followed by his wings and the rest of his body. Lava ran away in runnels down his breast, making crowns of fire where it dripped into the pool. He was an adult now, as wild and impressive as a dragon could be. He was showing no obvious darkling mutations, but the green had leached from his scales and wings and there was no hint of violet in his tortured eyes. He was the antithesis of all his kind.

A black dragon.

He stared at the newcomers in the chamber. When he saw David, his optical triggers contracted in a rush and he reared back, flaring his smoking nostrils. A jet of fire burst from his gaping mouth, split into forks by his enormous fangs. Even David must have feared being turned to ash. But the blast hit an unseen barrier between them and dispersed in harmless scribbles of flame. Gawain extended his wings to their fullest and with a whip of his tail went spiraling around his invisible cell.

"Impressive," David said, blowing out the air his lungs had been grasping. He brushed Rosa's hand to check how she was. Her auma was off the scale. "Not only infected but imprisoned as well."

"Better for you that he is," growled Zanna. "Oh, and in case you were thinking of trying, you can't commingle with him through the field."

"What have you done to him?" Rosa demanded. "Why is he in that . . . place?"

"Like you care," said Lucy, showing her teeth. "He's nothing but a myth in your imagineered world."

"Better a myth than a servant to *you*."

"He's digging," David put in quickly, trying to defuse any further conflict. He raised his hands in mock surrender and stepped up to the point where the fire had petered out. He prodded the force field, making it dent. Gawain put his dark head forward and roared.

I know, I know, David said in his thoughts. *I will get you out of there. But why are you so very angry with me? And how have they gained control of you . . . ?*

"Digging?" Rosa said, as if she'd eaten something sour.

"I use the term loosely," David muttered, looking at the glowing rocks in the crater. "They're trying to reach into the Fire Eternal. Nothing but a dragon could cope with the heat." He turned and rattled a question at Zanna. "How are you making him work for you? A dragon would rather go into stasis than give itself up to the Ix:Collective."

Zanna threw him an all-knowing smile. "If I *was* to allow you to commingle with him, David, you'd find that he's not completely . . . himself. You mentioned Gwilanna just now."

The color drained from David's face. He flashed another look at the dragon's eyes. "She's *illumined* — to Gawain?"

"A marriage made here, on the peak of the island, under the light of a crescent moon. Just like it always was in legend."

"In your dreams," snarled Rosa. "What have you done with Guinevere and Thoran?"

"Will you keep *that* under control?" Zanna barked.

Tam found a piece of cloth and snapped it tight between his hands. "Be warned, girl. Next time, I gag you."

"And Gretel," David added quickly. "What about Gretel? No room in this world for your potions dragon, *Pri:magon*?"

"Gone," she said, without remorse. "Written out of time. All of them. Elizabeth Pennykettle included."

She gestured at Tam to put David back with Rosa again.

David raised his hands and rejoined Rosa without the need for force. "That's not possible. I can feel the auma of Thoran within me."

"A weak Ki:meran echo," Zanna said. "A hangover from your Travels across the nexus. Try it, David. Try to shift into Ingavar. You must have felt him fading when you battled the wolves. The same goes for Grockle, your tame dragon. In this timeline, your connection to him is nonexistent."

Rosa shifted her feet, hopeful, perhaps, that David would change and fight their way out of there. But as it became clear that he wasn't going to risk it, she vented her feelings about Zanna instead. "Why me?" she hissed at him, under her breath.

"Shush," he said from the corner of his mouth. "They're not joking about the gag."

But she wouldn't give up. "Why *me* who fades out of time and not her?"

"What are you talking about?" Zanna snapped.

"We're confused," David said, loud enough to drown Rosa out. "If Liz was lost when the timeline altered, how do you explain the presence of Lucy?"

The darkling girl raised her chin.

"Or you, for that matter?"

"Lucy was selected. Like Tam. Like me. All of us were taken from Scuffenbury Hill and reinserted at this timepoint to aid the inversion."

"Inversion?" said Rosa.

"Do you repeat *everything* you hear?" growled Lucy.

"Let's come back to the 'inversion,'" David said quickly. "Tell me about Gwilanna and the . . . selection process."

Zanna pressed her hands together, making the bangles slip down her arm. Her scar was still prominent, but the lines were dark and scabbed right over. The darkling infection had tried to erase them, but had not entirely succeeded, David thought. Perhaps there was still a chance to reach the real Zanna underneath. "With Guinevere gone," she said, "the dragon soon lost his will to live. He settled on the island and watched the moon. We sent Gwilanna to hide among the rocks and wait."

"She caught his *fire tear*?" Rosa scoffed. "No way. It would have burned her inside out."

"His tear was shed though?" David queried.

Zanna nodded.

"Then how did he survive?"

"Because of me," said a voice.

Tam and Lucy stood to attention as a figure dropped down from a ledge above Zanna. A man so full of darkling twists that it was almost impossible to see any true humanity in him. A spiked tail dragged along the floor behind him. Pointed wings rose above his shoulder line.

Zanna turned to the captives and said, "David, Rosa, let me introduce you. This is my betrothed. The Shadow Prime. His name is Voss."

8. A Tale of a Listening Dragon

He could hear the hum of the universe, right down to the space within atoms. That's what Ganzfeld, "the listener," could do. Now I had seen him and learned his name, my memories of him were strong and clear. I remembered how Elizabeth would blow him a kiss every time she opened the refrigerator door. How she would ask him what was happening in the Crescent. How, with one subtle twist of his ears, he would always have some sort of answer for her. The thing that puzzled me most about him was why he'd never been referred to by name. But then, no one had ever asked.

That night, I let the question float in my dreams. And my dreams came back with a surprising answer. I found myself sitting on a pillar of ice, listening to the words of the polar bear Avrel. He had an engaging story to tell. He tipped his snout toward the northern sky. "One night," he began, "Gaia was playing with the dancing lights, when she caught an array of interested stars and joined them together in the shape of a dragon. This pleased her so much that she brought her creation down to the ice. Fearful that the wind would blow him away, she took clay from the land so his body would be solid. She colored him green with grass she had found. She tickled his feet until he drummed them into claws. She pulled his tail until he flicked it into a pleasing arrow. She caught two feathers from a passing bird and stroked them on his back until his wings folded out. Two ribbons of light, one green, one violet, she gave to him next to provide him with eyes. And when the sun came up to chase away the night, she let the first ray enter the dragon's mouth and burn there forever as a spark of fire. Only one thing was missing. Ears. Gaia looked for more stars with which to make them, but the night, by now, had blossomed into morning. She thought of flowers and their beautiful petals. But none were in bloom this far north at that time. Then her dragon did a very strange thing. He jerked his head as if he *could* hear something. He bent forward and touched the ice, then scraped a small chunk of it into his paws. *Hrrr*, he said, (for he could speak, of course). The ridges of his eyes came together in a frown. He held the ice close to his heart, as if he could sense it calling to him. Immediately, a white bear rolled into view. He was padding along with heavy paws as though he wished the ice would swallow him up. When he saw the dragon he staggered to a halt. He squinted in the way that only bears can. Gaia hid behind a nearby ridge, curious to see what this meeting would bring.

"The bear sniffed at the dragon. '*What are you?*' he grunted. His gaze suggested he had seen many dragons, but never one quite as unusual as this.

"The dragon tilted his head to one side.

" 'I am Thoran,' said the bear. 'Who are you?' There was a deal of impatience in his ruffled voice, but it was clearly hiding a mountain of sorrow.

"The dragon tipped his head the opposite way.

"A rumbling tumbling grumbling noise bobbled around in Thoran's throat. He could have walked on or swatted the dragon aside. Instead, he lowered his black-tipped snout and blew a great draft of air across his head. His aim was to clear the creature's hearing, but the result was a lot more lasting than that. His misty breath settled in two fine clouds, which the north wind set in the shape of ears. Magnificent ears. Big and bold. Twice the size of any found on a bear.

"Thoran stood back, wondering how this had happened. Already that day, he had seen a human companion die and break up into flying . . . *fairies*. Now there was this. A little green dragon with ears made out of his grief-stricken breath. What kind of magical world had he entered?

"*Hrrr!* went the dragon.

"Thoran gave a roar and shuffled back. He was not afraid, just mildly puzzled. The dragon had spoken in a strange variation of the usual tongue. In that brief warm puff of air, the creature had described everything Thoran had gone through that day — and the days before. His journey north, his escape with Guinevere, the fire tear that had created the ice they were standing on. What's more, he understood how Thoran was *feeling*.

"'How?' said the great bear. 'How can you know this?'

"*Hrrr!* went the dragon. *I heard your auma.*

"And now it was at work with its nimble paws, flashing away at the nugget of ice it had first scraped up. Somehow the chunk had doubled in size. The dragon split it open and breathed inside. A spark ignited and nestled at its center, yet the ice refused to melt.

"The dragon shaped the ice into a ball again. And it grew again. And again. And *again*. Until it was so large that he could only carry it above his head. *Hrrr*, he said, meaning, *Thank you for the ears. This is for you*. And he lobbed the ball at the mystified bear.

" 'What should I do with it?' Thoran asked. He was looking at the ball and paying no attention to the dragon now. When he looked up, the dragon was drifting away, hand in hand with one of the strange little fairies Guinevere's body had broken into. . . .' "

There, Avrel's story came to an end. In my dream, he began to turn away.

"Wait!" I shouted. "Is this how the listener came to be with Elizabeth?"

Avrel paused and blew a snort of air. "Ganzfeld has always been her guiding force. The others were made in the image of him."

Others. Others. My mind began to spin. "Why did she never speak his name?"

"Because she did not know it and she liked him as he was — her faithful listening dragon."

"Ganzfeld," I said. "Why did he tell me?"

"He wants you to lead us to Ingavar. Since the exchange of ears and snow, bears and dragons have been allies in all things."

"But how does knowing his name help me?"

"To speak his name is to know his power. . . ."

"Ganzfeld!" I shouted, while Avrel watched. "Ganzfeld! GANZFELD!"

The universe hummed — and I woke with a start. I sat up in a room with deep red walls. I was panting and frightened, a little confused. I felt Elizabeth's arm on my shoulder. She crouched down and held me. She was almost in tears. "Oh, Agawin, what have you done?" she whispered.

On the floor stood a row of dragons. I looked at them in turn and knew their names.

G'reth. Gretel. Gruffen. Gollygosh. Gwendolen. Gwillan.

Gadzooks.

9. A Sea of White Fire

He was at least another foot taller than David, his overall shape defined by a mass of swollen muscles that seemed to have burst through the bag of his skin — not red in color with the blood of a man, but a glistening turquoise-black, host to the Shadow in his corded veins. He walked on two legs, as humans did, but the weight of his brawny wings — which seemed burdensome, even in their folded state, despite the support of a collar of muscle high up his neck — suggested he'd prefer to crawl on four limbs or at worst scratch along with the gait of a bird. His strapping tail helped in this respect. It worked in the way that a dragon's did, aiding balance during vigorous movement. It was never quite still, the tail, twisting and turning and pointing at objects as if it possessed a life of its own. A serrated isoscele glimmered at its tip, a constant reminder of the Shadow

Prime's menace. What remained of Voss's face was fiendishly distorted. Helical shells had replaced his ears and his chin had grown down to a sharpened point. His nose was large and wide like an arrowhead, his teeth just a circle of badly spaced fangs. Flaring out of his slightly concave temples were two strange horns that gave him the look of a curved-claw hammer. David suspected that some of these changes were imagineered for demonic effect. But there was no mistaking the coldness in the eyes, like looking into swathes of endless space.

"I suppose congratulations are in order," he said. "When's the unhappy wedding taking place?"

"Do not mock me," the Shadow Prime hissed. His tail swung upward. For the second time that day, David found himself leaning away from a sharp object close to his throat. "A scratch is all it takes to begin your inversion. And I can make it very unpleasant. Even an illumined Fain construct couldn't fight the spread of the Shadow through its auma."

David rolled his eyes sideways. The barbed end of Voss's tail was stirring the air beneath his left ear. "So, you know a few things about me . . . Voss. But where exactly do *you* fit in?"

"You're looking at Gwilanna's father," said Zanna.

415

"Silence!" barked Voss.

Zanna lowered her head.

"So, you *are* human," David said. He moved the tail aside with the back of his hand. "Or you were."

Leaving David with a lingering look of contempt, Voss drew away and stalked toward Rosa. "So this is the clone?"

"Technically, yes," David said, following after him. He signaled to Rosa not to speak back, though the sight of Voss had all but muted her. "All the more remarkable because she's not a Co:pern:ican construct. She's a natural-born. Quite a rarity in her world. They could almost be twins, don't you think? Except one of them is . . ." He smiled at Zanna, who looked, for the first time, slightly uncomfortable with Rosa present.

Voss raised a hand to Rosa's cheek. Out of what used to be fingers came a set of bedded claws. Rosa screwed her eyes shut and turned her face away.

"Let her go," said David, coming to stand at Voss's shoulder. "She's no threat to the Shadow. It's me you're after. Why *do* you want us — me, by the way?"

"Tell us where Alexa is," Zanna said bluntly.

"Ah, yes. Alexa." David raised a finger. "Our lovely daughter. Lucy's only niece."

Lucy stared ahead without even blinking.

"Well?" said Voss, turning toward him.

David opened his hands. "I don't know."

There was a pause. Gazes flicked across the chamber like lasers. Voss was the first to speak.

"Take the girl to the upper ledges."

Lucy and Tam grabbed Rosa's arms.

"What? Hey! No. Let go of me! David?"

"All right, stop!" he cried.

Voss gestured them to halt.

David took a breath and ran a hand through his hair. "I mean it, Voss. I really don't know. Alexa is illumined. She could be anywhere in time."

Tam pulled on Rosa's arm again.

"She was at Scuffenbury with you!" David said, putting himself in front of the commander. He grabbed Tam's wrist and turned the palm uppermost. *"Find the bear inside you,"* he whispered, before Tam threw him off. "Why were you three 'selected' and not her?"

"She wasn't there," said Zanna. "Something moved her."

"Not me," David said, as sincerely as he could. He opened his jacket as if to prove he wasn't hiding her. "I swear, it wasn't *me*."

"Take the clone," said Voss.

"No!" David shouted. And this time, he tried to transform. He flickered between the shapes of Ingavar and Grockle before collapsing, exhausted, to the rock floor: human.

In his prison above the lava pile, Gawain roared.

David looked up, hearing Rosa's muffled shouts. She was being dragged away, with Tam's hand clamped hard across her mouth. David lowered his head. His hair fell forward. "What will you do with her?"

Voss suppressed a chuckle. "Do you really have to ask? You have until nightfall to think of all the interesting ways I could kill her. Tell us where the child is and the clone will be spared."

"Spared? For what?"

"She will be inverted."

A look of fury swept across Zanna's face. "Inverted? That wasn't what we agreed."

David propped himself onto one elbow. "Oh dear. Now, that *is* rich. A darkling demonstrating signs of jealousy. Unless, of course, it's the human inside her still fighting to get out?"

Voss responded to this jibe by opening his mouth and issuing a jet of dark fire. David rolled away from it just in time. When he looked back at where he'd been lying, the surface of the rock had been eaten away, leaving a shallow bed of steam.

"Final warning," the Shadow Prime said.

"I didn't take Alexa," David repeated. He stood up, loosening his collar. "There are other explanations. She was holding Gadzooks; he could have moved her."

"I told you," said Zanna. "The timeshift erased the Pennykettle dragons."

David shook his head. "I very much doubt it. The dragons weren't an act of random creation. Liz made them with definite intent. A record of them must exist within the Is. They could be in this timeline, just not in that form. Then there's Joseph Henry, of course."

Voss looked at Zanna. "What's he talking about?"

"Elizabeth Pennykettle's unborn son. He transferred his auma to one of her dragons. It was at the hill with us."

"Clever little soul," David said. "Powerful enough to turn a fully fledged darkling back to the light. Also unaccounted for . . . right?"

Voss stamped forward and pushed his callused face near to David's. "Your threats mean nothing to me,

Fain. Where was this unborn spirit when the Shadow was taking control of the Earth?"

"That's a very good question," David said quietly. "One you should give some serious thought to. What exactly do you want with Alexa?"

Voss stood back, cracking his joints. "Show him what we found."

"Is that wise?"

"I said *show him*."

Zanna gave an obedient nod and stepped out of sight for a moment. She returned carrying a large old book. "When we overran the Fain we discovered their secret." She showed David *The Book of Agawin*.

Trying not to betray anything more than casual interest, he reached out to take it. "Where did you get this?"

Voss's tail came down with a thwack across the cover. "You know of it?"

David shook his head. "I knew a boy of that name once. A seer's apprentice. He was taken by Gwilanna just before time changed. I don't know why. I assume you do?"

"The boy had a nasty fall," Voss said. "Off the slopes of Mount Kasgerden."

Agawin, dead? David bit back his anger. "I don't know this mountain. Why would Gwilanna take him there?"

"To resurrect me. To give me *life*."

"At Agawin's expense?"

The Shadow Prime leveled a weary smile. "A minor sacrifice to aid the rise of the Shadow."

David backed away, throwing out a hand. "That's what all of this is about? She altered time to save *you* from death?"

"What child does not grieve for its father?" Voss snapped.

David looked at Gawain. The dragon was silent now, moodily tenting his wings against the heat. "And yet she's subdued in the body of your enemy. How did that come about?"

"Voss, he's asking too many questions," said Zanna.

"And what can he do with the answers?" he sneered. "Our poor, weakened agent of the Fain?" He turned away from David and bellowed at Gawain. "She was a disappointment to me. She brought me back believing she could take her revenge for being made into the child she was. But the claw she had used dissolved to ash and she was powerless against the Collective. Even then, I offered her a chance of retribution. Because she had held the dragon's claw, her auma resonated powerfully with the beast. She was able to be close to him when he died."

"So she *did* catch his tear?"

Voss gave a quick snort. "When the moment arrived, she was fearful, penitent; she tried to use magicks to keep us away and send the fire tear back to the core."

Gwilanna? Penitent? David shook his head. This really *was* a bizarre timeline.

Voss's dark eyes blazed with triumph. "We captured the creature in its dying semistasis, moments after the tear was shed."

David glanced at the crestfallen dragon. Now that the rage had died away, the sadness in him was crushingly apparent. "And what did you do with Gwilanna?"

"She was a traitor to the Ix. She had to be punished."

"You killed her? You killed the daughter who'd saved your life?"

"I gave her what she craved, what she dared not take herself."

"We extracted her auma," Zanna put in, as if to offer some attempt at remorse.

"And the body?"

"Weak," Voss grunted, "unsuitable for inversion."

Thrown away, pecked at by ravens, thought David. For the first time, he pitied the crazed old sibyl. "How did you bind her auma to Gawain? True illumination requires both physical bodies to be intact."

Voss dismissed this with a wave of his hand. "The Shadow performed a trans:morphic implant."

"So, her auma drives his physical body?"

"Controlled through my command," said Zanna.

"*Your* command?"

"Her sibyl tendencies are still intact. Gwilanna obeys my greater will."

"No." David laughed this off. "He won't remain stable. Not for long."

"Long enough to do my bidding," snarled Voss. "Let me tell you the best part, Fain. When the dragon was turned, the tear's journey was suspended. We found it here, in this hollow in the island. We used its power to hasten the inversion. And now it's leading us straight to the core."

David looked at the pool of lava. He shook his head in confusion. "I'm sorry, but all this talk of betrayal has made me drift off the point somewhat. Satisfy my curiosity, Voss: Why does the Shadow want to destabilize G:ravity, disrupt the Earth's magnetic field, and bring the entire galaxy to the point of collapse?"

"We come from a world of fire," said Zanna.

"I've . . ." *Read that,* David was going to say, until he realized that Zanna had quoted from *The Book of Agawin*. His blood ran cold. "What do you mean?"

"What's *the* unanswered question, David? And before you come up with your usual fatuous response, I'll tell you. How did a universe as large as this appear from a singular microdot of space? Where did all this 'Is' come from? And please don't tell me you believe that nonsense about Godith. That was a story generated by the Fain to keep their inquisitive Premen at bay."

David steepled his fingers — a prop for his rather vacant expression. "So . . . ?"

"We're living in a microcosm. A blip that bubbled off from an infinite sea of white fire. The gateway to all creation is here. Right at the heart of this inconspicuous but rather special planet. It's all in the book."

Then why didn't I read that? he was thinking. And his mind flashed back to the great librarium, the last place he had seen the book. That thought reintroduced him to the firebirds and for some odd reason, Joseph Henry. "I wouldn't believe everything you see in print."

"Funny," she said. "Maybe this will change your mind." She turned to a marked page and opened it for him.

And there was a picture of a child with wings. Beside it, a squiggle of dragontongue. It said,

Alexa. Gatekeeper. Protector of humankind.

"Gatekeeper," said Zanna. "When we have her, we'll be able to open the core. The dragon is simply preparing the way."

"You have until nightfall," Voss said darkly.

"For the last time, I'm telling you the truth!" David barked. "I don't know where Alexa is."

"Then we move to our second option. One that might bring her out of hiding."

Zanna closed the book. Gawain let out a roar.

"We put you in the dragon's *den*," said Voss, gesturing toward the lava pool. "We sacrifice you instead."

10. Particles and Time

They were intrigued by me, that was plain from their unified stare. But the one they clamored for, of course, was Elizabeth.

"Oh dear," she sighed. She lowered herself, cross-legged, among them. She was pleased to see her dragons, but saddened, too.

They flew to her, making their hurring noises. G'reth and Gruffen each landed on a knee, from where they could reach up and touch her face. Gwendolen flew to the slope of her shoulder and started making braids of her growing red hair. Gollygosh picked up the hem of her smock and gently caressed a green paint stain. Gretel and Gadzooks simply stood before her, stretching their oval eyes to the limit. The other dragon, Gwillan, she picked up and held in the shadows of her lap.

In perfect dragontongue she said, "You know you shouldn't be here, don't you?"

Hrrr! went Gretel. She pointed at me.

"Yes, I know. Agawin shouldn't be here either. But he's a special case. It's not your time."

"I'm sorry," I said. "I found Ganzfeld —"

Hrrr!

All the dragons ducked.

"Sorry," I tutted, remembering now what Avrel had said. *To speak his name is to know his power.* But I didn't understand his power.

So I asked.

"Very well, I'll tell you," Elizabeth said. She signaled Gretel to be quiet. "Ganzfeld was made by the will of Gaia."

"From stars," I gushed. "I saw it in a dream."

G'reth raised an eye ridge. He seemed to like the idea of dreams (and stars).

"He has special significance," Elizabeth went on, "because he was the first of his kind on Earth, the first to be touched by the passing of Gawain."

Hrrr . . . Seven little chests deflated.

"Now, now. No fire tears here." She stroked Gwillan, who seemed the most upset. Gollygosh, likewise, was looking a little moist. With a sad-sounding hurr he put down his toolbox. An asterisk of light immediately flew out and formed itself into a small handkerchief. He put it to his snout and blew into it hard (leaving two scorch holes at its center).

"That's better," said Elizabeth. She went on with her account of Ganzfeld's influence. "The listener, like all of you, had a special power. He could 'listen,' of course, we all knew that. But if he listened hard, very hard indeed, he could lose himself in the auma of the universe, in the energy field after which he was named."

I noticed Gadzooks doodling on his notepad. Spiderwebs connected by dozens of stars. His impression of the energy field, perhaps.

Elizabeth pressed her fingertips together. At the same time, a tele:screen flickered into life. It put up a picture of the listening dragon slowly turning through starlit space. None of the dragons appeared to have noticed.

"You all know about the auma of the universe, of course." Elizabeth looked at each of them in turn. "You use it when Gretel makes a potion from her flowers, or Gollygosh imagineers something from his toolbox, or a wishing dragon grants a fall of snow."

She smiled at G'reth, who put his famous paws together and blushed.

Meanwhile, on the tele:screen, the same voice that had described the evolution of the firebirds began to babble about something called "neu:trinos," particles so tiny they could pass between the spaces in "atoms." A small animation faded up. It showed a band of neu:trinos flowing through and around a number of "solid" objects: a kettle, a table, a refrigerator door . . .

"Hey, did you see that?" I nudged G'reth. He twizzled his snout and looked at me blankly.

"Up *there*," I hissed. I pointed at the screen.

The neu:trinos were passing through a polar bear now.

G'reth looked over his shoulder — and shrugged. Like the rest of the dragons, he seemed oblivious to the tele:screen, as if the pictures were only in my head.

"Then what?" Gretel asked impatiently. "What happens when Ganz — the listener gets lost?"

Just as Elizabeth started to reply, Gruffen paddled an ear with his paw. Gretel checked it for signs of unusual auma. Finding none, she told him not to interrupt.

"Gretel, behave yourself," Elizabeth said. She stroked Gwillan's back. He shivered and seemed relieved to be in her hands. "The answer is very simple, really. Once Ganzfeld had entered the energy field he could begin to make connections."

The listener was back on the screen again, but he was made up now from thousands of points of colored light. A swarm of neu:trinos were sparkling inside him, like a host of tiny fire stars. To my annoyance, the screen began to flicker and buzz. Broken lines of static crackled across it. A scratchy image of an old man burst into view. He was rocking in a chair, saying over and over, *"Which has more auma, light or fire? Light or fire? Light or fire?"*

"C-connections?" I asked. My head was spinning.

"To anyone, anywhere, anywhen," said Elizabeth. "All he had to do was create an image of where he wanted to be or who he wanted to communicate with and the field responded. This is one of the enchantments of time."

"Light or fire?" the old man said.

The image of Ganzfeld appeared again, but now he was beginning to dissolve into the field. Arcs of dotted lines, which I took to be thought waves, were shown streaming out of his head. *Each neu:trino*, said the tele:screen voice, *carries a minute degree of energy. But scientists at the Merriman Institute believe that in sufficient quantity, and with sufficient intent, it is theoretically possible for a field of these particles to disrupt molecular structure in one of two ways. They might draw an object into their flow, for instance.* . . . With a spectacular whoosh, Ganzfeld was sucked out of sight like a feather in a breeze. . . . *Or, more amazingly, they might rearrange it.* Now he was center screen again, and something odd was happening with his ears. They were feathering, turning into firebird tufts. The screen crackled. The old man appeared in close-up, leaning forward out of his chair. The voice of the narrator was now coming from his mouth. *Could this explain the astonishing ability firebirds possess of passing through solid objects, as if they are moving faster than light and Traveling ahead of time itself* . . . *? Light or fire — which has more auma?*

"Fire!" I blurted at him. "Fire is the answer. The universe is made of *fire!*"

On-screen, the old man silently rocked.

My head began to thump. The dragons and Elizabeth were looking at me, waiting. I took a full breath and I said, boldly, "If I wanted to lead one bear to another, how would I use Ganz . . . the *name* to do it?"

Elizabeth said, "Do you know the name of the bear you want to find?"

"Ingavar."

We all heard a quiet snapping sound. Gadzooks had pressed so hard on his pad that the end of his pencil had broken off.

Elizabeth stood up. She placed a kiss on Gwillan's snout and snuggled him into a pocket of her smock. "Gwillan is going to stay with me. I must go to my room. My sculpture is almost ready."

"Please," I begged her. "How do I find Ingavar?"

She was drifting away, like Ganzfeld had. But I could hear her voice between the atoms. "Your intent has already been answered, Agawin. Everything you need is right before you." The dragons blew smoke rings or twizzled their tails. "It takes a particularly powerful being to draw others across the energy field. Now that the dragons are here, maybe you should show them who you really are."

The Pennykettle kitchen appeared on the tele:screen. I recognized it right away, just as if a cloud had lifted from my memory. For the first time, the dragons were seeing it, too. They were shown in a group on the kitchen table, watching a young girl draw. She gave a satisfied hum and put down her crayon. "We need to send the polar bears here." She pinned a finger to the center of her drawing. An island at the edge of a wild gray sea. Dark creatures peppered the sky around it. An image of the island filled the screen. We saw water crashing, heard darklings screeching, smelled sulfur in the spouts of fire from its peak.

The dragons turned away from it and looked at me.

Gone were my boyish hands. I could feel the soft fall of hair on my face, the reassuring tug of wings at my back.

I was Alexa again and fully aware.

"Time to go," I said.

Time to find Daddy.

11. A Strange Reminder
of a Library Garden

They hauled David outside and put him in the company of Voss's men. His hands were tied and he was marched, sometimes dragged, to a high point of the island. He was thrown into a damp and narrow cleft, facing the cold, wind-roughened sea. The sides of the cleft were too sheer to climb, and any thoughts he had of leaping for water were dashed when he looked at the maze of rocks below. Open cells didn't come much harsher than this. "What have you done with Rosa?" he demanded. But the men just beat him and kicked him and laughed.

"You so much as pick your nose," said one, "an' the watcher'll call down the fliers, you gottit?" He turned David around and untied his hands, then jabbed a finger at the glowering sky where several scrawny "fliers" were circling. Darklings, eager to drop down and feed.

The men filed away, making jokes about "pickings." A solitary raven was left to watch David's position.

"And if I want to tell Voss what he needs to know?"

"You tell me," said a voice. Lucy stepped into view.

The last of the men nodded curtly at her, then scuttled away out of sight.

Lucy perched on a rock, some ten or twelve paces away. Her amazing red hair was now ash-gray and black, tied in a bundle at the nape of her neck. She was wearing patchy remnants of human clothing, but the sleeves of her top had been torn away to reveal what looked like black tattoos all along the skin from her knuckles to her shoulder. David realized with some dismay that it was nothing more than the Shadow in her veins. "Sorry, don't have much to offer you." He gestured at his bleak surroundings. "Pretty chilly up here, too." He pulled the lapels of his jacket together. She quickly dipped to her belt for a knife. He lowered his hands into plain view again. "Thought you might have put me in the cave, at least."

Her hand relaxed, but only to check the bowstring running across her chest. "Cave?"

"You've been here before, in another time. You met a female polar bear in a cave. Gwilanna kept you there when she took you from the Crescent. When you were still a cute little girl. Remember that, Lucy, what it was to be cute?"

"Save your breath, Fain. I care for nothing I knew before my inversion."

"Yes, you do," he said. He drew up his knees. "You just don't know how to reach it yet. I can help you with that. It's what your mother would have wanted."

"I have no *mother*, only the Shadow."

"The Shadow isn't going to last." He cast a wary eye at the darklings all the same. One of them had landed on a ledge above the cleft and was peering down at him, showing its teeth. A hiss from Lucy stopped it creeping any closer.

"All I want from you is to know about the child."

"Oh, Alexa will come," he said. "Though what she'll find is open to debate." The wall of rock behind David shuddered as Gawain resumed his "dig." In its aftermath, a shower of cinders fell. David heard the darkling spitting out the sulfur, though none of it seemed to be affecting Lucy. "This folly with the core will blow the Earth apart. The Shadow won't want to 'mother' you then. The Collective will desert you and simply move on, until it finds another life-form to terrorize. You really ought to think about that."

"The child," she said. "You think about that."

But all he did was snap his fingers and say, "Do you want to play a game?" He gave her no chance to reply or refuse. "I say a word and you tell me the first thing that comes into your mind. Bacon."

"*What?*"

"Bacon. Henry. Next-door neighbor. Drove you crazy for fifteen years. Clever man. Total curmudgeon, but heart very much in the right-shaped . . . place." He made a poor drawing of a heart on his chest. "Bacon."

Lucy stared at him hard.

"Okay. Not Henry, then." He pushed a hand through his hair. "What about the library? The clock tower? The gardens? You must remember the library gardens?"

For the first time, she gave an encouraging jolt.

"That's it, the library gardens," he said. And as the wind blew a shower of raindrops across them, he lowered his voice to a captivating whisper. "It was a blustery autumn morning in —"

"Shut up," she said, reaching for her bow. "Shut up or I'll . . ."

Suddenly, she dropped her gaze and looked down at the space in front of his feet. A small gray squirrel had materialized there. It sat up and chirruped, flagging a tail as delicate as a dandelion puff. It lifted a paw and twitched its whiskers. One of its eyes was matted and closed.

The darkling on the ledge above David snarled.

Lucy gave a violent shudder. A vein near her elbow began to pulse. One of the coils at her temples blanched. A thin film of moisture clouded her vision. The raven beside her paddled its feet as though it ought to be doing something about this. A gust of wind rippled its feathers, which persuaded it, finally, to tip its beak and squawk.

"Conker . . . ," Lucy whispered, narrowing her gaze.

"Just hold on to his memory," said David. He maneuvered his feet, getting ready to stand.

The shadow of a darkling swept across the cleft.

In a flash, Lucy had an arrow in her bow. She tensed the string and trained the arrow at the squirrel's heart. But with a sudden upward movement she changed her aim and the darkling fell with a thump to the ground, skewered on a shaft of wood and steel.

The raven squawked and took to the air.

David jumped up. "Great shot. Let's —"

"Don't move."

Lucy already had a second arrow primed. The imagineered squirrel faded away. The arrowhead glinted at David's chest.

"Lucy, what are you doing? The bird will warn Voss. I need to find Rosa. We haven't much time."

"I was told to guard you. That includes against darklings."

David stepped forward.

She drew on the bow.

"Lucy, listen to me, please. I can bring you back. I promise I can make you human again. The squirrel came from your head, not from mine."

"I don't care," she said. "The Shadow is everything. We're going to take the nexus and break into the core."

"No. Together you and I can stop this."

She shook her head. "I know a better way, David." Her arrow flashed through the air and bedded itself into the hollow of his shoulder, knocking him onto one knee. He gripped the shaft and looked at her in horror.

"You come to us," she said.

12. UNLOCKING KI:MERA

Although there was nothing much out at sea, it was not uncommon for a solitary darkling to fly across the water in search of something worthy of torment — a fish, perhaps, that the Shadow hadn't reached. Or better still those galumphing brutes that gathered in piles on any shallow landmass. "Walruses," men called them. They were always fun to bully.

So it came to be that on the day that Lucy fired her arrow at David, one darkling was skimming the water when it noticed something extremely unusual.

The waves had stopped rolling.

There was surf and ripples, troughs and peaks, but it was all suspended. No movement.

None.

The darkling knew what it ought to do. It ought to

hasten back to the island and report. But curiosity had gripped its *shade*. It wanted to investigate.

And so it did.

Slowing its wing-beats back to a glide, it tentatively touched down on the surface.

The sea was *absolutely* still. Not a single bubble was rising. The darkling extended a claw and prodded the glassy cover. The sea responded with a satisfying *ching*, the chime fissuring out in several directions. The creature prodded harder. *Ching, ching, ching. Ching, ching, ching, ching . . .*

Clink.

The last noise was either an echo, or . . .

The creature looked around.

And then it saw the child.

She was sitting on the water some wing-beats away. A human girl, untouched by the Shadow.

The darkling sped toward her. As it circled her it saw she was not alone. A disgusting excuse for a dragon was standing in the cup of her outstretched hands. Its paws were huge and offensively green. Its oval-shaped eyes were tightly closed, suggesting it was deep in concentration.

The darkling landed, using its retractory claws as anchors. It bared its teeth and tilted its horns.

This, it thought, would not take long.

Surprisingly, the girl showed no signs of fear. "Go to your master," she said.

This made the darkling chatter and scowl, for the child had spoken in perfect Ix.

"Tell him that my wishing dragon has frozen the ocean and opened the way to Ki:mera. He'll know what that means."

The darkling spat a glob of oily black phlegm. "Wat is yaar . . . ?" Its ability with speech was confined to rasps; its vocabulary almost minimal.

"I'm Alexa," the girl said, tossing back her hair. "And this is G'reth. He grants wishes that benefit dragon-kind and anyone who cares for dragons. He's come to help me free Gawain. If I were you, I'd set off now, darkling."

The creature pulled back. Was this pathetic pink human speaking a threat? It flicked two poisonous stigs from its neck.

"It's going to get very cold," said Alexa, "and very crowded very soon. Go to your master. Tell him he must free my father and let the dragon go."

A snowflake floated between them. The darkling tried to snatch it out of the air, but one blow from Alexa's lips sent it dancing away to land well out of the creature's sight. At the same time, the surface of the water groaned. The darkling lifted a leg. The sea had hardened further — and cooled.

"That was the first one," Alexa said.

First one? First one *what*? The darkling snarled. It was tired of this. It splayed its claws and prepared to strike. But as it reared, something unexpected happened. The dragon in Alexa's hands changed shape. Not by much, but enough to stall the darkling's attack. The new dragon was even stranger than the first. It had a weapon of sorts, some kind of flattish object. The "weapon" was actually a book of instructions, wielded by a brave, if frightened, "guard" dragon. The darkling watched it flip through the pages, eventually stopping at the letter *P*. There was one instruction written there: *Point*.

The dragon slammed the book shut . . . and pointed.

The darkling turned around.

Towering over it was a huge white bear. In the background, more and more flakes were falling. Everywhere they landed, more bears appeared.

The darkling bared its teeth. Knowing no instinct other than conflict, it issued a threat which had scarcely grazed the back of its throat before the bear brought down a mighty paw and flattened it into a mess of ooze.

"Hate those things," the bear said gruffly.

A younger bear, sleeker than the first, drew up. "We could have captured that and questioned it, Kailar."

"You talk too much already, Teller." With a wallop, Kailar punched through the surface and washed his paw in the water beneath. "Which way to Ingavar, child?"

Alexa looked down at her hands. Once again the dragon changed shape, into noticeably softer lines. "Have you found David's auma, Gwendolen?"

The dragon blew a smoke ring and watched it drift. She pointed toward the setting sun. *Hrrr.*

Alexa nodded. "Go quickly, Avrel. Surround the island. Remember your training when the darklings attack. Don't let them into your mind."

The Teller grunted. "Did the dragon say anything else?"

"Nothing that concerns you," Alexa said, though it was of deep concern to her. Now that they were settled in the crucial timepoint, Gwendolen and Ganzfeld were using the field to search for traces of recognizable auma. Gwendolen's first report had been quick and heartfelt. *They're hurting Lucy.*

Avrel nodded and drifted away to join the pack.

"Why?" asked Alexa, when he was out of earshot. "What has Lucy done?"

Again the dragon changed shape. This time Gadzooks appeared. He was shaking and sweat was pouring off his neck. His green scales were turning black near one shoulder.

Alexa parted her hands. Gadzooks stayed on her left palm and Gretel materialized on her right.

Hrrr! went the potions dragon.

"Yes, they've infected him," Alexa said.

Gretel immediately reached for her flowers.

"No," said Alexa. "Let it build."

Hrrr? said Gretel. *And watch Gadzooks invert?*

"It's a form of dragonpox," Alexa told her. "And what do we always do about that?"

We call upon the auma of Gawain to transform it.

"*Mmm,*" said the child. "And David will do that. But *we* need to find a way to spread it." She closed her right hand and Gretel disappeared in a spark of light.

Then, bringing Gadzooks up close to her face, she politely asked, "May I?"

He gave her his pencil.

"Don't be frightened," she said in a lullaby voice. "Joseph will be here soon." And she wrote one word on Gadzooks's notepad:

kiss

13. Hands

Y ou liked me once, didn't you?"

Like David, Rosa was being held in a small indent on the high outer edges of the Tooth of Ragnar. More a scoop out of the scree than an actual cave, but slightly better protected from the wind and continuously warmed by the work of Gawain. She was comfortable enough, though fretfully aware of the setting sun, the dwindling curtain of light that measured the remaining hours of her life. She had to fill them somehow, and talk was cheap.

"Is this what you do when you write your poems? Just stare at the sea until inspiration comes?" He had his back to her in a silhouetted A shape. He'd been looking at the ocean almost since they'd arrived, as if his previous life was rowing in on a boat. " 'I wandered lonely as a darkling.' You might as well talk to me. I'm not gonna bite."

"Poems?" he said. He half-turned toward her. In profile, with the horns and coils concealed, he was deeply handsome. Almost human.

Rosa shuddered — and not just because her head was throbbing, though it had been since he'd brought her here. A swarming spiral of intense pressure that seemed to be chasing the blood around her skull. "You were creative, weren't you? The memories are patchy, but she liked that about you. The way you expressed yourself in verse. The way you read. The accent in your voice. She liked that a lot. Liked you a lot, really — until you betrayed her."

"Who?" he said. "Who are you talking about?"

"*Her*, who else? Zanna. Your 'Pri:magon.' The one you'd happily die for. Ohhh . . ." The pain again, as if something . . . wild . . . was trying to connect to her. Rosa pressed both hands to her head.

"I told you to stop that," Tam said coldly.

"And I'd tell you to go to hell — except I think you're already there. I have a headache, okay?" She tapped her temple. "Probably this toxic . . . stuff in the air. It feels like the dragon is blowing its *smog* straight in through my ears. The real Tam would have tried to help me. Don't you feel anything for her now?"

"I'm here to guard you, human. And whatever you think you know about me, I would never betray my Pri:magon."

"Hmph," went Rosa. She gathered her knees up under her chin. "Does it. hurt to know she's marrying Voss?"

"Be quiet," he snapped. "If the Pri:magon orders it, I will gladly throw you off the cliff at dusk. Think about that before you open your mouth again. It's a long way down to those points of rock. Pray you reach them before the darklings snatch you out of the sky."

Rosa gulped as one screeched past, the fourth or fifth she'd seen in the last few minutes. Was it her imagination or were they becoming more numerous, more active? "They seem anxious. Is something wrong?"

"Nothing can be wrong. The Shadow is everything." An unconvincing reply, Rosa thought. He sounded as if he was reading from a script.

"So why are you looking at the sea for so long — assuming you're *not* writing poetry, of course?"

Saying nothing, he crouched to the ground and roughed his palm in the gravel and dust. Then he stood again, shaking his hand, as if he was trying to throw something off. It was the second time Rosa had seen him do this.

"What's the matter with your hand?" She was remembering now how David had grabbed him and turned the palms upward, wanting Tam to find something. "What did David say to you? Back in the chamber?"

"Be silent," said Tam.

But this was important, Rosa suspected. She could hear footsteps loosening the scree. Someone was approaching at a speed that suggested urgency. As Tam went to meet them, she closed her eyes and concentrated hard. Somewhere in Zanna's memories there had to be something about Tam's hands. The Pennykettle kitchen swept into her mind. Zanna, making tea for him in . . . *the snow*? No, Zanna was imagining snowflakes falling, something to do with what he was saying to her.

"Commander . . . ," panted a voice nearby.

Rosa half-listened, but the messenger was too exhausted to report. *Concentrate*, she told herself.

Kitchen. Tea. Biscuits. Conversation. Then suddenly it came, a whole slew of information. Tam's voice, talking about something he'd received from David.

They weren't snowflakes, Zanna. They were bear flakes. A small pack of them, come to battle the Ix. Two of them landed on my hands. Since then I've remembered things about the Arctic — stuff I shouldn't know, legends I can't know — coupled with a crushing desire to protect you and Lucy.

"Bears," Rosa gasped, opening her eyes.

Tam turned and looked at her furiously. The man beside him nodded. "She's right. An army of bears is approaching the island from all directions."

"How could you know this?" Tam Farrell said.

"Your hands," Rosa said again. "Look at your hands."

Tam turned his palms up and gulped. Two polar bears were glimmering under his skin.

The messenger shook his head in confusion. He began to mutter something about reporting this abnormality to the Prime when Tam's fist punched his jaw sideways and the man collapsed like an empty sack.

Rosa saw her chance and leaped to her feet. "Where are they keeping David? Come on, we've got to free him. You are . . . Tam now, aren't you?"

He looked at her as if the truth had poisoned him. "Stay where you are. I don't know what I am."

"But . . . you've just knocked one of your men out cold. Very impressive, by the way."

Tam didn't seem to think so. "I bought myself some time before they kill me, that's all. When the Collective absorbs this mutation, Voss will seek me out."

"It's not a mutation, you idiot, it's a gift. If the bears are coming then you should — ohhh . . ." She fell to her knees again, cradling her head. The pulses were growing stronger by the second.

"I have to go," he said, turning away.

"Don't leave me!" she cried. "You're Tam. Tam Farrell. You swore to protect Zanna. Protect me now. Please, Tam. My head's exploding."

"I can't help you," he said. "The Pri:magon will decide your fate."

"Not without a *fight*!" she screamed. "Then I'll come for you, you useless piece of alien . . . *agh*." But he was already gone, leaving her clutching her temples again. There were voices far below, shouting danger. The screech of darklings. The rumble of the dragon. But none of this troubled Rosa as much as what was happening inside her head.

"No!" she argued, shaking herself. "No. Not you. Get out of me. *Go*."

Suddenly, there were images to go with the pain.

"I won't let you in. I will *not* let you in. You won't infect me. Get out, you witch!"

Then the sibyl's voice broke through, a ghostly relation of the snappy, croaking voice of old. Just two words entered Rosa's consciousness.

Help me.

14. A Vital Kiss

"Who gave you the authority to *attack* the prisoner?"

Another bolt of Voss's *shade* swept into the nodes at Lucy's head. She jerked in pain. It was all she could do to remain kneeling. If he upped the intensity any more, she was going to pass out, maybe even die. "I was acting for the good of the Shadow," she gasped. "He was trying to escape. What else was I to do?"

Voss leaned over her, twisting like a snake. "You used a tipped arrow. The kind of dose we save for *rats*. His inversion will now be slow and erratic; that's always supposing he *lives*."

"It's not too late to withdraw it," muttered Zanna. She was standing over David, checking him for vital signs. His motionless body had been laid out on a ledge on the far side of the chamber. The arrow had been removed, along with his jacket and shirt. From the center of the wound, a web of black veins was spreading up his shoulder and into his neck. He was barely breathing. "The infection isn't pure. If we stop it now, he will recover."

Voss cracked his knuckles. Leaning over Lucy again, he said, "Even if the Pri:magon brings him back, his connection to his daughter will be weaker than it was — though maybe *your* allegiance has changed, Commander . . . ?"

Lucy shook her head. "I only serve the Shadow —"

With a thwack, Voss's tail came down on her shoulder, the barbed end dangerously close to her skin. "A darkling was found with an arrow through its gut. Explain that to me."

Zanna spoke up in Lucy's defense. "He may have begun the conflict to distract her. It would be easy for him to draw down a darkling. They're natural enemies, Voss. She may have even done you a service. With his powers diminished, he wouldn't have survived a darkling's bite."

Voss pressed his tail under Lucy's ear. "Is this your claim?"

"Y-yes." She half-nodded.

He put himself close to her face and whispered. "I do not believe you."

"But —?"

"Do not *speak*." A barb nicked her skin, drawing out a dot of thick black blood. "If he dies . . . you burn." Lucy shuddered as he turned and looked at the lava. Gawain was now deep within the Earth once more.

With a snarl, Voss whirled away toward Zanna.

"I'll need to commingle with him."

"Commingle?" Voss didn't like the sound of that.

"He's too weak to be a threat. If I reach into his auma I might even be able to access his memories. It will be quicker than forcing him to talk."

Still Voss didn't seem sure. "You forget, you were close to him once."

"In another timeline," she said plainly.

A guard burst in then, shouting the alarm.

"Get out!" Voss roared. "How dare you disturb me!"

The guard fell to one knee. "Forgive me, Prime. The island is under attack."

"From what?" scoffed Voss. Every species on Earth had been dimmed by the Shadow.

"Bears," said the guard.

Lucy looked up.

"White bears," the guard added. He was a burly man with impressive muscles, but the odor of his sweat was drenched with fear. "They are running on the water. The sea has frozen."

"That would take powerful magicks," said Zanna, throwing an urgent look at Voss.

Voss spread his wings, making the guard cower. Battle stigs emerged all along his spine. "It's the child," he said, with malevolent certainty. "It appears she has decided to come to us. What direction are these bears coming from?"

"Every direction," the guard jabbered. "Even the bridge. They are falling from the sky in great number. The darklings are fighting but the bears are strong."

Lucy clambered to her feet. "Prime, I will defend you. . . ."

Voss stared at her and beckoned the messenger to stand. "Bind her and take her outside. Hide her in one of the caves."

"Bind . . . *her*?" The man pointed at his former commander.

"Unless you want to die on your overweight knees."

"But I'm Shadow," Lucy protested.

"No," he corrected her. "From now on, you're hostage."

Without dwelling on his options, the messenger stood up and attended to his orders. Within moments, Lucy's hands were tied and she'd been pushed outside on the point of a sword.

"Voss, wait," Zanna called as he prepared to follow. "If magicks are being used, I should come with you. I might be able to undo the freezing spell. The bears would still be able to swim, but in the water they would be easy victims for the flock."

He nodded and took a knife from his belt. He threw it across the chamber floor. It stopped spinning at Zanna's feet. "Do what you can, but kill the Fain first. He is no use to us now."

And he swept toward the opening and flew into the sky.

Zanna bent down and picked up the knife. An old hunting blade. Not overly sharp, but effective against the human template. She scraped it over David's body, making a nick in the region of his heart. "You should have come to us willingly," she whispered. "Who knows what might have been?"

David tried to speak. His lips parted and he made a quiet *zz* sound.

"Touching," she said, thinking he was trying to speak her name. She placed the blade flat to his lips to quiet him. "*Shh*, David. This won't take long. . . ."

And for whatever reason she cared to imagine, she took the knife away and kissed his mouth.

As she rose, he managed to say what he'd wanted to. "Z . . . ookie."

The Pri:magon touched her lips. They were tingling slightly. The Ix inside her swarmed to the point of alien contact. "What have you done?" she hissed. "What have you *done*?" The faintest smile broke over his lips. She gave a cry of fury. Clenching her teeth, she raised the knife. It had reached no farther than the height of her chin when something heavy thudded across her shoulders. She collapsed in a zigzagging motion to the ground.

"Cow," said Rosa, throwing the rock aside. "You leave my David alone."

And careful not to make any contact with her clone, she stepped over Zanna and shook David awake.

15. A Dialogue with Gwilanna

She had to slap him twice to bring him around fully. "David, wake up. We need to get out of here." She cradled his face. "Look at me, will you? Are you okay?"

He nodded woozily. "Umm. Just cold."

She found his jacket and draped it over his shoulders.

"Voss?" he murmured, looking around.

"They're all outside. We're safe for now. A messenger came saying bears were attacking."

"Bears?" That woke him like a shot of adrenaline. He refocused his gaze at the entrance to the chamber.

"They think Alexa sent them. They think she might be here."

Still bleary, he swung himself upright. He saw Zanna laid out at his feet and slowly worked out what must have happened. "Please tell me you didn't kill her."

"She was kissing you."

"That's no excuse to knock her senseless."

"Oh, and about to drive this through your heart." She slapped a supercilious grin to her face and twiddled the knife in front of him.

He found the nick in his chest and drew his hand across it, smearing the tips of his fingers with blood. "Yeah, well. She'd have a few good reasons."

And not all of them to do with this timeline, Rosa imagined.

David staggered to the entrance and carefully peered out. The gray sky was striated with flying darklings but there was no sign yet of bears approaching. Most of Voss's men had run to the shoreline, hands cupped above their eyes, unsure of what was coming or what to do. A few brave parties were advancing out to sea, stamping their feet to test the surface, their swords raised high like candlesticks. Voss himself was nowhere to be seen.

"We haven't much time," David said, drawing away. "If the bears reach the island, Voss's men will retreat here, into the chamber."

Rosa pointed at his arrow wound. He'd been feeling his shoulder ever since he'd woken up. "Are you . . . ?"

"Infected? No. Just a bit tender." He pushed the jacket aside to reveal the punctured skin. "The scars

461

will show for a while, but there wasn't enough poison in Lucy's arrow to invert me."

"*Lucy* shot you?"

"She thought she was doing me a favor."

"Some favor. What is it with the women in your life?"

"I don't know. You tell me."

When she couldn't find an answer she flapped a hand and said, "Put your jacket on. You're making me nervous."

He raised an eyebrow.

"Not in a good way. What do we do about goth girl here?"

He knelt down and rolled Zanna onto her back. Brushing her dark hair away from her face, he carefully opened the lid of one eye. A glint of green was showing in her iris. Her natural eye color, coming back. "It's started," he said, relief in his voice. He lifted her and carried her toward the lava.

Rosa stayed rooted to the spot, arms crossed. "What? What's started?"

"I had enough of Gawain's auma to begin a transformation on the Shadow. I passed it on to Zanna when we kissed."

"*She* kissed. There wasn't a 'we' involved."

"It's low-level," David said, ignoring her. "They'll crush it unless I get help from Gawain. He'll still have the power to multiply the antidote and spread it through the humans controlled by the Collective."

Appropriately, the dragon rose from the pool. When he saw the state that Zanna was in, he hammered his front feet against the force field. Sparks flew around his chest and head. Still the barrier between them held.

"Somehow, we have to get him out of there." David laid Zanna down again, taking care not to knock her head against the rock. Something about the tender way he nursed her prompted Rosa to take a breath and say, "Can I ask a question?"

David stood up and pressed the force field again. Fluid. Movable. There had to be a way to get into it. Had to be. "Not now, I'm thinking."

She asked it anyway. "What happens if Zanna returns to normal?"

"Sorry?"

"If you cure her, if you make her human again — what will happen once she's rid of the Shadow?"

"Zanna is one of us," he said, irritated by the need to state what he thought was obvious. "She's strong. She'll help us defeat —"

"That's not what I meant." Rosa turned a knee inward. "If Zanna's back in play, what happens to us?"

"Us?"

"You and me."

His gaze lingered over her.

"Will you be with her or will you come back home to Co:pern:ica — with me?"

He watched her nervously picking at her fingers. Her vulnerability was uncomfortable to see. All the same, he answered truthfully. "I don't know what's going to happen; I just know I have to save her." He saw her throat ripple and looked away. "Rosa, we can talk about this when —"

"I think I can help you."

"Help me? How?"

"Gwilanna's in my head. I've been hearing her voice."

"Gwilanna?"

"David, just shut up and listen. I had this seriously weird headache — then she broke through."

It took him a second to figure this out. Then he remembered Zanna's words from earlier and everything seemed to make perfect sense. *Her sibyl tendencies are still intact. Gwilanna obeys my greater will.* Which meant that Gawain did, too. "What did she say?"

" 'Help me.' "

"Is that all?"

"Isn't that enough? She sounded scared."

"Have you tried to speak back?"

She shook her head.

He came over and gripped her arms. "Zanna's been giving Gwilanna orders, which means that you can, too. If you concentrate hard enough you should be able to strike up a conversation."

"I'm not meeting her for morning coffee, David! This is a dragon's head you want me to enter. One that's been twisted by the Ix, remember?"

"I know," he said, raising his hands to calm her. "But you wanted to help, and this might be our only —"

Before he could complete his sentence, a loud screech echoed off the walls of the chamber and a darkling hurtled in. It plummeted down at a long, sharp angle, skidding haphazardly across the floor before tipping over, onto one shoulder. A trail of black fluid marked its landing.

"It's injured," gasped Rosa. There were gouges in its side. A hanging wing. One limp foot.

"Not injured enough," David said. And he was quickly proven right. Hearing the sound of human voices, the creature twisted its venomous head, rolled its berry-like eyes toward them, and launched an immediate attack. It flailed at David, slashing and spitting. He went down, wrestling its prickly arms, the needle teeth all the while snapping at his face. "Now would be a good time to use the knife!" As he yelled this he managed to lift the creature, bring his feet up, and kick it hard in the underbelly. The darkling was thrown against Gawain's prison. Its spine gave a crack as it slid down, winded. When it looked up, Rosa was there with the knife.

She plunged the blade into an existing wound, leaving it embedded above the fraying wing. The darkling shrieked but barely winced. To her horror, Rosa realized she hadn't done enough. Instead of inflicting a mortal blow, she had stood off too far and barely caused the creature any more pain than it was already in. Instantly, it coiled up and sprang at her. Rosa raised her arms to protect herself, but the darkling's leap only measured the length of its scrawny tail. Amazingly, Gwilanna had used Gawain's weight to warp their prison wall and trap the darkling's tail at its tip. The creature was pinned, but the danger wasn't over. The darkling looked back, assessed the situation, and bit clean through the tail at its base. Rosa screamed as it came for her again. But the second lunge was even shorter than the first. David by now had found the arrow that Zanna had extracted from his shoulder. As the darkling opened its jaws to bite, David thrust the arrow into its mouth, breaking its central teeth in the process. The darkling clamped on the arrowhead and gulped. A trail of black fluid oozed from one ear. The creature blinked, shuddered, and then fell sideways, dead.

Rosa took refuge in David's arms.

"It's all right," he whispered, stroking her hair. "It's done now. Gone. But there are going to be others. You have to contact Gwilanna. I think that demonstrates whose side she's on."

Rosa settled her nerves and stared at the dragon, who was flipping his bemused gaze between the two women. "What do I say to her?"

"Make contact, then I'll guide you. Commingling is just a form of advanced telepathy."

"That easy?" She pulled a trying face. "Don't know why I bothered reading the manual."

"Just think of her, Rosa. She'll come."

She looked at the dragon again. "I've got a question."

"You'll be fine. Just concentrate your mind."

"Do you love me, David?"

"Do I . . . ?" His chest deflated a little.

"Sorry," she said. "Later, eh?"

"Yes. I . . ." He glanced at Zanna, his face a model of pure confusion. "Yes . . . later."

So Rosa closed her eyes and focused on the voice. Within moments, she jerked her head and said, "Okay. I've got her."

"Good. Tell her we want to free Gawain. Ask her how the force field was put together. Was it imagineered or is it magicks?"

Rosa put the question into her mind. "Magicks, she thinks. She's not sure. Voss did it."

David clicked his tongue in frustration. If Zanna had put the barrier in place, it would have been easy enough to remove it. "Does she know a way out?"

The dragon shortened its gaze and blew a fireball at him. "No. She was hoping you knew a way in. By the way, she says you're useless."

David stared into the sad, jeweled eyes. *Like this is my fault*, he thought. "You said she was scared. Why is she frightened?"

Rosa's face screwed up in concentration. "She's close to the core. About to break through. She says there's something on the other side."

"Does she know what?"

"She says . . . 'Trick or treat, boy?'"

In other words, she had no idea. To make matters worse, a light groan from the floor alerted him to the fact that Zanna was coming around. Pri:magon. Sore head. Lethal combination.

Rosa seemed unaware of it and was still reporting back her conversation with Gwilanna. "She thinks whatever it is won't be keen on meeting a tainted dragon. She agrees she needs to get out. She says —"

"Forget it, Rosa. We have to go."

"But — ?"

"Seriously, we have to run."

She blinked in confusion. "As in 'away'?"

"Far away. We should try to find Alexa. Zanna's recovering. When she comes to she'll overcome the change and go back to the Shadow. We've failed here. There's nothing else I can do. Come on." He took her hand and yanked her toward the light.

Halfway there, she wrestled herself free. "Wait. Why don't you just kill her?"

"I can't," he said, looking back, pained. "She's the mother of my child. I can't do it. Please, Rosa. We have to go. Now."

"No," she said, standing firm. "You can't desert her. I won't let you abandon her."

"*What?* What are you talking about?"

"I hate what she is and I hate the fact you want her more than me, but if she has a chance at humanity again we ought to try for her. *I* ought to try for her. Maybe there's another way?"

"There isn't," he insisted, "and we're wasting time."

"Gwilanna had an idea."

That stopped him dead. "When?"

"Just now, while we were commingling."

He threw up his hands. "Why didn't you say?"

"Because you stopped me." She folded her arms. "It's dangerous anyway. You wouldn't approve."

"Tell me. Quickly." Outside, voices were calling the alarm. The battle was closing in.

She swallowed and gave a tight-lipped nod. "All right. But there's something I need to do first."

He looked away, distracted by a polar bear's roar. When he turned back, Rosa was right in front of him. "Do you remember when we sat by the well on Co:pern:ica and I made you a bracelet of violet-colored daisies?"

David grimaced. There was no time for this. All the same, he let his mind drift back. He'd been twelve years old, happy and relaxed with her, taking time off from their work in the librarium. "Of course I remember. It was . . . a beautiful day."

"The best," she said.

"Special," he agreed. "Rosa, what's the matter?" Her eyes were glistening with tears.

"I made the bracelet to tell you how much I loved you, because I wasn't brave enough back then to do this. . . ." And she pulled him toward her and kissed him passionately. Then she stepped back, and kept on stepping back. "I'll miss you, David."

"Rosa, what are you *talking* about?"

"Gwilanna knows a way to speed up your cure. All it needs is a powerful burst of auma."

And at last he understood what she planned to do. "Rosa?! No!"

But she was already running.

Zanna, by now, was bent over but on her feet.

Hearing someone approaching, she turned and saw Rosa standing over her. "Need a hand?" Rosa asked, extending hers.

Without thinking, Zanna gripped it.

Above and below their hands, a vertical flash of light emerged. Then the universe hummed and their bodies came together as the timeline moved to heal the paradox. A pressure wave pulsed in all directions. The light contracted to a single point. And when it was done, there was only one girl left in the chamber.

Zanna.

16. OF BEARS AND DARKLINGS

In the early stages of the battle at sea, the conflict between the bears and the Shadow had gone very much the way of the bears.

Another lone darkling had raised the alarm. From a height well above the motionless water, it had seen the bears forming like giant blocks of ice and witnessed the ease with which Kailar had dispatched its reckless companion. Straightaway it had turned and headed for the island, calling out a warning that had initially gone unheeded. Then the first snowflakes began to fall on the chain of rocks to the north and west of the main isle. The brood of darklings nestling there were immediately scattered by the roars of the bears that materialized among them. Many were cut down before they could fly. One of those which got away badly mauled was the one that had made it to the chamber, and David. The shock of surprise had given the bears an early advantage, which could be measured by the carcasses strewn across the sea and the trails of black fluid running down the rocks. But it wasn't long before Voss's creatures began to hit back. Only then did the battle begin in earnest.

In theory, everything favored the darklings. They had the medium of air for a start. Greater speed, better maneuverability, complemented by a startling array of claws, stigs, toxins, and teeth. Their ability to paralyze the nervous systems of organisms such as bears and humans was known to cause instantaneous blindness and several other forms of sensory disarray. Plus they had the option of self-division. Their rapidly developing genetic footprint supported a form of self-cloning called budding. Ten darklings could become twenty in minutes.

Despite their early losses, they were confident of victory.

So they attacked with arrogance at first, strafing the bears with jeers and hisses and gobbets of vile acidic spit, aimed at delicate parts of the body: the eyes, the shells of the ears, the tail. Then the first darkling landed on the hump of a running bear's back. It rode along for a few rough strides, gaily swinging its ugly head to

the scooping rhythm of the bear's gallop. It goaded the
enemy with taunts of a terrible, agonizing death. Yet
the bear made no attempt to throw it off. Annoyed by
this haughty show of indifference, the darkling decided
to move to the kill. It cranked its jaws and sank its
numerous retracted teeth into the scruff of the bear's
thick neck.

Crunch.

There was a nauseating crack of bones. White spikes
sprang out of the darkling's head, as if it had swallowed a ball of thorns. Black stains flooded its bulging
eyes. Spittle trickled from the sides of its jaws. Its
vicious hooked claws relaxed their grip. A few more
seconds elapsed before its lifeless body leaned sideways
into the wind. Then it tumbled down the polar bear's
shoulder, falling away to be kicked aside and trampled
to mulch by the next set of paws that came pounding
along. Those darklings that witnessed this bewildering
fatality swept down and attempted to exact revenge.
The outcome for most of them was the same. One by
one they fell away dead or injured, or leaped off their
victim, screaming in pain. In one spectacular case, a
rider exploded. This pattern was repeated all over the
sea, and many more of Voss's multitude perished before

he could transmit the vital information that the bears were protected by some kind of magicks. In fact, the truth was more straightforward than that.

The bears had been taught to imagineer.

On Earth, in the dominant timeline that had seen them evolve from the brown bear, Thoran, on a bed of frozen water made by Gawain, bears had ruled the Icelands for thousands of years. When the risk of dark fire had become a real threat, the Higher had removed this iconic species into the safety of the thought plane of the nexus they called Ki:mera. There the bears had remained in stasis, ready to return when the threat was removed and the timeline was stable. One of them, however, proved a little troublesome. The bear known as Avrel refused to cooperate. Despite the Higher's most intensive efforts, the self-styled "Teller of Ways" would not (or could not) close down his mind. The Higher subjected him to rigorous testing. Avrel's capacity for information storage amazed the Fain beings, who had only ever noted this level of ability in Collectives such as theirs (or the Ix Shadow). The ice bear was carefully nurtured. His extraordinary mind was allowed to move freely within the Is. In time, certain *developments* were noted. Interesting constructs began to appear, unlike anything the Higher had seen before. The entire history of the Icelands of the North began to float out of Avrel's memories and take physical shape as it spun around his head. This went on for as long as it needed to, until one exceptional memory stood out: the shedding of Gawain's fire tear. As it dripped from the dragon's eye, the image froze and the tear hung in the Is like a jewel. The Teller opened his eyes and squinted. Something could be seen inside the teardrop. A sculpture, in ice, of a woman holding hands with a boy. A bear was spread-eagled at their feet. The Teller blinked. The scene in the fire tear immediately changed. Suddenly, a girl with wings appeared, sitting cross-legged on a static sea. In her hands was a small green dragon that was constantly blurring its shape, moving quicker than light itself. "It's time," said the child. The dragon in her hands opened its enormous paws and hurred. Avrel blinked again. To the Higher's astonishment, a fire star opened in Ki:mera. Even more bizarrely, they were helpless to stop the ensuing exodus. Polar bears drifted to the Earth as snowflakes, led by Avrel and the fighting bear, Kailar.

But they were changed, these bears. On their journey, through a kind of morphic resonance, Avrel had taught them how to use their minds like his. Their first test was to protect themselves against darklings. Temporarily hardening their fur into spikes was a tactic adopted by most of the pack. And even when the darklings learned to avoid making physical contact, the bears grew more ingenious again. They imagineered blizzard "nets," which could freeze a wing and make the creatures drop from the sky. Once a darkling was on the surface, one swipe of a bear's paw did the rest.

Of course, there were losses on the bears' side, too. Sometimes, out of fear or recklessness, a bear would forget the Teller's training and revert to brute strength alone. On one distressing occasion, Avrel witnessed a hotheaded yearling underneath a skriking cluster of darklings. For that bear, there was no hope of survival.

On the island itself, opposition was minimal. This was partly due to confusion. Even as news of the bears began to spread, men could be seen wandering aimlessly about, examining their skin or their companions' eyes. Something was draining the Shadow out of them. They were becoming human again. Snow fell on every shoreline all the same, greatly outnumbering the men who were there. They were faced with simple choices: fight a physically superior opponent, hide where they could, or lay down their weapons. Under Avrel's orders, those that fought were dealt with mercifully. Those that surrendered — the vast majority — were shuffled into groups and guarded. Those that hid were simply ignored.

One of those who managed to escape the roundup was the man who'd been ordered to hold Lucy hostage. His plan had been to keep her in a cave at sea level. She was a feisty, kicking wretch, and a journey to the windswept higher ledges with an ex-commander who was constantly spouting all the different, colorful ways she could kill him was deeply unappealing.

The arrival of the polar bears changed his mind.

"Up," he ordered, jabbing her ribs with the butt of his sword. Though wary of her old authority, he was still far broader and stronger than she and there was little she could do to resist — except talk.

"Let me go, you idiot! Voss needs me to fight."

"There ain't no fighting."

"Let me see!"

He allowed her to stop and shuffle around. Sure enough, he wasn't lying. Voss's men were being herded into groups by bears. One bear, a young-looking animal with a deeply intelligent air about him, was set apart from the rest. He was scanning every dent in the lower escarpments. A sudden rumble drew his gaze to the peak of the island, offering Lucy a better look at his face. "I know him," she murmured.

"'Course you do," the guard said. He bundled her around and forced her up the slope. "I was very good friends with the fish I had for lunch. *Walk.*" They had gone ten steps when another rumble sounded, causing a quake that chased a flurry of rocks into their path. The guard slipped and cussed as he tried to avoid them. "What's wrong with that idiot dragon?"

Lucy's reply was to turn and kick him under the chin. She heard the crisp smack as his jaw snapped shut. He staggered backward, swimming in air, then eventually lost his balance and fell. Lucy scrabbled down to finish him off. One more kick, she hoped, would knock him out. But the guard was more shocked than hurt. He caught her foot and with a roar upended her, leaving her close to a serious drop. She wriggled away from the draw of the edge, desperate to find a snag of stone she could use to cut the bindings from her hands. But he was up again, dragging an arm across his mouth. He spat out a tooth and picked up his sword. "You'll wish you 'adn't done that."

He taunted her with a sweep of the blade. Instinctively, she scrabbled away. But as she swapped her gaze between the drop and the sword, she saw an opportunity to reason with him. "Your hand. Look at your hand."

He snorted with laughter. "I ain't falling for yer tricks. You ain't livin' to tell no tales of this. When I'm done here, trust me, no one's gonna find yer."

"I mean it. Your hand. You're changing. We all are." She could feel it — and definitely see it in him. The weblike patterns of the Shadow were fading.

Still he ignored her and whirled the sword. He might have been approaching humanity again, but he was dredging up the very worst side of it. "Never liked taking your orders neither."

Then a new voice said, "You should be careful, soldier — making admissions like that."

The guard whipped around and immediately took another blow to the chin, this time from the end of Tam Farrell's fist. The man pirouetted once and fell without a sound, into the maw of rocks below.

On the distant clank of the sword, Lucy said, "Technically, that's treason, Commander."

He knelt and untied her. "Correct me if I'm wrong, but don't I have a history of saving your life?"

She gripped her wrist and flexed some bright red blood into her fingers. Green veins. Pink skin. Red blood. Red *hair*. "What happened to us?"

"Don't know exactly. Maybe these guys can tell us." He showed her the polar bears glowing in his palms.

Before she could comment, the ground around them juddered and the sky was set alight by a plume of flame. "Look out!" cried Tam, as a shower of ash and white-hot debris came fizzling down like angry rain. He grabbed Lucy and flattened her against his chest.

If I'm going to die, let it be now, she thought.

"Cover your mouth. The fumes are getting worse." He tore a strip off his shirt and offered it to her. She almost fainted at this act of mild heroism. Had she really been this crazy about this man before the Ix had got to her? Then again, he *was* mouth-meltingly handsome.

"What's the matter?" he asked, seeing her looking.

"Me and you. Do we go out together?"

"*What?*" he coughed. The thickness of the air was pressing on his lungs. "Do we what together?"

She covered her mouth with his shirt piece. "Nothing."

"Come on." He bundled her around and pulled her down the mountain, with nearly as much intolerance as her previous captor. Only this one, she would have stayed with forever.

They reached sea level in minutes, met right away by four large bears.

"Okay, this is scary. . . . ," Lucy whispered, nudging right up to Tam's shoulder.

The leading bear rolled its lip back and growled.

Tam showed it the images in his hands. "I need to speak with Avrel and Kailar." No human present could have understood the grunt, but the bears around him did.

The leading bear spoke quickly to the others. They parted to let Tam through, but escorted him closely as he marched across the scree. Lucy trotted on close behind, still with Tam's shirt across her mouth.

They found Avrel sitting on a patch of clear ground, his head low down in his bright white chest. He heard the crunch of pebbles and raised his gaze.

Again Tam showed his palms. "Avrel. My name is Tam Farrell. I am a friend of Ingavar. He blessed me with your image."

"I know who you are," said the Teller of Ways.

"He's in the heart of the island. I can take you to him."

Avrel nodded. A slight breeze picked at the fur around his ears.

"Commander!" a distant voice called.

Tam heard it and said, "These men you are guarding are no danger to you now. Something has reverted the Shadow in us. Let them take arms. They will help you fight Voss."

Avrel glanced at the men, the sleek lines of his jaw so sharp against the sky. "The fight is over," he said.

Tam peered across the sea. He could still see darklings wheeling in the sky, albeit some distance away. "Voss is dead?"

Avrel shook his head. "His darklings have multiplied in number and the Shadow has absorbed enough of our auma to begin an inversion of our species. We cannot fight anymore."

Lucy prodded Tam's shoulder. "What's going on?"

Avrel turned his brown-eyed gaze on her. "You must take the girl away. Any child of the dragon is bound to suffer."

"Hey, did he speak to me then?"

"Why?" said Tam, ignoring her. "What's happened?"

"Voss was seen with the flying girl."

"Alexa's out there?" Tam spoke this aloud.

"Alexa?!" Lucy shoved Tam aside and put herself in front of Avrel. "Where? Where is A-lex-a? You-have-to-find-her."

Tam translated her outburst, adding, "You have to fight, Avrel. Ingavar will lead you, with Kailar at his side."

Avrel tipped his snout into the wind. "Look at the water, Tam Farrell."

Tam looked and saw the tide was rolling in. In his haste to bring Lucy down to the shore he hadn't noticed that the sea was fluid again. His heart sank when he saw a wide slick of blood.

"For us, the battle is done," said Avrel. "Kailar is dead."

17. Opening the Lock

All David could do was stand and stare. It was her, from the beautiful hips to the snaking hair. With no ugly adornments from the Shadow. Human again. His Earth love.

Zanna.

She looked at the dragon, her bangles, her arm. Her fingers settled lightly over her scars. From that, she seemed to learn everything at once. "Oh my god . . . ," she whispered. "Rosa. Oh my god . . ."

The first of the judders Tam and Lucy would feel on the slopes of the mountain happened at that point. Gawain flapped his wings and spiraled around the pool. A single point of flame went rocketing past him on its way to the dome of the island.

"Something's happening," said Zanna. "Gwilanna's

reporting waves of energy emerging from the other side of the core."

"I have to go," David muttered, shaking his head. "There are bears. They'll be looking for me." He backed away.

"Wait," she commanded. Her devastating green eyes pierced his heart. "You know that Rosa would want you here."

Now he could only hold his face. Steepling his fingers around his nose, he tried to staunch the threat of tears. "Can you feel her?"

"Of course I can." The words were softly spoken. Zanna placed her fingers in the scars again. They began to glow blue. "Your antidote's working. It's spreading through the matrix the Ix created to control the humans. Gwilanna was right. The energy from the paradox was enough to force the change. Rosa has saved a lot of lives. But it won't revert any of the darklings — or Voss. He's too far gone. Only a dragon could take him down."

"That's why I need to go."

The island rumbled again. This time, David felt it in his gut.

"No," she said. Once more he paused. "When Gwilanna messed with the timeline she got the added bonus of screwing up your connection to Grockle. You can't call him. You're out of phase. I can give you some of your old strength back but it won't protect you against Voss's magicks."

"Then take down this barrier and give me Gawain."

The dragon was following this conversation like a confused but faithful dog.

"I can't. Voss set it. Only he would know the encryption."

David whirled away, driving a hand through his hair in frustration. "This is ridiculous. I can't just hang around waiting for this lump of rock to explode." As he spoke, shale was cracking off the walls. "There must be *something* I can do."

"There is. They were right about Alexa. She's close."

"How close? Where is she?"

"I don't know yet."

"But you can feel her?"

"Yes. The dragons, too. The Pennykettle dragons. She must have moved them here, through time."

"What's she *doing*? If you can sense her, Voss must

be able to. She might as well have painted him a 'look here' sign."

Zanna nodded, grim faced. "I have a horrible feeling she intends exactly that."

David rubbed his fingers against his temples. "You said I could do something. What did you mean?"

"Call them. Call the dragons here. Your links to them overrule Alexa's. If we get them away from her, Voss might go off the scent — and we'll have a chance of freeing Gawain."

David gave a hopeful nod. There were very few problems in the known universe that couldn't be solved by Liz's creations. So he closed his eyes and pictured Gadzooks. Straightaway, he saw the writing dragon in Alexa's hands. Gadzooks felt the auma wave and sat bolt upright. He put away his pad.

"Come on-n-n," muttered David, "look this way."

Gadzooks frowned and turned his head.

"Good boy. Come to Daddy. . . ."

The dragon blew a puff of smoke and shook his head. *Hrrr.*

Typical, thought David. He concentrated on G'reth instead. To his surprise, he saw Gadzooks morph into the wisher. "She's combined them," he said. "How's she done that?"

"Stay focused," said Zanna. "Just get them here." She came to him and put her hand to his heart. "Gawain is the key. Concentrate."

There was a fizzle of light, and suddenly G'reth had materialized before them.

For a third time, an ominous rumble shook the island. Gawain beat his wings and bellowed a warning. The lava pool opened in the shape of a crown and began to spit white-hot rocks into the air.

"Quickly," Zanna said, "before Alexa calls them back. We need to get Gwilanna out of there."

"How? What should I do?"

"What you always do when you want to crack a nut."

"Use a sledgehammer?"

"No, you idiot. You ask Gollygosh."

The healing dragon. The moment David thought of him, he'd taken G'reth's place. "There, look. What's with the morphing thing?"

"I don't know," said Zanna. "But in case you hadn't noticed, this whole island is about to go up. Ask him what he can do about the force field."

David dented it so Gollygosh could see the problem.

And the dragon did what he always did. He put down his toolbox. It opened and an asterisk of light zipped out. The toolbox closed. Gollygosh disappeared. But just when David was thinking they had failed, the asterisk exploded into a shape. And suddenly, the answer to their problem was obvious.

Only one thing in the universe could pass through a construct. A firebird.

Gideon had come.

18. NEVER BORN HUMAN

Tam Farrell burst in with Lucy at his side. "David? Zanna?"

Lucy ran to David and threw her arms around him. "They've got Alexa," she whispered.

David met Tam's gaze. "Is this true?"

Tam nodded and gave him a very quick rundown, pausing on the difficult news about Kailar. "He was last seen protecting Alexa. Voss attacked him with a jet of dark fire. It blasted a huge hole in the surface, destroying the freezing spell in the process. Kailar . . . didn't come up. Any bears that survived the early battles must be in the water by now. I'm not sure what we can do for them. It gets worse, David. Voss is gathering darklings way out at sea. According to Avrel's best reports they've tripled in number."

"Why aren't they attacking the island?" asked Zanna.

David looked at Gawain and said, "They're waiting to see what happens to it."

Tam nodded in agreement. "We should get to the mainland. It's safer there."

"What about Alexa?"

"I'm guessing Voss has her."

"I doubt it," said a voice.

Everyone turned to see a shimmering boy sitting on the rock where Gideon had been.

"Who are *you?*" said Lucy, in her usual semi-scornful way.

The boy raised his angelic face to her. "I'm Joseph Henry, your brother."

Zanna plucked at David's arm. Despite her considerable sibyl strengths, she was struggling to take this in. It didn't help that the boy was the image of David — or how David might have been when he was twelve.

Likewise, Lucy tottered a little, not quite able to believe what she was seeing. "But you're . . ."

"Dead?" He shook his mop of hair. "No, just never born human. It's different."

"Then you're a spirit?" said Tam.

"Who's moving through time as a firebird," David added.

Joseph lifted his shoulders. The white robe he was wearing rippled like silk. "I 'am' what everyone imagines me to be. It's easier for you to see me this way. Easier than talking to Gideon anyway."

"Where's Gwillan, Joseph?"

The boy tapped his immaculate fingers together. "You sound disapproving, David."

"I just want to be sure we're all working in harmony. The last time I saw you, you'd taken his form — and stolen powers from the other dragons."

Joseph smiled and imagineered a conker, as if that might somehow help his cause. "Gwillan is safe. He's with my mother."

"I remember," Lucy interjected suddenly, recalling echoes of the previous timeline. "Mom was ill. The dark fire was in her. I had to leave her and go to Scuffenbury with Tam."

"Is Liz all right?" Tam asked.

"I was looking after her," Zanna muttered, as the memories began to come back to her, too.

"But you were at Scuffenbury with us," said Tam.

Zanna nodded. "I left her in Agatha Bacon's care."

"That was not Agatha Bacon," said Joseph.

Behind him, Gawain gave a pitiful roar.

David put two and two together at once. "You," he said darkly. He was looking at Gawain, but from the tone of his voice addressing Gwilanna. "What have you done to Liz? If you've harmed her, I'll find a way to drag you out of those scales and I'll kill you and everyone here can be my witness."

"Killing Gwilanna will not change anything," said Joseph. "Unless the timeline changes, what happens to my mother and Arthur is fixed."

"Can we change the timeline back?" asked Tam.

Joseph took a moment before replying. "Yes, but Gwilanna must agree to it."

"*Gwilanna must?*" Zanna stared at him in shock. For the last few moments, she had been trying to commingle with the sibyl, whose silence was only compounding her guilt.

"She began this, she has to end it," he said.

The chamber juddered again and the whole bedrock of the island moved. Gawain, by now, was swimming in a constant stream of fire.

"I hate to break this party up," said Tam. "But we have *got* to get off this island." He took Lucy's hand and pulled her a little closer to the entrance. She needed no persuading.

"The core is reached," Joseph said. "Alexa must be brought here. Only she can control the gateway."

"Then she's alive?" Zanna pressed forward in hope.

"Yes, but in danger. You are all in danger."

"How do we fight them?" Tam Farrell asked.

"You don't," said Joseph. "There is no battle for any of you."

"But the tapestry?" said David.

"Ended at Scuffenbury Hill, with Gadzooks. When time resets, you will all be returned to a natural life — and all that that life entails."

"You can't take on Voss and his darklings alone."

The boy smiled. "I don't need to, David. In following the fire tear down to the core, Voss has organized his own destruction. As for the darklings . . ." He closed his eyes, and moments later a spume of lava erupted from the pool, helped on its way by a bellow from the seat of Gawain's huge lungs. "That will bring them down. Avrel and his bears will do the rest."

Tam coughed and spluttered and beat his chest. "How can they fight when they can hardly breathe?" The gaseous mixture in the air was horrendous.

"The bears will breathe well enough," said David, guessing now at Joseph's intent. "But the change in air

composition, the added sulfur, will block the darklings'
spiracles, right?"

Joseph nodded. "Good-bye, Ingavar. We will not
meet again. Tell your bears to look for a miracle. Enjoy
your future life."

"Wait," cried Lucy. She let go of Tam's hand and
ran to her brother. "Where will you be, when time
goes back?"

"I will be here," he said. And he touched her heart
with a spark of white fire.

In an instant, he turned into Gideon again. And
they barely had time to admire his plumage before
he flew through the force field and disappeared into
Gawain's body.

19. The Fire Ascending

Although his primary reason for flying off the island was not to get involved in the grind of the battle, it had irked Voss to see his darklings losing. There were only so many *stains* he could take before the need to fry a bear got the better of him. Their subtle attempts at imagineering were a laudable addition to their basic strengths (of hitting and squashing and being large), but none of them could cope with his own dark fire. He had taken out . . . ten, a dozen, maybe more, when the first real trace of the gatekeeper's auma had begun to trickle into his sensory detectors. He had tried to lock on to it right away, but the signal strength was carefully encrypted and the frenzied twisting of locator stigs was actually beginning to hurt his head. He suspected that the girl was merging in and out of the timeline at random. Or dissociating into the *ganzfeld* as required. She was clever. He admired that about her. The very fact she had Traveled the nexus was impressive. Here was an opponent worthy of respect. An intelligent hybrid. Gatekeeper to the core. If her mood was right, he might let her survive. She would make a valuable addition to the Shadow.

In the end he found her by chance, during what must have been a lapse in concentration — hers, not his. At the time he was considering one more kill, to eliminate an irritating monster of a bear that had had the bizarre audacity to track him — a ludicrous exercise on the bear's part. He, Voss, could easily outfly the most fleet-footed lump of white gristle. This one was only keeping pace with him because of his height and angle off the sea. It would have been amusing to zigzag a little and watch the brute die of a sprained neck. But a burst of dark fire or a poisoned barb would settle the issue much quicker. Then he could focus on his search again.

And then he felt it. A surge of auma that only a being of superior intelligence would have the power to transmit. He forgot the stupid bear and turned his sensors to their maximum sweep. The signal was intermittent. But when it was there it was strong and clear, as if the girl had peeked out from her hiding place to look for something she might have lost. Voss was not to know that his island enemy, David Rain, was working on his behalf just then. It was David, calling the dragons away, that had made Alexa expose her position. Through his best intentions, he had put his daughter's life in peril.

Voss swooped down, big and menacing, every bit as ugly as he was chilling. "Hello, Alexa," he said, making the greeting seem as dark as the ooze that pumped around his veins. "Please don't try to escape. Now that I have your auma trace I can follow you anywhere, even into the field. I don't want to hurt you — or your dragon."

Alexa glanced at her hands. The dragons (plural, Voss had yet to discover) had come back a moment too late for her to flee. She was surprised to see Gollygosh was active, and worried that Voss might ask about the toolbox. For now, the dragon was keeping it hidden, tucked away awkwardly behind his knee. "This island belongs to the bears," she said.

Voss larruped his three-forked tongue. "No," he assured her, "it's definitely mine. I am the Prime. Your mother is my Pri:magon. Your father is being . . . converted to the Shadow. I'd like you to join us in our adventure. Why don't you stop this temperamental nonsense and take my hand so we can all be one?"

"What have you done to Gawain?"

"Ohhh, dragons," he sighed, flicking his tail, "such a flawed and rather outdated design. Why are humans so obsessed with them? Ah, but I'm forgetting. You're not entirely human. What *do* the Higher label you, child?"

"Angel," she said. "They call me Angel."

"A good term," he conceded. "A powerful name. Angel: part dragon, part Fain, part human . . . part bear, even?"

She felt Gollygosh gulp and prayed he wouldn't rattle. "No," she said. "I couldn't be a bear."

"And why is that?"

"I'm not very good at sneaking up on people."

Voss was quick to note this deceit. Was that a hint of eagerness in her voice? Certainly a glitch in the corner of her eye. Treachery was subtly at work in the girl.

Something was approaching him from behind. . . .

Too late, Kailar was on him. And unlike the previous attack on the darkling, Voss was allowed no time to turn. Kailar had stalked him since his landing, using every skill his mother had taught when hunting for slippery, nervous seals. The long, low crouch. The brush of paws hidden in the sigh of a breeze. The silent, deadly leap.

He was exploding through the air as Alexa was finishing her final sentence. Any normal creature, even one of above-human height like Voss, would have crumpled under his immense weight. But Voss had speed and preternatural strength. Not only did he absorb the impact, he opened his wings and lifted the gallant bear off the sea. Out from the notches in his stooping spine came four venomous triangular thorns. Kailar howled as the spikes ground in. (Bears reporting to Avrel later claimed they could feel the fighting bear's pain, even though they were miles away.) Blood emerged in spurts from each wound, turning Kailar's undersides red. When the thorns had done their grisly work, Voss withdrew them, letting his attacker slide off his back and fall down with a sorry *crump*. In his enraged state, the Prime turned and blasted the sea around Kailar with a wide spray of dark fire. It traveled a hundred searing paces. G'reth's amazing wish was shattered. The Great Sea roared and ran wild again.

At the same time in all directions, bears were pitched into open water. Those who made it back to shore (carried on the huge incoming waves), told how Voss had attacked without mercy, killing bears freely — to be sure, perhaps, that Kailar was dead. Whatever the reason, their champion, their noble leader in battle, descendant of the bear who gave the Tooth of Ragnar its name, was not seen by any of the survivors. He was dead, they claimed. Assumed drowned.

It was not just bears thrown into the water. When Voss struck, the Pennykettle dragons were swept right out of Alexa's hands and sent tumbling through the heaving waves. Swimming was not something that came naturally to them (there'd been very little call for it at Wayward Crescent). They could do it, of course. Any dragon could. And they were experts at shielding their fire in water (holding their smoke, they called it). Even so, a lot of shape changes took place before they decided that Gwendolen was the one to get them to the surface, where they could look for Alexa again.

The dragon spread her wings and stabilized their fall. But as she kicked her feet and arrowed her tail she was aware of Kailar sinking beside her. Her heart wrenched as she saw his paws moving, stirring up the blood spilling out of his wounds. Despite the severity of his injuries, he was still bravely fighting for life. Still, in his mind, defending Alexa. Gwendolen called on the others for assistance. What could be done to help the bear? *Nothing*, was the distressed answer from Gretel. The water had washed her flowers away. What did the guard dragon's book suggest? Gruffen took shape and opened it. Amazingly, the pages did not become water-logged and none of the printed words were blurred. He repeated Gwendolen's question: What could be done to save the bear? The pages fluttered and stopped at *I*. One word appeared there: *Isenfier*.

Isenfier. None of them knew what it meant. And time was running out for Kailar. The bear, though instinctively treading water, was still going down, not up. Bubbles were streaming out of his nose. There was only one possible option left. Gadzooks took shape and wrote the word on his pad.

The response was a little vague. All the same, the universe heard his intent and sent him an instant reply: *BLOW*. The word arrived in his ear like a mote of dust (or maybe an off-course plankton), spoken, he thought, by Elizabeth Pennykettle.

"Blow," he transmitted to the others.

"What?" said Gretel, ever the skeptic.

Gadzooks didn't bother to repeat the word. He just did what dragons do best: breathed fire.

Out into the water went his breath. Instantly, it turned to ice.

HRRR!

The others saw it and quickly understood. They were born of Gawain, the maker of ice. And ice, they knew, floated on water. They swam under Kailar and made the largest raft they could. Lo and behold, as it began to take shape, it lifted the stricken bear to the surface.

And bobbed up under their worst nightmare.

Voss had been carefully scanning the water for signs of Alexa or her body. His surprise at seeing Kailar, on a tablet of ice, was only bettered by his intrigue about Gadzooks.

Gadzooks backed up to Kailar's flank. The bear was breathing thinly, too weak to stand.

Voss flashed his tail and circled it tight around Zookie's middle. He yanked the little creature close to his face. "The mysterious tapestry dragon," he said. "So, we meet at last. What is your name, creature?"

"His name is Gadzooks," said an unexpected voice. "A foolish-sounding name, I grant you. But it literally translates as 'claws of Godith.' Which makes him rather powerful, Father."

Voss whirled around to see Gwilanna on the far side of the ice. Beside her was a boy in a shimmering robe. No other humans were near. Voss's attention was briefly taken by a darkling spluttering out of the sky. The third he'd seen drop in as many minutes. "How did *you* get here? How are you even *alive*?"

"I was called," she answered truthfully. "The dragon you're crushing invoked my auma. He does things like that. Elizabeth, I now see, was very blessed. Surely Zanna warned you about them?"

Voss twisted Gadzooks like a pepper grinder. Yes, the Pri:magon had talked about these creatures. Dragons from clay. He'd paid it no attention.

He did now.

"Who's the boy?"

"My grandson . . . in a manner of speaking." She pinched his perfect cheek. "Joseph is also remarkably powerful. It was him who freed me from your construct and gave me back my . . . shape."

Voss eyed Joseph Henry with suspicion.

"He's kindly offered me a chance of redemption for all the misdemeanors I've committed."

"Grandma?" he tutted.

"Oh, very well. I suppose I was plain *bad* sometimes."

In the distance, the island finally erupted. Fire arcs lit the sky. Wave after wave of them. Trail upon trail. Breaking up steadily into stars.

The boy said, "Alexa has opened the core."

"She sends her apologies," the sibyl added. "She came to the island seeking help from her father and had to avert a major crisis. There's been a little problem with G:ravity, apparently. Thanks to you, our universe is in danger of collapsing into Quantum."

"Quantum?" sneered Voss.

"Your sea of white fire. The world we mistakenly 'budded' from. Oh dear, am I sounding like Arthur Merriman?"

"Yes," said Joseph.

"A little knowledge and we all become scientists," she sighed.

"Be silent!" said Voss.

"Oh, do calm down," Gwilanna said coldly. "You're upsetting the bear."

Voss's response was to turn and attempt to kill Kailar for good. But the blast of dark fire he'd gathered in his throat emerged as a slowed-down plasma bubble.

Gadzooks had to duck as it clawed at the air, then retreated with a sucking noise into Voss's mouth. The Shadow Prime grimaced in pain. "What's hap-pening?" he said, though the words were difficult to speak. He gurgled slightly and the corner of his mouth began to bend inward. One of his thorny hands went to his throat.

"You're imploding," said Gwilanna. "Is that the right term?"

"Yes," said Joseph. "All dark energy is being restored to permissible levels."

A searing oval of violet light swept out from the island at sea level. At the same time, one of Voss's knee joints buckled. The line of his waist began to warp. Zigzagging cracks appeared in his chest.

"I don't understand it either," said the sibyl, noting the perplexity in Voss's gaze. Or was that his skull beginning to compress? "You must hate me, Father. This is all my fault. I can't even offer you a decent *skirmish* because you're going to struggle to fly."

Fittingly, his wings wrapped into his body, pressuring his rib cage against his organs. He cried out as something burst in his gut. It bulged for a moment, then was sucked back in. A shoulder joint failed. A hip caved in. The tail began to wither and shrink. Gadzooks, still caught in the tail, began to struggle.

Joseph tapped his grandmother's arm. "It's time, Grandma. The guardians are waiting."

"Gar ... dy ... ans?" Voss slurred.

Gwilanna pointed to the sky. The stars that had formed, and were still forming, were popping like fireworks, exploding into sparkling, colorful dragons, no bigger than the size of Gadzooks. One of them dropped down and hurred on Voss's tail, freeing the grateful Pennykettle dragon. He tipped his snout and hurred back at it. Every one of the guardians suddenly gained a pencil.

"They've come to restart time," said Gwilanna. "They've allowed us to keep this sector of the universe as long as time begins in its proper place."

"At zero," said Joseph. "All that Is will be restored, with some minor differences."

Voss's legs were suddenly sucked into his middle. His head began to melt into the whirlpool of his body.

"That's got to hurt, hasn't it?" Gwilanna muttered, pulling an expression of mild abhorrence. "You've probably realized, Father, you won't survive. I don't suppose there's any chance that I will, is there?"

"No," said Joseph.

Gwilanna sighed. "Ah, well. I had a good run. I met dragons. I commingled with the finest one on Earth. I even lived to see where they really come from." At her back, a silver-colored fire star rose above the island. She stared at Voss, who was now just a howling scrunchbag of darkness. She took a deep breath and raised her chin. "I'm glad the real villain wasn't me in the end." And with a whoosh that threw up a minor blizzard, Voss disappeared into a point of no return.

Gwilanna opened her hands. A beautiful fire tear blossomed inside them. In the sky, the sparkling guardians of Quantum all held a fire tear of their own. "So this is it, boy. This is the end for me now?"

"For me, too," said Joseph, taking her arm.

"Will it be painful?"

"No. Just strange. Think of it as your gift to the world."

"I will see Elizabeth again, you promise?"

"I promise. I believe she's expecting us."

Gwilanna extended her hands, letting the fire tear bobble within them. "A new ice cap. It doesn't seem much of a gift."

"It will to him." Joseph nodded at Kailar.

But the bear had closed his almond eye. And as the north wind stroked his fur and mourned, it was all Gadzooks could do not to shed his spark into the waiting ocean.

Even Gwilanna shuddered. "Stupid lump of fur," she muttered. "Couldn't even stay alive for my moment of glory. He was the one who freed me from an ice block when the Ix turned me into a raven, you know."

"Then now is your chance to thank him," said Joseph, "and earn the respect of Gaia."

And so Gwilanna walked over to Kailar's body and clamped his ear in her one free hand. "Here you are, ice bear, this is for you. Let me be an angel once in my life."

And legend would record that as the tear of Gawain fell into the ocean, the bear, the sibyl, and the boy who took her hand became immortal.

Frozen in the ice and fire of time.

PART EIGHT
THE LOAF EVERLASTING

Wayward Crescent
In the timeline set by the Guardians of Quantum

"David, it's nearly half past ten. The cars will be here in fifteen minutes."

"Still looking through the albums," he called.

A floor below, he heard Zanna sigh. "Lexie, go up and fetch him. No. Wait. What's that on your head? How've you managed to get *orange peel* stuck in your hair? I don't care. Never mind, just go and get Daddy."

Feet pounded up the stairs. Seconds later, Alexa ran into the study and plunked herself onto her father's lap, facing his computer screen.

"You look pretty," he said, adjusting her so he

could still read his manuscript. She was wearing a violet-colored dress and shoes. A green bow wobbled in her wayward hair. "Hmm, oranges," he said, sniffing her curls.

"Mommy says you've got to hurry up."

" 'Twas ever thus," he hummed.

"What's this?" She jabbed a finger at the screen.

"A new story. Well, the start of one."

"About Bonnington?"

"Not this one, no."

"Daddy, you *promised* you'd do a story about Bonnington."

He pinched her around the waist and said, "It's not your birthday, yet, is it?" He checked the desk calendar. Dangerously close though.

She dropped her shoulders and simultaneously lifted her perfect chin. A gesture that always made Zanna cry, "Action!"

Alexa picked up a pencil and chewed the end.

"Don't do that."

"Why?" she demanded.

"You'll give yourself . . . pencil poisoning."

"Mommy says *you* do it."

"No, I don't."

"Then why are there teeth marks here and here and . . . ?"

He took it off her and dropped it in his cup with the others.

"Who's Rosa?" she asked, shaking her hair imperiously. She touched the name on-screen, denting her finger. In a separate window, the character's avatar appeared.

"She's a girl. You'd like her."

"She looks like Mommy."

"Ten years ago, maybe."

"Do you love her?"

"Who, Mommy? Of course I love Mommy."

"Nooo, *Rosa*."

"She's a character, Lexie."

"Yes, but Mommy says when you write about *heroines* you're really writing about *her* because you find it easier to tell Mommy you love her in a story than when you're . . . out shopping."

"Shopping?"

"Or something."

There was really no answer to that. *I love you, Zanna. Do we need eggs?* "Where did you learn a word like 'heroine'?"

"Mr. Henry taught me."

"Oh, him again." Mr. Henry was her "computer tutor." "Aren't you tired of the Mr. Henry game? Don't you want to play some adventure games like . . ." *Normal children*, he almost said. "The ones Aunt Lucy makes?"

"Aunt Lucy's games are *all right*," she said, dragging her finger along the edge of his desk. "But Mommy says 'Librarimum' —"

" 'Librarium,' " he corrected her.

"— is good because it *teaches* you things."

"Not if it gives you a better vocabulary than me."

"Anyway, you haven't answered my question."

"Which one of the multitude did I miss?"

"The one about Rosa."

"What about Rosa?"

"Do you *love* her?"

David looked at the avatar again. She did bear a strong resemblance to Zanna, though he wasn't sure Zanna would wear a bracelet made of daisies. "I love them all in a way, even the baddies."

"The baddies? That's silly."

"Well, when you write your first . . . blockbuster you'll probably feel the same."

"David, ten minutes!"

The welcome relief of maternal authority. "We're on our way!"

Though they clearly weren't.

Alexa rolled her eyes.

"Okay, guilty as charged." He scrolled the story off-screen, tapping it to bring up the albums database. He double-tapped one called "Mom." "You can help me choose a picture of Grandma."

"All right," said Alexa, resetting herself.

"I've narrowed it down to six." He showed her a montage.

She looked at them carefully and pointed to the one in the center at the bottom.

"Yes, I like that one as well," he said. It was the oldest picture of the bunch. His mother must have been in her midtwenties. Slim and green-eyed. A beautiful waterfall of red hair was falling halfway to her waist.

"Is that you?" Alexa pointed at the baby in Liz's arms.

"No, how could it be me? That's Aunt Lucy. And that's your great-aunt Sibyl standing behind Grandma — looking like she's chewed on a lemon, as usual."

Alexa drew her lips in but didn't smile. "Why isn't Grandad in the picture?"

Without thinking, David said, "Grandad Arthur wouldn't have been there then."

"Why not?"

"Well —" Hole. Shovel. Deep dark pit. Fortunately, she threw him a rope in her very next sentence.

"Was he in his labradory making spells?"

"*Lab-ora-tory*. A labradory is . . . a fancy person's dog. And Grandad Arthur doesn't do spells — no matter what the scientific community believes."

"What does he do, then?

"He swivels in his chair and thinks about things."

"What things?"

"Oh . . . little things, mostly. And how the little things make up bigger things, like . . . toast."

"Toast?!"

There was a half-eaten piece on a plate on the desk. Not the best example David could have come up with.

And she wasn't going to let it go. "Grandad Arthur goes to work and thinks about *toast*?"

"Well, no, I might have been exaggerating there. But if he did think about toast, he'd think about it in a very special way."

She gave him that "explain to me" scowl.

This was getting worse. He took a deep breath and looked along his bookshelf for inspiration. *The Five-Year-Old's Guide to Quantum Physics* appeared to be out on loan again. Drat. "Well, in Grandad's universe the loaf of bread the toast came from would have an infinite number of slices."

"What does 'infinite' mean?"

"Lots. Everlasting. As many peanut butter sandwiches as you can think of."

"Grandad's got an everlasting loaf of bread?"

"Well . . ."

"I thought you said he didn't do spells? He'd have to be *magic* to make a loaf go on for*ever*. And, anyway, that's stupid, because lots would go stale."

"Yes. Good point. I'll mention that to him. He might want to dismantle the entire foundation of theoretical physics based on that conclusion. Anyway, you like this picture?"

"Yes. Why do we need a picture?"

He let the air settle in his lungs again. It was strange how she could disarm him so quickly with such a seemingly innocent query. "People at funerals like a picture. It helps them to remember."

"I remember Grandma."

"I know you do." He bent forward and kissed her head. "I hope you always will."

Then she hit him where it really hurt. "We haven't got a picture of Joseph Henry."

"No," he said quietly. "No, we haven't." He glanced at a piece of paper secured to the pin board above his desk. Written on it were the numbers 3:15:22. One tragic point in time that would be etched through the middle of his heart forever.

"We could pretend, couldn't we?" Alexa said suddenly.

"Sorry?" he said, shaking that awful memory away.

"We could pretend *that's* him." She pointed excitedly at baby Lucy.

A tear pushed itself over David's cheek. "I don't think that would be right, Lexie."

She heard the drip on the arm of the chair and prodded the wet stain with her finger. She looked up at his face, then again at the blot. "Daddy, why are tears hot?"

He intercepted the next one before it could fall. "Oh, it's just . . . the dragon coming out of you."

Alexa looked up at one of the sculptures. Four of her grandmother's award-winning creations were ranged on the shelving above the computer. "Does a dragon keep its fire in its *tears*, then?" She gasped in that extraordinary way a child does when it knows it has made a great discovery.

"Oh, yes," David heard himself saying. No matter the mood, his storytelling functions always kicked in. "Not many people know about it though."

"Can I tell Bonnington?"

"I think *he* probably knows."

There was a pause. Then she said, "Are you going to do a story about them?"

"What, dragon tears?"

"Yes!" She bounced with glee, as if she'd already placed an order for the first edition. "I want to be in it. I want to be a fairy. No, a boy. No, an angel!"

Boy? That intrigued him. He slotted that away for future musing. "You're already an angel," he told her.

"Well, sometimes."

"David, the cars are here!"

"Time to go, *Angel*." He lifted her down.

"Do it tomorrow."

He laughed and tapped the screen, sending the photograph to his printer. "No. Not tomorrow."

"The day after, then!"

"No."

She huffed like mad. So Lucy. So Merriman. His mother had always loved that.

"What about — ?"

"After Christmas, okay? I'll think about it then. When I'm done . . . writing about Rosa."

"And Joseph Henry's got to be in it."

David picked up the print. "You want Joseph in the dragon book, too?"

"Yes!"

"Why?"

"Because then we'll have a picture of him, in *here*." She was pointing to her head, but looking past her father as if she had seen the boy's face at the window.

"What is it?" said David. "What can you see?"

Alexa shrugged and let her gaze drift into the future. "Nothing," she said. "It's snowing again."

PART NINE

INTERVIEW

The Nathan James Television Show, eighteen years later

The lights dim on a lavish television studio. A desk is
positioned to the right-hand side, angled to face a comfortable sofa and coffee table. Behind the desk is a
panoramic backdrop of the New York skyline. To the
left of the studio a music stage is set for a band: micro-
phones, drum kit, tuned guitars glistening on their stands.
A red light blinks on an amplifier. A stage manager in
a headset comes out. He silences the audience, then
counts from five to zero with his fingers. At zero, the
lights come up, the entrance music begins, and a pair
of doors slide open. Nathan James, the well-known talk
show host, steps out to greet his whooping audience.

He is dressed in an immaculate gray suit and over-
extravagant matching tie. He waves and says "thank

you" several times to the crowd, smiling as if he has won an election. He passes a hand through his shoulder-length hair, which is almost as well-groomed as his suit. He walks to his mark and straightens his cuffs. A smile as bright as Times Square lights his face. A woman wolf-whistles. He says "thank you" to her. The audience laughs.

For the next two minutes, he delivers some weak, anecdotal humor, based on topical issues in the news. Then he invites the audience to look toward the studio screen to see who is appearing on his show this evening. They see Eddie Supple, the popular gymnast, four-time Olympic gold medal winner, and face of *Stretch*, the best-selling moisturizer for men. Next to him is the TV chef and occasional magician, Pierre Crouton. He greets Nathan with a conjurer's flourish and produces a large blue egg in his hand. The audience claps. Nathan asks Pierre if he's planning an omelette for his next trick. Pierre waggles a finger and flips his hand. The egg disappears (making Nathan go, "Whoa!") but there is nothing in the magician's hands. His eyes, however, suggest that the camera should pan sideways. Nathan buys it and says, "Okay, let's see what we've got. . . ."

The camera alights on what appears to be an empty seat, but slowly drops down to show a small clay dragon. It is Gadzooks. The audience claps and cheers. "All right," says Nathan. "I think we all know who *that* belongs to. Assuming Pierre's not moved her into a parallel universe, let's get her out here. Ladies and gentlemen, please welcome my first guest, a rising movie star. The one and only, the gorgeous, the super-talented, Angel Merriman!"

Enraptured clapping fills the studio. Angel appears at the sliding doors. She nods warmly to the audience. Her electrifying smile lights up the set. She is indeed gorgeous. Her famous cascading hair has been tied back to look like a fox's bushy tail. She is wearing an elegant gown, dark blue, perfectly matched to her eyes. She walks on to the sound of her father's song, "Fire Star," which is riding high on the download charts. She exchanges a pouting air-kiss with Nathan, then walks to the sofa as if ice itself could not unbalance her. She sits down, picks up Gadzooks, and puts him on the table, turning him to face the interviewer's desk.

Nathan leans forward, reaching out a hand. Affecting an air of worry, he whispers, "Is he real? Does he bite?

Does he, y'know . . . ?" He makes a reasonable attempt at a hurr.

Angel smiles. She adjusts her dress so she can sit back comfortably. "Only if you don't believe in him, Nathan."

The audience chuckles.

Nathan leans back in his leather chair. "I take it he's just . . . ?"

"Acting solid — for the cameras, yes."

The audience chuckles again.

"And is he the real one, the original Gadzooks?"

"This is him," Angel says adoringly. "Gretel wanted to come as well, but we might not have kept her under control."

Nathan grins, showing off a set of piano keys for teeth. He likes the fact that he's being teased. "Gretel, she's the one with the flowers, right?"

"The feisty one. The one you don't want to mess with."

"I wouldn't want to mess with any of them," he says. He peers at Gadzooks. "Is he looking at me?"

"Probably. He does like you. He watches your show all the time at home."

Nathan laughs and pats a hand on his desk. "Knock it off, will you? Now you're freaking me out."

Angel raises a taunting eyebrow.

The audience laughs at Nathan's pretense of discomfort. He glances at Gadzooks again, then stacks his notecards and cheerily says, "So, what do I call you? Alexa or Angel? Or Agawin?!" he adds before she can respond.

She laughs and says, "Anything you like — maybe not Agawin. It's usually 'Angel.'"

"How did the name come about? I'm assuming, of course, you don't actually have wings."

She puts out her hands and flaps them a little.

"Stop it-t-t," he says.

The audience laughs again.

"There was another Alexa in my class at drama school. Calling myself Angel seemed a good way of avoiding confusion. It just stuck. I like angels. They're cool, don't you think?"

Nathan is clearly not sure how to answer this. He opts for, "This is the essence of your father's books, isn't it? They play around with the idea that dragons and angels and so forth are real."

"Careful," she says. "He's got very good ears." She nods at Gadzooks.

The audience laughs as Nathan sighs. "Will you give this up now?"

"Okay," she peeps.

He prepares to ask his next question, but amuses the studio by checking on Gadzooks again, just in case. "Is it okay to talk about the books? I know your dad's not very forthcoming about them."

Angel sits back, crossing her legs. "Oh, I wouldn't say that. He just hates the idea of taking his writing apart and putting it back together again. He wants people to read them and think."

"They are pretty deep," Nathan prompts. "My eldest daughter, Jess, has read them all. She says they're challenging."

Angel nods. "Kids often write in and say they've read them four or five times before they've grasped what Dad was getting at, or what they think he was getting at. But the true fans seem to like the intrigue. The movie will make it clearer."

Nathan swivels his seat. "You're talking now about *Icefire*, of course."

"Have you seen it?"

"I have. I loved it. I thought you were fantastic. My kids were enthralled."

"Thank you."

"We'll see a clip from the film in a minute. But I have to ask, was it strange, playing the role of your mother? The characters, I believe, are based very much on your family setup."

"Pretty much, yes."

"So, Mom? How was that?"

"Fine," Angel says with a shrug of modesty. "I got to boss my 'dad' around. That was cool."

The audience approves of this.

"You also had to kiss him. That must have been weird?"

"Kissing Johnny Delph? Oh, no, that wasn't weird."

The women in the room clearly appreciate where Angel is coming from.

Nathan tells them to calm themselves — then raises the temperature for the men. "We've got a photo of you and your mom at the premiere."

"Really?" Angel turns to look at the screen. Sure enough, a picture comes up of herself and Zanna on the red carpet, linking arms. Zanna, in all black, looks amazing — ice cool and very chic. A point not lost on Nathan.

"Wow, she is a good-looking woman, isn't she?"

Angel gapes at him now. She can't quite believe what he just said. Then she reveals, "She's in the audience, actually."

"What?!" Nathan is genuinely shocked. "No?"

"Yeah. Dad's here, too." She scans the faces. "There."

The camera picks them out. David smiles politely. His hair is shorter than his eponymous hero's and there is a neat line of stubble on his chin these days. Zanna doesn't smile. She simply melts the camera with her gothic stare.

Nathan wiggles his tie. He blows a breath to cool his exaggerated rapture. In a conspiratorial fashion he says, "Do you think you can put in a word for me . . . ?"

"With Mom?"

Nathan makes his eyebrows dance.

"You're not her type."

The audience howls as Nathan feigns hurt. He tries again. "I've got this polar bear outfit I wore for the office Halloween party. . . ."

Angel laughs and chews her lip. "I see you more as a squirrel."

"Awww . . ." Nathan throws up his hands at this rebuff. But he laughs and takes it all in stride. "Seriously, could I meet her? I use her products!" He smooths his face. He's referring to the fact that Zanna has a successful line of natural health and beauty products, used by men and women alike.

Angel nods. "She'd approve of that. I'm sure she'd be happy to chat with you afterward."

The camera picks out Zanna again. She barely raises a smoldering eyebrow.

"Was that a yes?" begs Nathan.

"As close as it ever gets."

"All right." He straightens his shoulders, tosses back his hair. He's a happy host now. "Let's have a look at you being your mom. This is one of my favorite scenes, where David and Zanna first meet the villainess of the piece, Gwilanna."

They turn to the screen again.

We see the interior of Wayward Crescent, specifically the Dragons' Den. Zanna has picked up a bronze-colored egg, claiming she can feel something moving inside it. David snaps at her to put it down, saying Liz, his landlady, will go crazy if she comes homes and finds anything out of place. Little does he know the alarmed face of Gruffen is already watching from a shelf in the background. Zanna refuses. Experiences like these are what she was put on this Earth for, she says. They argue, but she won't give up the egg. Despite the bickering, the romantic tension between them is obvious. Then the doorbell sounds. David and Zanna freeze. Gruffen is seen to gulp. David hurries downstairs, certain that Liz has forgotten her keys. Zanna follows. All the way, the bickering continues. David yanks the door open. There is Gwilanna. Stern and scary. On the suitcase beside her sits the potions dragon, Gretel. David says, dumbly, "You're not Liz." Gwilanna replies, "No, boy, I'm not. Trick or treat . . . ?"

The clip ends. The audience applauds.

"She *is* scary, isn't she?" Nathan opens up. He means Gwilanna, of course, played to perfection by the grande dame of cinema, Helena Meeren.

"Almost as scary as the real thing, Dad reckons."

"Tell me about this," says Nathan. He undoes one button of his suit, feeling, perhaps, that he has gained a little more intimacy with his charming guest. He leans forward again, focusing the intrigue of the entire studio on to Angel's eyes. "Is it true that Gwilanna is based on your great-aunt Sibyl?"

Angel nods. "The whole family is more or less written as they are."

"But the books were intended for you?"

"Kind of. I gave Dad the idea, but his ultimate motivation was to give his brother, Joseph Henry, a life."

Nathan takes this in and immediately adopts a more somber tone. "I want to tread lightly here because this is quite tragic, isn't it?"

"I don't mind talking about it," Angel replies.

Nathan nods. He puts his notes aside. "Correct me if I've got this wrong, but your grandmother, Elizabeth, the one who made these beautiful dragons, died giving birth to a stillborn son who would have been named Joseph, right?"

"Joseph Henry, yes." Angel picks it up from here. "It's just one of those awful tragedies that families suffer from time to time. I don't think any of us ever got over it. Dad dealt with it the best way a writer knows how: in words and stories. He told me once that when Grandma first found out she might die, she held his hand and told him a dark fire had entered her." (There are heartfelt sighs from parts of the audience.) "He never forgot it. The loss was very hard for him."

"He was adopted, wasn't he?"

"*Mmm*, when he was twelve, which is why he made himself a 'tenant' in the books, though when he wrote some of the timeline changes he became their son, just to satisfy that need in him. Liz and Arthur adored him and treated him as their own. But if there was one thing Dad really wanted them to have, it was a 'proper' son."

Again, the audience makes their empathy clear. The camera picks out Zanna, who is close to tears.

"That's very moving," says Nathan. And he means it. Not wishing to dwell on the subject too long he moves the conversation sideways a little. "And Lucy, your aunt. There's some . . . mystery surrounding her as well, isn't there?"

"Only that we don't know who her father is. Grandma would never talk about it. She had Lucy young, long before she married Arthur. We suspect that Great-aunt Sibyl knew the truth, but she took it with her to the grave. If asked, she always claimed that Lucy was hatched by a dragon."

The audience are relieved to stutter with laughter.

"Yeah, but she was *how* old then . . . ?"

"Oh, pretty wrinkled."

"So she was . . . ?" Nathan twists a finger next to his temple. He whistles, like a meerkat popping up and down a tunnel.

"Well, you *say* that . . ." Angel opens her hands.

"Come on, she was nuts!" Nathan is riding a mischievous wave. But he's confident he has enough of her trust to be allowed to say something this outrageous. "She was as potty as him." He points at Gadzooks.

"But she said it with such conviction, Nathan. I think that rubbed off on all of us."

"So Gwilanna — if I may call Aunt Sibyl that — believed in dragons?"

"Oh, totally." Angel slides her hands to the front of her knees. "She encouraged Grandma to make the clay models."

"Really?"

"Oh, yes. And the idea that the universe was made by a dragon came from Aunt Sibyl, too."

Nathan grins. He's pleased she's brought this up. "And your grandfather famously quoted this." He turns to the audience. "I should explain, for those who don't know, that Angel's grandfather is the outspoken theoretical physicist Arthur Merriman, who once said, if I remember rightly, we know so little about the exact moment of the big bang that the idea of a dragon creating the universe isn't that far-fetched."

" 'We come from a world of fire,' " says Angel, cleverly quoting her father's text.

But Nathan wins the round with another quip, "No wonder he never won the Nobel Prize."

The audience claps, spurring the presenter on. "Can we talk about Professor Merriman? 'Cause he's *great*, isn't he?"

"Don't you dare suggest he's mad," she warns.

"As a hatter," Nathan says from the corner of his mouth.

Angel scowls.

Nathan protests. "Oh, come on-n-n. He's got cats called Higgs and Boson! Who in their right mind names their pets after an undiscovered particle?"

The audience, by their laughter, are clearly with him. But Angel moves her gaze toward the seats as if to threaten Nathan with a no-show from her mother. He gets the significance and confesses he'll behave. "Okay, eccentric. Can we settle on eccentric?" He takes her silence as a yes. "Can I ask you, seriously, about his work?"

"Sure."

"He believes it's possible to 'imagineer,' doesn't he? To actually construct or materialize objects from thoughts?"

"Yes, he does."

"That's a bit creepy, isn't it?"

Angel brushes her thigh. "Grandad would say there are lots of unexplained forces in the universe, especially in the quantum world. His team feels they're close to a breakthrough."

"Really?"

"*Mmm.*"

There is a pause. The audience giggles at Nathan's look of incredulity.

"Seriously," says Angel, laughing herself.

"You're putting me on."

"No. Really. Ask Dad afterward."

Now Nathan is hooked again. "Your dad's involved in this, isn't he? And so is Anders Bergstrom, I believe, the famous Norwegian . . . What is Bergstrom, exactly? I've never really understood what he does."

"Officially, a psychologist. But he's done a lot of things."

"Including exploring dangerous glaciers."

"He gets around, yes."

"No," Nathan argues, tapping his desk. "I bike here in New York City. That's *getting around*. The Canadian High Arctic is a whole different ball game. Is he *really* a polar bear?"

"Probably." She laughs. "I wouldn't put it past him. He's an interesting guy. One of the most charismatic men I've ever met — present company included, of course."

Nathan wiggles his tie. A deliberate act of self-effacing vanity.

"Anders is a free-thinking spirit. A very bright and gifted man. He helps Grandad to rationalize his beliefs. He's the perfect complement to the scientific approach."

"I'm told he wasn't in the final book."

"Who, Bergstrom?"

"Yes. According to Jess, he doesn't appear in *The Fire Ascending*."

Angel shrugs. "I guess he just wasn't needed."

Nathan accepts this at face value. "Let's go back to the imagineering thing. There's been a buzz going around the Cloud for years that your dad is a guinea pig for Professor Merriman's research into 'active consciousness,' which I believe is the basis for imagineering."

"Well, that's a bit *X-Files*," Angel says, referring to her father's favorite television program, an old show in which an FBI agent, Fox Mulder, investigates paranormal events. "When Dad started the books he asked Grandad Arthur's permission to include him as a character. Grandad agreed on two conditions: one, that Dad stayed true to his beliefs —"

"Your grandfather's beliefs?"

"Yes. And two, that he wrote the books organically."

"Meaning they should come out as they wanted to. Unplanned."

"Yes. This is why there are some loose ends or seemingly impossible complexities in the stories: They reflect the nature of spontaneous creation, the chaotic universe of a writer's mind. Whenever Dad wrote, he wore a small device that recorded the pattern of his thoughts and the synaptic energies involved. I've seen the graphs. They're particularly spiky when Dad has moments of genuine inspiration. The auma of the universe is most empowered when he's apparently creating something out of nothing. If you can harness that energy, theoretically you can imagineer."

"Right." Nathan sets his shoulders square. He closes his eyes and concentrates. After a second or two he blows a breath of failure. "No, still can't produce a clone of your mother."

Angel rolls her eyes. The audience appreciates the joke, all the same. Nathan, all teeth and schoolboy smiles, tosses his hair off his forehead again. "What?"

"Mom is *so* going to tear you down."

Nathan says, "I'll look forward to that. So where does *he* come in?" He nods at Gadzooks.

"Well, he's a dragon. He's in perfect harmony with the universe. He helps Dad when he's stuck."

"I love that," says Nathan, curling a titter around his words. "That you talk about him as if he's real."

"To the family, he is. Grandma felt the urge to create him because Dad was always scribbling stories. All through the novels, he used Gadzooks in the same way David Rain does. When he was stuck, he talked to Zookie. In his mind's eye he'd see him write on his pad and that would kick-start his imagination again."

Nathan leans forward to point something out. "In his mind," he says quietly.

"It's a perfectly valid tool," says Angel. "I know writers who talk to trees to help them through a mental block."

"Yeah, but the tree doesn't talk back!"

"How do you know?" she counters, laughing.

"Because . . ." But Nathan is flummoxed now. He merely points at Gadzooks and says assuredly, "They're a myth."

Angel smiles in silence. But she isn't done yet. "Grandad's got a nice take on myths. Do you want to hear it?"

"Is it quick? I could debate this with you all night, but we have other guests and I want to show another clip from the movie."

"Real quick," she says. "Arthur would argue that what we call myths are events that happened in their own timeline. But if the timeline changes, an etheric trace of those events is left behind — and that becomes the basis of a memory, or a legend."

"Didn't understand a word of that."

"Play it back later."

"I will."

"Slowly."

"Thank you." His laughter acknowledges a point on her scorecard. "Let's see another piece of the movie, shall we?"

The audience claps their approval.

"This is from the beginning of the film, when Bergstrom talks to the polar bear. My daughter says this isn't in the book."

"No. Dad has always acknowledged that it would be difficult to film the books individually because they don't lend themselves to discrete movies. So he and Rod, who wrote the screenplay with him, cherry-picked parts from later in the series, particularly *Dark Fire*, to help explain the overall plot."

"This is Rod Duncan?"

"Yes."

Nathan gives an approving nod. "I am such a big fan of his zombie movies." He glances at Gadzooks and points. "Did he just do the zombie thing? I swear I saw him hold up his paws and sway."

Which prompts Angel to lean forward and whisper to Zookie, "Behave, you're scaring Nathan. That's Mom's job."

The studio erupts in laughter.

"Okay, here we go!" Nathan shouts. "This is from *Icefire*, out in general release next Thursday. Go and watch it. Trust me, it's a terrific film."

The screen flares into life. We see Bergstrom, the enigmatic explorer, approaching a sitting polar bear, who appears to be guarding a pocket watch. The watch is ticking louder than it should, as if it's in harmony with the universe. It's Bergstrom's timepiece. A precious heirloom. He stares at the bear and asks for it back. The bear speaks, telling Bergstrom he can have the watch back, but only if he picks it up and follows the bear north. When Bergstrom asks why, the bear reminds the explorer of what he discovered earlier that day: dragon-tongue, burned into the walls of a cave. A record of the meeting of the last twelve dragons. Bergstrom is the first human to encounter evidence of dragons on Earth. The mark of Oomara suddenly appears in the polar bear's head. Bergstrom looks back at the life he once knew. He steps forward and picks up the watch. He flips it shut and puts it in his pocket. "Lead on. . . . ," he says.

The clip ends. The audience applauds with great enthusiasm.

"Wonderful scene," says Nathan. He addresses the crowd. "Be honest. How many of you would pick up the watch and go with the bear, and how many would just get the heck out of there?"

Judging by the rumble, the audience is divided.

Before Nathan can respond, Angel sits upright and says, "Hey, you know Uncle Tam, don't you?"

547

"The journalist who married your aunt Lucy? I play golf with him. Bad loser. Owes me five bucks."

"No, he doesn't," says Angel. "Uncle Tam's great. Shall I tell you what he'd do in this situation? He says he wouldn't pick up the watch. He'd just offer the bear a couple of grand to publish his story."

"Nice," says Nathan, laughing with the audience. "That's very him. Listen, it's been a pleasure talking to you. Good luck with the movie. Will there be another?"

"Two more, we hope. Dad's roughing out the next one now with Rod."

"Fantastic. We'll all look forward to that. Ladies and gentleman, Angel Merriman!"

They stand and air-kiss again. Angel picks up Gadzooks and kisses his topknot, a scene that will later spark another incredible buzz around the Cloud. Just for a moment, as Angel waves good-bye, the camera manages to blur Gadzooks. But what was written on the dragon's notepad? It looks like the three-lined mark of Oomara.

Though it could have just been *Hrrrrrrr.* . . .

PART TEN
GADZOOKS

The studio lights come up and the floor manager announces a break in recording. "Do you want to go down and see him?" David asks.

Zanna, who has had her arm looped in his throughout, says, "She'll be disappointed now if I don't."

"If it's all right with you, I won't. I'd like to go and visit Mom."

Zanna nods. "Of course."

"Mr. Rain? Sorry, I mean Mr. Merriman?" An embarrassed fan has shuffled along the row in front of them, holding a pad she hopes he'll sign. "Would it be all right if I had your autograph?"

"Of course," David says. He takes the pad.

"I just love your books, and I *do* believe in dragons."

"I should hope so," he says, making Zanna smile.

"Can I ask you a question?"

"Uh-huh."

"Why did you call yourself Rain in the stories?"

David hands the pad back with his signature. "I always wanted to write paperback books, and the Beatles had a tune called 'Paperback Writer.' On the opposite side of the record was a track called 'Rain.' That's my favorite song of theirs. That's where it comes from."

"Record?" says the fan.

Zanna laughs. "Now you're showing your age," she says.

"Enjoy the movie," David says to the fan.

"Oh, I will." She clamps the pad to her chest. "Thank you *so* much."

She shuffles away.

"You've still got it," Zanna says.

David smiles. He stands up and kisses her cheek. "Tell Lexie she was great. See you back at the house."

And he disappears out of the theater, noticed by many, questioned by none.

When he arrives in Scrubbley later that day, he takes a cab to the small graveyard on the hill outside the town where his mother and Joseph Henry are buried, stopping on the way to buy a few lilies. They are Liz's favorite flower. He pays the driver but asks him to wait, saying he will only be ten minutes. He opens the swinging picket gate and walks along a winding path that will shortly bring him to his mother's grave. It is autumn and the path is speckled with leaves. Appropriately, a squirrel bounds across the gravel. It bounces onto a wonky urn, then a tilted headstone, and disappears into the shadows of an oak. David smiles and scents the flowers. They smell heady. He thinks that Gretel would approve.

Liz's headstone faces the afternoon sun. A simple arc of granite. No real frills. There was talk at the time about fixing one of her dragons to the plot, but the risk of theft put an end to that.

David crouches and removes the existing flowers. They are long dead, needing to return to Gaia. "Hello, Mom," he says, laying the lilies down. "I've just come from a TV studio. Lexie was being interviewed about her role in the movie. She did well. She's a big star now. You would have been so proud of her."

He brushes some moss off the epitaph wording, the part that says MAKER OF DRAGONS. He traces the last word with his fingers, making sure the grooves in the letters are clear. He does the same with the small bit of corbeling that decorates the top of the stone.

He speaks some more about Alexa, and is about to move on to Zanna and Arthur and Lucy, when he hears footsteps farther down the path. This is not unusual, even in midafternoon, but the visitor's identity does surprise him. He stands up as Anders Bergstrom joins him at the graveside.

"I thought I might find you here." Despite his many years in Massachusetts, there is still a strong hint of the Arctic in Bergstrom. "How is she?"

There is nothing strange about this. Both men hold the strong belief that the spirit survives the body after death. So David says, "Calm. She's calm."

Bergstrom nods. "I'm glad to hear it." His hair, like David's, is closer-cropped; his skin a little thinner on his cheekbones, perhaps. As always, despite the threat of winter, he does not appear to be feeling the cold. David is wearing an open overcoat; the Norwegian has his sleeves rolled up to the elbow. A jacket, at least, is slung across one forearm.

"What are you doing here, Anders?"

Bergstrom stares at the grave. "I visit when I'm in

the area. I liked your mother. She was a wonderful woman. How did the interview go?"

"Good. Alexa handled herself well."

"Did Nathan speak of the experiment?"

"A little. Why?"

Bergstrom hunkers down and picks up a lily. "Why have you stopped using the implant?"

David instinctively feels in the region of his heart. He seems to come to a decision and slips his hand inside his shirt. When he withdraws it, there is a small spike of transmorphic crystal between his forefinger and thumb. It could almost be a piece of ice. At one time, the invisible neural fibers running through the implant would have been pulsing neon blue. Now, there is nothing. He shows the crystal to Bergstrom. "I haven't. It stopped working two days ago."

"Have you told Arthur?"

"He's away, at the Oslo Conference — where I thought you would be. I was going to tell him when he comes back. Why aren't you in Oslo?"

"Because I'm here."

This is a fairly standard response. Bergstrom is a man of few words, and likes to cultivate an air of detachment with them.

David looks across the graveyard. In the distance, a gardener is mowing the bumpy strips of grass between the graves. David thinks of Henry Bacon, his long-dead neighbor, and how squirrels once wrecked the old man's mower. The memory is strong and almost over-powers him. He hears the gardener bellow something. But the man is too far away to make any sense. David shivers and looks at the sky. There are no clouds pres-ent, and no real warmth from the orange sun either. He lets Dr. Bergstrom come back into focus. There has always been an odd kind of tension between them, which David has never fully understood, though he's written about it accurately in the books many times. He offers Bergstrom the crystal. "Take it. Maybe there's a fault."

"Or maybe the experiment has run its course?"

There is a sense of accusation here, as though David is holding something back. But Bergstrom doesn't pur-sue it. He relaxes and pats David's arm. "We'll talk about this when Arthur returns. Now I'll leave you in peace, with Elizabeth." He takes the crystal and puts it in his pocket. Before he leaves, he switches his jacket to the other arm and touches his right hand to his lips, releasing a silent kiss for Liz. It's then that David sees something he's never seen before. On Bergstrom's temple, revealed by his receding hairline, is a three-lined scar.

David grips the Norwegian's arm. "How did you get this?" He points to the temple.

Bergstrom stares at him without blinking. That powerful icy squint, straight out of the polar bear handbook. "I had minor surgery when I was younger. It's nothing, David. A scar, that's all."

But it doesn't look like nothing to David. It looks very much like the "sometimes" symbol. The trademark of dragons. The sacred sign of ice bears, the Inuit — the North. "Why have you never shown me this?"

"Because some things are better not said," says Bergstrom, gently but firmly freeing his arm. He looks at the grave for a long moment before adding, quietly, "Be with your mother." As he walks away, he pulls an old driving cap out of his jacket. He puts it on, covering the scar.

David watches him all the way to the gate. It creaks as he opens it, clatters as he leaves.

Another leaf falls from another tree.

The smell of mown grass is in the air.

David turns to his mother again. There is so much he wants to talk to her about. So much he'd like to know. He crouches again and thinks about the mark on Bergstrom's head, all that it has meant to him over the years. And perhaps because he can't let go of that symbol, his mind begins to flood with dragon auma. One by one, they all flash through. The natural dragons — Gawain, Galen, Grockle, Godith. Roaring at him from every angle. Then firebirds in the great librarium, flitting back and forth between the shelves of books. But, inevitably, his mind grows calm and only one kind of dragon fills his thoughts. His mind does a tour of his mother's creations before settling on the one most personal to him. He pictures Gadzooks, as he has so often. The dragon, as usual, is poised with his pencil, ready to scribble a note on his pad. David's heart begins to thump. He can't explain it, but he feels much closer to Gadzooks today. Yet they haven't written a story for years. What message could the dragon have for him? What could be so important at this odd juncture of their lives?

In his mind's eye, he watches Gadzooks lick the pencil tip. Slowly, but steadily, the dragon starts to write.

H . . . E . . . L . . . L . . . O

"Hello," mutters David, and opens his eyes.

Gadzooks is sitting on Elizabeth's grave.

Hrrr! he says, and blows the perfect smoke ring.

It drifts upward and catches in David's nostrils.

The scent of dragon fire.

Powerful.

Real.

THE END

A Q&A with Chris d'Lacey

• Which is your favorite character in the series?

I usually split this up into two categories — human and dragon. Let's deal with the human first. It's very hard for me not to choose David, as he is based on me when I was a young man. If the series had gone no further than *Fire Star*, I probably would have chosen him. Of course, there are many characters I could opt for. Gwilanna has been fantastic to write — villains always are. And Anders Bergstrom intrigues me as much now as he ever did in *Icefire*. But the human I really like is Zanna (and her alternative in *Fire World*, Rosa). She has a lot to deal with throughout the series. I love her spirit, particularly the way she copes with David's disappearance in *The Fire Eternal*. And she's a great mum. I would have loved to have met her when I was David's age!

As for the dragons. I'm in danger of being seriously scorched here by the ones I leave out. Seriously, I love them all. They make me laugh and cry in equal measure. Sentiment says I should pick Grace, because she will probably never get over having her ears broken by David. In the end, if I'm forced into a corner, it comes down to two. Gretel is just brilliant. Her feistiness, especially in *Icefire*, is legendary. I like the way you can never be quite sure about her and how she thinks the other Pennykettle dragons are "useless." But even she would forgive me for choosing the one and only Gadzooks as my favorite. How could a writer not choose the writing dragon? Notice that *The Fire Ascending* is dedicated to him. That just about says it all.

- Which is your favorite book in the series?

Again, very, very difficult to choose. For a long time I would have picked *The Fire Within*, because it's not a book about squirrels and it's not a book about dragons; it's a book about creativity and where ideas come from — a subject close to a writer's heart. When I wrote *Dark Fire*, that took over as my favorite for a while. It has so many lovely twists and turns and it was great to write about Gawaine, the queen dragon, coming out of stasis. Then came *Fire World*, and my feelings changed again. At the end of *Dark Fire*, I knew I had to come up with something spectacular to explain the ending at Scuffenbury Hill. It was a real gamble to dive into the alternative world of Co:pern:ica, but, boy, was it good fun! A small number of readers just didn't get it. But those that did couldn't praise it enough. I absolutely adore *Fire World*. I don't think it's the best book of the series, but it is my favorite — just.

• So which book *is* the best of the series for you?

The Fire Ascending, without a doubt. It wraps everything up so beautifully. Again, I took risks. I knew I wanted to go back in time and examine the story of Guinevere and Gawain, but I wasn't expecting to write a 20,000 word chunk of prehistory without any chapter breaks, that didn't include any of the known characters (or barely any), and introduced a villain we hadn't met before! That spirit of adventure set the tone for the rest of the book. It was just a question then of how to mix the old with the new and bring everything to a satisfying conclusion. I think *The Fire Ascending* contains some of the best bits of writing I've ever done.

• Where did you get your character names from? Are they made up or did you choose any of them in homage to anything else?

The only two characters that weren't entirely made up are David and Zanna. David is a name I've always liked and wouldn't have minded being called. Zanna came about after I met a girl at a signing who called herself that. She was a Goth and very striking. I asked her if "Zanna" was an eastern European name, to which she replied, "No, it's short for Suzanna, you . . ." I won't repeat the rest! I thought it was such a cool name and immediately wrote it into *Icefire*. Nearly all the other names, including Gadzooks, just floated into my consciousness when their character was first introduced. It rarely takes me more than a minute to find something I like or that seems appropriate. And the character will soon tell you if the name is wrong; they dig their heels in and refuse to be written. I was really struck with Ingavar (the polar bear), because it conjures up an image of a hugely powerful and courageous bear. It was always good fun making up names for the Inuit characters. Tootega was my favorite. Voss was interesting. I wanted to give the opening section of *The Fire Ascending* a vaguely Scandinavian feel. I typed "Norway" into Google and one of the first words I saw was "Voss" (an area of Norway). I liked it and it stuck. Henry Bacon, I have to confess, is a slight homage to Mr. Curry, the annoying neighbor in the Paddington Bear books. Curry? Bacon? See the connection? Many people have asked if the use of the names Gawain, Guinevere, and Arthur is some kind of nod to the Arthurian legends. No, not at all. I just liked the sound of them. Gawain, particularly, is a wonderful title for a dragon. And why do all the dragon names begin with a "G"? Well, read *Dark Fire* or Jay's *Rain & Fire* guidebook! The answer's in there.

• When did you know how the series was going to end? Did you plan it from near the beginning?

There's an old saying that goes, "every story is as long as it needs to be." I don't think anyone quite expected seven books at a time when trilogies were all the rage, but I always felt that if the story was there, I would be happy to continue adding to the series. I did consider writing *The Fire Ascending* as two books, where book one would have dealt with the historical stuff (Agawin, Grella, etc.) and book two, the Ix inversion. But after a little discussion with my editors, we felt that one volume would be enough. I did cut out a long history of Co:pern:ica, and I would have seriously liked to have dedicated more chapters to Gwilanna's illumination to Gawain. But I'd rather people have a book, not a doorstop. I'm happy with the way things worked out. As for the ending, would you believe I didn't know the exact ending until a few days before I wrote it? I decided from the start (well, from *Icefire* onward) that I would write these books "organically." In other words, I wouldn't plan them at all, but would just let them take me wherever they wanted to go, to keep them "true" to what David does when he writes *Snigger and the Nutbeast* for Lucy. With every book, I always knew what the beginning would be, and I had a *vague* idea of the ending. Everything in between was an adventure! It's a scary way to write, but for me, it's the only real way to do it. I placed my faith in the Universe — and let Gadzooks do the rest! Of course, there is a great responsibility on a writer to wrap up a big series in a satisfactory manner. I'm well-known for leaving dreadful cliff-hangers at the end of my books. I couldn't allow that to happen with *The Fire Ascending*. It had to have a definite end, and it had to be good, but more than that, it had to be different. I came up with the idea of the interview sequence before I started the book, but didn't tell anyone except Jay about it until it was done. I'm absolutely thrilled with the way it came out. It puts the whole series into perspective and is both funny and moving in equal measure. The closing lines didn't really come to me until very near the end. What I like about them is how they address the two main themes of the series, i.e., the power of the mind to create ideas and whether dragons exist — or not.

• What have been the highs and lows of the series?

It's been a delight to unwrap so much wonderful story. As I said above, when you write the way I do, you're never quite sure what's going to happen. So it's really exciting when fantastic scenes pop up out of nowhere. Developing the covers has been another thrill. Angelo [Rinaldi] has done a fabulous job with the artwork, which has become iconic. My favorite cover is *The Fire Eternal* (love the planet in the eye), closely followed by *Fire World*. Someone jokingly suggested that I couldn't write any more books because we've run out of colors! Pink dragon, anyone? Maybe not. If I had a low at all, it would be the feeling that over a period of years, books like these tend to be taken for granted. People see three, four, five come out and assume they know what they're getting. My answer to that would be, read *Fire World*. How many series take a complete sideways step, six books in, and manage to pull it off? I'm sometimes told, as well, that the plots are confusing or complicated. Yes, they are, probably because of the way the books are written. And maybe it's partly due to the fact that my two favorite television series were *The X Files* and *Twin Peaks*, which had so many layers of intrigue that it was virtually impossible to finish them conclusively. I learned a lesson there. I think *The Fire Ascending* does have a strong conclusion, one which brings the whole series together.

• What will you miss most about writing the series?

I've lived with these characters for over ten years. It's going to seem odd not writing about them. I've always felt happy in Wayward Crescent and will miss visiting the kitchen at number forty-two. I can see Bonnington at his food bowl as I type this. More than anything, I will miss the Pennykettle dragons. Their innocence and humor and occasional mischievous behavior were always a joy to experience. I used to believe I was better at writing domestic dramas than full-on fantasy. Part one of *The Fire Ascending* has changed my mind about that. But although I could see me writing another book about dragons, it almost certainly wouldn't be about *those* dragons. There is a degree of sadness about that. But no matter what else I do, I will always be associated with David, Gadzooks, and the Dragons' Den, which is fine by me. They have made me what I am and I would miss telling their stories at school visits — not that they'll ever let me ignore them (they're *hrrr*ing in my ear even now . . .).

• What *won't* you miss?

Writing a lengthy series like this brings its own kind of pressures. To keep the momentum going, the books have to be delivered regularly. That has not always been easy. I could have written a different ending to *Dark Fire* and quit the series there, but it would have left too many unanswered questions. I could never have put the Chronicles away without feeling entirely happy about the ending. Other than that, I don't think there's anything I would miss. These books opened me up to a new genre. They have taken me to places in the world I might never have visited otherwise, and brought me into contact with lots of wonderful people. But I guess the last word should go to the fans. I've had thousands of messages over the years from boys and girls (and, yes, many "grown-ups") who've told me the books are amazing and even life changing. That's a humbling feeling when you get right down to it. I want to thank them all and say I hope you enjoyed the conclusion. One day, we will get a movie (or three) for you. Then you can say you were there at the beginning, before the whole world knew the meaning of *hrrr*!

Chris d'Lacey
January 2012

Chris d'Lacey is the author of several highly acclaimed books for children and young adults, including the Last Dragon Chronicles: *The Fire Within*, *Icefire*, *Fire Star*, *The Fire Eternal*, *Dark Fire*, *Fire World*, and *The Fire Ascending*. He has also written The Dragons of Wayward Crescent books, including *Gruffen* and *Gauge*.

Chris lives with his wife in Devon, England. Visit *www.scholastic.com/lastdragonchronicles* to learn more about Chris and his dragons, or Chris's own website, *www.icefire.co.uk*.